"How high?"

With a roar of triumph, a pyluk sprang from a tree behind them. Turning, Thru drew an arrow, took aim and released. The pyluk gave a sharp cough as the arrow suddenly sprouted from his shoulder. Another green-skinned monster appeared, and more were coming.

The mots ran, but they had nowhere to go. Another hundred steps brought them to the steaming cool cloud that edged the ridge above the falls. The rock was slippery and wet, cold to the touch. The river below arched out into nothingness.

"Jump," said Thru. "We have no choice." The mots stared at him, eyes drained of hope.

"It is death to jump."

"Maybe. But it is a worse death to stay here."

A spear flew forth from the trees and flashed over Thru's head. Then the mots jumped, launching themselves out into the waters. . . .

DOOM'S BREAK

The Third Book of Arna

Christopher Rowley

A ROC BOOK

ROC
Published by New American Library, a division of
Penguin Putnam Inc., 375 Hudson Street,
New York, New York 10014, U.S.A.
Penguin Books Ltd, 80 Strand,
London WC2R 0RL, England
Penguin Books Australia Ltd, Ringwood,
Victoria, Australia
Penguin Books Canada Ltd, 10 Alcorn Avenue,
Toronto, Ontario, Canada M4V 3B2
Penguin Books (N.Z.) Ltd, 182–190 Wairau Road,
Auckland 10, New Zealand

Penguin Books Ltd, Registered Offices:
Harmondsworth, Middlesex, England

First published by Roc, an imprint of New American Library,
a division of Penguin Putnam Inc.

First Printing, December 2002
10 9 8 7 6 5 4 3 2 1

ROC REGISTERED TRADEMARK—MARCA REGISTRADA

Printed in the United States of America

PUBLISHER'S NOTE
This is a work of fiction. Names, characters, places, and incidents either
are the product of the author's imagination or are used fictitiously,
and any resemblance to actual persons, living or dead, business
establishments, events, or locales is entirely coincidental.

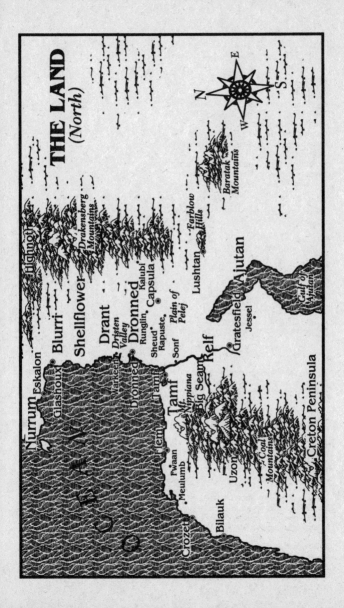

Prologue

His name was Pulbeka. He was a stone breaker and the largest man ever seen in Shasht. In height he stood nearly seven feet tall. He tipped more than three hundred pounds on the scale, and very little of it was fat. Nor was he stupid, Pulbeka. He broke stone in the quarry for his living, but he was known as something of a savant.

When they came to him with word that he was wanted at the pyramid, Pulbeka was silent for a moment.

"Do they want just my heart?" he said at last.

"No, they want all of you."

"Then I will go," he said, setting down his hammer.

They brought Pulbeka to the temple pyramid, and he prayed to the Great God and prostrated himself on the temple steps. He expected death.

Instead, he was brought inside to a vault in the heart of the temple and laid out upon a stone table. He was tied to the table with heavy ropes, beyond even his enormous strength.

He waited.

After a while the door opened to admit a pale, feeble figure. Indeed, it had to be helped into the room. It stood beside Pulbeka and stared into his eyes. Pulbeka felt the force of the mind behind the dark, penetrating orbs. Pulbeka understood the purpose of this fell being.

Pulbeka screamed.

Chapter 1

The storm had passed. The *Sea Wasp* was still afloat, riding on the stubborn swell. The huge, mountainous seas were gone. The terrifying winds were but a memory. Now they tore at the waters far ahead, beyond the wall of dark clouds that lay across the horizon.

Aboard the *Sea Wasp,* the men and mots crawled out of their hiding places and surveyed the damage.

The foremast was gone, snapped off six feet from the deck. A tangle of rigging was strewn across the barque's waist. With the mast had gone the bowsprit, ripped out during the tempest's climax. The remaining mast, the mizzen, was relatively undamaged. The big triangular sail had been securely reefed well before the storm hit.

Thru Gillo's bare feet gripped the deck, which was beginning to dry under the hot tropical sun. Like the others, he felt the damage to the ship almost as wounds to his own flesh. Five months of sailing on the *Sea Wasp* had made him feel the ship was a part of himself.

At the wheel, defiant, stood gray-haired Mentupah, the brother of Emperor Aeswiren.

Thru gave a happy shout. "You're alive!" He ran lightly up the steps to the upper deck.

"You bet I'm alive," growled Mentu. "Take more than the waves to be rid of me, my fur-bearing friend. How about the others?"

Thru picked at the wet knots holding Mentu fast to the wheel. "Nobody washed overboard, but Juf got hit on the head with a block of wood."

"I saw that. He was on deck trying to tie up a loose line when the mast went. I thought he was a goner."

"Not our Juf. He's down below with a gash in his head."

"You mots have the hardest damned heads, eh?"

Finally, Thru gave up on the wet knots and cut the line with his knife. "Some of us, anyway," he murmured. Unconsciously, he put a hand up to the scar on the back of his own head.

Mentu held up the rope with a grin. His white teeth split the strange facial hair that showed him to be man. "Without this, I'd be feeding the fishes now."

Thru clasped Mentu's hand, reflecting briefly on how dear this man had become to him. Truly they'd become like brothers, despite everything.

Five months at sea had accomplished that, and more. They were five thousand miles from the dread Empire of Shasht, cruising in the tropical Maruka isles to take on fresh water and banyam fruit before they crossed the equator. Then they would head out across the vast reach of the northern ocean toward the homeland of the mots, brilbies, and kobs.

"Pity to lose the mast," grumbled Mentu. "Ship will be hard to steer now."

Thru was studying the damage. The other mots were doing the same. "We'll have to erect a temporary mast," he said.

"With what?"

"We have that old boom down below. It's broken, but there's a good twenty feet of it left."

Mentu pursed his lips. "Better than nothing, I suppose."

Thru clapped him on the back. "Compared to what

we went through after Maringa, this will be easy work."

"Please, don't remind me!" said Mentu with a shiver.

While taking on water at the Isle of Maringa, they had also taken on some most unwelcome stowaways: a swarm, several thousand strong, of tropical fire ants. The struggle to eliminate the ants took up much of the succeeding week. During that time, the sound of oaths and screams of pain had been commonplace aboard the *Sea Wasp*.

Those on the deck were clearing the torn rigging and examining the bow and the gash in the decking left by the bowsprit when it was ripped away by the storm.

Simona climbed the steps a little unsteadily, took Thru's hand for a moment, then turned to examine Mentu. She'd cut her dark hair short and she wore a set of baggy trousers and vest just like the mots.

"I was sure we'd lost you," she said with a smile.

"Take more than a storm to be rid of me, Mistress Gsekk."

Simona smiled and patted his shoulder, an unheard of gesture by a woman of Shasht, but Simona was that incredible rarity, a woman of the upper class who had renounced purdah. Indeed, since leaving Shasht and abandoning her veils, her face had tanned a deep brown.

"You really are a survivor, brother of the Emperor."

Thru went down to help the others clear the wreckage.

"Keep anything that might still serve as rope," Mentu called after him. "We don't know when we'll be resupplied."

Janbur of the Gsekk appeared from below. He was a younger man with straight brows, dark hair, somber of eye but light of heart. An aristocrat who'd lost everything in his efforts to save the mots from death at the hands of the priests of Shasht.

"There's a foot of water in the hold."

"That's all?" said Mentu with some surprise.

"You wanted more?"

"Bah," snorted Mentu. Janbur's humor rarely worked on the older man.

"A little water is still coming in from the bow, where the bowsprit was torn out," reported Jevvi Panst, a mot from Old Sulmo.

"I hope it can be repaired," said Simona.

"Oh, for sure," said Jevvi, one of their best at carpentry. "We can seal her up. Needs a new bowsprit, that's all. I've told you before, Mistress Gsekk, this boat is well built."

That was a comfort, since Simona had paid for it with the jewels of her family inheritance.

"We could use some help down here," said Ter-Saab, a big brown kob, in a loud voice from the waist. Everyone, including Simona, joined him in hauling up a cable to which was attached a spar and a mass of wet rigging that had caught on the spar after being dragged overboard. Carefully they pulled the tangle apart.

The mots began to make repairs. Mentu and Janbur, lacking experience in using tools, could only stand aside. In their world, such work was done by slaves.

The leak in the bow was plugged and sealed with tar. A bowsprit was fashioned out of a gaff brought up from the hold. After a lot of work, an old boom was fished into what remained of the foremast. To this runty mast they attached a small spar. Lines were run out to the new gaff bowsprit, and a small jib sail was set.

With the big triangular mainsail deployed on the mizzen and a square foretopsail placed on the new small foremast, they hoped the barque would respond to their efforts to steer her.

Meanwhile, everyone took a turn on the foot-powered pumps. While they worked, they sang. It made the time pass more quickly. Janbur had been teaching them the old songs of Shasht, and in return they were teaching him the songs of the Land.

Down below, Thru found Simona putting a bandage on poor Juf Goost's head. The back of his head was swollen from a three-inch cut. The wound had been cleaned and treated with salt, but despite the pain, Juf was his normal cheerful self.

"I suppose it could have been worse." His smile creased his battered face, destroyed by vicious thugs in the Shasht temple.

"You could have broken your foolish head," said Simona, who would have missed Juf's infectious good humor.

"Well, you'd have had one less mouth to feed."

"Yeah, and one less pair of hands to haul on a line," said Thru.

A strengthening breeze in the late afternoon drove the *Sea Wasp* eastward through the Maruka channel. As the daylight dwindled, they prepared a meal of banyam and salt fish. They soaked the fish to soften it, then boiled it and ate it sprinkled with a little lime juice. The starchy banyam fruit was baked in its husk. It was hardly eating in the manner of the Land, but it filled their bellies.

As usual, Simona, Mentu, and Janbur sat slightly to one side. The rapid-fire conversation among the mots in their own tongue was still hard for them to understand. Even Simona struggled at times.

So, as was also usual, they fell into a familiar conversation of their own, in Shashti.

"I dream sometimes that I am all alone, in a world of them," said Janbur quietly.

Simona nodded. She had actually lived that dream, briefly, some years before. A girl lost in a world of fur-covered people with strangely colored eyes and inhuman faces.

"We will adjust."

"Damn, I hope so," said Mentu, sopping up the juice in his bowl with a piece of banyam.

"My mother tried to warn me," said Janbur with a wry smile.

"Bah," said Mentu. "You young hothead. You should have listened to her and stayed at home."

Janbur never let Mentupah's annoyance bother him. Which annoyed Mentu even more, of course.

"We were young hotheads, but we saved our friends here."

"For which," murmured Simona, "I am profoundly grateful."

Finishing quickly, as he often did, Mentu went to the cabin and thence to the upper deck where he took sightings with the quadrant. The storm had ruined their reckoning of position and so it was necessary to come up with some idea of where they were. He used a sighting of the giant red star Kemm, which came above the horizon shortly after sunset. Kemm's ruddy glow was many times brighter than any other star in the heavens.

Later, the planet Igen—"the bright one," as it was called by the men of Shasht, also known as Zanth in the language of the Land—rose above the horizon and could be used for further measurements. Then the readings obtained were checked against the tables in the book of variables. With two figures in hand, their north-south location could be determined. East-west was another matter.

Thru went back to the main cabin to see the results of Mentupah's sightings. He found him with the lantern lit and a chart of the Eastern Marukas unrolled on the table. Mentu greeted him by pointing to the chart.

"From the readings I took, I'd say we're about two hundred miles north of where we were yesterday. But how far to the east we've been blown I cannot tell. We couldn't track our speed, and even the log and line were torn away." Mentu looked back to the map. "I think we must be fairly close to this arc of islands here, the so-called Lost Marukas. If I'm right, we'll pass through them in a day or so. Once we're past them, we enter the great ocean."

"So, this will be our last chance to find more banyam."

"Unless we want to turn back and search the other Marukas."

"Our voyage has been long enough. Everyone is keen to push on."

"Right, of course." Mentu looked down.

Thru guessed what was troubling him. "I know you're concerned about what it will be like when we reach the Land."

"Well, yes. Where will we fit in? I certainly don't want to join the Emperor's army. But then again, I don't know how I'd feel fighting against it either."

"I don't think you'll be forced to join our army."

"Well, that's a relief, I suppose."

"And you won't be alone. There will be other men, maybe even women. We had taken some prisoners, even by the time I was captured. By now there will be more."

"So you foresee a little village of us?"

"Perhaps. I don't know. It will be a decision for the Kings. Perhaps the Assenzi will invite you all to live in Highnoth."

"Ah, this Highnoth, you mentioned it before. You trained there, you said."

"I did. It is in the far north, and it gets cold in

winter. You will learn many wonderful things at High-noth. The Assenzi will teach you."

"Mmmm. I see." Mentu managed not to sound too dismissive.

"I know it will be hard at times. But you knew that from the moment you decided to come."

"Yes. That's true."

"If you or Janbur had stayed in Shasht, you would have had to stay hidden for the rest of your lives. Or you would have been killed."

Mentu nodded. He had been imprisoned in a remote tower for twenty years on his brother's orders. In doing so, the Emperor had been protecting him. But then the Emperor had fallen, and no one knew where he was or if he still lived. The priests would have come for Mentupah sooner or later.

Suddenly they heard a pounding of feet on the deck, and Juf burst into the cabin.

"We have a light, very distant."

Mentu hurried up the mast, spyglass in hand. Janbur climbed the boom they'd fished into the wreck of the foremast.

Thru climbed into the crow's nest, too. Far away to the north he saw the glimmer of a distant lamp.

Mentu frowned as he lowered the spyglass. "We had better douse our own lights and steer away from them."

"Why?" asked Thru.

"That will be a fishing boat. But the distinction between fishermen and pirates is none too fine in the Marukas. If the fishing isn't good enough, there are other ways of making a living."

They set their course south, steering by the constellation of the Porpoises with the bright blue star Bilades to the fore. Through the night they kept an anxious watch for a light behind them, but none was seen.

By dawn they were scudding south and east on a fine westerly wind. The *Sea Wasp* was riding well despite the imbalance between her two masts. Unfortunately, no sooner had they set to eating their banyams and dried fish than Pern Glazen, the mot in the crow's nest, spotted a triangular sail to the west.

Mentu studied it for a while then pronounced the worst. "That rig tells me they are Maruka fishermen. They are following us, no doubt of it."

"The fishing wasn't good enough, then?"

"They can see that we were dismasted in the storm. Perhaps they think they can catch us."

"Well, we have eight fighters," said Thru. "We can give a good account of ourselves."

"No, we are seven," said Mentu. "A woman cannot take up arms."

Simona looked at him with exasperation. "This woman has taken up arms before," she said.

Thru nodded in agreement. Simona had fought Red Top priests on more than one occasion during their strange odyssey together across Shasht.

Mentu's face tightened. "It is against all tradition, all precedent."

"Dear Mentu, you are such a conservative at heart."

Janbur said nothing, but Thru could tell that he agreed with Mentu. All Shasht men were like this about women.

Their main problem, however, was their lack of weapons. They had but a single bow, and it was small and weak. A couple of swords, some knives, a pair of axes from the ship's tool kit, and that was about it.

Thru searched the contents of the hold. Useful clubs could be fashioned from a broken spar, but of metal for arrow points there was none.

The *Sea Wasp* sailed on, and the triangular sail gained slowly but steadily. By late afternoon, the pursuer's hull was visible above the horizon.

Then came the welcome cry of "Land ho!" from
Janbur in the crow's nest. Soon they spied the outlines
of several small islands. Then more appeared to the
south and a vast coral reef became visible. Beyond it
they glimpsed a wide lagoon and a central volcanic
island.

By tacking first to the north and then turning
sharply south, they worked their way between two
rocky isles and into a channel that was out of view of
their pursuers. They steered between two outreaching
arms of wave-swept coral, fled across a wide bay, and
entered the lagoon. Now they were hidden from the
open sea by a headland leading off the main island.
They found a sheltered backwater and dropped
anchor.

Above and all around them grew a riot of tropical
vegetation, deep green with bursts of scarlet and yellow. Birds greeted their arrival with raucous cries and
then fell silent.

Everyone went ashore. While the others looked for
a tree that would be suitable for a new mast, Thru
and Simona climbed to the top of the headland to spy
out the sea to the north. As they climbed, Thru examined all the trees and bushes, keeping an eye out for
limbs to use for bows or spears.

Although the ground was full of sharp volcanic
shards, the slope was gentle for the most part, and he
and Simona soon reached the top. Pressing forward
through a dwarf forest of penhueche trees, they came
to the edge of a thirty-foot cliff and below that a steep
slope down into the forest skirting the northern shore
of the headland. A mile away, across the lagoon, surf
pounded on the reef. Beyond that, blue water
stretched into the distance. Other islands loomed here
and there, each surrounded by a ring of surf marking
its reef.

They scanned the sea carefully. Thru opened the

spyglass and studied the horizon. "There," he said at last. "Found them."

A small scrap of white sail danced in the spyglass.

"Where?" said Simona as he handed her the tube.

Thru guided her to the spot, farther down the channel to the east, well past the island they were on.

"Then they missed us?"

"Looks that way."

They took turns studying the distant sail until it vanished over the horizon. Then they moved back through the dwarf forest until they had a view of the main island. The volcano dominated everything, its slopes clad in green almost all the way to the top several thousand feet above the sea.

Beyond the mountain, extending off to the south and west, were long tongues of land. Again they studied the landscape with the spyglass.

"I see some big stands of banyam trees down there," said Thru.

"Yes," said Simona. "It's just like that first island, where we found so much. The same flowers are blooming."

"If we can get enough here, this will be our last stop. We'll go on to the Land."

Simona nodded. "It's a long way across the ocean."

"That's why your people never found us before."

"Do you think we can do it? In our little ship?"

"The *Sea Wasp* survived the storm."

They were so close together they were almost touching. Their eyes met. They had known the deepest levels of intimacy and remained friends. But there would always be something slightly more than friendship between them.

"What do you think will happen to us?" she said.

"You mean you, Mentu, and Janbur?"

She nodded.

"I don't know. The Assenzi will help you."

He could tell that this wasn't what she wanted to hear.

"I think I would like to live in a village."

Thru chuckled. "Simona, my friend, you are not a farmer. The work never ends, you know."

"I can work hard!" Her face was flushed with indignation.

"I know, but Highnoth will be much more interesting than a village."

"You think the villagers won't accept us, don't you?"

Thru shrugged and took her hand in his.

"Whatever happens, you will always have at least one friend in the Land." Simona squeezed his hand back. If there was one person to have as a friend in this world, Thru Gillo was a very good choice. When she considered what Thru had brought the two of them through during that long winter in Shasht, she was left amazed. The mot had an unquenchable fire in his heart.

The mots were knowledgeable about different kinds of wood, but the trees they knew grew in the Land, thousands of miles northeast of the Marukas. Mentu was their only guide, therefore, and they clambered all over the rugged slopes seeking a particular pine tree that Mentu knew was sometimes used for masts. The wood of this tree was not brittle like most tropical conifers. After surveying the scene carefully, they decided on a specimen growing in a patch of deep soil close to the edge of the cliff.

"Once we have it down, we can pretty much lower it all the way to the water," said Mentu, pointing below to the various stages in the fall of the cliff. That notion confirmed the decision.

Soon they'd brought up ropes and line and began to construct an intricate set of ropeworks that would allow them to lever the fallen tree into the air and then drop it down the steep slope in a controlled manner. Blocks and tackle, pulleys and guy ropes were all eventually used.

Next they took up the saws and began the process of carefully felling the tree. It had to be cut so that it came down close to the cable but not on top of it. They had two saws, one six feet long and made primarily of wood edged with steel and a smaller one made entirely of metal.

By careful work they brought the tree down to within a foot of where they wanted it. Then they set to cutting off the branches, removing the bark, and trimming away imperfections with the adze.

They had been at work like this for only a few minutes when Juf Goost gave a howl of pain. He jumped up and ran around slapping at his skin.

"The ants, the damned ants!"

Soon they were all busy killing the little red pests, which had swarmed out of a small nest at the foot of the tree. It took perhaps half an hour, but eventually the ants were suppressed, and work was resumed.

At ten-foot intervals along the tree, they attached a cuff of rope around the trunk. Other ropes were then relayed through the cuffs and pulled up over the cable that was stretched down the cliff. At every point in the chain of ropes were blocks of pulleys employed to increase the efficiency of the line. To gain extra braking power, they set a cradle of wood on the main line, just ahead of the tree. When they pulled down on a line leading to this wooden cradle, they jammed the tree downward toward the ground and halted its movement along the big cable.

They took up the rope and raised the tree well off the ground. Ter-Saab, Juf, and Thru seized hold of cuffs along the trunk and with considerable effort got the tree moving and out to the point where it hung over the edge of the cliff. They slowly lowered the tree down along the guiding cable some thirty-five feet to the next stage. Then they dismantled the cable and blocks from the top of the mountain and carried it all down the cliff and set it up for the next stage, a more or less vertical drop of fifty feet.

Once more they lowered the log slowly and carefully down to the next stage. The following stages were on less vertical slopes, where the vegetation grew thickly. The difficulty here was passing the log down between the tree trunks. They slung their cable, tree to tree, on relatively short hops as they juggled the trimmed tree along. It was hard work, and they were sweaty and dusty when they paused on a rocky ledge.

They hadn't sat down more than a minute or two before the first ants found them. Simona gave a squeal and slapped at her calf. Janbur followed suit.

"Oh, not again," groaned Jevvi.

This time they found the entire hillside around covered in ants.

"Look at them!" said Simona in a trembling voice. There were millions.

"What we could do with a dozen chooks around here!" said Juf.

"Chooks?" gasped Pern Glazen, slapping at ants on his ankles. "Chooks would have run to the hills by now."

The trees, the ground, the rocks—all were deep, dark red with ants, a red that moved and shifted constantly. An angry roaring sound came up from this vast army's mandibles.

It became a race with death. While four of them fanned out with branches and brush pulled together into crude brooms, the others worked frantically to set up the tackle, lift the tree, and slide it over the cliff for the next stage, about forty feet down to a spot that overlooked the lagoon below.

The ants were very determined. The work was punctuated with a roar of oaths and shrieks of pain until they were able to get the log over the edge where it rattled down through the underbrush to the next stage. Then they ran, crawled, flopped, and slid to get down the slope as quickly as possible and distance themselves from the red horde.

Everyone was feeling the effect of so much venom. Poor Ter-Saab actually fainted at one point. They had to pick him up and carry him, or the ants would have killed him. If you stayed still too long, they went for the eyes.

At last they had the tree positioned at the top of a sandy slope that went straight down to the water.

"To hell with the ropes," snarled Mentu. "Let it roll the rest of the way."

No one cared to argue with that idea. They lined up along the tree trunk, gave it a heave over the top of the slope, and then stood back while it rumbled down the sand and splashed into the water.

They noticed that ant scouts were starting to appear around them. The whole island was alive with excited colonies.

"I'm getting off this damned island," roared Mentu, running down the slope and throwing himself into the lagoon.

Juf was the last to follow him, but only by a few seconds.

By the time the sun was beginning to set, they had hauled the log out to float alongside the *Sea Wasp*.

With considerable discomfort, they washed off the grease, dirt, and dust and gathered to eat a somber little meal by the light of a single lamp.

Even in that dim light Thru could see that they were all sporting dozens of hot blisters.

"Well, at least they didn't get onboard this time," said Juf.

"I hope that's true. I really do," replied Pern.

"I can sure understand why nobody ever settled on these islands," muttered Mentu.

"Anyone for a round of 'The Jolly Beekeeper'?" said Juf in a lame attempt at humor.

"Oh, shut up!" said half a dozen voices.

The next day they moved around a little slowly, gingerly. They worked with saws and drills, hammers and wooden spikes to outfit the mast before they raised it over the side and then, with a line from the top of the mizzenmast, lifted it slowly and carefully, and planted it in the mast hole.

They used the remains of the old mast to help buttress the new one, which was slightly narrower than the old. Spars were attached, block and tackle added, and soon they were fitting the mast into the rigging of the ship, with lines fore and aft and a pair of spars.

In the meantime, Simona and Janbur went ashore and searched the island for food. They found two big stands of ripening banyam. In addition, thick-stemmed sugar grass was growing densely by the lagoon. It could be harvested and dried. It was poor quality food, but it would keep them alive if necessary.

They began harvesting banyam and sugar grass that same day. By then, Thru had another project to keep him busy. While they were carrying banyam back to the ship, Mentu had pointed out a klimm tree.

"Such wood is used for making bows. It's very springy, very strong. Has to be cut along the grain. Takes a fine hand and a good saw."

Thru visited the tree the same afternoon and came away with a pair of nice-sized branches. He cut and trimmed them, removed the bark, treated the wood with spirits, and began honing it down with a plane and a sharp knife. Since the wood could not be treated at length, or even dried out, he cut the bows deliberately large, almost bulky to the hand. They would have seemed heavy, even ugly, to his father, Ware, he thought, but Ware always used well-aged yew with its great strength and resilience. All that mattered to Thru was that these bows would drive a heavy arrow a good distance.

As the afternoon lengthened, he turned aside from the bows and prepared some stout lines for use as bow strings. He cut them precisely, worked the nocking loops up, and sewed them tight. Then he greased the string lightly and rubbed it through a cloth.

By the time the sun was dropping toward the western horizon, Thru had finished one bow and was close to being done with the other.

He had a handful of arrows, small ones designed for the little bow he'd brought all the way from Shesh Zob. Now he strung the bow and practiced with these light arrows. The bow worked well, perhaps a little clumsy in feel, but it was strong. Barely pulled halfway back, it drove one of his hunting arrows deep into the mast. Thru set it aside for the day, pleased with his efforts.

The sun slid toward the horizon. Simona and Jevvi had not returned from an expedition to the southern part of the island. Thru became concerned.

When the moon rose, Thru and Juf lowered a boat, pushed off, and rowed out toward the channel. The winds were light, and the lagoon was as calm as a lily pond. To their left loomed a continuous wall of white coral, marking the reef. To their right the land was a dark mass, fringed at the base by a strip of pale sand.

As they rowed, they discussed the likely fate of their mission.

"Well, you know what will have happened," said Juf. "They'll have got back not ten minutes after we left. That's the way it always goes."

"I know what you mean," agreed Thru.

Fool's errand or not, the night was beautiful, the rowing was not difficult, and they continued to slide south across the smooth sheet of dark water. Ahead loomed the high south point, part of an extended ridge from the central volcanic core of the island. Beyond the point, the lagoon opened out into the wider water of the channel. A slight breeze stirred the air here, and on the farther banks of coral they could see the phosphorescent glow of surf.

They came around the point and almost immediately shipped their oars.

Inside the point, anchored under the headland, was a single-masted fishing schooner. The same sort of craft that had been chasing the *Sea Wasp*.

"I don't like the look of that," muttered Thru.

"I think I know where Jevvi and Simona are," replied Juf in a somber voice.

Chapter 2

Thru unshipped the oars and had Juf hold them while he wrapped rags around the oarlocks. When he was sure they wouldn't betray them, he rowed carefully to the ship.

There was no one visible on the deck. Thru thought it unlikely that no one was keeping watch, so he continued to approach cautiously. He slowed their approach with cautious dips of the oars. As they got closer, they caught the reek of rotten fish.

They slid in close beneath the stern of the fishing ship until they were able to actually touch the hull and hold the boat steady against it. The light was coming from a half-open port on the right side. Gruff voices were arguing up there.

Listening carefully, Thru began to make sense of the argument. His heart sank when he heard a particularly loud, deep voice break in: "Witch mark! All over her tits!"

They had captured Simona.

He made a sign to Juf and continued listening.

"Well, you fellows may do what you want," the big voice continued, "but I say she's bad luck, and we're better off selling her as untouched as possible. Take her right back to Shasht now and put her into the market. Make up for the lousy fishing we've had."

"What? And leave that barky out here? She's from that ship, what else do you think?"

"As well as the thing, the monster?"

"Well, who knows what the hell it is, but we'll cook it tomorrow and get some use out of it, eh? Haven't had meat in I don't know how long."

"Hope it's not too tough a chew," said someone.

"Heh, heh, we tenderized it pretty well, I'd say."

"Enough! What if we can find that barky? We could be selling a barky and a few more slaves."

"So we'll look around tomorrow. But I don't see any harm in poking the girl. That's all that's coming for her anyway, once she's sold."

"Look, if we all use her every day from now until when we get her to the market, she's going to be worn out. If you want good gold for her, then we have to agree to leave her alone."

"Ach, how often do we get a chance to poke something this good?"

Thru listened with deepening foreboding. Then he shifted forward to whisper to Juf.

Shortly afterward, he left the boat and began to climb up the side of the ship's stern. Over his shoulder he took the new bow, with six shafts in a small quiver tied high on his belt.

Juf remained where he was, hidden under the stern in case any of the crew came on deck.

The vessel was somewhat smaller than the *Sea Wasp*. Once Thru could peer over the top of the gunwale, he sized up the situation. The ship was steered by a tiller that ran out to a cockpit set under the foreside of the sterncastle. The small upper deck was bare except for a rail and lines running up to the mast. In the cockpit was the watch, a single man smoking a pipe.

Upon closer study, Thru realized the watch at the tiller was far more attuned to the argument going on in the big room behind him than to the ship and its surroundings.

"Witch mark!" yelled another voice down below.

There was a loud chorus of groans.

Thru found a useful seam in the outer hull near the gunwale and slid around from the sterncastle to the waist of the ship. He pulled himself over the gunwale and slipped silently into the foresection. The watch had not seen him.

The fishing boat was a popular type, with a small hold forward for the catch. The man at the tiller guarded the dark entranceway leading to the interior cabins inside the sterncastle. The men arguing over Simona's fate were somewhere behind him. So, most likely, was Simona herself. Thru cast a prayer to the Spirit that she wasn't able to hear their horrible talk.

Thru's nose twitched. The foul fishy smell was coming from the bow. He moved silently forward. The mainsail was furled, and a long, dark object was hanging from the mast on a line run to the forespit. He frowned and hoped it was not too late.

By the side of the ship, near a coil of rope, he found the source of the stink, a chum pot the size of a man's head. Thru peered over the side. The water in this cove was deep, and the fishermen had anchored close to the shore. It was no more than forty feet to the narrow strand of moonlit sand. Thru nodded to himself.

Then he went back to investigate the hanging object.

As he had feared, it turned out to be poor Jevvi Panst, strung up by his heels. However, he was not dead. Thru detected a pulse, faint but steady.

A glance showed him that the man at the tiller was still engrossed in the argument. Emboldened, Thru hunted along the side of the forward hold. He found a sail cache and pulled out a heavy bundle of spare jib sails. Bound up, he imagined, they were not too different in shape from a badly beaten mot hanging by his heels.

Thru returned to the mast, selected a line that would normally raise a sail, and tied the bag full of jibs to it. Carefully he hauled it up and swung it close to the hanging shape of poor Jevvi.

When it was parked next to the mot, he tied the line on a cleat at the side rail. He lowered the line bearing Jevvi and slowly laid him out onto the deck. Jevvi sputtered once, then returned to silence. Thru listened to his breathing, slow, shallow, but steady.

A sudden noise came from the tiller side, a loud grunt, as of disapproval. Thru froze. Had the watch noticed something at last? Thru peered over the near-side sail cache and was reassured. The man had simply reacted to something said in the backroom. Thru returned to his task.

With Jevvi lowered to the deck, Thru could see more clearly the extent of his injuries. He had been beaten to a pulp. Staying low, Thru pulled Jevvi across the deck to the side while keeping the mast and the pin rail directly between himself and the man at the tiller. Thru dared a quick look over the side.

Down below, Juf saw him at once and silently moved the boat over so it was directly beneath.

Thru took hold of Jevvi and lifted him into his arms, then set him on the rail. Jevvi was a deadweight, but lighter than Thru had expected. Working the line through a cleat on the rail, he carefully lowered the injured mot down the side of the fishing ship until he felt Juf take hold. Thru cut the line and tied it off at the cleat.

Now he slid back toward the man at the tiller, who was turned halfway into the passage so he could hear more clearly what was being said. They were arguing about who would get the first turn with the girl. They had decided that they would all have a turn with her, but then they would leave her be until she was sold at the slave market. A drawing of straws was proposed, then the throwing of dice. Each concept had its supporters.

Thru crept closer, behind the ship's small boat, which was stowed aboard by the mast. He was wondering if he would be able to shoot the fellow without alerting the others. Then he could get past him to investigate the cabin where, he suspected, Simona was being kept.

Just then, however, a door opened, and two other men emerged to stand in the cockpit by the tiller rod.

"Hey, Mergas, you get fourth turn. All right by you?" said one of them.

"And Tricko gets first, I suppose?"

"No, he came second this time. Supor gets the cherry."

"Well, well, well, that makes a change."

Thru crouched down, ready to nock an arrow if he had to. But the men opened another door and disappeared inside for a moment, then reappeared carrying bottles.

"Oh, drinking up the wine, too, are we?" said the man at the tiller.

"You'll get your glassful, Mergas, don't worry."

"Just my luck to pull watch on this night."

"You're always griping, Mergas, you know that?"

Another door opened and closed.

The one addressed as Mergas gave a sigh and stepped into the cockpit and looked around.

Nothing struck him as being out of place at first, but then he spotted a line left tied to the side-rail cleat. Mergas stepped forward, intent on tidying up that line.

Thru fell back, hiding behind the pin rail until Mergas passed. Then he rose and struck the man on the back of the head with a wooden bucket. Mergas fell to the deck and did not move.

The man was heavy, much heavier than Jevvi Panst.

Thru got a shoulder under the weight and, staggering a little, dragged the body forward and laid it down near the chum pot.

Then he hurried back to try the doors of the cabins.

A rumble of voices arose in the cabin on the left side as he stepped into the dark passage. He froze for a moment, ears straining. But the rumble merely presaged a coarse bellow of laughter.

"Holds liquor by its ears!" roared a voice, and the laughter redoubled.

On the right were two doors, a small one, which obviously led to a closet of some kind, and a full-size one leading to a cabin.

He tried them both. The smaller one opened easily and revealed tools and bottles set inside container rails. Furled sailcloth was stacked in bolts at the back. The larger door was locked. After quick examination, Thru saw that it was stoutly made and would resist his efforts to kick it in. Long before he could rescue Simona, the other men would take him prisoner, too.

He backed down the passage to the cockpit and took a look over the side. The ports on that side were shuttered and fastened from within. There was no easy way to get inside that cabin.

At the bow he took another look at the nearby land. Forest came down right to the edge, with trees forcing their way out over the rocks. The nearest was no more than fifty feet away.

That gave him an idea. Thru lifted the big coil of rope at the bow and tossed it down to Juf. Then he wound a line around the chum pot and carefully lowered it over the side. Juf received the smelly pot of fish guts with both big eyebrows lofted in curiosity.

After recovering his bow, Thru climbed over the side. When he was down, Juf pushed the boat out from the ship and then began to row, with care but with power, to take them back out of the cove and around the point.

"You will leave me on the far side of the point, then go back to the *Sea Wasp*. They must raise the anchor and bring her down here."

"What will you do?"

"They have locked Simona in a cabin. To free her we have to distract these pirates and then board them."

Juf, still puzzled, looked to the pot of chum. Thru turned to him with a grim smile.

"I'm going to make things interesting for them. Which is why you must press on as hard as you can. Tell Mentu to make haste. It won't take long, I think, to get things stirring."

Clutching the heavy chum pot, Thru clambered out of the front of the rowboat and splashed ashore. He set it down carefully and went back for the big coil of rope.

"Every minute is precious, Juf."

But Juf needed no reminding. He drove the oars into the water and propelled the boat back out into the sea.

Thru watched Juf go, then shouldered the rope, took up the smelly clay pot, and ran up the rocky point to the trees. There had been no cry of outrage from the ship yet, but it couldn't be too long before the pirates found they'd been boarded by stealth and robbed of the meat they'd planned to roast the next day.

Thru had much to do in that time.

He left the pot on the beach, took one last look at the fishing vessel sitting at anchor just fifty feet away, and went up into the tangled forest. He found a stout enough tree just ten feet or so up from the sand. With several low branches it was easy to climb. He took one end of the rope up with him and tied it around the trunk some twelve feet up. He dropped down quickly, then pulled the rope behind him out through the lower bushes and down to the beach.

Now came the least pleasant part of the task. He removed the lid of the chum pot and, using a leafy twig stripped from a bush, began to splash the rope with the sticky muck. The smell was appalling, but he could see by the moonlight that the chum left a dark stain on the rope wherever it landed. In a couple of minutes it was done. The rope was thoroughly stained.

He walked out into the water with the stinking rope over one shoulder, slid in on the other side, and swam sidestroke out toward the ship. As he went he unreeled the rope from his shoulder and played it out behind him. When he reached the ship, he pulled himself up at the bow on the anchor cable. The cable passed through an oval hole in the gunwale before fastening to a bollard just aft of the bow. Thru slipped the end of his chum-stained rope through that hole, then crawled back onboard and heaved on the rope to pull it clear of the water. It came up quickly, and he wound it around the bollard with a double hitch. Now it stretched above the water all the way back to the tree on the shore and, being stained, was hard to see in the dark.

Mergas was still unconscious on the deck behind the mast. Back in the cabin, the men were still singing some bawdy song. They broke into guffaws with the conclusion of each verse.

There was still time to save Simona.

Thru climbed back over the bow, and this time he dove in headfirst, knifing down into the water. They weren't likely to hear him now. He stayed under the surface all the way back to the shore, coming up only when he could put his feet down.

Still, no sound of uproar from the ship. The fates

were with him. He hurried up the beach, grabbed the chum pot, and slipped into the forest.

Back at the bottom of the tree, he dipped his branch in the pot and smeared the awful stuff onto the trunk all the way up to the rope. He put a thick gob or two on the rope as well. Then he climbed down and took the pot farther inland.

Through the undergrowth he spread the stuff, flicking it here, there, and everywhere, on bark and ground and fallen leaves. Within a few minutes he'd spread the stench far and wide above the narrow beach. Then he traced a path back to the tree, redoubling the spatters on the ground, right up to the trunk of the tree.

The powerful smell hung under the trees. Everything that lived there was immediately aware of it.

He did not have long to wait. He saw the first ants scurrying across white sand under the moonlight before he got back to the tree. A moment later, a sharp pain on his left ankle warned him that it was time to get out of the bushes. Several more stings were delivered before he could get down to the beach and throw himself back into the water.

He stayed in the surf, keeping low, and swam for the point.

He was halfway there when the ship erupted at last into roars of rage. The men had finished their wine, emerged from the cabin, and found Mergas out cold. Being excited by wine, they misinterpreted the scene at first, thinking him merely malingering.

"Should've known you'd try and sleep through your watch!" one of the men charged. Mergas did not respond, even to a less than gentle nudge by Tricko's boot.

Then someone noticed the substitution of a bag of sailcloth for the creature they'd planned to eat for breakfast.

They howled in anger. In sudden dread they turned

and all tried to get into the passage at once in their
haste to assure themselves that the girl was still captive. That set them to squabbling, even exchanging a
few blows. Finally someone announced that she was
still there, untouched, and they gave a universal sigh
of relief.

By this time, unseen by the fishermen, the first ants
had reached the ship. The chum-soaked line was a
highway covered in ants, and they were heading one
way.

Thru swam around the shallow headland before
emerging onto the rocks. Fortunately, the wind was
keeping the surf off the headland that night. He
scrambled up into a position from which he could see
both the fishing ship and the eastward side of the point
to the northern part of the lagoon, where the *Sea
Wasp* lay at anchor.

The aftereffects of the previous half hour struck him
now that he was sitting down. He shivered, feeling a
sudden chill. He worked himself back into a crack in
the rocks from which he could still keep watch.

He was sure that Juf should be back at the *Sea
Wasp* soon. Mentu would hurry. They had a chance
of saving Simona.

Back on the fishing boat, the men, still arguing, were
about to set down their dinghy to search for any sign
of their missing breakfast, when someone discovered
that they had an invasion of ants.

By then the ants had found the contents of their
hold: a ton of well-dried flatfish, taken on the Basalt
Banks. News of this discovery among the ant nests on
the island had produced an explosion of activity. The
tide of ants scurrying along Thru's rope thickened
until it was three and four deep.

It was the worst nightmare for a fishing crew in the
ant-infested Marukas.

Yells of anger, horror, and, soon, of pain rang out

on the ship. Using whatever came to hand, the men flung themselves on the ants. Brooms and boots, palms and feet—everything was employed to smash them.

The line was finally discovered and cut, but by then the ship was inundated with ten thousand little red horrors. The battle intensified. Every pirate had been stung again and again, and still the struggle went on while shouts of pain and rage echoed around the lagoon.

Thru caught a gleam on a taut sail and then another coming out of the north. Hurrying down the lagoon's length came the *Sea Wasp* with sails full, on a freshening seaward breeze.

Never was a sight so welcome. As the *Sea Wasp* approached, he ran down to the water's edge and tore off his shirt and waved it above his head.

They were watching for him and soon spotted him. The *Sea Wasp* came about while the sails were lowered. The boat was set down, and Juf rowed swiftly over to the point. Thru swam out to meet him halfway, and they returned in haste to the *Sea Wasp*.

Once onboard, he took a swig of warmed coconut juice and explained the situation. "I arranged for a little ant invasion of their ship. They're still dealing with it."

Unconsciously, everyone in the room blinked and shivered. The pain of their own experiences in battling the ants were all too recent.

"So, right now they're probably not being very observant. They know that Jevvi is gone and that somebody boarded their ship without them knowing, but they have a more pressing problem on their hands."

"So that's what the stink pot was for," exclaimed Juf.

"But we still have not freed Simona, and we will have to take their ship to do it."

"Then it's best if we swim to the ship and attack by stealth, while they are occupied with the ants."

"Unnnh," groaned Pern Glazen. "You mean, their ship is covered in the ants?"

"Yes. Just listen—you can hear them cursing."

And it was true. Howls of pain wafted over the rocky point.

"I wonder if that was such a good move," grumbled Pern.

"If it keeps them from seeing us until we're onboard, then it's worth it."

"And if we get onboard, are we going to kill them?" asked Janbur.

"If we have to, we will kill them. Jevvi may not recover from the beating they gave him. The best swimmers will swim out. Juf and Janbur will follow in the boat, and we'll use that to make our getaway."

Plans made, they selected weapons. The swimmers took the swords and knives and tied them tightly to their waists before they dropped from the boat and began to swim.

Aboard the pirate vessel, the fight with the ants was still very much alive. Four men were down in the hold swatting and wielding brooms. Even with the line cut to prevent any more of the little horrors getting aboard, the men faced a terrible ordeal. The worst thing would be for a few hundred ants to escape and start a nest. One of them would be selected to become the queen, and the ship would never be free of the infestation.

Ter-Saab was the first to reach the ship. Thru was close behind him, alongside Mentu and Pern Glazen. They gathered there, listening carefully. Thru crawled up the sternpost and found a seam in which to plant his feet and slide over the rail. Ter-Saab quickly joined him, with Mentu and Pern close behind.

"I count five men down there."

"The others are in the hold, I'd say," whispered Mentu.

DOOM'S BREAK

"Then we have a chance," said Thru.

"Now!" said Ter-Saab, and they got up and hurled themselves forward.

The fishermen saw them coming only at the last moment and turned in stunned surprise at the attack. Ter-Saab walloped the closest over the head and threw him headlong down into the hold.

A general melee followed while the men in the hold looked up astonished. With a shout they jumped to the ladder, but Ter-Saab was already there, wielding a broken oar, and the first man on the ladder paid the price.

Thru pitched another man down to the hold, and Pern Glazen hammered a third to the deck. The two who remained on deck drew back into the bow, holding out their knives. Their faces were contorted in terror, for in the moonlight they perceived they were fighting inhuman foes.

"Demons!" one of them shouted. "They're fornicating demons!"

"They look like the thing we caught in the woods. Apes of some sort," shouted Tricko from down in the hold.

"They're apes who know how to fight," shouted back the man on deck.

Thru Gillo leaned over the lip of the hold and called down in the tongue of the men of Shasht. "If you try to get out, we will kill you, do you understand? You will stay in the hold until we are gone."

The men fell silent.

"It speaks?" said one.

"I do indeed," said Thru very clearly. "You have done us a great wrong and severely hurt our comrade. For that you will pay, but we will not have your blood on our hands if we can avoid it."

"You saying you ain't going to kill us?" said Tricko, the leader and de facto captain of the ship.

Just then Janbur came running up, for Juf had brought the boat alongside the pirate vessel. Janbur carried one of the bows that Thru had made, and with it Thru's quiver of arrows. He gave this to Ter-Saab, who notched an arrow and held it ready above the men in the hold.

"We will not kill you. But we will be avenged."

The men stood there, clenching and unclenching their fists, their faces twisted in frustrated rage.

The two men at the bow still held out their knives, prepared to sell themselves dearly. Pern at one side and Mentu at the other confronted them with hammer and sword. Janbur went forward to join Mentu. Juf had climbed up at last, and he joined Pern.

The men in the hold seethed.

"Who the hell are you?" roared their leader.

Mentu leaned over the hold.

"We are men of Shasht, with our friends here, who are a folk from a distant land."

"They are furred demons. What do you do with them? You are unclean."

"No, they are a good-hearted people. We can learn much from them."

"Abomination! You speak abomination. We are men—we cannot learn from animals!"

"So you say. I think you are wrong."

Thru spoke to the men who crouched in the bow with drawn knives.

"Put down your knives. Jump down into the hold, and we will not harm you."

The men looked to each other with wide eyes.

"What should we do?" shouted one of them down to Tricko, the leader.

Tricko hesitated, undecided.

"Move down!" said Thru. "Or we will kill you." He gestured to the bow in Ter-Saab's hands.

At twenty feet, Ter-Saab couldn't miss. The men

realized this. Both of them laid their knives on the deck and swung over into the hold and dropped down.

The ants were still boiling below, and the men could not stand still. They had to defend themselves from the red hordes.

Ter-Saab chuckled, watching the men stamping their feet and slapping their hands against the walls of the hold. "So that's what it looks like when you're fighting ants," he said to the others.

They all laughed. Another man gave a howl and swatted at his neck.

Thru and Janbur went back to the cabin. Breaking down the door, they cut Simona free of the post to which she'd been tied. She was unhurt but for a few cuts and bruises.

They helped her to her feet and she embraced Thru, thanking him for saving her from a dreadful fate. As they held each other, a frown formed on Janbur's brow.

"So, dear Simona," said Thru, "can you walk? Are you hurt?"

"I can walk. Thank you, Thru, you came back for me . . ."

"Of course. We all did."

He helped her into the passage, past the frowning Janbur.

Suddenly the opposite door opened and Mergas emerged, having finally woken up with a splitting headache. He gave a shriek at the sight of them and swung blindly at Thru, clipping him on the ear. A moment later, Mergas's knife was out, and he drove in at them, growling.

Taken by surprise, Thru reeled from the blow. Simona gave a scream and fell against the pirate. His knife cut her along her side as she went down, but his thrust at Thru's belly went wide. Mergas stumbled over Simona and lost his balance. Thru shoved him backward, and he fell over in the passageway.

Thru landed on top of him immediately, caught the knife hand, and delivered a hard blow to the man's chin. Mergas went limp once more. Thru took his knife, then turned back to Simona.

Janbur was helping her up. There was a line of scarlet along her side.

"How deep?" asked Thru.

"I don't know," she said. "Not too badly, I think." Her hand came away from her side dripping blood, and she fainted into Janbur's arms. Janbur carried her to the ship's side and, with help from Juf and Mentu, lowered her down into the boat.

Ter-Saab kept his position at the head of the ladder with an arrow drawn. The pirates dared not try to get past him.

Thru came out of the stern cabin carrying a lantern blazing high. "You will live," he told the men, "but you will suffer, and you will rue your evil actions here."

With that he smashed the lantern against the mast. The burning oil flowed out and onto the lowered sail.

The men screamed as one when they saw the bright flames flicker along the sail and catch.

Pern Glazen broke another lamp on top of the sterncastle and then dove overboard. Thru and Ter-Saab were the last to leave, jumping over the side together as the flames took hold. They swam for the boat, which Juf had taken out about fifty feet.

Behind them, the pirates fought frantically to put out the fires, which blazed high in the tropical darkness.

As they rowed for the point, with Ter-Saab hanging on in the back, they heard the men cursing them horribly. The rescuers said nothing, but exchanged grim smiles.

Back aboard the *Sea Wasp,* Janbur and Mentu examined Simona's wound. It was a slashing cut, a quarter inch deep down her rib cage and along her hip.

"It will need to be salted," said Mentu, "to keep it from infection. And we must sew it up. That will hurt horribly."

Simona bit her lip. "I am not a weak woman of purdah anymore. I will not cry out and beg you to stop."

A closer examination of Jevvi's injuries left them far less sanguine, however. Jevvi's labored breathing brought up bubbles of blood. He remained unconscious, and there were terrible swellings on his skull.

They raised the sail once more, catching the last of the offshore breeze. As they drew past the point, they looked back into the cove and saw the pirate vessel ablaze from bow to stern. The men had swum to shore and were standing in a glum line in the shallows.

Once they were out in the open sea, Mentu turned the *Sea Wasp* north. For the rest of the following day, they sailed across the Maruka channel. A day later, they had left the Marukas behind and were launched upon the huge northern ocean.

It was plain by then that Jevvi would not recover.

That evening, Thru found Mentu and Janbur sitting together in the bow while the sun sank in the west. "Why did they hurt Jevvi so much?" Thru asked.

Both men sighed and looked out to the horizon. "Why?" murmured Mentu. "Because in their lives any sign of compassion would be taken as weakness. The others would tear them apart."

"More the question, really," said Janbur, "is why you wouldn't be like them."

Thru blinked, reminded suddenly of the great gulf between mot and Man.

Two days later, far from any land, Jevvi Panst died. They had done what they could for him, but he never awoke.

Pern Glazen sang the sad songs of the Sulo Valley, which was their home, and they consigned Jevvi's body to the deeps, wrapped in a piece of old sailcloth with a ballast stone tied to his ankles.

They continued northeast, out into the vastness of the ocean with only the Land itself far ahead.

Chapter 3

It was the fifth summer of the war. The fifth summer in which red flames licked up from burning villages. The fifth summer in which the sounds of battle rang out beneath the trees and on the beaches. The fifth summer that saw the grim burials of the fallen, whether by solemn mots in village burial grounds or lines of men aboard the Shasht fleet as the dead, with rocks tied between their ankles, were dropped overboard.

By this fifth summer, no one in the Land wondered why the army of men had been sent to haunt their lives. It was simply accepted in the way of any other catastrophe.

Aboard the Shasht fleet, the war had become a nightmare without end. But no one ever thought about pulling up anchor and sailing away to find some other place to start the colony. Too much blood had been spent fighting for this land already. They were men, and they had been sent to take this land for the Empire. They would do it, or they would die trying.

Toshak, the former professional swordmot who had once rebelled at the training at the Royal Academy of Sulmo, was now the acclaimed commanding general of the army of the Land, both North and South. Having driven the Shasht army out of Sulmo before they could burn the city, Toshak and his soldiers had enjoyed plenty of leverage in establishing that unified command.

Relations were still difficult with King Gueillo and his inner circle, of course. Some members of the Sulmese nobility would always nurse the old grievance. For them, the dream of Old Sulmo would not die. Among their circle, cooperation with Dronned and the other Northern kingdoms was regarded as subjugation.

For this and other reasons, Toshak had kept his army's base in Dronned. But within the past year he had been forced to spend most of his time in Sulmo again, where the Shasht fleet had chosen to place its forts.

Fortunately, the disaster of the battle of Farnem-Chillum had helped the Sulmese people to see the need for cooperation. Outside of the royal court, the friction that had occasionally troubled Thru Gillo and other Northern officers during the second summer of the war had vanished.

But for Toshak, it was always present. The King had never forgiven Toshak for resigning his commission in the Royal Army of Sulmo and leaving the realm to become a vagabond in the North.

He refused to let it bother him. He had a war to fight. It was a difficult campaign as well, for it forced him to keep large forces in the field all the time. Toshak understood the enemy's rationale. The men were far from home, and they were desperate to keep their casualties low. They had suffered terribly in the first two years of the war, even worse than the folk of the Land. The war of forts was a clever strategy for the Shasht fleet, for it built on their strengths. With the freedom of the seas they had the ability to land and build a strong point before the army of the Land could respond and destroy it. Thus, it was a war of sieges, which allowed the Shasht to continue the war without risking many lives.

On a warm evening of early summer, Toshak sat on the bluffs below Criek's Rock on the coast of Blana.

With him was a group of special troops, gathered from the mountain towns of Creton. Known as the Mountaineers, they were all good rock climbers.

Toshak had brought them there to study the fortress the men of Shasht had built on the top of the Rock. The eighth such fort the men had built, it was well situated to dominate the surrounding country, yet Toshak had already destroyed three others.

Having seen the high stockade and the towers, the Mountaineers' attention was directed to the cliff beneath the Rock.

"Those towers really don't look down on the cliff, do they?" said Captain Oarg, of the Creton Mountaineer Company.

"Right. You can see why we wanted you to take a look at it," said Toshak.

Oarg nodded. He could indeed. The cliff was impressive, but not so difficult for mots such as his.

"The fort itself is well built. Ten-foot-high stockade wall, which is what they normally build. The towers are twelve and fifteen feet high. They even dug a ditch up there, though the ground is half rock."

Oarg continued to study the men's fort. He could see that it was a formidable place. "Not easy to attack with the siege towers either."

"We have kept them busy with fire from our catapults, but as you saw, the ground is steep below those walls, and it isn't easy to approach with siege towers. But, on this side the cliff is so steep, they haven't bothered to put up a wall."

"And the towers are well back from the cliff side, too. The climb will not be an easy one, but then again, it will not be that hard either. Look, there is a stretch on that diagonal crack that would be very quick."

Toshak studied the rock face. The big crack reached up to a place about ten feet below the edge.

"And after that?"

"Well, it looks a little tricky. But I can see some smaller cracks. I think it will take some time, that is all."

"That's what I was hoping you might say. I think we can give you the time you need."

Oarg, a phlegmatic sort, shrugged. "Then, sir, I'd say we can do it. Can you keep anyone up there from looking over the edge of the cliff for about half an hour?"

"Mmmm." Toshak scratched his chin thoughtfully. "I think we can arrange that. If you begin the ascent before dawn, on a foggy morning. We will test the outer walls after dawn and present them with a dragon to keep their interest focused."

"A dragon?" asked Oarg.

"Yes, made of wood and painted cloth, very lifelike. Of course, we won't let them see it very clearly. But they'll all be watching the forest in the hope of seeing it again. We'll keep them busy with that for a while, and then we'll attack with the new siege towers. That will really keep their attention and give you the time you need to climb the cliff."

"And then?"

"Can you take the gate from inside?"

"Two hundred of us, sir?"

"Yes."

Oarg was nodding with pursed lips. "I think we might, sir."

The plot was a daring one, but it would avoid a lengthy siege. Toshak left and traveled upstream through the woods, then across the river and up to the heights just below Criek's Rock.

The mots working on the "dragon" were housed in a ring of huts beside a grove of wild hazel. As he strode up, they spotted him and stood to attention beside the hulking shape they had been building.

"Stand easy," he said, returning their salute.

The dragon was made of cloth, bushpod paper, withe, wood, thongs, and dried grass. The wooden frame, shaped like a barrel cut in half lengthwise, was sixteen feet long. The tail, also framed in wood and withe, was another twelve feet. The dragon's head, painted with enormous eyes and a ferocious cast of teeth and red, curling lips, was five feet by three.

The project leader was a brilba named Kuli. She quickly organized a demonstration of the dragon for the commander.

They took their places, twelve mots inside the dragon body, three more controlling the tail, and Kuli holding up the head.

The dragon was now deployed. With head held at a very lifelike angle, the huge thing stepped forward, moved sideways, and then settled as if crouching on its haunches.

"By the Spirit, it looks as if it's alive!" exclaimed Toshak, impressed. "Excellent work!"

The dragon shimmied forward and gave a bow, dipping its huge, fierce head while the front half bent down and the back half and tail rose up.

Inside the temple pyramid in the city of Shasht, Basth waited, kneeling in the corner of the great room. Beside him was the water jug and the tall, silver drinking vessel that the Master preferred.

The world had changed in the most unaccountable way for Basth. Whereas before he had had to help the Master just to stand up, all that kind of physical assistance was now unnecessary.

The Master was now a giant of man, with the physique of a wrestler and the vigor of a racehorse. Basth had witnessed the transformation, heard the screams of horror as the Master climbed onto the huge body. When it was done, the Master arose in the huge young body and cast aside the old one. Basth had supervised the removal of the old body and its cremation. He had brought the pot of ashes to the Master in his new, giant body. Then the Master had cut out Basth's tongue, to ensure that the secret would always be kept.

Sometimes Basth wished fervently that he had never left his village, never even become a Red Top.

Today the Master met once more with a small group of wealthy men. They were the heads of the great banks and trading houses, and they were being squeezed mercilessly to pay for the new fleet.

Their faces clearly displayed the tension they felt.

"Worms!" snarled the Master. His huge hands, created from many years of breaking stone, clenched into fists in front of their faces.

On one recent occasion, Basth had seen him tear a recalcitrant banker out of his seat and beat him half to death in front of the others.

"I will have forty ships, or I will have your heads on poles while your hearts go to the Great God. Am I understood?"

The Master had thrown off all camouflage and emerged as the power behind the throne, and these men had had to accustom themselves to this. Tyrants, all of them, now they cringed before a greater tyrant and wondered how they had let themselves fall to this desperate state.

They had not raised a hand to save Aeswiren, and now they were paying the price.

"Any complaints?"

The small tyrants kept their mouths shut.

The Master glanced to Basth, who hurried to bring him water.

Admiral Heuze, commander in chief of the Shasht fleet, sniffed the air and noted a slight freshening of the wind. Instinctively, he looked up to check the sails,

saw they were furled, and laughed at himself. His ship,
the *Anvil*, was anchored in safe harbor, and he was
about to go ashore.

Once he'd sworn never to set foot on the accursed
land of the monkeys again. Those forests of huge
trees, dark and endless, had seemed a trap. But all of
that was behind him. For the past year, he had been
waging the war in his own fashion, now that Nebbeggebben, the Scion of Aeswiren, was under his thumb
and the priests' power in the fleet had been smashed.

The shoreline loomed half a mile to the east.
Wreathed in the usual mists, the tops of the huge trees
became visible where they erupted out of the fog.
Cliffs, dramatically black, soared three hundred feet
from the narrow beach. The fort was at the top, protected by cliff walls on two sides. The bowl-shaped
bay beneath made an excellent deepwater harbor.

Heuze congratulated himself on the qualities of the
place. He had chosen it from the map. Deep water,
close to shore, well protected from storm winds.

He'd built eight forts on similar locations around
the southern part of the monkey coast. This one was
close to where he'd won his great double victory over
the monkeys almost two years before.

Three forts had been lost, but lessons had been
learned with each loss. No fort had fallen in the past
three months, though all were besieged. It was a different way to fight the war, a way that played to the
advantages Heuze held over his enemy, the mysterious
commander of the monkey hordes.

Based on an island south of the land his fleet was
seeking to colonize, Heuze held the sea and could
operate upon it with relative impunity. Ashore, the
Shasht army faced an enemy with uncommon tactical
skill. Heuze had faced that enemy himself and been
forced into a desperate retreat to the sea.

So Heuze had turned to a war of forts. By coming

ashore, building a strong point and keeping a garrison big enough to hold it, he forced the monkeys to react. The territory all around each fort was at risk of his raids. So it emptied until the monkeys placed troops around the fort to invest it. A war of sneak attacks and raids it was, but it kept the monkeys on the defensive and perpetrated the idea among the colonists that the war was being prosecuted toward some end.

Sometimes, though, even Heuze wondered if they could ever succeed. This was their fifth year here, and for almost two years they had not even dared put an army ashore, just the small garrisons in the forts. The truth was brutal. The colony could not suffer any more casualties and remain viable. Between the terrible plagues and the fierce battles of the first two years, they had lost half their number. Heuze had barely nine thousand soldiers fit for battle.

But, he consoled himself, as he often did, there were only three Gold Top high priests left in the fleet, and the hordes of Red Top priests had been decimated. Their power was broken forever. Worship of the Great God among his men had become much more muted since that time.

Heuze, himself an unbeliever, didn't care much what anyone believed. As long as they obeyed his orders, they could worship Canilass or Buliferri or anything they liked. And as long as the Red Tops stuck with their ceremonial duties, he would let the survivors live.

His barge was ready. While he was lowered on a stout line, a horn blared to announce his departure for the land. Heuze prided himself on not being an invalid, even though he'd lost one leg from the knee down. The sailors, the backbone of the fleet, knew that their admiral was still a seaman. His personal aide, Ensign Combliss, had readied a spot for him, but he knew better than to try helping the admiral sit down.

Once he was seated, the barge shoved off. Rowed by twelve men, stout and true, it raced over the water to the beach. Heuze splashed ashore and was met by General Polluk's aide, Fode.

"Welcome to Fort Aeswiren, Admiral," said Fode, eager to help Heuze up the black shingle beach.

Heuze shook off the man's hand. He'd not be helped by some whelp like Lieutenant Fode. "This isn't the fort, Fode."

"Ah, no, sir. Step over this way, please."

Fode was reasonably sensitive, and he immediately toned down his fawning.

Heuze stumped up the stones of the beach and across to the lower station on the rope hoist. Heavy cables rose from the beams and pulleys in the beach station to the cliff top. A squad of a dozen burly slaves, many of them former Red Tops, stood ready to work the capstan.

It was a long way up. For a moment, Heuze questioned whether he really wanted to do this. Then he realized it was too late to back out. That would ruin him with the men.

Besides, his suggestion to put the fort up there had been a brilliant stroke. The place was damned near impregnable. He ought to take a look at it, enjoy the sense of accomplishment.

So, with a deep breath, he pressed on. Men could ride up the cliff on a simple loop attached to the main cable or they could go up in a chair. Heuze, thinking further about his reputation, put his good foot into the loop and took hold of the rope with both hands.

"All right, Fode. Lift me up there."

Fode turned to the sergeant in command of the station. A whip cracked, and the slaves heaved on the cable.

Heuze left the ground with a lurch and swiftly ascended. The capstan turned quickly with just his weight on the line. Heuze felt butterflies in his stomach as he contemplated the rock wall whizzing past him. Then the rope spun him around and he saw the seaward view. In the middle distance loomed the *Anvil.* Farther away, out beyond the headland, he could see the white pyramid of sails of the frigate *Cloud,* which was on station to ward off any fireships that the monkeys might try to send in against the flagship while she was moored in the bay.

Farther away still, white clouds rimmed the horizon to the south. Weather was blowing up from the sea.

The rope spun him around again. The walls of rock rose to the upper platform. He was almost there. Men were lined up, peering over the precipice at him as he came up on the cable. Heuze chuckled to himself at the figure he was cutting. Troops had to be inspired, and they could only be inspired if they respected their commander.

At the top of the cliff, the cable ran to a twelve-foot crosstrees. Below this was the landing stage and the main platform. The cable came to a halt. A soldier hooked the admiral's loop line and drew him safely across to the landing stage. Heuze stepped off the line onto his peg leg and stumbled, but he did not go down.

Cursing softly under his breath, he got his crutch under his arm and straightened up. A horn was blaring to greet his arrival. The officers saluted, and behind them was a line of men awaiting his inspection.

Heuze saluted back, then stumped along the line, staring into each man's face for a moment. They liked him, and he knew it. He was popular with the ordinary troops, mostly because he'd broken the damned priests, but also because they recognized something of themselves in him. They trusted him in ways they didn't trust their own generals, who they knew were all lapdogs, chosen for their obedience.

The men in the fort were veterans of the Third Regiment. They'd seen action in three battles against the monkeys and taken their share of casualties. As Heuze passed them, they exhibited the faintest of wintry little smiles.

At the end of the line, Heuze spun about on his peg and saluted them. "Looking good, Third Regiment, looking good. A great bunch of grim-faced rogues if ever there was one."

They smiled a little more broadly at that.

General Polluk accompanied him on a tour of the fort. There wasn't much to see. While the sense of airiness and space from the location atop the cliff was very strong, the interior of the fort was mostly dug into the ground. The men had to live in bunkers in almost all the forts, because the monkeys invariably built trebuchets and catapults and threw rocks over the walls. Except for the palisade and towers that blocked the side facing the neck of land, Heuze looked over only the entrances to the dugouts and the reinforced ground shelters.

However, the imperial banner waved above the big gate tower. Heuze smiled at seeing that white flag with the red fist of Shasht, the fist of the Great God, Orbazt Subuus. He didn't give a pin for the Great God, but another banner planted on the enemy shore was a symbol of his own success.

Heuze plunged into the inspections of the underground sick bay, then the kitchens and a scrubbed-down barracks, all dug into the hard ground of the cliff top. At each stop, Heuze exchanged banter with the men. Morale was good, even though they were under siege. The food supply was adequate; there was water and even ale now and again. The monkeys weren't terribly aggressive either, though they were building those siege towers. The soldiers didn't take too much notice of the small rocks; every so often, however, the big trebuchet out in the forest would launch a boulder. Those could be dangerous.

Their spirits had been raised by the strong rumors

that they were going to launch a sally into the woods and scupper the machines. Everyone itched for the opportunity to get to grips with the monkeys again.

After seeing the barracks, Polluk accompanied the admiral on a progress along the battlement. The palisade had taken a few hits over the months from the big trebuchet. The wall had been broken here and there and repairs patched in. The parapet and battlement had been shattered on one side of the gate tower. The footway behind the wall was still jury-rigged.

Up on the gate tower, they studied the terrain inland. The ground was broken by small hillocks. Trees covered everything in a deep green mantle. Heuze was always shocked by the fertility of the land here, so unlike his homeland. In the near distant trees he could see the enemy's siege towers. They were still unfinished, but not too far from completion. Something was going to be done about that, swore Heuze, and very soon.

Later, when Heuze and Polluk were alone in Polluk's quarters, a dugout about ten feet across, Heuze relaxed and took a mug of ale.

"Safe as houses in here," said the general as he yanked the stopper from a flagon. Heuze cast a glance at the tree trunks that had been laid end to end to form a roof over the dugout.

"Well, General"—Heuze raised his mug—"here's to Fort Aeswiren!"

"To the fort!" Polluk raised his mug, then drained it and poured again.

"And, so, General, you've had a week to get ready. When do you strike?"

Polluk had the look of a capable fellow, tall with a square head and a dueling scar on the right side of his face. He was the last of the generals selected by Nebbeggebben for the expedition. All the others were gone now.

Polluk was looking nervous. This inquisition by the

admiral was something he'd been dreading. Perhaps the fate of so many other generals was in his mind.

"Well, Admiral, I think we are finally ready to make an armed sortie against the towers."

"Good news. I have been impatient, General. It's a fault of mine, but this campaign has been a long one, and I wish it were over."

"Yes, Admiral. Everyone looks forward to the day when we have peace."

"Hmmm. The road to peace must be made from our victories, as you know."

"My command is ready. We have massed almost eleven hundred men in the fort. The enemy has not visibly reinforced. We suspect that they may not have seen our reinforcements, who all came in the night as secretly as possible."

"Excellent."

Heuze smelled victory. He had been involved in the planning of this from the beginning. The only way to get anything done well was to do it yourself.

Polluk warmed to his theme. "I intend to attack both siege towers simultaneously. We think the enemy has only a few hundred troops in our area. His patrols are rarely done in strength. We can see the same two or three hundred soldiers in visible positions."

"By the great purple ass! You can tell them apart?"

Polluk colored. It might be dangerous to admit such a thing, but it was the truth.

"Well, yes, Admiral. We have studied them very carefully. There are differences in the faces and ears. The eyebrow tufts are often different, too."

"Peel 'em and fry 'em, that's what I say. They're all the same when they're cooked, eh?"

"Yes, Admiral. Do unto them as they would do unto us, so it shall be."

"Have you been able to scout?" Heuze touched on a difficulty faced by all the fort commanders.

"Not very well. The enemy always seems to spot our men. They hardly ever get back."

Heuze nodded. Like everyone else he wondered what happened to men who were captured by the monkeys. If they behaved the way Heuze and his men customarily did with captive monkeys, then the scouts would have been killed and eaten.

"Horrible to think of being captured. They eat their prisoners, no doubt."

"Disgusting animals, daring to eat human flesh. We must exterminate them."

Heuze chuckled. "May the gods give us strength!"

"Sing the praises of He Who Eats!" General Polluk spoke loudly from the habit of a lifetime of truckling to the goddamn priests.

Heuze sighed and waved a hand. "Yes, yes. But the fact remains you have little information about what lies out there."

"We have seen their camp. Just a few primitive tents. They don't seem to use wood for construction."

"Only one camp?"

"Well, there are others, but as I've said, our scouts rarely survive to tell us what they've seen."

"A pity. But you're sure that you're seeing the same pack of monkeys day after day?"

"There's only a few hundred of them, it seems."

"Good. So, tell me, General, what are you planning to do when you capture these infernal towers of theirs?"

"Burn them and retire into the fort."

"I see."

Heuze had finished his mug of ale. He held it up for Polluk to refill from the jug on the table. It was poor stuff compared to the wine and rum they'd had when they set out from Shasht, but it would have to serve.

"Here, General, let's drink to victory!"

Relief surfaced on Polluk's simple face. It looked as if he was safe. One could never be sure with the admiral. He had a harsh reputation among the generals of the army.

Heuze was watching him carefully, waiting for just the right moment.

"But, I must say, General Polluk, this plan of yours is not especially ambitious, is it?"

Polluk goggled for a moment. The general felt that he was taking a huge risk. He planned to attack both towers at the same time, using surprise as his weapon. That wasn't ambitious enough for the admiral?

Heuze put a hand on the general's shoulder while favoring him with a patronizing smile. "You see, General, if the enemy is as weak as you think, then it may be possible to trick him into a confrontation that we can win without much loss to ourselves."

Polluk stared back, puzzled.

"And if we can kill a lot of them, it will help us take control of this region. We need victories. We need the taste of meat!"

Polluk still stared.

"So we will attack only one tower. Do you see?"

Polluk remained silent, irresolute, fearful of some trickery on the part of the admiral. He remembered Dashun, who'd been hanged after the loss of his fort. "I'm not sure," he finally replied.

"Well, it stands to reason, if we capture one of these towers, the enemy will reinforce the other one."

"Yes?" Polluk was still full of questions.

"So then we will kill more of them when we attack that tower with all our force."

The creases on Polluk's brow vanished.

"Oh, I see," he said. The admiral had a plan! In that case, Polluk would be happy to abandon his own. He preferred executing someone else's orders. Let someone else take the blame if things didn't go right.

"If his numbers are as low as you think, then we may be able to rub out his entire force."

"Yes, yes, an excellent plan!" Polluk nodded his head vigorously in agreement, another trait that had helped his rise through the ranks. "And it is less risky than mine. Because only half our force will be used in the initial attack."

Heuze nodded heavily. The generals were all obsessed with conserving their forces. After the casualties they'd suffered since they'd first arrived, such conservative thinking was inevitable.

"Yes, of course, caution is quite understandable. But when a first-class opportunity comes our way, we must seize it."

Polluk had a question. "What if the enemy is more numerous than we believe at this moment?"

"Then he will have to reveal his strength and we will still destroy one of those damned towers. After that they will have to reinforce the other one more strongly, and that will risk increased losses."

"Yes, yes," said Polluk with enthusiasm.

Heuze took another gulp of the ale. "There is another matter. We aren't going to burn the tower when we capture it."

"Not burn?" Polluk looked so dumbfounded that Heuze had to struggle not to burst out laughing.

"Yes. We're going to dismantle it and take the materials. The monkeys are very good at finishing off beams and planks. Haven't you noticed? Well-sawn planks they make, with even sides and smooth finishes. We can use that sort of quality material on the island."

"Oh, uh, yes, Admiral. Of course."

Heuze sighed inwardly. Really, the general staff was made of poor stuff. That had been very plain on this accursed expedition.

Heuze wondered where his old confidant, Filek Biswas, was at that moment. Filek had gone back to

Shasht, with his daughter Simona and that eerie message she'd brought from the monkeys. Filek was in the big city now, at the center of things, completing his research projects. Heuze envied Filek and wished he still had him to hand. It had made for more interesting conversation.

"So we don't burn, we take. Let the monkeys labor for our benefit, eh?"

"Yes, sir."

"Now, I plan to stay ashore tonight. I want to oversee the battle tomorrow and then be back to the ship by tomorrow night. A tight schedule, Polluk. Think you can keep to it?"

"Yes, sir."

"Good. When is dinner?"

Chapter 4

The following morning, Admiral Heuze awoke from a sound night's sleep feeling refreshed and unusually clear-headed. Indeed, he was a little surprised that he had slept so well. Usually he slept badly the first few nights on land, missing the familiar motions of his ship. He was, however, itching in a few places. The dugouts were home to a lively population of fleas.

He groped through the underground gloom of the dugout and found the steps up into the light. Outside, dense mist was rising from the river gorge. The sun burned pale and watery beyond the vapors.

A few men were moving about. The cook shack was serving up early breakfasts.

Something in his gut told Heuze that this was the time to attack. Not in two hours, not at noon, as they'd discussed the night before over mugs of ale. If they sallied forth soon enough, they would catch the fornicating monkeys napping, and annihilate them!

Roaring for Polluk, he turned back into the underground complex. Ensign Combliss tumbled out of his bunk and hurried to Heuze's side.

The general was drinking some hot soup when Heuze found him.

"Polluk! Get the men out now! Give them some bread and get them on their feet and ready to fight. We're going to charge now, right now!"

Polluk goggled, eyes big and round. Before bed, the

admiral had been very cautious. They were not to attack until the sun had burned off the treacherous fogs
of this coast. They would wait until noon if they had
to.

But Polluk had learned not to question the admiral
when he was enthused like this. "Yes, Admiral, of
course." He gulped down the soup and tore a chunk
of bread on his way out the door.

Within a minute, the men were tumbling out of their
dugouts, lining up for bread.

Heuze, with Combliss behind him, was ready and
waiting as the men began to form up. Of the twelve
hundred men in the fort, a thousand were scheduled
to take part in the assault on the siege tower.

"Come on, hurry it up!" snapped Heuze at every
opportunity. The men, from generals down to the
rankers, did their best to look lively. Within half an
hour, the assault force was ready.

From the walls they could see little sign of the
enemy, other than the tops of the two siege towers
projecting among the trees in the near distance.

Heuze waved aside all objections. Polluk gave the
orders. The gate swung open, and the ramp was lowered over the ditch. Out marched the assault force,
with no drums or trumpets. On the open ground they
deployed into a column ten files wide. Immediately
they increased their pace to a trot, while a few scouts
hurried ahead, bows at the ready.

The mists grew thicker as the trees came closer.
Scouts reappeared. All was quiet in the enemy lines,
from what little they had seen.

On went the assault formation, eyes fixed on the
prize looming in the misty woods.

For a while, they marched inside a bank of thick
fog, with nothing but the dim mass of the trees ahead.
Each man could see only his immediate neighbors.
Admiral Heuze was bringing up the rear, with a party

of four guards and Combliss. Polluk had gone forward
with his own staff, since he had to keep in direct contact with the force.

The admiral's confidence was high, and he worked
hard to keep up a good walking stride. He could not
trot with the peg leg, but he could walk, even though
the stump would get sore after a while. But he wanted
to stay in touch with the assault force just in case.

The mists were exceedingly thick, muffling sound,
trapping each man in a bubble five feet across. Heuze
was thankful that the ground was pretty level, covered
in grasses and moss.

Suddenly the first loud cries from the enemy lines
went up. Spotted!

Scouts came hurrying back to report to Polluk.
Arrows started flashing out of the white mists as the
enemy archers took ranging shots.

Polluk waited no longer. "Cha-aa-arge!" he bellowed, stepping out in front and waving his sword into
the mist.

The men couldn't see him, but they could hear him,
and they knew which way to go. They gathered themselves and rushed at the monkey lines. Along the edge
of the forest, they found the trenches, just as had been
observed from the walls. But what surprised them was
the absence of defenders.

A handful of monkeys discharged arrows and then
took to their heels, running into the woods.

Polluk dropped back personally to inform Heuze
about this.

"Hardly anyone there."

"Must all be working on the siege tower. Press on,"
said Heuze.

Polluk nodded vigorously and hurried forward.
Heuze walked on, ignoring the slight soreness in his
stump. Aboard ship he didn't walk that much anymore. The stump wasn't used to this kind of exercise.

Heuze was growing a little anxious. There should have been at least some resistance. Was it some kind of trap? But how could the monkeys have anticipated his attack? He hadn't even decided to attack so early until this very morning. No, he dismissed the idea. It had to be a genuine stroke of luck. He'd caught the fornicating monkeys napping! It wasn't easy to do that.

The men pressed on under the trees. Ahead lay the siege tower. Surely, they would meet some resistance there.

Under the trees, Heuze found the going considerably more difficult since the ground was uneven and tangles of tree roots spread above the soil. He fell at one point and was struggling to get up again when Combliss and a guard helped him up with strong young hands.

An angry flush filled Heuze's cheeks, but he bit his tongue. He dug his crutch into the bank and hauled himself over the next bunch of roots.

Suddenly they came up on General Polluk and his immediate staff, with a banner raised above them.

"What's happening? What is going on?" Heuze demanded.

"We've made contact—" Polluk began.

There came a roar of noise up ahead.

"Told you, didn't I, Polluk?"

"Yes, sir, you were right."

The noise intensified, and now there was that familiar ringing sound that spoke of steel striking steel. Heuze felt that old flutter in his belly. There was nothing like the fog of war to make one as nervous as a young tomcat.

"How many?" he kept muttering. Polluk, who wanted to know the same thing, had no answer.

They waited there, torn by the tension while the fighting intensified.

At last messages started to come in from the front-line commanders.

"We caught them by surprise. There are only a few hundred of them. It's just like I told you, Admiral."

"Yes. We've got them, for once. Press on. Take the tower!"

The noise ahead continued unabated, but slowly it changed. More of the noise was coming from the left side of the field, as if the axis of the battle had shifted ninety degrees.

They were brought the news that the siege tower had been taken. Heuze exulted with a roar and thrust a fist into the air. Orders were sent forward for men to start tearing down the tower. They were going to carry the wood back into the fort.

Heuze himself went forward. He had to witness this triumph.

Fifty yards brought him to the line where the original battle had been fought. There was a scattering of dead men and mots. As before, Heuze found the sight of the enemy a little unnerving. They were so much like men, except for the grey fur. But past this line he saw few bodies. Out of the fog loomed the tower, with men all over it, tearing it apart.

Beams were cut loose and dropped to the ground. Parties of men then stacked them so they were ready to be carried back to the fort.

Heuze stumped about the tower, encouraging the men and enjoying the triumph. He was still there when General Polluk came up looking very concerned.

"What is it, General?"

"Very strange report, sir. On our new front, the men report seeing some enormous animal in the woods ahead of them."

"What?"

"Yes, sir. It's green and brown and very big. That's what they're telling me."

"Have you seen this thing?"

"No, not yet, but I'm going up to the front now."

"I'm coming with you."

Heuze was determined to see this "animal," or whatever it was, himself.

Was this why there were so few monkeys around? Were they being devoured by some monstrous beast?

The terrain was hard for Heuze here, very broken up with rocks, roots, and hollows. At one point they had to cross a deep gulley with steep walls, and Heuze had to accept a little help from Combliss, but he was well past complaints about that. His stump was sore and his back hurt from the unaccustomed exercise.

They emerged out of the mist into a meadow that was almost completely clear. Men were lined up here by companies. Their officers were gathered in a group, arguing.

Polluk, with Heuze just behind, hurried up to this group.

"Where is this 'animal'?" snapped Polluk.

"Over there, sir." Several lieutenants raised their arms together.

Polluk and Heuze studied the far side of the clearing. There was nothing to be seen but trees.

"You're sure it's over there?" asked Heuze suspiciously. He half suspected the men of malingering. The fog was spooky, and these forests terrified the men. They had fought two campaigns on this land and lost them both. A lot of former comrades were buried in this alien ground.

"We all saw something, sir," said one captain. "We just don't know what we saw."

"It's a beast, I tell you," said another captain. "Lieutenant Grees and I both saw it at the same time. Must be thirty feet long, with the tail. Huge eyes."

"Then where is it?"

They stared across at the wall of trees some fifty

yards distant. No "beast" was showing itself right then.

"I see no beast," said Heuze.

"We did see it, sir. Everyone saw something."

"Well, are there monkeys over there?" grumbled Heuze. "Why don't we press on and see what they're getting up to? It's best if we keep the initiative."

The officers hemmed and hawed for a moment or two and then dispersed to their companies. Orders were given for the advance to be continued. Drums beat, and they stepped out into the clearing.

Suddenly, in the trees at the far side, they all saw the huge head poke out from between two massive trees. Behind it slithered a neck ten feet long. The eyes of the monster were the size of dinner plates. It opened a mouth that could easily take a man in a single bite.

The companies ground to a halt.

Heuze stared, muttered an oath, and took a step back. "What in the name of the Great God is that?"

It disappeared again. The woods ahead loomed dark and ominous. Polluk's eyes had grown huge. "A snake? A huge snake?"

Heuze knew there were some gigantic serpents, mostly on the tropical isles, but he'd never heard of anything that large.

"I'd have sworn it was a dragon, but those are strictly creatures of legend."

"So I've always believed, sir." Polluk's voice shook a little.

Heuze realized how ridiculous it looked. A thousand men standing irresolute in the meadow between the trees.

"Goddamn it! Attack! I don't care what it is—if it's alive, we can kill it. Archers! Prepare to take it down if it shows itself again."

The admiral's angry words broke the spell. But the men were still uncertain. The orders went out, the drums beat, and they set off again but at a noticeably slower pace.

They had taken five strides when the head appeared once more, this time about a hundred paces to the left of the previous spot. The huge head slid out of concealment and then rose just like a serpent's might.

The men quailed and came to a halt.

The head rose up, swung from side to side as if it were studying them, sizing them up for its next meal.

Officers shouted at the men. Heuze screamed at the officers. Polluk went white-faced with indecision and fear.

The head had disappeared again, back into the dim recesses of the forest.

"I don't care what the fornicating thing is. Get your men into those trees and find those monkeys."

"Yes, sir."

Once again the men set off, and this time the head did not appear. On into the trees they pressed, until they came to a ravine with a small stream at the bottom. The slopes were steep and strewn with boulders. The formations broke up as they scrambled down.

Then the head reappeared, upstream a little ways. This time it showed itself only for a moment and then vanished.

Everyone froze.

"It's up there," a soldier said.

"Silence in the ranks!" roared a captain.

The men were frozen. They hunched forward, spears in hand. The archers nocked arrows and prepared to fire. Everyone expected an attack from the thing.

Nothing happened. A long ten seconds passed, and then Heuze bellowed at them to get moving. Once again they obeyed, scrambling through the streambed and up the far side. Still there was no sign of the enemy, nor of the huge head and neck.

Heuze paused, undecided. To go farther into the unknown, unscouted woods was foolhardy. He knew what that might lead to. The chance of slaughtering a few hundred monkeys was not enough of a lure.

"All right," he said at last. "Turn them around. Let's get back to that siege tower and dismantle it."

"Yes, sir." Polluk was visibly relieved. The men were quite happy to turn about and retrace their steps, and in just a few minutes they were moving back through the woods.

Back across the gulley they went, with some chatter about the damned "beast" and its probable sexual habits. Officers yelled at the men to shut it, but still the chatter went on, though in whispers and grins.

They recrossed the wider meadow and returned to the scene of the siege tower. The carpentry team had been hard at work. Piles of neatly cut beams and planks were stacked at the bottom of the siege tower.

Orders went down the line. They would work in their usual units, five men making a squad. One man would carry all their shields and spears. The others would take up the beams and planks and lug them back to the fort.

In a few minutes a steady line of men, paired off to carry the beams, headed through the woods toward the fort.

Heuze was still puzzled. Why had the monkeys reduced their forces around the fort? Had they gone somewhere else?

With a little help from Combliss, he got back to the cleared space in front of the walls. He accepted Combliss's aid now without grumbles. His stump was far too sore for that.

Once he was out of the woods, Heuze noticed that something strange had happened. "The gate is shut. Who told them to do that?"

"No one, sir," said Polluk.

The men carrying beams were still marching toward the gate, expecting it to be opened at any moment.

Heuze also noticed that the imperial banner was no longer waving above the gate tower. "Who told them to take down the banner? I want to celebrate our triumph, damn it!"

With sickening suddenness, the top of the stockade filled with dark figures. Bows bent and arrows came hurtling out into the ranks of the men bearing timber.

Screams of rage and then terror broke out in the ranks. Beams were dropped hither and thither as the men scrambled back.

Heuze stared, dumbfounded. "The sodomistic monkeys have taken the fort," he breathed, scarcely able to believe it. "While we were out chasing that will-o'-the wisp in the forest, they captured the fornicating fort!"

"So it, uh, seems, sir."

Heuze flung his hat down into the dust and stamped on it with his peg leg, ignoring the sudden spurt of pain from his stump. "How in the name of the Great God did your men let this happen?" he roared at Polluk.

Polluk's eyes flashed in outrage. He was being blamed for this?

Heuze, for once, had the decency to look away and swallow his next words. Indeed, it was hardly Polluk's fault. He'd wanted to leave four hundred men. Heuze had insisted on leaving just two hundred.

"Sir?"

"Yes, Polluk?"

"What are we going to do now?"

Heuze reflected that he probably deserved that one. He gave a grunt and stood there, working on the problem, when a shout directed his attention to the woods on the far side of the clearing. A large formation of mots was marching out under their own banners. Pikes and spears formed a forest above their heads. Their shields were painted brown with a green wave, which made their united front look like a single living thing.

Heuze gave a strangled cry. He was trapped again. He was outside the protection of the fort and the enemy was launching a frontal attack.

Chapter 5

Panic would be disastrous, Heuze understood that. But it was hard not to panic as rank on rank of monkeys came on with their shields held up.

He forced himself back from the brink of panic. He had a thousand men. In theory, that would be good enough to counterattack. But he knew that they were tired and out of formation. They'd been chasing the monkeys through the woods for an hour or more. And they were cut off from the fort, which had fallen in some mysterious fashion to the enemy.

Now his tired men were about to be attacked by what looked to be a force larger than their own. Heuze had learned from bitter experience that while the men of Shasht were better soldiers than the mots, they could not always overcome them.

A glance to his right showed that Polluk was waiting for him to make a decision. The officers behind Polluk were waiting, too. They were all waiting for him. He had taken command of this mission, and now it was up to him to get them out of this jam.

Heuze spun around. "We have to fight our way down to a beach. What is the nearest, practical route down from these cliffs?"

A young lieutenant with red hair shouted, "The backhead trail, sir! It's almost a mile north of here."

"Good. What's your name?"

"Cump, sir."

"General Polluk, I suggest you put Cump here up for promotion, if both of you survive the rest of this day."

Polluk said nothing to that but turned away and began issuing orders for the companies to face right and march quickly for the trees.

"At the treeline we will form into column by company and march up the coast to the backhead trail."

Earlier the men had wanted a fight, but now they weren't so keen. There seemed to be a hell of a lot of the fornicating monkeys over there. And there might be more in the woods trying to get on their flank.

At the edge of the forest, Heuze looked back. The monkeys were still coming, moving at a steady pace, keeping their formations crisp. There were no gaps to take advantage of with a quick counterattack. Heuze cursed steadily under his breath. He felt his stump starting to burn unpleasantly, while in the small of his back there was a sullen ache.

He went on, hurrying as fast as he could manage. The ground before them broke up into gulleys and pits where the underlying limestone had eroded away. It became harder for either side to maintain formation. Within ten minutes, the men were hopelessly mixed up in a mob that was on the verge of breaking into a rout.

Heuze was struggling to keep up. He sensed the gathering panic. Whenever he caught a glimpse of his men, he saw they had a lost, frightened look about them. Not that Heuze had any ideas. If he had, they fragmented every time he jammed his peg leg down into one of the cracks in the ground.

Suddenly Ensign Combliss and another soldier came up on either side of him, took hold of his arms, and carried him across the next pit. They set him down a moment, then took him up again and helped him over a set of natural steps in bare rock.

Heuze was beyond any embarrassment now. If he had to be half carried, then so be it. He went on, sweat running down his back, his stump burning in the socket.

Thankfully, the trailhead was discovered a few minutes later. Polluk organized a rearguard of two hundred and fifty men to hold the top of the trail while the rest made their escape to the beach.

Heuze came up just in time. When he heard Polluk's plan, he sensed the potential for a disaster.

"Wait a minute, General. No point in us all going down to the beach if there's no boats to take us off. We must signal the ship."

Polluk nodded. "Yes, sir, of course. I have a detachment setting a fire now."

"Good man. I should've known you'd do that. Do we have any signal flags?"

That was a point that Polluk had not gotten around to, and he was quick to order a search. Soon a set of army communication pennons was found, and a man went up a tall tree with a line. Arrows were falling among them by the time the first line of flags fluttered up on that line. The monkeys were gathering in the nearby woods, forming up for an assault.

By that point, the fire in the thicket was going pretty well. Clouds of white smoke were rising from it. Heuze had his spyglass trained on the *Anvil.* Surely Captain Pukh would have noticed the fire by now?

The smoke was thickening, and flames could be seen shooting up here and there. Still no flags were visible on the *Anvil.*

The monkeys attacked.

A solid column, ten across and perhaps ten deep, came storming forward. Their formation was loose enough to allow them to keep some semblance of lines as they covered the rough ground.

The Shasht rearguard rose up to meet them. The men were angry after the fright and humiliation of the

chase along the cliffs. They came up with fire in their
eyes, and the mots' first assault was stopped cold. A
clatter of weaponry went up along with a roar, and
the mots recoiled and stepped back. The rearguard
thrust them back farther, and the assault column got
mixed up on the bad ground. The men made the mots
pay then, for they caught groups jammed together in
pits or in the process of climbing up out of them. And
there mots died, cut down from behind.

Polluk kept a close rein on his men, though. He
didn't want them pulled too far out into the woods.
He knew there would be archers waiting out there,
not to mention other columns of infantry. When the
enemy was definitely on the run, Polluk called his men
back. They formed a line in cover and waited.

By then the fire in the cliff-top brush was blazing
high along a hundred feet of the cliff line. Many men
had reached the bottom and were massing on the
beach, which was reduced to a strip by the high tide.

At last a line of flags broke out from the *Anvil*.

"Prepare for boats," read Heuze. "Well, thank the
gods for that. I thought Pukh would never see us!"

He could see boats being hurriedly lowered from
the ship. Still, even though the *Anvil* was carrying
more boats than usual, they could only take a couple
hundred men at a time. The rearguard would have to
hold the top of the fort for an hour or more while the
boats made several trips. Heuze realized that this
might be difficult. It began to seem like a mistake to
try and hold the monkeys off with only two hundred
and fifty, but it would be hard to get men to come
back up the cliff path.

Flights of arrows began falling like hail on the men
of Shasht, who were forced to take shelter wherever
they found it, in pits, behind trees or boulders. Again,
Heuze sensed a disaster taking shape.

"Look, General, we have to find some way of get-

ting all the men off the beach. Once the monkeys take
the top, they'll turn the beach into a slaughterhouse."

Polluk looked at the narrow beach down below and
saw doom approaching. He gulped and looked back
to the admiral. There was no doubt about it. They
were in a very tight spot.

A roar arose from the direction of the burning
brush, and another assault column of mots and brilbies
came pouring forward. Because the brush in that direction was partially ablaze, the men hadn't been
watching it carefully. The nearest men were resting
when the attackers broke from cover and sprinted at
them.

Powerfully built brilbies wielding pikes and axes
crashed through the lines before they could form
properly. Men died by the dozen, going down under
a sudden overwhelming tide of the enemy. The rearguard was shattered, and the fighting became a free-
for-all around the top of the cliff trail.

Heuze himself, swinging a sword taken from a dead
man, was caught in the thick of the fighting. He saw
Lieutenant Fode killed not five feet away. Splatters of
the man's brains fell across his legs. The huge monkey
whose sword had felled Fode turned in Heuze's direction, but before he could close in on the admiral, two
men engaged him. Their shields resounded from heavy
blows, but they fought on. Heuze stumbled away, horribly aware that he'd just pissed himself from the terror but glad not to be facing that huge monkey. A
few steps farther on and he reached the top of the
downward trail to the beach.

There was no more to be done on the cliff top. The
monkeys were all over them. With a terrified scream
a man fell over the precipice, then another. The monkeys were pushing the men right to the edge and then
out into thin air.

Down at the beach, meanwhile, the boats had arrived. Men surged out to meet them, and would have swamped them but for the remains of their discipline and a lot of bellowing from officers.

The first three hundred were taken off the beach. The boats headed back to the *Anvil,* which had raised her anchor and set a few sails to shift position toward the beach. With a practiced eye, Heuze calculated the time it would take for the ship to come close enough to exchange the rescued men. Still too long for those on the beach.

Heuze suddenly understood what had to be done. It was the only chance. He turned and fought his way back through the crowd to General Polluk, who was standing on the trail beneath a rock overhang that gave some protection from the rain of missiles falling from above.

"Polluk!" snarled Heuze. "Where are the fornicating flags?"

Polluk stared at him. The general was trying hard to keep control of the remaining men fighting at the head of the trail. They were losing the fight, but they were stubborn men of Shasht, and they would hold their ground for a long time.

"The signal flags? Lieutenant Cump has them."

"Cump!" roared Heuze.

Young Cump was there, toting the pack with the signal flags and lines to string them on.

"Send a message to the ship: 'Send ropes. Seven hundred men have to move.'"

"What are you planning, sir?" Polluk had hold of his elbow.

"The fornicating monkeys have taken the cliff top. Look!"

A rain of rocks and logs, stones and arrows was hurtling down from the cliff onto the men packed on the beach below. The men had no choice but to walk out into the waves.

Cump and two men worked frantically to sort out
the flags. A line was dropped over the edge of the
cliff, and flags were fed onto it with desperate speed.

The *Anvil* got the message. Additional sails spread
within seconds, and she accelerated toward the boats
bearing the first three hundred.

As the ship swept down on them, the men were
ordered out of the boats and made to swim. The boats
turned about immediately and started back to the
beach. The *Anvil*, slowing, with an anchor splashing
into the water, caught up to the boats, and coils of
rope were hurled down to them. Meanwhile, rescue
netting was being lowered over the sides and stern to
the swimmers.

Heuze gave thanks for Captain Pukh's wits. The
man had been slow on the uptake originally. This was
the Pukh whom he trusted in a fight. The first swimmers were clambering up the side. Sailors dived into
the sea to help the wounded and those who couldn't
swim very well.

Above him, the men at the top of the trailhead had
been forced to retreat almost as far as Polluk's post
under the overhang. More rocks, pieces of burning
brush, and occasional men's bodies kept flying off the
cliff and hurtling past.

Heuze had seen how it was going and was already
hurrying downward, stumping as fast as he could go.
Ensign Combliss was with him, while Lieutenant
Cump had recovered the signal flags and was right
behind. Combliss found a discarded shield and held it
up to protect the admiral. It was good that he did so
because a shower of small rocks came down almost
immediately and banged off the shield.

About halfway down was the most dangerous
stretch. The trail ducked in close beneath a near vertical drop from the top of the cliff. There was absolutely
no protection. Even with the shield held above him,

Heuze could not get past unscathed. A couple of stones struck him, one on the shoulder and one on the back. The second one almost knocked him over.

Then a bigger rock hit the shield, overwhelming Combliss and driving the shield down onto Heuze's head. He went down. Other men helped him get up. One of them was struck on the head by another rock and fell backward off the edge of the trail and plummeted down to the beach.

Horrified, Heuze got his crutch underneath him and drove himself across the next few feet to the relative safety of an overhang just past the turn. Combliss got in behind him.

"Admiral, are you all right?"

Heuze thought his heart was going to burst from the exertion, and his head was still ringing from the blow, but he muttered, "Of course," between gasps for breath. He hoped he looked better than Combliss, who'd lost his helmet and had blood trickling steadily down one side of his face. Then Lieutenant Cump joined them, still carrying the bag of flags, with rope coiled over his shoulder. He opened his mouth to say something but was interrupted by a shriek as a body flew past from above, bounced off the trail, and went on spinning downward. Far below, the men had abandoned the beach entirely and were bobbing in the waves as far out as they dared to go.

"Complete, fornicating disaster," muttered Heuze.

More men were coming down the trail, many of them wounded. The fight at the top had moved down past the overhang, and the retreat accelerated because the men could only fight while under a hail of rocks from above.

There was no way to stay under the overhang. Hundreds of men had to get past. Heuze got his crutch beneath him and shoved off once more, hurling himself from rock to rock, the crutch slamming up under his arm, his stump burning.

Bruised, battered, breathing hard, his vision fading to a red haze, the admiral finally reached the beach, where the hard trail gave way to soft sand. On the uppermost dunes the sand was deep and soft, and his peg leg sank in an inch or two with every step.

A rock the size of his head struck not three feet away, creating a crater in the sand.

Heuze dug deeper with his crutch and hauled himself over the sand. Stones spattered down around him, but he was still spared. Lieutenant Cump had the bag of flags on top of his head, which saved him when a rock clipped it a few moments later. Cump went down, however, knocked out cold by a fist-size piece of slate.

Heuze stopped with a weary shake of the head. They were all going to die in this miserable spot, he was certain. But he couldn't leave young Cump lying there. A soldier had leaned over the lieutenant to check his pulse.

"He lives."

"Damn," muttered the admiral. "Ah, well, can't be helped."

Some stones clattered off the beach nearby. Heuze bent over with a wheeze, grabbed Cump's trailing arm, and helped Combliss and the soldier carry the lieutenant toward the waves.

"Can you swim, Ensign?" asked Heuze.

"All my life, sir. I come from Gzia Gi."

"Good man. Then we'll just take him with us, eh?"

Somehow, Heuze found the strength to get down that soft dune while helping to carry Cump. They had just made the transition onto the softer mud flats when a tree stump about three feet across slammed into a pool a few feet away and covered him with gobs of muddy sand. Mouth full of grit, barely able to see, he kept pushing forward, felt the water splash over his boot, and dug his crutch in one last time.

The water was up to his waist, and Cump was floating. Heuze abandoned his crutch, tore off his coat and remaining armor, and kicked.

Combliss and the soldier had pulled Cump out through the waves. A wave lifted him off his foot, and he kicked off his boot. A duck of the head cleared the worst of the muck from his eyes. Something raised a big splash on his right, and there was a chilling scream. He didn't even look, but kept on, with the water now up to his waist.

He retained his peg leg, knowing he'd be helpless without it, and he was reluctant to abandon the sword, even though he felt its weight. Heuze was a strong swimmer, even with only one foot, and he caught up with Combliss soon enough. He took hold of one of Cump's arms and swam sidestroke, helping to push them all out through the surf into the deeper water.

He could see behind him. The cliff top far above was lined with dark figures, still hurling a rain of rocks down on the men scurrying across the sand and swimming out through the waves.

A rock fell just on the other side of Combliss, and several stones hit the water just behind them, but at last they were at the edge of the throwers' range.

Surrounding them were other men struggling to stay afloat. The good swimmers were doing their utmost to help the others keep their heads above water. Everyone had been forced to abandon their shields, armor, and weapons.

Heuze's luck continued to hold, however. Within a minute or so, the first boats came back in range, hallooing and throwing out lines to the men in the water.

"Five men to a line. Take hold and we'll tow you back to the ship."

Heuze tried to raise his voice to catch their attention. He was the admiral and he wanted to be taken back to the ship that very moment. But they didn't hear him in the general uproar. He bellowed, but everyone else was shouting, too. The boat went past him.

So, when a line drifted within range he had no option but to take hold and be dragged like all the rest. The line tightened with a sudden jerk, and then he was tugged away, with Combliss and Cump beside him. Ensign Combliss had put a loop of line around Cump under his arms, and the unconscious man lay on his back with his face above water.

The great mass of men clinging to ropes began to move more quickly as the rowers bent their backs to the task. They gave huge grunts as they dug deep with their oars. A quarter mile out from shore lay the *Anvil*, sails furled, anchors deployed, busy taking up the swimmers from the first three hundred rescued from the beach.

Once again Heuze looked back to the cliff. To his surprise the dark mass of mots had vanished. He couldn't see anyone left standing on the beach. The monkeys had gone back into their trackless forest. Damn them!

A familiar rage suffused the admiral's thoughts. Just when he'd had them on the run, the fornicating, sodomistic monkeys had sprung a surprise on him and turned the tables. It was insupportable, but he was going to have to live with the humiliation.

Turned around by the motion of the boat, he saw that the *Anvil* was appreciably closer now. The greater question, he realized, was how to keep this latest disaster from being perceived as such. He would have to make it sound like a success.

The fort had been lost. At least two hundred men were gone. But the rest had been saved, and that had been Heuze's work.

Yes. He had it now. That would be the focus, how he had stepped in and saved the rest of the army after Polluk had made a complete mess of things.

Heuze no longer gave defeated generals to the priests. Instead, Polluk would be hanged from the yardarm of the *Anvil*. After a trial, of course.

It was unfair, but it would be necessary to placate Nebbeggebben and the rest of the fleet. Either that or Heuze's own hide would be at risk.

The chill in the water was starting to get to him by the time he was finally hauled into a boat and recognized.

"It's the admiral, by gum. Sir, we had no idea."

"Thank you, boys. Take these men out of the water and then row us to the ship."

Chapter 6

"Land ho!" rang down from the top of the mainmast. Feet thudded on stairs and decks.

Among the men of Shasht who ran to get a glimpse of the new land was one figure, decidedly different. Undeniably female, and undoubtedly not human, Nuza of Tamf ran up the rigging into the foremast crosstrees like any other sailor. She wore matelot pants like all the men, though she'd reworked them to fit her wider hips, and a shirt made from good Shasht cotton, but soft grey fur covered her from head to toe, except on the front of her face around the mouth, nose, and eyes. She was a mor of the Land, not a man of Shasht, and she beat all the topsail men to the crosstrees, even the best of them.

They'd grown to expect that, having sailed with Nuza for ten months. For her weight, she was as strong as most men, and she had far better balance than any of them. On a dare she had often walked out to the ends of the topsail spars, spun around, and come back on her hands.

For her, such stunts were actually easy. She'd been an acrobat and a tumbler all her life. The men of the *Duster,* even though they were veteran sailors, had had to adjust to the sight of her skinning up a line arm over arm and running out to the end of a yardarm like one of them.

But after a month or so, they had accepted her. It

was just the latest of the strange developments brought upon them by their loyalty to the Emperor Aeswiren. Fortunately, there were no fanatical worshippers of He Who Eats among them, with all the prejudices and hatreds of that dire cult. Still, there were those who looked askance at the peculiar relationship Nuza shared with the Emperor. Endless gossip it had provoked, and even a few fights, but now even that was largely accepted. Nuza was somewhere between a wild animal and a concubine, but she was clearly athletically superior to any of them, and they respected that.

And, though it had never been tested, it was understood that she could fight. She practiced her kyo, mor's kyo, on the afterdeck every morning to loosen up her muscles. The men had all observed her swift moves, the whiplash speed of her feet when she struck a high kick. No one aboard had ever thought to challenge her.

Now she sat in the crosstrees and stared at the eastern horizon. There it was, at long last, a distant smudge of brown along the terminator. She felt her heart thud in her chest as she caught sight of it.

Home.

Once she had thought she would never see it again. Back in those dark, dreadful days of early captivity, when she was one of a dozen mots and mors jammed in the hold of a Shasht ship. Back then she had thought no more than a day ahead. Only squalor and death seemed to lie in the future.

But there was home, so close she could see it.

She was racked by sobs as her mind filled with thoughts of her family. Mother, father, brothers, sister, everyone she had left behind. More than two years had passed since she'd last laid eyes on them, back in Lushtan, the town in the Farblow Hills to which they'd fled after the burning of Tamf.

Tamf! Oh, by the wounds of the Spirit, poor Tamf! She cried again as she recalled how that beautiful old place had been burned to the ground by the men of Shasht. The towers, the houses, the ancient streets, all gone, destroyed by the hand of Man the Cruel.

But the Land still endured. She knew that the mots had held their own for two years and that no major battles had been fought in that time. She knew that the great Toshak must have come to the rescue of Sulmo in those dark, terrible days of the summer of defeat.

What she had learned since then had come directly from Aeswiren himself. She knew that the mots had avenged the defeat at Farnem and saved the city of Sulmo from the flames. The war went on, but on a smaller scale, with raids and the creation of Shasht forts on the coast.

She stared at the distant land. All the questions, all the hopes she had, were tangled in her mind like noodles in soup, and she knew she couldn't sort them out just yet. It was enough to feel her insides churn with a desperate yearning, to think that she would soon breathe that air and feel that ground beneath her feet.

Soon she would have the pleasure of being among her own people once again and hearing her native tongue and not the harsh sounds of Shashti. To have someone other than the Emperor to whom she could speak in her own language. He tried his best, but his accent was always going to be strange, and he still scrambled the order of words.

As if on cue, she heard a shout from below. She looked down and saw him standing on the forecastle, the Emperor of Shasht, Aeswiren the Third, himself.

"Come up!" she called with the easy familiarity that had grown up between them.

So he did, hauling his heavy frame up the rigging, then through the lubber's hole until he could join her on the crosstrees above the foresail. The sailors around her moved away to give him room.

"There!" she said dramatically and pointed to the east.

He squinted at the horizon. "So," he said quite calmly, "there it is, the fabled Land you have told me so much about."

She glanced at him for a moment and then looked away again. Many things would change now, she realized. When she set foot on the Land, she would be in her own world, not in the world of men.

Soon after that she hoped she would have an answer to the most burning question of them all: Was Thru alive?

The last she had heard of him, two years before, he and his brigade had left Glaine, heading for Farnem.

After the battle there was little news from the army. The word of the disaster had passed over Sulmo like a foul wind from an opened grave, and on its heels came the army of man. Nuza had endured the siege of Sulmo and was captured in the fall of the outer city.

When that had happened, she'd still had no word about the fate of Thru Gillo, who was lost and presumed dead.

Now she hoped to know for certain, either find him alive or extinguish the spark of hope that had lingered, despite everything, throughout these years of exile.

Aeswiren was looking at her. She could not ignore him.

"Almost there," he said and leaned closer. "I know this will change things, dearest Nuza. We will not be as intimate as we have been. But you must know that my feelings toward you will not change."

"And I to you, Lord," she said automatically.

That led to another question. How was she going to handle her strange relationship with this great man? He had brought on his own downfall in part because he would not hand her over to be killed. He had shown himself, time and time again, to be a firm friend.

She knew that the feelings of friendship went further on his side of the abyss that lay between them, man and mor. She could not return those feelings, but she did feel love of a sort for him, not in a sexual sense but in the way she loved her father, or Toshak, her former lover.

She found it all very confusing.

Finally, there was the colder understanding that Aeswiren the Third was the only hope for ending the war without more bloodshed. For he was the true Emperor, and the man the soldiers of Shasht would always follow.

In Shasht itself, his son, Aurook, had taken the purple mantle and the title of Norgeeben the Second. But the common soldiers would turn to Aeswiren, if given the chance.

"We have much work to do, you and I," he said.

"Yes, Lord," she said, using the honorific constantly employed by the men aboard the ship. He was the Emperor, after all, even if he did not insist on ceremony. Aeswiren was a man with great dignity, but also one who was comfortable in his own skin. His men loved him for it.

Nuza wondered how it would go when Aeswiren finally met Toshak. Two giants brought together like that could raise sparks, even a conflagration. Yet they shared a common need, to end the war. Plus, Nuza knew both of them and how their minds worked. She could defuse any conflicts.

A wide swathe of land was rising into view. Captain Moorsh was up in the mainmast topstory taking observations. Soon he would try to match what he was seeing with what the charts depicted. These charts had been drawn up by the invasion fleet and sent back to Shasht in the first year of the war. They offered considerable detail concerning shoals, rocks, and headlands. The interior was simply labeled "unknown."

Aeswiren climbed down to the deck and began pacing. Nuza had to smile. His impatience was so clear. He was itching to get back on land.

But sometimes even Emperors have to wait. So he paced back and forth while Captain Moorsh completed his observations and scrambled down with a chart tucked inside his coat.

Nuza watched them go, the Emperor beside the captain. Aeswiren intended to move very quickly once he reached the expedition forces. They were known to be harbored on an island south of the main mass of the Land. From the description of this island—nearly circular, dominated by craggy peaks, with a harsh, hot climate—Nuza knew it had to be Mauste. The mots there were mostly fisherfolk and shepherds, since the rivers were too steep and rocky for the farming of polder land. From what she had heard from Aeswiren, the Mauste villagers had either fled to the neighboring peninsula of Fauste or were dead, slain by the men of the expeditionary force.

Nuza prayed that Aeswiren could end the war and take the expeditionary force away. He said he would take it back to Shasht to be the core of the army he would build to take back the throne.

Nuza and the four men who were going to row her ashore were lowered down the side of the *Duster* in the ship's small boat. As the boat was lowered, Nuza felt his gaze upon her. She looked up, and their eyes met. Aeswiren, as Emperor, could not wave, but Nuza could.

"I will come back," she had told him. She thought he believed her, but perhaps not entirely. The trust between them had never been tested like this. She had always been the one forced to trust him, and, of course, her trust had been rewarded. Once she was free on her home soil, though, there would be nothing to stop her from remaining there.

She looked across the water to the town. Her heart skipped a beat once again. With its steep gray roofs, the buildings packed tightly into a narrow space beneath a great brown bluff, it was undoubtedly a town built by mots. She would be among her own people again, for the first time in two years. By the breath of the sweet Spirit, it would be wonderful just to see a crowd of mots and brilbies in the street.

Nuza had insisted that she be the first person to contact the townsfolk. Aeswiren and the others had accepted this. The ship had put in at a couple of villages so far, only to find the folk had fled inland at the first glimpse of their sails.

"What else would you expect?" she'd said to them when their boat came back with the news that no one had stayed to greet them. "Mots are not fools. We learned that your ships come seeking meat, not friendship."

At those words, every man had had the grace to drop his gaze.

So they'd had to accept that she was their only real chance of opening communication with the folk of the Land.

The boat splashed gently on the water. The men unhooked the chains and settled over their oars. Soon they were moving steadily away from the *Duster*.

It was a cloudy day, overcast but without rain. Nuza kept her gaze on the town. From the charts, Captain Moorsh was certain they had made landfall in the Northern part of the Land. Certainly the vegetation on the hills was of a Northern variety, pines and firs almost exclusively. Nuza did not know the region. She had never really traveled farther north than Dronned, which had to lie some distance to the south.

The inner harbor ahead was crowded with shipping: single-masted cogs, the predominant style of ship among the mots. The presence of so much shipping had made Captain Moorsh nervous. The *Duster* had not even put down an anchor, since he feared fireships such as those that had caused havoc in the first summer of the war.

The town was a sizable place, she could see, but smaller than Dronned or Tamf. The black roofs were made of slate, and they were steeply angled to shed the snow that would come in winter. She couldn't see anyone on the jetty or in the streets, but she had the feeling that many eyes were watching the boat as it entered the harbor.

Those eyes would have noticed by then that though men rowed the boat, a mor sat in the front of it.

A few minutes later, they approached the stone jetty. This was a dangerous moment. Arrows or spears might greet them. But the boat ground against the jetty without any sign of life in the town. A seaman named Kunkus, a gentle giant who reminded her in some ways of dear old Hob, the brilby that had been a part of her acrobatic act for many years, formed a step with his massive hands and she vaulted lightly to the top of the jetty. She stood there for a moment, struggling with powerful emotions.

"Thank you," she said to Kunkus and the others in Shashti.

"We will wait here, if we can," said Kunkus.

"I think they will leave you alone. I will tell them that you mean them no harm."

She took a step and almost tripped over her own feet, unused to stable land after so many months at sea. Recovering, she steadied herself on a bollard and then, taking careful steps, walked into the town.

The streets were deserted, though a flock of gulls wheeled above with their harsh cries echoing off the building fronts. While there was not a soul to be seen, she could feel concealed eyes following her movements. This was not a small village. There would be a militia ready to resist a landing from the ship.

She sniffed at the strong smell of fish. There could be no doubt of the town's primary occupation.

"Hello?" she called.

Her voice echoed back to her. She'd never been this far north. She hoped she could understand the Northern accent. Down in Tamf, they'd often joked about the clipped Northern way of speaking.

She wandered up the widest street leading off the harbor. Sunlight broke through the cloud cover for a few minutes. She noticed the glass windows all along the street, indicating that these were shops rather than homes. This town was clearly a commercial center.

The street was clean, with whitewashed curbs. A small pile of rubbish, bushpod husks mostly, had been swept up on one corner awaiting removal.

Someone had just moved into one of these houses, she realized, and grinned. It was common all over the Land to use bushpod husks to wrap around one's valuables when you packed them for a move.

She wondered where the sweepers were, running for the hills or crouched inside one of these buildings with a bow in their hands and an arrow trained on her.

"Hello?" she called again, but the silence continued. The sun slowly faded behind the clouds again.

She came to the corner. A side street cut across here on both sides, narrow and dark. She turned right. "Hello?"

Down this street there was no glass. The windows were all firmly shuttered with wood. Painted designs on each shutter spoke of candle makers, cobblers, and a hat maker. The designs were exactly the same ones used in Tamf.

Suddenly doors opened on either side. A half dozen mots and brilbies came out and surrounded her.

"Who are you?" said a tall mot with streaks of white in his cheek fur. He did not seem friendly.

"I am Nuza of Tamf."

"You came from a man ship. Why did they not kill you?"

"I was captured by the men at Sulmo. They took me to their own land. That ship brought me back."

The mot gave her an inquiring look. "To say the least, this is unusual treatment. We of Eskalon have only known the men as killers, not as hosts."

"I understand. Before I was made captive, I had seen the work of men. My own family lost everything when Tamf was burned. When I was taken captive, I expected death at their hands. They put me on one of their ships and we sailed to Shasht, which is what they call their land. I was very fortunate. Perhaps the Spirit took pity on me, I don't know, but the Great King of Shasht himself protected me. He befriended me. When I told him what his army was doing to our people, he understood. He had already decided to stop the war. He has now come to Shasht to put an end to it."

There was a long silence from her ring of listeners.

"You're saying that the Great King of the men is on that ship?"

"Yes. He is not like the other men. He is a good man."

"I have never heard a man described that way before."

"I was as surprised as you are now when I was first told I was not going to die. I had been separated from the others as soon as we landed in the city of men."

The mot had noticed Nuza's beauty and lithe presence. "They took you because you are beautiful."

"Perhaps. I have a gift at acrobatics. That's what I

used to do, in the old days. It pleases him to watch me. When I learned that the Great King wanted to meet me, I had little to say in the matter, so we met. He told me many things, explained much about the world that I did not know. He had decided to stop the war."

"Then why has it not stopped?"

"There are other forces involved. The Great King rules on sufferance of another authority, an ancient being called 'the Old One.'"

The mot drew back with a hiss. "That sounds like sorcery."

"It is. And the Old One moved against the King."

"So the Great King fell from power, and now he comes to us seeking forgiveness?"

"The Great King fell, but he comes here to take command of the army of men. He will reorganize them and then take them back to Shasht."

"And win back his throne with it?"

"Yes."

Her listeners drew back. Three of them huddled together to exchange views. Finally the first one turned back to her.

"Your tale is fantastic and would be dismissed as nonsense except that we have seen you come from a man ship."

She shrugged. "Whether you believe me or not, what is important is that you take this message." She handed over a sealed envelope.

The mot scrutinized the envelope carefully. "It is addressed to the great Toshak."

"It is. He is a friend of mine as well. He once worked in my troupe of acrobats. He was the sword fighter."

His eyes widened. "Truly, you are a well-connected mor . . ."

"Fortune has forced this on me. I would prefer to

still be earning my living tumbling in the villages of Tamf and Dronned. It was a good life, and I loved it."

There was further discussion.

One voice, that of a brilby with prominent eyebrow tufts, arose in dissent. The spokesmot turned back to her.

"The message will be sent to the South at once. Jilba here thinks you should be sent to the Assenzi at Highnoth. What do you say?"

"I will see the Assenzi soon enough, I'm sure," she said. "But first I must escort the Great King south. I must be there when he and Toshak meet. It is vital that they be able to work together. I can help them, because I have learned the language of the men."

The mot was incredulous. "Are you saying that you want to go back to that ship?"

"I have been treated well on that ship. Yes, I want to go back, and I hope I can take back some food with me. We have been at sea for a long time, and our rations are running low."

The mots and brilbies drew back with a collective hiss. "You want us to give them food?"

"I know it sounds crazy, but yes. You must understand that the Great King is our best chance of ending this war without further bloodshed."

For a long moment the crowd stared at her, then at each other. At last, the spokesmot turned back to Nuza.

"It is fell chance that brought you here. None of us would wish it known that we had given aid to the enemy. But you pose us a difficult choice. How can we turn down an opportunity to help bring about an early peace?"

And so, when Nuza returned to the jetty an hour later, a cart was driven up behind her and casks of flour, jars of oil, and cartons of cheese were set down there. The mots and brilbies would come no closer than ten yards, though, and remained nervous.

Kunkus and the other men rolled the barrels across and lowered them down to the boat. A few minutes later, they pushed off from the jetty and, now heavily laden, with Nuza in the prow, rowed back to the ship.

Chapter 7

Nuza could not fail to notice one striking change about the city of Dronned. A pall of smoke hung over the city, rising from newly built iron foundries. When she looked more closely, she observed that large new buildings had arisen, too, though whether they housed forges or their workers it was impossible to tell.

Standing near the top of the tall sand dunes that lined the bay south of the city, she was able to over-look the city walls, about two miles north. The bloody battle of Dronned, in the first summer of the war, had been fought right there, on the flat plain that lay be-tween the dunes and the wall.

Which made it an oddly fitting place for this meet-ing. She squared her shoulders and took a deep breath. Toshak was waiting nearby. She knew that her role in this was small but essential. She was the only person in the world who knew both of these huge, masculine personalities. She was the only one who could keep them from butting heads at this all-important en-counter.

Just ahead of her, Aeswiren climbed the slope, and just behind her came the heavy tread of Klek, the bodyguard. There were just the three of· them, the agreed number. Their boat, with six rowers, had re-mained behind at the water's edge.

One reason for such a small meeting was that Filek Biswas, the former chief surgeon of the fleet, and a genius of medicine, had begged the Emperor to keep all contact with mots, brilbies, and other folk of the Land to a minimum. He was convinced they were the source of the plague that had slain one in three of the Shasht colony.

Aeswiren had heeded the good doctor's warning, of course. In coming here alone, Aeswiren had accepted the risk that the mots might take him prisoner. Nuza said that General Toshak's word could be trusted, but Aeswiren knew that the exigencies of war could overwhelm the best intentions. Aeswiren had taken the risk, nonetheless. The gains were too great to be missed, and at this point in the game Aeswiren needed information that only this General Toshak could give him.

Besides that, Aeswiren wanted to meet this mysterious figure from Nuza's life. Aeswiren had heard much of him from Nuza, enough to know something of their history together. He wanted to put a face to the picture her words had painted.

When they were a few feet short of the dune's crest, Klek halted. Aeswiren and Nuza went on, carrying no weapons. Ahead, alone, waited a figure clad in a blue jacket with three red pins on one shoulder. The general wore no helmet nor a sword, but he radiated a sense of authority. The face was leaner than that of Nuza, harder, with deeper cheekbones and a gaunt fierceness to the eyes that Aeswiren noticed at once. Where Nuza was a dove, this mot was a hawk.

As they drew close, the mot opened his arms, stepped forward, and hugged Nuza, lifting her off the ground.

"Nuza! Nuza! Nuza!" he called out, swinging her around in complete abandon. Aeswiren gave Klek a look over his shoulder. General Toshak was obviously a character. Here was the Emperor himself, and the general was ignoring him.

"Nuza, my dearest, I thought I'd never see your face again."

Toshak crushed her in his grip.

"Toshak," she murmured, pushing him back slightly, concerned about Aeswiren's feelings. It was vital that this meeting went well. Jealousy could cloud things, ruining the clarity that they needed to have.

"Toshak," she said again. "Here, you must meet the Great King. You must not be rude to him; he is a great man."

"Bah," snorted Toshak, still holding her tightly.

"Toshak, listen. The Great King, he is a good man. You must talk with him. You can make peace."

Toshak didn't seem to hear her. "I have never heard a man described as 'good' before this. They are killers, hungry for the flesh of our children. They leave us nothing but piles of heads."

Nuza recalled the horror of that day in Bilauk. "I know, I know all that. But, Toshak, this man is different. He offers us a chance for peace. We must seize it."

Something cold and dangerous gleamed in his eyes for a moment. She saw how wide was the abyss that had opened between them. She and he, who had once been lovers, were now almost strangers, separated by her exile to Shasht and the war he had waged in the Land. He studied her with chilly precision, then relented.

"Yes, yes, dear Nuza, I know."

His shoulders sagged, as if a great tension went out of him.

"Toshak, dearest, you have saved the Land."

"No, dear Nuza, the Land is not yet saved. The men still threaten us. They still hold forts on the coast of Sulmo."

"That is why I am here to interpret. The Great King has been learning our language. Speak slowly to him, and he will understand most of what you say."

Toshak struggled with something, but could not say it. Instead, he turned to Aeswiren, who had waited patiently while Nuza and this fierce-looking mot had hugged and babbled at a speed far past the Emperor's ability to comprehend.

Nuza watched the two of them as they studied each other at close range. The man was the taller by an inch and heavier, too, but she doubted that would help him in a fight with Toshak. She knew all too well that Toshak was a master of the sword and all other edged weapons. For years he had been the swordsmot of her troupe of acrobats, jugglers, and entertainers. And yet there was something very similar about both of them, mot and man. They were leaders, steeped in the ways of war.

"General," said Aeswiren, using the language of the Land.

Toshak's eyebrows rose at hearing that tongue from the mouth of a man. Nuza had taught this one well. "Great King. You will have to pardon me, I cannot help my feelings. I find it hard to offer any man a welcome to the Land. We have suffered nothing but horror from men."

Toshak spoke too quickly, however, for Aeswiren to understand. Confused, the Emperor looked to Nuza. She translated into Shashti.

"General Toshak says that it is a difficult moment for him. There is great emotion, great pain from our losses."

Aeswiren nodded slowly, then spoke in the tongue of the Land. "I know. I wish to end all of that."

Toshak blinked on hearing these words. Some of the fury that burned in him turned to curiosity.

"Those are the best words I have heard in a long time. I give thanks to the Spirit." This time he had spoken much more slowly. Aeswiren nodded to show he understood, then replied, "How much do you know of the situation?"

"Which situation? On Mauste?"

Aeswiren shot a glance to Nuza at hearing this name.

"Lord," said Nuza, "Mauste is our name for the island where the fleet has set up its base."

"Ah, yes, that situation, too, but I refer to the larger scene involving myself."

Toshak looked to Nuza. She had seen him react to her use of the men's tongue. Now he heard Aeswiren's words and wondered at them.

"What does this mean, dearest Nuza?"

She gathered herself. Toshak must know the whole truth.

"The Great King is in exile himself. He has been overthrown. They tried to kill him, but he survived, and he still has the power to end the war. He has come here to take control of the expedition army, then take it back to Shasht and defeat his enemies with it."

There was a long moment of silence as Toshak absorbed this. He had suspected as much when he'd received Nuza's message.

"Well," he said dryly, "that rather reduces his value to us, but, better he is here late than that he never came at all to visit the scene of carnage his forces have unleashed."

Aeswiren understood enough of this to know it was time to keep his silence. Toshak must make up his own mind. The anger was to be expected.

Toshak had balled his fists so tightly, the muscles stood out on his neck. He stared upward as if seeking some advice from the heavens, or a whisper from the Spirit. Nuza watched him, not knowing whether he would accept Aeswiren's offer.

At last he relaxed and, with no further ado, took the Emperor's hand in his and they shook, brown-skinned hand of man and the grey-furred hand of mot. Nuza saw Aeswiren's eyes tighten as Toshak revealed his strength.

"Welcome, then, Great King," said Toshak, speaking slowly. "For I have just now learned that you are a fugitive and in need of shelter."

Aeswiren cast a sharp glance in Nuza's direction. She saw that he had realized that his ability to manipulate the situation was limited by his need for her to translate. That he was a deposed fugitive was information he would rather not have had Toshak know just yet.

"Thank you, General Toshak. I do not intend to trouble you more than is absolutely necessary. The men in my army will listen to me. I am confident of that. They will give me a hearing, and then I think they will rally to my cause."

"What will you offer them?"

Aeswiren's face creased into a grim smile. "Years of suffering, toil, bloodshed. War, in a word, but in the end the opportunity to overthrow the priesthood and change Shasht forever."

Toshak blinked, then glanced at Nuza.

Aeswiren continued. "I will offer them a war of liberation. I have learned a great secret, which I shall pass on to them."

Toshak looked to Nuza once more to be sure he was hearing this correctly. "Secret?"

"Yes, please listen to him, dear Toshak."

Aeswiren now spoke passionately, and when he stumbled, Nuza helped the words along.

"Once our land was almost as lush as yours. Our peoples were mostly peaceful. There were wars, but they were small in scale. Our population was stable, and we had both gods and goddesses. Our lives were governed by the round of festivals in their name and the liturgy of their worship.

"Then came the Empire. A man named Kadawak arose in the Old Kingdom of Shasht. At first he was but an officer of the small army kept by the royal house. He usurped the throne and began a war that lasted ten years. When it ended, he became the First Emperor. In the city he erected a pyramid to the new god, He Who Eats, Orbazt Subuus.

"He changed many things. Women could no longer go forth in the street. They lost all rights and became chattels of their husbands. Thousands of prisoners of war and captive women were used as breeding stock for slaves. Slaves became cheap. It was a popular policy."

Nuza observed that Toshak frowned at hearing of such evil.

"We do not have this thing, slavery, that you speak of."

"I know. Nuza told me."

And there it lay, the polar difference between the world of Shasht and that of the Land. To exploit one's fellow beings in such a way was unworthy, degrading to both sides of the division.

Toshak gave her another sharp look. She knew he was wondering about the relationship that had grown up between the Emperor and herself.

"The real problem, alas, was that the increase in slavery was popular with certain social classes among the population. Common property was seized under the law. Old traditions were overthrown and women enslaved. On the altars of the temple to He Who Eats, they began to tear open men and rip out their hearts to offer to the Great God."

Nuza shivered, just listening to Aeswiren describe all this. She saw that Toshak winced before replying.

"We have learned of this from men taken prisoner. They tell us of your so-called 'Great God' who demands fresh hearts from his worshippers. Your world seems to have nothing but ugliness and horror. Bare land, poverty and starvation, endless war and slavery."

There was a long moment of silence. Aeswiren, just in sailing this coast, had seen the differences between the two lands. This world was verdant, alive with life, lush with great forests, and already peopled. Shasht was a dry husk.

"Yes," Aeswiren admitted. "However, many live in luxury, especially in the cities, and they have gained great wealth. They support the Empire and the priesthood.

"But what they don't know, what nobody knows except the Emperors and a tiny group among the priesthood, is that there has always been a secret ruler, a hidden power that has ruled over all the Emperors since the beginning."

Toshak's eyebrows shot up for a moment. Then his eyes tightened to slits as he looked to Nuza for confirmation of these words. She nodded. This was Aeswiren's understanding, which, though it sounded incredible, he believed wholeheartedly.

Aeswiren continued, "It is a power that sits inside the pyramid. It rules through the priesthood, and it always has. It is the intelligence that informs Shasht society."

"What form does this thing take?"

"It is that of a man, very old when I saw him. He has ruled for hundreds of years, living on while dynasties have come and gone."

Toshak muttered to himself, then spoke clearly. "The Assenzi were right, then. I think this is what the old ones spoke of. They called it 'Karnemin.'"

"The Assenzi?" said Aeswiren. "They are the very old ones, who help your rulers. Nuza has spoken to me about them."

"They are not mots and they are not men, some say they are not actually alive like you or me. They are built of magic, perhaps."

"And they know of this man I speak of, which we call 'the Old One'?"

The name struck them both with its implications.

"Yes. They say they knew him long long ago, in the time of ice." And they, too, are the "old ones," Toshak wanted to say, but did not.

Aeswiren stood stockstill, drinking in the enormity of what he was hearing. The ice was barely a memory in Shasht, a thing of legend from long ago.

"Then this thing has lived far longer than our Empire. Far longer than the Old Kingdoms."

"And your people know nothing of it?"

"Only the inner circle of the high priests really knows. It is most dangerous knowledge to have."

"I see." And Toshak did.

Aeswiren looked at Nuza for a moment. He had seen the strange symmetry of the two forces. Nuza saw it, too.

"The expedition to your land was not my policy. It was a policy I inherited when I took the throne. For many years I bottled it up. I refused to spend money on a huge fleet of ships. But in the end they got around me. Politics is like that. When there's money to be spent, a way will be found to spend it."

Toshak understood this very well. Since the war's beginnings he had been forced into the financial and economic planning circles of both Dronned and Sulmo. The politics surrounding a royal budget had become crystal clear to him.

"But the Old One wanted it, that was the essential thing. He always pressed me to finish the fleet and send it. He wanted this war."

Toshak was nodding. "This thing you talk of, it wants to destroy us and the Assenzi."

"We are but pawns on an ancient chessboard."

Nuza watched the two of them as they came to grips with this vast, terrible realization.

The ancient thing that ruled in Shasht had forced the men to build an Empire and then used that Empire to build a fleet that was designed to destroy inhabitants of the Land and the Assenzi.

"The Assenzi are its real target, then. But there is a difference between our wise old helpers and this 'Old One' of yours. For this figure behind your Empire does his work in secret. We can judge from its results that it is foul work, the cause of endless bloodshed. But the Assenzi have usually done their work among us in the open."

"Usually?"

"At times there have been crises that have called for them to intervene in hidden ways. They have sought stability above everything, and our world has been without change for aeons."

"You have been held back. The men of Shasht have been pushed forward. We have all been made into puppets." Aeswiren slammed a fist into a palm. "I say it is time to end it. Let the ancient ones fight their own battles."

"I have a question," said Toshak. "Who made the policy that causes men to kill my people and eat them? Why do men eat our children?"

Aeswiren blanched. He remembered when the orders for that policy were given. He remembered that he signed them blithely, thinking that it meant nothing. The inhabitants of this mythical land that the priests wanted to conquer were but animals. If the men ate them, then so be it. Men got hungry, and animals were food.

"It was a policy put forward by the priests. They said that animals of abomination inhabited the new lands and that they should be consumed as food."

It was hard to translate "abomination" into the language of the Land. With Nuza's help, they came up with "evil in the form of unbearable wrongness."

The hate came back to Toshak's eyes.

Aeswiren met it, accepting the dark cloud. Then he put his right hand to his chest before speaking. "The guilt for this evil will never leave me. I accept my responsibility. I say only that I signed the order in ignorance. But this I swear: I will put an end to all killing. Men under my command will no longer attack your people without suffering just punishment."

After a long moment of silence, Toshak nodded, accepting the Emperor's words on their face value. "I would expect you to do no more than that. But what, I wonder, can be done to make up for what your men have already done to us?"

"It can never be made up. I know that. But when I regain my throne, I will begin a program of compensation for your injuries. If it is within my strength and power to do it, I will make things whole again. For the lost lives, and other injuries, there is no power in the world that can repair them."

It was a long speech for Aeswiren, and his control of word order was not exact, but his sincerity glowed in his eyes. Nuza saw that Toshak had been moved by it. She gave thanks to the Spirit.

"So," said Toshak, "how can I help you, Emperor?"

"I need to know how my forces here are disposed. They are based on an island to the south, called Mauste, I believe you said."

"Yes. Most of the ships are moored there. But others raid our coasts and supply the forts on the shores of Sulmo."

"Yes, you mentioned these forts before, to Nuza. How many are they and where can I find them?"

Chapter 8

The audaciousness of it was the key. That's why the men would know it was him. Who else would dare something like this? Only old Aeswiren, the legendary fighter who came back three times from defeat to win everything in the end. Only Aeswiren, who'd taken ten thousand beaten men and made them into an army that won an Empire. Only Aeswiren, who'd risen from defeat to win victory at Kaggenbank.

Audacity and his own legend, that was what he had in his favor.

His guides had faded back into the undergrowth. These young mots were clad in a camouflage fabric so effective that he could hardly see them in the woods at a distance of twenty feet.

It was time.

He strode out from behind the last tree and started for the fort. The ground was rough, stippled with tree stumps, littered with broken branches. When he was less than two hundred yards from the gate, somebody on the tower gave a yell.

Aeswiren noted that the fort was well built. The gate was solid, with proper stockade construction. The ditch was deep. Aeswiren smiled at seeing the professional quality on display. Good fortifications had always been something he'd prided himself on.

He wondered how many archers on that wall had him in their sights right then. At this range, the sharpshooters would not miss. He waved a hand, continued a steady walk.

They'd seen that he was a well-dressed man with a shining helmet and burnished breastplate. Those would tip them off that he was an officer, at the least.

"Who goes there?" roared a voice from the gate.

He stopped, raised both arms and roared back, "I am Aeswiren."

This produced a harsh bark of laughter, followed by: "Oh, sure, and I'm a monkey's arsehole. Stop playing around. Who are you? And how did you get here?"

Aeswiren laughed, waved a hand, and kept walking. "Meet me at the gate," he called. "Are there any veterans among you?"

"Veterans? Plenty of 'em. We're Third Regiment here."

"Ah, the fighting Third. I know you well. You were at Kaggenbank."

There was a sudden silence on the top of the wall. The gate opened a crack.

"All right, approach the gate. Let's have a look at you."

A number of men had climbed up to the parapet gatehouse to take a look at this phenomenon, a man come alive out of the woods. It hadn't happened before. Men went out into the woods, they died in the woods.

"You don't look like a scout," said a voice from the wall. "How'd you make it out of there? The monkeys kill our scouts."

"Look at that breastplate," said another voice. "Look at that helmet. That's gold chasing, my friend. Very expensive."

"It's one of the generals, then? The ones that were captured."

"Maybe. You, step closer."

The man with the gold chasing on his helmet stepped up to the gate.

The corporal of the gate detail, old Pils Heeber, pushed forward to do the talking. "All right, all right. Now, excuse me, sir, whoever you are, you have to forgive us. We've never seen anyone walk out of the forest like that. Scouts have only come back at night. The monkeys are always out there."

"Ah, yes. Well, boys, I think we're going to see an end to all that pretty soon. I expect you're tired of being stuck out here."

"Sir, as long as they feed us, we're proud to do our duty. Ain't we, boys?"

They gave loud assent.

Sergeant Kaffee had dragged himself away from lunch, a kedgeree and a fish pudding. "All right, what's all this? Why is this gate open? Are we going to let in every sodomistic monkey in the fornicating woods?"

Corporal Heeber turned around quickly.

"Ah, Sergeant, we got someone here who just walked out of the woods."

"What?"

Then Sergeant Kaffee got a clear look at the man in his high-class metal finery. The sergeant felt his jaw drop. He felt his pulse race. His knees wobbled.

Sergeant Kaffee had served in the Emperor's personal guard five years back. He'd volunteered for the colony expedition from the guard. It had been regarded back then as a privilege, a chance to get out of Shasht and forge a new life in a land without the weight of Shasht society holding a man down.

"Open the gate!" the sergeant bellowed. He slammed to attention and thrust his arm up in the imperial salute.

The others stopped laughing and looked at him aghast.

"Sir!" roared Sergeant Kaffee in his best parade-ground voice. "Begging your pardon, sir. I had no idea, sir. Sergeant Kaffee, Third Regiment, reporting, sir!"

Corporal Heeber was looking at Kaffee like he expected the sergeant to start barking next. "What's that about, Sergeant?"

"You idiot," hissed Sergeant Kaffee, "that *is* the Emperor Aeswiren. I served in his guard. I know that's him."

Aeswiren allowed himself a little grin as he heard this. It had been a hell of a gamble, but the first piece of luck had come his way. He'd run into a veteran right off. Someone who had actually seen the Emperor Aeswiren at close quarters and recognized him at once.

The other men still hesitated. Kaffee spoke up again in his parade-ground voice. "Sir, begging your pardon, sir. I was in your personal guard during the time of the fishermen riots."

"You was in the guard, Sarge?" asked Corporal Heeber.

"Oh, shit!" said someone a little too loudly.

"Sir!" said Corporal Heeber, finally coming to attention and raising his hand in the imperial salute.

"Sir!" chorused the others.

The gate swung wide. Aeswiren acknowledged their salute and let them stand easy.

"Don't sweat it, boys. Hell, I'm the last person I'd expect to come walking out of these woods. Your disbelief was understandable. But, thanks to Sergeant Kaffee here, we've established who I am. It's a long story, and I will tell it all very shortly. But first I have some things to do. Now, who's the commanding officer here?"

The men stared at the gold chasing on the breastplate. Worth a small fortune on its own. And they saw the heavy gold rings on the man's fingers, and they heard the words and felt the bearing of the man.

"Uh, that will be the colonel, sir. Colonel Breuze."

"Excellent, and where will I find the colonel?"

Chapter 9

Admiral Heuze paced up and down the floor of his stateroom aboard the flagship *Anvil,* his peg leg making a dull clunk with every step. They had spotted a distant sail approaching hours before, and the ship had been beating up to them through an irregular breeze ever since. Heuze was worried, and impatient, which was not a good mixture.

The first news had come from Ensign Combliss, shortly after the distant ship's hull became visible. "It's the *Duster,* sir. Frigate that went back to Shasht year before last. Was replaced by the frigate *Wasp,* sir."

"What are they doing here, then?"

"Say they have a special passenger. Request a meeting with you, sir."

Heuze did not like mysteries like this. Coming on top of the bizarre news from his forts it was unsettling. Who was this "special passenger"? Was there a connection with this madness from the forts? A man had appeared from the forest, claiming to be Emperor Aeswiren. Three forts had gone over to this man.

Heuze didn't know yet if the men had gone barking mad or if he had a rebellion on his hands, though it certainly sounded ominous.

"A message, sir." The door had opened after a knock. A hand passed in a slip of paper.

"Identity of special passenger, Filek Biswas," he read with astounded eyes.

"Any return message, sir?"

Heuze hesitated, befuddled by surprise. "No. No return."

The door closed.

Shaken, with mounting concern for what all this might mean, Heuze sat down by his desk. This news was the last thing he might have expected.

Filek Biswas had come back? But what about his research program? What the hell had happened in Shasht? And if the *Duster* was bringing Filek Biswas to see him, who was this man who had convinced three forts that he was the fornicating Emperor Aeswiren the Third?

Rousing himself at last, Heuze took his spyglass and went up to the quarterdeck and studied the approaching frigate carefully. Her rigging was worn but seaworthy. To Heuze's expert eye, she had the look of a ship that had been at sea for a long time.

Tacking into the wind, her crew were setting sails with an expert efficiency that brought a small grunt of approval from him. Like most frigate crews, they were natural-born sailors. Soon afterward, the frigate made a final tack and slid smoothly between the much larger ships of the colony fleet.

A boat was set down, bearing a single figure rowed by four men. It moved swiftly across to the *Anvil*'s side. In a few minutes, the passenger had climbed the netting to reach the deck.

"Biswas!" Heuze could not contain himself.

"Admiral."

They clasped hands. There were a thousand questions pressing.

"My dear fellow, this has been something of a surprise."

"Yes, Admiral Heuze, I'm sure it must be."

"Come up to my stateroom. We can talk there."

A few moments later, they were secure behind a locked door.

Seeing Biswas once again brought back memories for Heuze. The two had become friends when Surgeon Biswas had been brought in to take off Heuze's leg from the knee down. A tiny wound on a toe had grown into gangrene, threatening the admiral's life.

Surgeon Biswas espoused novel notions about cleanliness and anesthetics. Heuze had been pleasantly surprised by how easily the amputation had gone. The two became fast friends, for it happened that the admiral was able to rescue poor Biswas from an unfortunate situation on another ship. Indeed, if not for the admiral, Biswas most likely would have been castrated and sold into slavery.

"What in the world are you doing here?"

Biswas held up a hand with a weak smile. "I thought you might ask that. It's a long story. Let me explain . . . I sent you a letter after my return to Shasht. Have you received it?"

"Yes, a year ago. You had been well received by the Emperor. He had shown his favor on you and rewarded you with—"

"Oh, he was most generous. I had the run of the hospital. The research was going very well. But, well, nothing that good can last forever."

Heuze nodded. "Yes?"

"Admiral, tell me, how much do you know about the temple in the pyramid?"

"What?"

"The Gold Tops, the high priests, what do you know about them?"

"Hate their sodomistic guts is all. We killed them. You remember. You helped me do it. Killing those buggers was one of the best things I've ever done."

"Uh, yes, Admiral, but have you ever heard of the 'Old One'?"

"No, can't say that I have."

Filek nodded. "They keep it well hidden. Do you

recall the message that my daughter brought back from her time among the native people?"

"Biswas, stop that 'native people' stuff. They're monkeys. We went through all that long ago."

Filek laughed. The admiral was still his fierce, irrepressible self.

"Well, Admiral, if you recall that message, you may have heard a name mentioned during it."

The name came back to Heuze as if it had been but a moment before. That strange, terrifying vision. A place of vast towers, of bright pennons that burned upon a blue sky. And that small voice in his ear.

"Karnemin?" he said.

"Yes. That is it."

"Who does this refer to, this name?"

"It is the Old One, Admiral. The Old One is the hidden ruler of the Gold Tops. From the heart of the pyramid he rules Shasht."

"But . . ." Heuze's face expressed a mixture of astonishment and disbelief.

"Believe me, Admiral, the Old One exists. He has lived in the pyramid since the beginning of the Empire, but he is far, far older than that."

Heuze's curiosity was aroused. "What is this thing, this Old One?"

"In form, he is said to be a man. Every Emperor has to meet him. They learn that they rule only so far and no farther. They learn that the Old One is the ultimate ruler of all Shasht."

Heuze was left groping for air. All kinds of horrible realizations were slipping into place. "Biswas, has the Emperor been overthrown in Shasht?"

"Yes. Aeswiren was overthrown by the Old One."

"By the purple ass of the Great God, don't tell me . . ."

"Yes, Admiral, the Emperor is here. He has come to the Land."

And he had already taken three of Heuze's forts.

"Oh, my god." Heuze stared at Biswas while his mind spun.

"He is here, Admiral, and he has need of you. I have been sent to ask a question. Will you be loyal to Emperor Aeswiren now that he calls upon you?"

Heuze sucked in a breath. This was a most dangerous moment. If he put a foot wrong here, he could easily end up being handed over to the priests. How they would love that! The admiral who had broken their power, given to them to be tortured before they tore his heart from his chest and offered it to their Great God.

"Well, of course." Heuze tried to think of some way to dissimulate. "I have always been loyal to Aeswiren."

"Yes, I thought so," said Biswas with a smile. "You know by now that most of your men in the forts have gone over to him."

"Yes, I had heard this. I didn't believe it."

"He went to the forts alone, Admiral. He just walked up out of the forest and the men took him to their hearts."

"I . . ." Heuze heard Filek's words and understood.

Aeswiren had truly come. The men in the army would respond to him like no other. The tide would be unstoppable.

"What about Nebbeggebben?" The Emperor's son, who remained in nominal command of the colony.

"We hope to arrange it so that there is no time for him to do anything. If you will stand by the Emperor, he will land on the island tomorrow and speak directly to the troops."

Heuze whistled. The audacity of it. Sailing in under Nebbeggebben's nose and taking his army, just like that.

The admiral snapped his fingers.

"By the Great God's purple ass, I like it."

It was just like the daring Aeswiren of old. When he'd lead a rebel army to unexpected victory. Heuze could feel the coming wind. There was no way to play it safe. And loyalty to Aeswiren would be recognized and rewarded.

"Damn it all to hell and gone, I'm Aeswiren's man, you can tell him that."

Chapter 10

When Aeswiren sailed to Mauste, Nuza had stayed behind in Dronned, among her own kind. As she'd watched the *Duster* sail out of the bay, she'd known that she might never see the Emperor again. The thought left her sadder than she ever would have imagined.

She'd returned to her room in the palace, struggling through the throngs that crowded Dronned because of the war. Even the palace was jam-packed, as the royal civil service struggled with the huge demands of the army.

Back in her little room, she sat quietly on the bed, writing letter after letter to her family in Lushtan. She had still not received word back from them, which left her in a state of mild anxiety. There had been no raids as far as Lushtan, but Nuza could not help but feel uneasy.

She would have set off for Lushtan as soon as Aeswiren had gone, but there had come messages from the Assenzi requesting that she remain to speak with them about her adventures in Shasht and her relationship with the Emperor. They were hurrying to meet with her. On the roads to Dronned, from the north, south, and east, there were ancient frail figures on the move, each accompanied by nothing more than a donkey and a young acolyte or two.

On several occasions, she had been invited to dine

with the King and Queen of Dronned and their guests. They could not get enough of her stories about Shasht, even though she protested that she had seen very little of the place, having been virtually a prisoner most of the time in an apartment in the capital city. Still, His Majesty was interested in whatever she'd learned. A land turned into a virtual desert was almost incomprehensible to him. As were tales of giant pyramids, huge palaces of stone, and cities so vast you could not see beyond them.

As for the Emperor, the King was filled with an eager fascination, as well as a certain resentment. The speedy visit of the Emperor to the dunes, to meet with Toshak alone, had not been taken kindly by the King of Dronned. Often in an evening, he would return to this point in the conversation.

"I must admit that we have wondered why the Emperor did not ask to meet with us. We are, after all, the titular ruler of this realm. To request to meet only with General Toshak seemed almost insulting to us."

Nuza would try once more to pour oil on the troubled waters.

"We tried to explain all of that in our letters to you, Your Majesty."

"I know, I know," the small fat king would grumble. "This plague you wrote about. It kills them, the men, and he was afraid we'd give it to him. That didn't please us very much either, to be thought of as disease-ridden."

And so Nuza would have to work hard to rehabilitate the Emperor's reputation with the King and Queen, who remained quite prickly on the subject of Aeswiren's swift visit to their land.

"What we have to remember, Your Majesties," she would say, over and over, "is that the Emperor must move very quickly now. He has to act before his enemies even know he is here. If he succeeds, then the war will end."

That happy thought was always enough to still their protests and soften the hard feelings left behind. Ending the war was paramount. Even though the war had shifted its focus south to the coastline of Sulmo, the strain on Dronned was still enormous. All the realms of the Land were involved to some degree in the effort to defeat the invaders, but Dronned was one of the most prosperous realms and therefore the burden had fallen disproportionally on the house of Belit to provide material for Toshak's army.

Sometimes the strain showed at the dinner table. Important nobles, Gryses of the Realm, were usually present. They, too, were paying more than they ever had before, but not as much proportionately as the King, and his resentment would on occasion boil over. The Grys Nurrum was practically driven from the dining table by the King when he foolishly attempted to protest the necessity of delivering twenty tons of dried fish.

"What the hell do you expect our soldiers to eat then?" had been Belit's response. Nurrum had no good answers.

Such dinners were hardly relaxing, and Nuza did not welcome the invitations, yet still they came, and still she went. She had no worthwhile excuse for refusing an invitation from the royal house of Dronned.

Beyond all these matters, neither the King nor anyone else had been able to answer Nuza's own most pressing question. She could get no fresh information about Thru Gillo's death. Then, one evening at dinner with the King and Queen, she was introduced to the Grys Norvory, who had once been Thru's nemesis in the weaving guild. Since those days in the prewar past, he had fought in the army. He had even served under Thru's command in the battle of Dronned. At some point after that battle, the Grys finally became aware that he had been completely mistaken about Thru Gillo.

Nuza listened to his account of his great change of mind. When he had finished she spoke. "Thru and I were lovers." She was frank as always and took no notice of Norvory's embarrassment. "We spent a great deal of time together. I remember the 'Chooks and Beetles' of his that you sold. It really was his. I saw him make another of that pattern, and other work, too. He was gifted."

Norvory had recovered his poise.

"Yes. Another Misho in the making, I think. He would have brought a revolution to our weaving arts. For what happened in the matter of the 'Chooks and Beetles,' I can only beg for your forgiveness. I was wrong. Worse, I was so caught up in my own view of the matter that I behaved with unpardonable arrogance. In mitigation I can only say that I was taken in by Pern Treevi, who I have learned was not a mot to trust."

Nuza nodded mutely. She remembered the heartbreak for Thru back in those days. This aristocrat had ruined Thru's dream. But that was before the war, and more important matters had swallowed up that time.

"It is hard not knowing for sure whether Thru is dead."

"I am afraid he must be. I was not at the battle of Farnem, which is probably why I'm still alive. Almost all of the officers from Dronned who were there perished."

Nuza gave a sigh of sorrow. "I saw Thru that summer. In Sulmo City, whenever he could leave his command."

Norvory's face took on a grim cast. "That battle was such a disaster; our army engaged piecemeal. Gillo's brigade and another were forced to fight the entire enemy army. They were overwhelmed. I was devastated by the news of his death in particular, because I had finally understood how mistaken I had been in the matter of the 'Chooks and Beetles'; I had wished to apologize and to offer him some form of restitution. His death took that chance away, and now I am left with this stain on my good name and no way of removing it."

So, Thru was dead. She said good-bye to her last faint hopes. Mourning was easier than not knowing.

"Perhaps, Grys, if the war ends, as I now hope it will, you might open a legal office dedicated to helping the small and the weak pursue just claims against the great and the powerful?"

He looked at her as if the idea intrigued him. "I thank you, Mistress Nuza. That is a very good suggestion."

That dinner ended more pleasantly than some. The Grys had offered her room to stay at his country house should she ever want a respite from the crowding in Dronned. They had parted on good terms. She'd left hoping that Thru would have approved.

The next evening, a mot came to her room with a message. On reading it, she jumped up, pulled on a light coat, and followed the mot through the winding passageways of the ancient palace.

Toshak was waiting for her in a small office chamber. They embraced and then sat across from each other at the table.

"Toshak, dearest, I have prayed that I would see you again."

"Many things are in motion. It has been a very busy two weeks."

"What news have you from the Emperor?"

"He has landed on Mauste. If he has succeeded, then the war will end, for now."

"He will win. Aeswiren is filled with an elemental force. I have seen it."

"Yes, I believe you, but you also know what he faces. What we all face. This thing, the Old One, that has lived since the days of the old world, of the time of Man-the-Cruel. It will have anticipated the Emperor's plans. It must know that he has come here."

Nuza frowned. Could they never be rid of the fear? The terror of war?

"But, enough of that. I have good news from Sulmo. The men have abandoned three of the forts and moved into a single fort on Pelican Point. We have agreed that they will erect a larger place there, from which they will disembark when they leave our shores forever."

"Where will they go then?"

"To Mauste for a while, at least a year, perhaps two, and then they will sail away, back to their homeland."

"May that day come!"

"They will need our help before then. We will have to help them outfit their fleet, and dry and store enough food to keep them alive. We do not have the animal foods that they like. They will have to adjust to bushpod and bushcurd."

"Let them. It is nothing compared to what we have had to live with because of them."

Toshak nodded, then took her hand in his. "You will be visited soon by several Assenzi. They have a great many questions for you. They also want to meet with the Emperor. Do you think he will allow it?"

"I think so, but he does not completely trust them."

"Yes, he does not know them. He thinks they are like his enemy."

"Our enemy, Toshak."

"Yes."

"Toshak, dearest, did you ever learn what exactly happened to Thru? His body was never found."

Toshak's face fell once more. He squeezed her hand. "His brigade was annihilated at the battle of Farnem." Toshak was struggling with the hate in his voice. "We found very few of our people afterward."

Her eyes widened. "Do you think?"

"Yes, they were taken by the men for food."

Pelican Point, the mots called this place. A sweeping hook of sand and gravel extending from the forest out into the bay as if it were an arm attempting to gather up the riches of the water and drag them ashore.

Aeswiren stood atop the little knoll at the end of the hook. His boat was beached on the shingle down below. Klek was standing by. There were no pelicans on the point that day, just six thousand men. A great mass of faces, hushed, expectant, looking up at him like children.

Aeswiren grinned. This was where his power lay. Let the Old One fiddle with its evil magic. He—Ge Vust, humble fisherman of the Gzia coast—now known as Aeswiren the Third, Emperor of all Shasht, had the power to arouse and motivate fighting men.

"All right, boys!" He raised his hands and spoke in a firm voice. It was better to make them strain to hear him, especially at the beginning. "Among you there must be a few who served in the imperial guard at some time or other. Would some of you old veterans step out and come a little closer?"

Some jostling here and there broke up the mass of eyes, beards, noses. Seven, then eight older fellows emerged. All but one were sergeants with red plumes on their helmets.

"Come on over," said Aeswiren, more loudly. He made a big gesture with his arm. In front of this many, you had to pantomime a bit, exaggerating everything so they all saw it.

They crowded up. He recognized a couple of them, and he struggled to recall their names.

"You!" he bellowed. "Aktinus, isn't it? Aktinus of Gzia Gi?"

"Emperor!" roared the fellow, a massive bull of a man, six and a half feet tall, with a face like a rocky crag. The others were quick to follow his lead, slamming to attention. "Emperor!" they called in unison, arms flashing up, fist clenched in the imperial salute.

"Emperor!" echoed the response from the first rank, who had seen Aktinus's reaction close up. A moment later, the rest of them took up the cry.

Aeswiren raised his hands and called for quiet, but it took three or four more "Emperors" before they would quiet down.

"Come up here, Aktinus."

The huge sergeant lumbered up the slope. Before he reached the top, Aeswiren stopped him with a gesture. He didn't want to be dwarfed by the fellow. It was a piece of sorcery he was trying to pull off here, and every angle had to be considered.

"Aktinus was in the guard a couple years back, isn't that right?"

"Correct, Lord."

"You must have volunteered for this expedition. You all volunteered, right?"

"Volunteers, sir!" they roared back.

"So, Aktinus, how would you say the mission has gone so far?"

Aktinus swallowed, looked Aeswiren in the eye. "Permission to speak my mind, sir, in a frank and open manner?"

"Permission to speak, Aktinus."

"It's been a complete, sorry mess, sir, from beginning to end."

A hush came over them. Aktinus had dared to express what they all thought but never dreamed of telling a superior; he had been allowed to complain directly to the Emperor. It was an intoxicating notion to every soldier.

"That bad, eh?"

They let out a collective sigh. Aeswiren heard it but refrained from smiling.

"Yes, sir."

"Why was that, Aktinus?"

"Begging your pardon, sir, but the generals we had were dolts. We only won one battle, and after that we ended up being chased off the mainland by the fornicating monkeys."

"Dolts?"

"Yes, sir."

"Well, boys, I want you to know that I didn't choose the generals for this mission. I didn't even want this expedition. It was the priests who wanted it."

"Kill the sodomistic priests," said a soldier at the back, and everyone laughed, including Aeswiren.

"That's exactly what I plan to do. The priests have had their way with old Shasht for too long. It's time we straightened things out and took them down a peg or two!"

The men before the Emperor exploded into long, loud cheering.

Chapter 11

The army was Aeswiren's. Wherever they were, the men went over to him as soon as they saw him and heard his voice.

He offered them an immediate end to the useless war against the mots.

"These folk, whom you call monkeys, are not our enemies. Our real enemies are the fornicating priests; they are responsible for this mess. I came here to get you boys out of this shit and back to Shasht, where you can help me bring an end to the whole damned priesthood and their tyranny. What say you?"

"Aeswiren!" they roared, flinging their right arms up in the imperial salute.

The army was his, but the fleet was another matter. Admiral Heuze and a few of the ship captains were ready to go over to him, but the majority were not. Ship captains were a different breed, accustomed to ruling their own little realms. Thousands of miles from home, after years of failures by the commanders of the colony expedition, they were not quite ready to accept that the Emperor himself had come all this way to join them.

Nebbeggebben had denounced the man now running the army as an impostor and put a price on his head. No one had dared to try and collect it, not with the six thousand men ashore ready to die for their Emperor. Yet the implications were clear to every captain: Nebbeggebben would have their heads at the slightest sign that they were going over to Aeswiren.

Meanwhile, the men ashore withheld water and food supplies from the ships.

A stalemate ensued. Days went by. Aeswiren understood the dangers very well. If the fleet pulled up anchor and sailed away, he'd have to build new ships from scratch and crew them with soldiers. In the meantime, elements of the fleet would return to Shasht and pass on the news of what was going on in the Land.

He had to move quickly.

And so, in the dead of night, a small boat rowed out toward the *Shark,* fourth in the line behind the flagship *Anvil* in the inshore squadron.

In the stateroom of the *Shark,* several nervous ship captains had gathered at Heuze's request. They were not a happy bunch, frightened of making a mistake in this situation and losing their heads.

"Damn you, Heuze, why didn't you just kill this bugger and keep it hushed up?" groused Captain Groth.

"Besides the fact that he's got six thousand men backing him? Let's just say this: I would rather fight with one hand tied behind my back for Aeswiren than for his son with both hands free."

There were wary nods of agreement. Nebbeggebben had never been popular.

"Well, I don't care who this fellow is who claims to be the Emperor. I have to have provisions. My crew are hungry."

"Damn your provisions," snapped Captain Egemel. "I need fresh water. Unless I can refill my casks in two days, my crew will be without anything to drink."

"We all have problems," said Heuze, raising his hands.

"We all have problems, all right," groused Groth, "even this Emperor of yours."

"He isn't mine alone, Groth. You swore your oath of fealty to him."

"I'll believe that when I see him, and not before."

The door had opened while Groth was speaking, and two men had entered. One was Filek Biswas, the well-known former chief surgeon of the fleet who had gone back to Shasht years before but had been rumored to have returned recently. The other was a taller man, broad-shouldered, with hair turning grey and features that were familiar to every man of Shasht who'd ever used an imperial coin.

The captains—Groth, Egermel, Herbest, and the rest—froze. Until this moment they had not really believed that it could be possible. Despite all evidence to the contrary, they had clung to the notion that this was an impostor who had the idiots in the army in his thrall.

"Your Majesty," said Heuze, hitching his crutch, bending at the knee, and bowing low. With alacrity the rest followed suit, even the clearly stunned Groth.

"At ease, gentlemen." Aeswiren strode farther into the room. He wore his breastplate, red cloak, sword, and greaves. He carried himself as if he were going into battle.

The captains remained agape.

"I gather that some of you don't quite believe that I'm me," said the Emperor with a fierce grin. Captain Groth, he noticed, had gone pale. "Well, get used to it, because I am me, and I am standing right before you."

Groth practically fell over himself in his effort to be first to kneel and kiss Aeswiren's hand. "Begging your pardon, Your Majesty. I couldn't imagine that you'd really come all this way."

"That is understandable. There are times when I can't quite believe it either."

They were still thunderstruck, staring at him with disbelieving eyes. Aeswiren turned to face Heuze again.

"Well, Admiral, what do you think? Am I Aeswiren, or am I not?"

"You are, Lord." Heuze bowed again. So did everyone else.

"Well, in that case, if we're agreed, then we need to have a little talk."

The ship captains listened as Aeswiren explained what he intended to do.

"Go back to Shasht?" asked one, when he was done.

"Yes," said Aeswiren. "We are not going to waste another drop of blood here. We will sail back to Shasht either next year or the summer after that."

There was no doubt in his voice. They all felt the heat of Aeswiren's will in those words.

"So be it," said Heuze. "From what you've said today, Your Majesty, it sounds like we're needed back there a lot more than we are here."

There were mumbles of agreement from most of the others.

Less than an hour later, it was done. One by one, they renewed their oaths of allegiance to the Emperor and then slipped out onto the quarterdeck of the *Shark.* Boats were readied to take the captains back to their ships. Their plans were laid.

But the best-laid plans may still go awry.

Just as the boats were about to be lowered, lights suddenly blazed up from below. Hoarse cries could be heard along with the sudden thud of drums. A swarm of boats had crept up unseen around the ship, and Red Tops were climbing up the side netting. There were hundreds of them, probably all the Red Tops remaining in the fleet.

"We are betrayed!" wailed Groth.

A huge voice bellowed from below, "Arrest them all in the name of His Majesty Nebbeggebben. They are all to be questioned by the priests."

"Damn," said Captain Temerar, "that's Beshezz."

"Well," said Heuze, "that answers the question about his loyalties, all right."

The captains stood irresolute, frozen in horror.

Aeswiren broke the spell with a roar: "To hell with this. I'm not going to slaughter like a fool calf." His sword flashed in the torch light.

"Come on, the rest of you," he yelled at them. "They're just a lot of Red Tops. We can beat them. Fight!"

The captains hesitated, so intimidated by the rule of the priests all their lives that even now they hardly dared resist.

A Red Top started climbing over the side. Aeswiren sped across and punched the fellow in the face. With a startled whoop, he went backward down to the water below.

"Come on!" bellowed Aeswiren.

And the spell was broken. The captains charged forward, drawing swords, picking up whatever lay to hand for weapons. If they were taken alive, the priests would hammer their fingers flat and then tear their hearts out of their chests while they screamed their last. Better to die fighting.

Even Filek Biswas took up an oar and swung it two-handed to knock Red Tops back into the sea.

"That's it, Biswas," roared the admiral, who was swinging his sword with a will.

The ordinary seamen of the *Shark* had come on deck at the sounds of the attack. At first they had stood still, numbed by what they were seeing, fearing to do anything lest it lead them to the altars of the Great God. They observed that there were a lot of captains onboard. The quarterdeck was jammed with men in blue and red coats. They looked to them for leadership as the Red Tops scrambled over the gun-wale.

Then the figure clad as the Emperor on all the coins jumped forward and started attacking the Red Tops, and the men went crazy.

There was nothing in the world they hated more than the Red Tops. They met the young priests with swords, knives, belaying pins, mattocks, and hammers.

It was a thumping, scratching, bloody fight. The young Red Tops had spent much of the last two years in a state of humiliated rage. The power of the priests had been smashed by Admiral Heuze. The Gold Tops had been almost annihilated, and the number of Red Tops had been cut down by three quarters, with the majority castrated and sold into slavery.

The surviving Red Tops had been itching for this chance ever since. They were so close to arresting the hated admiral and his closest captains and giving them over to the inquisition. Thus, they fought with everything they had, and they would have cowed and defeated the sailors if not for the amazing rumor that was sweeping through the ship.

"The Emperor is here! On the *Shark,* now!"

Eyes bulging with amazement, the sailors turned on the Red Tops with fury in their hearts and renewed strength in their arms.

"Aeswiren!" they roared.

They stopped the attackers dead in their tracks. Then they began to clear the decks, pushing the maniacal Red Tops back, cutting them down, hurling them overboard.

On the quarterdeck, the captains, the admiral, and the Emperor had withstood the efforts of the Red Tops to get among them. The deck was slippery with blood.

The sound of the fighting, the glare of two dozen torches, the chants of "Aeswiren"—all had been noticed by the rest of the fleet. Dozens of boats had been set down, and now these boats, crewed by sailors, came up on the boats of the priests.

Admiral Beshezz roared orders at the newcomers, telling them to take up the attack and overrun the *Shark.*

The crews rowed in, hardly slackening their pace, until they were abreast the priests' boats, where the Red Tops, wet and nearly defeated, were climbing aboard.

The arriving sailors attacked, driving spears and swords into the exhausted Red Tops. Beshezz roared in anger. So did other officers, but they were ignored.

"For Aeswiren!" howled the sailors. The rumor had already swept the fleet that day, and now the fighting confirmed it. The fornicating Red Tops were trying to kill the Emperor, and the ordinary seamen would not have it.

The Red Tops were caught between two fires and could do nothing but fight and die. Many drowned after being knocked into the water and prevented from climbing out again. It was over in less than an hour, and Admiral Beshezz, hog-tied and soaked, was delivered to the quarterdeck in front of the Emperor.

The word was passing through the fleet, borne on a tidal wave of cheers. Aeswiren was among them. The war was over. They were going home.

Best of all, the hated Red Tops were finished.

Chapter 12

The Old One sat in meditative seclusion. The blinds were drawn, the candle doused. His breathing was very slow, seven breaths a minute.

Meditation was both a retreat and a trap for him. A retreat, because in the dark silence he could find the peace that was otherwise elusive. A trap because if he was not careful, he could lose himself there in the quiet dark and not come back. After one hundred thousand years of life, the quiet dark was very seductive. Life was an enormous burden sometimes. It would be very easy, he thought, to lay down that burden and cease to exist.

Why live?

The question hung there, shimmering in the silent dark. Why suffer any further in the material world?

A moment passed. Thousands, millions of smaller lives hung in the balance.

The answer welled up from a small residual core of anger and hate. Because he would be avenged on them! On the leaders of long ago, who had cast him down and expelled him from their world. He would carry on his war until he had exterminated every trace of their work. So he had vowed on the day of his escape. So it would be!

The Old One stirred and broke the trance state. He took a deeper breath and opened his eyes.

The room was as it had been before, close, comfortable, warm even in midwinter. It was time for him to practice magic. Time to read minds on the other side of the world.

Once, he would have needed help from Basth to move around, even in the middle of the day, but in the new body he had taken that was not a concern. He rose in a single fluid movement and stood for a moment, enjoying the new body.

It was the strongest he had ever had, a joy to control. When he practiced with a sword he exulted from the strength and speed that he now possessed. This body had belonged to Pulbeka, a stone breaker. But Pulbeka had never known the way of the sword. Only Karnemin knew that.

The Old One tipped back his huge head and roared with laughter.

He pulled aside the curtain and stepped out of the alcove. In the outer room, warm water and clean towels were waiting. He refreshed himself, swung his arms in the air, threw a few mock punches, reveling in the power these huge shoulders provided.

He had stayed in the old body far too long. The previous transit had been most difficult. He had almost died in the process and lost everything after so long. That experience had made him afraid to move on to the next body. Death for that body had been a kindness.

He stepped down the hallway to another room. Several oil lamps had been lit and the airshaft opened to let out the smoke. It was night outside the temple pyramid.

A quick examination of the scene showed that Basth had prepared everything as ordered. The grey ritual slab of stone had been wheeled in on a heavy dolly.

Across the stone lay an old woman, naked, bound to the plank at her ankles, knees, waist, chest, and neck. Her arms were tied painfully behind her and under the plank. She had been thoroughly bathed, oiled, and perfumed, as if she were going to a lover.

He gazed down on her. She was just an old scrub slave. He'd specified only that she be reasonably healthy. Years before her face had been broken with the brand. Since then she had lived chained to a huge brush with which she scrubbed the streets. Her old stringy arms were thin but wiry. What crime had she committed? The Old One did not care a whit. Her life spirit, her death energy, that was all he required.

On the table next to the slab was a pile of perfectly cut slates, each two feet by one and no more than a quarter inch in thickness. Each weighed five pounds. He laid the first slate on the old crone's chest and began to chant the curious rhyme that governed this spell.

As he chanted he felt colors swirling in his mind. First green, a stain that covered everything. Across the pure green grew a lacy network, a riverine system of dark threads. The threads connected, then grew together into knots and masses and finally clustered into blobs, growing darker and bluer and finally purple before they suddenly flushed red. With the color of blood flowing through his eyes, he turned, took up a second slate, and laid it carefully on top of the first on the old woman's chest.

She looked at him wonderingly. He continued to chant, the singsong syllables swinging back and forth while the red conglomeration glowed like heated wires.

After he placed the third slate, the wonder in her eyes turned to fear. She could move her head easily enough and had seen the pile of slates placed nearby. The stack was three feet high.

In Pulbeka's hands, the slates were not much more than large playing cards. The Old One snapped them down, one every ten seconds, singing all the while. The old woman began to scream, understanding her doom. She strained at her bonds, seeking to move her chest, but the ropes were iron tight.

The eighth slate brought a different timbre to her screams. She was finding it harder to hold up the weight. The fifteenth virtually silenced her. Little more than gasps and croaks came up after that, until with the thirtieth there began the gurgles.

The Old One kept singing while he held her eyes and absorbed her terror. The slates piled higher. She could not move. She could not breathe. She struggled to hold up the weight. He stared into her eyes, sucking out her life energy.

The gurgles gradually faded, the skin dulled, the eyes lost their shine. He took in the whole of her death with a tight smile on his great face.

His heart soared with the perfection he had achieved. His eyes closed while his mind exploded from the confines of his skull and flew outward, taking flight like an eagle of the dark.

Below him he could see the city of Shasht spread out around the temple pyramid. The harbor and the river snaking inland were etched darkly beneath the moon. Lights in thousands of windows picked out the outline of the great boulevards.

The world curved away to the horizon and the distant mountains of the south. To the north the oceans beckoned. He flew on, arms outswept as if they were wings.

Above the world glittered the stars, hard and sharp in this view, unobscured by the atmosphere. This world would belong solely to Man once more. The evil begun by the academy would be expunged.

Like some giant dragonfly of pure energy, he arrowed northward and into the east, hurrying over great cloud masses lit by moonlight. Far below, the ocean sparkled darkly in its immensity. On these gossamer wings of magic he passed faster than a sound, faster than anything but the gleam of the sun, and soon far ahead he perceived the dark mass of the northern continent.

The eastern edges were tinged by the first touch of dawn.

Down now, swinging over the mountains into the sweet green interior. Then, in a high valley, he spotted an encampment of pyluk. A dozen green-skinned fighting machines, lying by their simple wooden spears.

He felt laughter soar in his throat. He hadn't seen pyluk in a long, long time. Pyluk, his creatures, his playthings, his weapons.

But, it was not time for that. He had other work in mind.

The pyluk were soon far behind. Now the mountains rose up from the wrinkled hills. And there was Highnoth.

The ruins of the ancient city, the last city, the last place in the world that men lived as of old.

The place where he had been held captive for so long.

And there he found them, the creatures of the Leadership. His enemies in all things.

They felt him!

There was sudden panic among the ancient gnomes.

Chapter 13

The smelters weren't fired that day, so the blue sky over Dronned was clear for once. Folk from all across the kingdom were drawn to each month's biggest market day, visiting vegetable stalls and art galleries and everything in between. Drummers and tumblers from as far away as Reif were playing for the crowd in the southeast corner of the Dronned market. From the far corner came the shrill pipe music of sheepherders from Blurri.

The midday bell rang from the tower of the Guild Hall. The cook shops along Pike Street were firing up their grills. At the Laughing Fish tavern the barmots were breaking open a fresh barrel of beer.

From the lookout tower, built on the harbor mole, came a cry. With so much commotion in the old town, no one took that much notice.

A youngster in the blue shirt of the messenger corps soon came running up the mole. "A ship!" he cried as he went past.

"A ship with two masts."

That news caused an immediate stir. Two masts meant a ship of men, not a stout cog of the Land. Ships full of men had always signaled a raid. Hundreds of mots ran down to the harbor to see for themselves. In many homes there began an immediate surge of panicky packing. Donkeys, carts, chests, and boxes were all in motion.

A bugle began to sound in the courtyard of the palace. The town criers took up their places on street corners to bellow a message. The royal civil service was suddenly boiling over with activity as messengers by the score exited the palace.

A pair of messengers were already haring up the north road to find the Commander of the Third Regiment, currently in Dronned Camp for training. "Seven hundred mots and brilbies will be ready within ten minutes, sir!" roared the sergeant at arms, though he was barely to be heard over the sound of the camp springing to life.

Nuza heard the message while working in the royal library, editing the transcripts of her memoir of Shasht. Also in the library were the two Assenzi that had been visiting with her for the past week, digging out everything she recalled about Shasht and her time there.

Nuza had never been exposed to Assenzi like this before. In person, they were unnerving. They seemed to know or sense everything. Most of the time they exhibited a slowness of movement that was almost unlifelike. But they also possessed perfect memory.

The messenger was a boy with a piping high voice, and she caught the words "a ship, two masts" very clearly.

The Assenzi, Utnapishtim and Acmonides, both down from Highnoth, certainly came to life. They got up from their own projects with alacrity. Their gnomish faces with the huge eyes were a study in alarm. They reassured each other in gentle voices.

"We need not be overly alarmed," said Utnapishtim.

"Indeed, there is a full regiment here. And many veterans in the town population at large."

"But there should be no more raiding."

"*Could* is the word, dear Utnapishtim, not *should*. They still could raid."

"The Emperor promised an end."

"But Aeswiren did not gain control of every element among the men."

"It is quite bothersome to have to pack up all these papers," muttered Utnapishtim as he stuffed scrolls and parchment into a satchel.

"Surely, ancient Masters, there must be another reason for a ship of men to come here. Perhaps they bring a message from Aeswiren?"

"Yes, Nuza, you are probably correct," Acmonides replied.

Aeswiren had taken control of the Shasht fleet and army. Only three ships had broken away, carrying his son, Nebbeggebben. The fighting was over. The men had evacuated Sulmo entirely. They were still occupying Mauste and would do so for the next year while they cultivated supplies to keep them going on the long trip back to Shasht, but they were wielding shovels and hammers, not swords and spears.

Another messenger came running through the palace. "There are mots and men on the ship. Mots and men, they can be seen together."

This provoked another wave of curious folk to hurry down to the harbor, mors among the mots now. They formed a crowd along Dock Street and around the inner harbor.

The city waited breathlessly. Small boats had already put out and circled around the strange ship as it came in, sailing on a scrap of sail on the foremast. From the lookouts on the headland north of the city came word that no other sails were visible. The small ship was alone.

The two-master came on, slowly but directly into the harbor. A space was kept clear on the inner side of the mole. Cogs with heavy cargo could unload there before moving off to their own berths farther down. The ship was clearly heading for that spot. This implied that the ship expected to be welcomed peaceably.

As yet there was no sign of warlike intent, but the watching crowd remained uneasy despite their curiosity.

The little ship had slowed considerably now, her last sail taken down. The rudder pulled hard to starboard, swinging her right in to nestle against the side of the dock.

Several figures onboard were waving madly. Others were up in the rigging.

Stepping forward onto the dock came the harbormaster, a brilby in traditional costume of gray, fuscous fustian. "What ship?" he called in the tongue of the Land.

"The *Sea Wasp,* of Gzia Gi" came back the reply from a mot high up in the crosstrees of the foremast.

The crowd gasped. There really were mots aboard the ship!

Other figures onboard were moving forward with oars and poles in hand as the boat sidled slowly up toward the dock. A brilby ran up to the forepeak and threw a heavy line ashore. It was caught by the harbormaster, who turned it quickly around the big bollard. The ship came up against the line with a hard tug, then stilled and backed up against the dock.

Another line was thrown ashore astern, by a tall grey-haired man. The sight of a man caused the crowd to recoil a step or two, but a boatmot took the line anyway and made it fast. Here and there in the crowd behind him, mots and brilbies instinctively checked their belts for knife and shortsword.

"Mots and men on the same ship?" said many voices in the widespread confusion.

The *Sea Wasp* was hove tight against the dock, her gunwales four feet above the stone jetty.

A figure jumped up onto the gunwale. They clearly saw him, a mot with a scarred face, wearing the scraps of what had once been an officer's coat. Beside him was a brilby with an even more battered face. Then a third joined them, a mot whose face looked as if it had been beaten in with a club, which it had.

This trio of the battle-scarred made folk uneasy, too.

"Who are these scarred strangers?"

"Be they mots of the Land? They have the look of demons."

Then Thru Gillo jumped down from the ship and knelt and kissed the stone of the jetty.

At that very moment, Nuza came running up from Dock Street to join the crowd. She heard nothing but muttering around her. On the stern of the vessel she could see a tall figure.

The ship was decidedly not of the Land. And the figure at the stern was a man. More than that, the man had an incredible resemblance to the Emperor, Aeswiren the Third.

Nuza felt her heart thudding in her chest. A tremor went right through her body. Why was the Emperor here, and in such a ragged state?

She was still staring at Mentupah Vust, brother of Ge who had mounted to the purple many years before and become Aeswiren the Third, when the crowd thinned in front of her and another figure came stumbling forward. His eyebrows had jumped almost over the tip of his head.

It was Thru.

Nuza locked eyes with him for a long, astonished second, while her mind circled helplessly around and around like a whirligig. Then everything blanked out as she slid to the ground.

Chapter 14

Thru Gillo's reappearance in Dronned sparked a huge celebration. Bonfires burned on the dunes while mots and mors, drunk on early summer brew, whirled and twirled. Ostensibly this outpouring of joy was to celebrate Thru's return, for he was still recalled as the hero Seventy-seven-Run Gillo, of the bat-and-ball game. But, in reality, the folk of Dronned were celebrating the certain end of the war.

If a ship crewed by men mixed with mots had sailed all the way from Shasht, then anything was possible. The Emperor had withdrawn his forces. The raids had ceased, though the army of the Land still watched the coasts. Now it seemed they really could trust the reports. The war was over.

The mots from the *Sea Wasp* were treated as heroes, and the men, after a cautious period of examination by the throng, were welcomed in the manner of the Land, which meant with food, ale, and song. The party went on all night, sputtering out only with the dawn.

Thru awoke with the first light. Nuza was sleeping beside him on the narrow bed in her room at the palace. They had had a great deal of catching up to do. They had had no time to spare for anyone but each other as they renewed their love. Sometimes they just lay there and laughed in each other's arms.

"Fate has played a strange game with us," said Nuza at one point.

"I suppose we should regard it as an honor."

They laughed again, giddy with joy.

"Nuza and Thru," said Thru. "We'll end up as a saga sung at winter festival."

The memory of winter stopped the laughter in Nuza's throat. She squeezed his hand between hers, and tears flowed down her cheeks while he kissed them away.

Thru told her what he had seen in Shasht, the sheer desolation of their land. "They use the world, plundering, never giving anything back. Their land is bare. There is no game in their forests."

When Nuza told him of her own strange adventures, Thru fell silent for many minutes. Nuza had become a favorite of the Emperor and been kept hidden in his palace. Thru did not know how to respond at first, and he was troubled by a strange sense of jealousy. Nuza had performed to entertain the Emperor. The Emperor had told Nuza he loved her.

The twinges of jealousy left Thru shaking his head. Nuza had told him everything. He understood that she had not reciprocated the love of the Emperor. Nuza was a mor, Aeswiren was a man, and in Nuza's words they "were not meant to be lovers in this world." And yet Thru was still jealous. He disliked this smallness in himself, and when he thought of what he and Simona had shared, he felt a pang of guilt such as he had never suffered before. It confirmed the wisdom of his decision not to tell Nuza the complete truth about what had taken place between Simona and himself.

When she kissed him and asked him why he was so quiet, he shrugged and dissembled, and in this he hated himself, too. "I can only give thanks that we survived. The Spirit must have been watching over the two of us. The Spirit must have a purpose in mind. No, it must be true. Consider this: You met the Emperor, and I met the Emperor's brother and became his friend."

Nuza gaped at him. "Brother?"

"Mentupah, the younger brother of Ge who is now called Aeswiren."

"I am amazed."

"You came back here on the Emperor's ship. I could not have made it back without the navigation skills of Mentu."

Nuza gasped and clapped her hands together. "You must be right about the Spirit. But the Emperor never mentioned his brother to me."

"Perhaps he was too ashamed. Because he imprisoned him for twenty years."

Nuza blinked, brought up short. Was Aeswiren capable of that?

"Why?"

"To prevent someone using him as a pawn or an impostor to replace the Emperor."

Nuza nodded, understanding the kind of intrigue that could flourish in Shasht politics. "Yes, that I can see. It is the way of their world."

Later, by great good fortune, Nuza was facing away from Thru when he told her that Simona had been aboard the *Sea Wasp*. When she looked back to him, she was able to hide the things she'd guessed at just from the way he spoke.

"She came back to the Land?"

"She wants to live here among us."

"I see." Nuza deliberately kept her voice neutral. Simona was a friend of Thru's, and so he must never know the truth. Nuza realized at once what her friend had done for her. If Simona had told Thru about Nuza being in the custody of the Emperor, he would have gone back to the city and been murdered on the altar of the dire God of Shasht. Simona had saved Thru's life, and Nuza knew she must protect that secret.

"And the others?" she asked.

"Janbur will probably go and live among the Emperor's men. Mentu has a more difficult road ahead. He does not trust his brother all that much."

While Nuza slept, Thru arose and scouted through the palace for the kitchens. He secured a tray of hot buttered scones, two tubs of chowder, and a pot of tea, which he took back to Nuza's room.

"This is the first breakfast we've had together since that morning in my house in Sulmo," she said with a smile.

"On Whiteflower Lane, I remember it well."

Nuza looked down, struck by sadness once more. The house and everything around it had been burned when the outer ward of Sulmo was captured by the Shasht army.

After breakfast, a message came for Thru. He was requested to attend a meeting with the Assenzi. They had many urgent questions for him. Thru had expected the call. He knew it would be the first of many. Others would want to talk to him, Toshak among them.

He kissed Nuza farewell. She had her own tasks to attend to, and they would meet again at the end of the day. He navigated the mazelike corridors of the palace and found a long, narrow room on an upper floor of the east wing.

Three of the ancient little beings were waiting to see him: Melidofulo, Acmonides, and Utnapishtim. Of this trio, Thru knew Utnapishtim best. At Highnoth he had taken Utnapishtim's classes and then accompanied him on a perilous trip into the Farblow Hills.

Utnapishtim was overcome with emotion at meeting Thru once again. He embraced his former pupil while his eyes glistened with tears of happiness. "It is a miracle, and I thank the Spirit."

Thru laughed. "A miracle indeed, in fact several of them. The Spirit intended all along for me to survive long enough to come back."

Three young mors with earnest expressions entered the room with trays of parchment, ink, and quills. They set them on the table to write down everything that transpired. There was no escaping the importance the Assenzi attached to this meeting.

"What do you want to know, Utnapishtim?"

"We want to know everything, Thru Gillo, everything you can remember."

Thru, well taught in the Assenzi way, had expected this answer. The questioning was in minute detail.

Hours went by. Occasionally young mots and mors in palace livery entered with trays of hot tea and wedges of bushpod pie or salted beeks with pots of mussel stew. At such times, the young mors set down their quills and ate heartily, and Utnapishtim or Acmonides took up a quill in their stead. The Assenzi ate but lightly, a bisk here, a mouthful of stew there. The young mors of the Dronned civil service were stunned to see the old Assenzi take their place, but Thru was not. He knew the Assenzi were not averse to work.

After Thru had described the canal trip across Shasht and then his precarious life through the winter, holed up in caves and lodges in the mountains, Utnapishtim wiped his eyes with a handkerchief.

"It is just as I'd expected, Thru Gillo. I knew you were destined for some great undertaking. Don't you see? You have become our eyes and ears, peering into the world of our enemy."

Thru smiled. "I think I was merely the agent of the Spirit. Because now the war is over. There will be peace, thanks to the Emperor."

Utnapishtim put away his handkerchief. "Ah, well, that may not be so. Our real enemy has not made peace."

Thru stared at them for but a moment. He understood. "You mean that thing we saw in the pyramid? The Old One?"

The Assenzi said nothing, regarding him with their huge eyes.

"The message you sent, which Simona took, it was not for the Emperor, was it?"

"No. Our message was ineffective. Karnemin ignored it."

"Yes, that was the name you spoke once before. Who is this enemy that we never knew existed?"

"Who is Karnemin?" repeated Utnapishtim softly, and he looked over to the other Assenzi, who shrugged.

Utnapishtim turned back to Thru. "As to who he is today, well, none of us has any idea. As to what he is, of that we are better informed."

Acmonides spoke as if reciting a well-known text: "Karnemin is the last survivor of the Groybeel Vaak, a clique of wizards, shapechangers, and mindstealers. This clique was one of many that flourished in the last days of Man. Social morality had broken down. Sorcery obsessed the last wizards. They formed secret societies devoted to necromancy, cannibalism, and dark forms of magic."

Thru shivered. What great evil was this?

"Men felt the cold chill of extinction coming upon them. Their numbers had dwindled steadily for many centuries. In their despair, they turned to evil."

"Then what is this Karnemin you speak of?"

"An evil wizard, Thru. A thing that is no longer really human, yet inhabits a human body. There were others, terrible creatures such as Pinque or Namooli of Thoth. But they had all died off by then. Karnemin is the last."

"It is a parasite," said Acmonides, "a man who delved too far into dark arts and became debased. It learned to move its mind into the bodies of others, thus it could defeat death. It became long-lived and lost all sense of humanity."

"It lives on forever in the flesh of other men."

Thru stared at them, horrified.

"Once," murmured Utnapishtim, "we knew him well. Our masters at Highnoth imprisoned him."

"It was in the first period of the ice," said Acmonides. "Karnemin was already very old by then. He was kept locked in a high room in the Red Tower."

"I remember," added Utnapishtim. "The High Men numbered only ninety-nine then, and they were beginning to die off. Karnemin was insane. But he was cunning. He inveigled Cusewas, whispered words of poison in his ears."

"Cusewas helped him escape, there is no doubt of it," said Utnapishtim somberly.

"That was but the beginning. The struggle went on for thousands of years. Eventually his power was smashed. We thought he was lost in a crevasse in the great glacier of Kabal Mountain. But it was not so."

"He fooled us. It was some poor devil, one of his slaves. He escaped and fled south. We knew no more of him."

"Somehow he got along. Perhaps he dwelt among the pyluk, though we think they would have eaten him, having no memory of their creator. However he did it, he crossed the world and found the primitive men of Shasht. He must have dwelled among them for tens of thousands of years, taking one of them every so often to renew his own life."

Thru stared, openmouthed. "*He* made the pyluk?"

"Yes, they were meant to be an army for him. He saw himself as the Lord of the World. All others were to be his slaves. This is when the High Men imprisoned him in the Red Tower, however, and most of the pyluk were destroyed."

"Alas, a few escaped and became a plague upon the Land."

Thru thought back to his own encounters with the pyluk and had to agree. The green-skinned lizard men had earned their terrible reputation.

"Were there mots and brilbies then?"

"Yes. They were few in number, though, and all lived in Highnoth."

Thru shivered as he recalled the words of the Book; the ancient dogma of his people:

They raised us up
from bowls of purest glass, with teeth of shining steel.
They made us what we are.

The ancient lines confronted him with a glance back across an aeon of time to the very origins of his own kind.

"Karnemin is behind the current war," said Utnapishtim. "He will not stop unless we destroy him."

At once Thru could see the fuller dimensions of the problem. "It will be hard to keep our armies up to strength. Our folks are not warlike unless faced with annihilation."

"True enough, and there will be many difficulties. But we can work to keep up the tradition of self-defense. All youngsters will receive training. Swords and spears must be kept sharp and ready. Shields and wicker armor, too."

"And we will become more like them, like the men," Thru said sadly.

Utnapishtim nodded sadly. "Alas, I fear you are right."

Old Melidofulo, one of the most peaceable of all the Assenzi, spoke up at last. "This will be the greatest evil yet that Karnemin has wrought."

"Perhaps," said Utnapishtim in a distant voice. "And then again, perhaps not. If Karnemin ever succeeds, then he will annihilate all of us. We must make what preparations we can. Aeswiren will take his army back to Shasht next summer. Can he prevail with a mere ten thousand soldiers? We do not know. He has won many battles in the past, often against the odds. If he is victorious, then we can strive for some peaceful coexistence with the men of Shasht. There is much we can teach them."

Thru nodded. "We can learn from them as well."

"Yes, Thru Gillo, you have already told us a great deal. The land of Shasht is worse off than I had imagined. Your insights have been invaluable. Again I thank the Spirit that preserved you."

"I second that thought," murmured Acmonides.

"But"—Utnapishtim held up a bony finger—"if Aeswiren is not victorious, what then? Clearly, Karnemin will not give up. Sooner or later he will send another fleet. We must be ready when it comes."

Eventually the meeting broke up, and Thru set out back through the warren of passages in the palace to Nuza's room. She was not there, so he headed out again on an errand. He had many letters to write and he needed quills, ink, and paper. Ter-Saab would be heading south to Sulmo. He would take letters to the Sixth Brigade in Glaine. Thru was still a part of that brigade, and he had to send in a report as soon as possible. And a quick message needed to be sent up the coast to Warkeen village. Thru knew that his family had to have given him up for dead. They were in for a pleasant surprise.

Out in the streets of Dronned, Thru was almost overwhelmed by the rush of sights and sounds. Back among his own folk, back in this city where he had so many memories, his feet flew over the cobbles and his heart soared up to the sky.

It was busier than ever. Building work was going on all over the place. The strong smell of wood smoke in the air brought with it a whiff of brimstone every so often. At the major intersections, Dronned had always had gardens in the squares. Now some of these had been taken over by cookshops and beerhouses.

At the junction of Slope and Seam Streets, a large

beershop had been erected on one side and a cook-shop on the other. Thru discovered Juf Goost standing by the lamppost, leaning on his staff.

"Well, well, greetings, Thru. How does it feel to be back home?"

"My feet are scarcely touching the ground. I keep pinching myself to make sure it's not a dream."

"It's no dream. We got back alive. We're home!"

Thru patted Juf on the shoulder. "But you're not all the way home yet. Are you going south with Ter-Saab and the others?"

Juf nodded, then burped. "I've been drinking beer," he said happily.

Thru laughed. "And singing, too, I expect."

"Care for a round of 'The Jolly Beekeeper'?"

"Get out of here with that beekeeper! Never again. Not after that damned island."

"Oh, yes, forgot about that. Well, I 'spect you're hurrying somewhere."

"I've letters I must write and send south with Ter-Saab. Army matters. Don't forget, we're all still soldiers in the Army of Sulmo."

Juf's forehead furrowed. "But the war is over. Why do we need to be soldiers anymore?"

"You were in Shasht, Juf. You saw what they're like. We will have to keep a standing army from now on. We will always have to be ready to defend ourselves."

"Friend Thru, you know how to take the fun out of the daylight, don't you?"

"Sorry, old Juf."

"Think I'll go back for another beer. Care to join me?"

But Thru was already leaving, intent on finding Nuza before the dinner gongs began to ring. The streets were alive with folk. Thru had returned to the Land.

*   *   *

Aboard the *Sea Wasp*, as the lamps began to be lit in the city, a message was brought addressed to Simona. She opened it with trembling hands. Ever since she'd seen Nuza on the dockside, Simona had kept to herself, tormented by the inevitable loss of Thru's affection once he had found out that she had lied to him.

The message was written in the tongue of the Land, and Simona struggled as she read it.

> *I know what you did, dear Simona, and I write to thank you from the bottom of my heart. Thank you for bringing my Thru home to me safe and sound. I will always be in your debt. And be assured, Thru will never know the truth from my lips.*

She set it down on her bunk. Tears were running down her cheeks, and she looked out the porthole toward the city of mots, where more and more lamps were being lit.

Simona mumbled her thanks to the Spirit. Dear Nuza, so wise and yet so naive. But how could she even begin to suspect the truth?

And Thru, dear Thru, who had been her only lover in this life . . .

They would have to keep their secret locked in their hearts forever.

Chapter 15

The first year of the Peace of Aeswiren was regarded as a miracle year. The winter was mild, and the sea-ponds provided a great bounty. The spring came early, and the summer was perfect for the growing crops, with rain arriving at least once a week.

All over the Land there was a great movement to rebuild. The determined survivors of a thousand coastal villages and towns returned to their homes, or in some cases to the ashes of their homes. Spirits were higher than anyone could remember, as if, having survived the horrors of four years of war and peril, the warm summer had brought back a time many had thought lost forever. The dreams of the folk were soaring like hawks on the warm winds of summer.

The harvest was one for the annals. They called it Aeswiren's Harvest, despite the fact that Aeswiren was the Great King of the men of Shasht. Aeswiren had earned a different reputation; he had not only ended the war, he had slowly but surely brought about cooperation between his men and the folk of the Land.

And so, the mots and brilbies of Dronned and Sulmo had seen another side to the hand of Man. Handpicked parties of soldiers had come ashore to help with the work of rebuilding places such as Tamf, which they had burned to the ground a few years before.

Of course, at first there were long and difficult negotiations about these matters. Many mots were against having anything whatever to do with the men of Shasht. But others took a longer view. In this they were encouraged by the Assenzi, who advised cooperation with Aeswiren.

On the island of Mauste, men worked alongside the mots and brilbies to bring in a huge harvest. The men were also working to stock their fleet for the following year, when they would set sail for Shasht once again. Temporary fields and extra polder had been cleared in the effort to feed the men and prepare them for their great journey.

Everyone understood that these men carried a huge responsibility. They had to go back and defeat their common enemy and return Aeswiren to his throne. The success of this mission was of paramount importance. And so they worked with Man the Cruel himself. And they found that those men could work hard.

Aeswiren's Harvest started well, with early wheat crops in Dronned and Tamf. The oats in the North were excellent, and the barley was wonderful, though a little late in ripening. The wine regions of Sulmo reported bumper crops ripening on the vines.

Then came three days of rain and mist, and, when it cleared, the harvest continued at a rapid pace. All across the Land the polder was alive with workers taking in waterbush. Apples were thick upon the trees in Blurri, and the wine grapes were the pick of a hundred years down in Ajutan and Sulmo. The harvest for bushpod on the fertile plains of the Sulo Valley was the greatest ever seen.

The new beer was made for the harvest moon, and the young wine was set to ferment, while fiddlers, drummers, and horn players took up their instruments—and the Land set to dancing and feasting. In Warkeen village, Thru Gillo had many reasons to celebrate: the war's end and his release from the army of Dronned, the abundant harvest, and also the announcement of his engagement to Nuza of Tamf. She had accepted when he proposed and had even come North with her mother to join the Warkeen harvest festival.

Her father, Cham, and the rest of her family had remained in Tamf. The survivors of the city had returned that spring and summer, and with help from all the neighboring states, as well as the men of Aeswiren, they had begun the task of rebuilding. Alas, New Tamf would not be as beautiful as the old—nothing could bring back the grace of thousands of years—but Tamf would rise again.

In Warkeen, Nuza and her mother picked bushpod from morning to night along with everyone else. When it was done, they picked the grapes and took them in barrow loads to be crushed as the young wine was pressed. While they were so engaged, Thru and his father, Ware, were working with a gang of six other mots, going from field to field to mow the late harvest oats. Working together with a group of youngsters and two donkey carts, they were able to cut the oats on every farmer's field on the northern side of the village.

When it was all done, even while the cider apples were still being pressed, the festival began. The tenth moon of the year was riding high and full. The fiddles and drums were going, and as always the first dancing began at the town tavern.

The first barrels of young beer were rolled out. The beer had only just cleared that morning, barely ready to be drunk, but the folk of the village were more than ready to drink it.

That evening, a bonfire was lit on the village green, and the singing and dancing went on until the moon went down.

Thru and Nuza danced, drank the young beer, and, when they were tired of the gaiety, went back to the house and sat up talking of the future for hours.

"We must live in Tamf, my dearest Thru, I have

promised Mother that. But we shall come to Warkeen for harvest time. Never have I seen a village let itself go like this one!"

Home village was the wife's choice, so custom said, and Thru agreed. They would live in New Tamf, Nuza would work with her mother, and Thru would have a workshop in which to weave.

"I want to have our children quickly. I want a mot and a mor."

"We will live in New Tamf so long, we will forget there ever was a war."

They laughed, but in their eyes each saw the truth. They would never be able to forget. Everything had been changed by the war.

The next day, they repaired to the village green. The old batting tree had been freshly painted red, and the boundary lines were laid with chalk. The last game of the season was a game that usually brought out most of the village to watch, if only for a little while.

Warkeen played their oldest rivals in a local grudge match, neither having succeeded in going on to the championships in the city. Warkeen played well but were beaten nonetheless by an inspired Juno village team who put up 123 runs on the board. Thru Gillo batted for the village, but it was not his day. He was caught for the final time after scoring only 18 runs. Warkeen village managed no more than 102, and Juno carried off the vine garlands of triumph.

That night, while dancers whirled on the village green, a party was held to announce Thru and Nuza's engagement. Ware Gillo broached a barrel of new ale and wished the couple well, though he lamented that they would live as far away as Tamf. The evening ended with a great feast. Thru's mother, Ual, and his sister, Snejet, had worked long and hard to set out the delicacies of the Dristen Valley. Everything was superb, and the crowning glory was a great bewby pie.

The family chooks, of the clan Tuckra, were on hand to eat their fill and dance like a whirlwind to the fiddles and the drum. Chook dancing was too wild and fast for mots to imitate, but it was wonderful to watch. When the roosters had finally tired of bouncing with legs extended far and wide, Ware filled everyone's mugs again for a round of the old songs. While the ale flowed from the barrel, Thru and Nuza were toasted a dozen times. Then the musicians took up their instruments again and the dance resumed, but now at the more stately pace of mots and brilbies. Thru and Nuza led the ensemble through the pretzel patterns of the engagement dance. Next came the Lushtan Reel and the age-old Chook's Dance, where mots tried to move their legs with the speed of chooks, and everyone laughed at the general silliness. None more than the chooks themselves, enlivened by a little ale on their feed corn.

Suddenly there came a commotion in the outer yard. Mots had come up from the tavern. There were visitors. A voice fueled by a little too much beer called out, " 'Tis Aeswiren himself, as I live and breathe."

The dance was forgotten. Everyone crowded to the door.

Two figures stood by the gate. Thru felt a sudden shiver, as if some chill wind had blown out the candles on the cake. There stood General Toshak in a grey cape and Mentu, Aeswiren's brother.

Thru clasped hands with each of them and welcomed them in, though the sight of General Toshak here in Warkeen village filled him at once with foreboding. Thru had been Toshak's emissary the previous year and had logged thousands of miles, many of them aboard the *Sea Wasp*, in his service. Thru knew how busy Toshak was, all the time.

"This is the night of our engagement," said Nuza as she hugged Toshak.

"Then my mission is especially blessed," said Toshak. "For I can wish you both the best of fortune in your lives together."

Thru hugged Mentu after explaining to the folk that the man was not the Great King of Shasht but his brother.

"The ship?" asked Thru.

"Anchored off the point," replied Mentu. "Juf is aboard, keeping an eye out."

Mugs of ale were pressed on them, and they joined the company. The presence of a man at the party drew mots into Ware's yard from all over the village. Despite the peace and general goodwill, some angry shouts among the crowd were heard.

At first the rumor had been that it was Aeswiren the Emperor, come himself. Then it was learned that it was his brother, the one who had befriended Thru Gillo on his epic travels and sailed home with him from the evil land of men. Still, everyone wanted to see this marvel, a man who had befriended their Thru Gillo.

For Thru, Toshak's presence was the more worrisome. Thru knew that Toshak would have come only if he wanted something very badly.

After a round of dancing, when Toshak and Nuza looked particularly fine on the floor, came another set of toasts. Ware was unstinting with the barrel, and more songs were proposed. Soon the company was lost in "The Fields of Home" with its many verses.

Toshak took the opportunity to draw Thru aside. Mentu followed them to the old parlor, near the kitchen in the rambling Gillo house.

Toshak got to the point. "My friend, I grieve that I must come to you at such a time with my news. But I know that you will understand at once the gravity of the situation."

Thru felt his eyes harden. He knew. "They have come again?"

"Yes. There is a second fleet. We learned just a few weeks ago. A small ship, like the *Sea Wasp,* appeared at Mauste. It got out of Shasht harbor just ahead of the new fleet. The men who sailed it here are brave, true-hearted servants of Aeswiren. We know we have less than a month now to prepare ourselves for the onslaught."

Thru felt the tender shoots of hope wither in his heart. He had half expected this renewal of the darkness, but during the wondrous year he had put it out of his mind at last.

"Foolish me," he murmured sadly.

Toshak glanced at him, his eyes beady in the gloom of the parlor.

"Well"—Thru shrugged—"the Assenzi warned me that something like this could happen."

"The Assenzi know our enemy well."

"I always feared that this would come."

"So did we all."

Thru nodded. There was a long moment of silence.

"What do you want from me?"

"I need you back as my emissary. From your previous work for me you have learned everything such a figure needs to know. You have met all the functionaries and Kings, all the generals and melds. No one else quite fills the bill like you. I want you to come back to the army. In fact, I want you to leave with me right now aboard the *Sea Wasp.*"

Mentu leaned close and put his hands on Thru's shoulders. "We can leave with the turn of the tide."

Thru closed his eyes. The glory of the summer, the bounty of the harvest, the delight of being with Nuza—all began to fade away like a dream.

"Are the reserves being mustered?"

"It begins tomorrow. By the end of the week, it will have spread to all Dronned, Tamf, Creton, and Relf. I hope to have twelve thousand back in training within a month."

Again Thru fell silent. With each turn of the gyre of war, the armies got larger.

"What will the Great King do?"

Toshak pursed his lips for a moment. "He will prepare to fight. We met with him two weeks ago. He expressed his regret that he was unable to prevent this second round of invasion."

"We are better prepared this time."

"Our enemy knows that, and much more. Neither side will begin in such a state of ignorance as we did following the raids on Creton."

Toshak studied him with those piercing dark eyes. Mentu brooded in the doorway.

"Well, of course I accept. My duty is clear. Though I am saddened by the loss of my dream."

"Yes," said Toshak after a moment. "We are all saddened. But we both suspected this day might come."

It was true.

"I must also speak with Nuza," said Toshak. "We have need for her as well."

Thru protested, "Surely she has given enough!"

They all glanced outside where Nuza could be glimpsed dancing now with her mother and Ware Gillo on the edge of the throng.

"We are building a hospital. I think she should administer it, at least in the first couple of years. Nuza has more energy than three ordinary people."

Thru had to agree with that.

"The hospital will be in New Tamf. The great Filek Biswas, the father of Simona, is coming to advise us on the construction and to begin training our new cadre of doctors."

Thru's eyebrows bobbed up and down when he heard this. "That is good news. We can use such skill in the Land."

"There is more than skill. When I visited Aeswiren

on Mauste, he showed me some of the things that the great Filek has made."

Thru nodded vigorously. "Yes, the micro-scope." Simona had spoken often of Filek's projects.

"Then it will be a worthy cause for Nuza. She will make it work."

Chapter 16

The *Sea Wasp* rode northward on a thin wind out of the west. There was a light chop on the sea and a handful of small clouds scudding east toward the Land. The sun was past the zenith, but Mentupah felt confident that they would make Dronned before nightfall. The Lower Alberr rocks, a long stretch of shoals, lay just ahead.

The ship's permanent crew—Juf, Janbur, and Mentu—were all aboard, and with them once more was Thru Gillo, carrying messages again for General Toshak.

Juf and Janbur had both tried to make new lives for themselves ashore, but both had retreated to the barque. Juf's family and village had been destroyed in the war. He'd become a lost soul, drinking himself to oblivion in Sulmo City when Thru had found him and persuaded him to come back to the *Sea Wasp*. He'd settled in to the life of an itinerant sailor.

Janbur was another story. He'd gone to Mauste with Simona and hopes of a bright future. But somehow he didn't fit in with the men from the army. He was an aristocrat, from a higher level of society than any of them, and they knew it and resented him. At the same time, the rough-hewn life in the sheds at Mauste wore on him. He had risked everything for his principles, and he had lost. He would never see the ancestral home again, never be Janbur of the Gsekk in that world where it meant so much to be wellborn. The hay pallet and ill-cooked food of the sheds was a poor reward for what he'd given up.

Then his courtship of Simona Biswas had been rebuffed. She had dedicated her life to her work for the Emperor. She was the Emperor's courtesan in all but name. When he was ordered to return to the *Sea Wasp* as the Emperor's personal representative, he was glad to obey. He had never realized that Simona had seen his desperation and pressed the Emperor to act.

Mentu had welcomed them both back. He'd had crews of sailors from Heuze's fleet and even a couple of fishermots—the Bellekay brothers from Dronned, who'd come to know Mentupah on his visits to the Old Harbor tavern in Dronned—but none could stay for long. With his old shipmates back, the barque felt complete once again.

Mentupah, too, had struggled with feelings of loss and alienation. After spending twenty years locked up in the tower he had been freed, in a sense, by Thru Gillo. Abandoning his own land, he had set out across the oceans to an uncertain future because he could not join the Shasht colony. His brother, Emperor Aeswiren, had originally imprisoned him, and Mentu did not trust him not to do it again if allowed the opportunity. At times, Mentu felt truly alone in the world. Fortunately, he had the *Sea Wasp*. When Simona stepped ashore in Mauste, Simona had made him a gift of the little ship.

When Mentu had returned to Dronned, he found the mighty General Toshak waiting to interview him. Toshak needed a swift vessel to carry messages around the land, and the *Sea Wasp* was so much faster than the little cogs and fishing boats of the mots that it was a natural choice. Toshak also surmised that Mentu needed something to do.

Mentu gladly accepted. And soon enough Toshak had roped Thru Gillo back into service. Having done

the job before, Thru already knew the Kings, the
Melds, and the Gryses of the Southern kingdoms. He
had taken messages to all of them. Merchants in
Creton and Ajutan gave him purses of gold coin to
be taken to Toshak for the army. At that very moment, he carried a reply from Aeswiren to Toshak
concerning their joint plan of action in the event that
one of them was assaulted by the Old One's fleet,
which they knew could not be far off.

The *Sea Wasp* had come up to the edge of the
Lower Alberr rocks, where odd currents helped to
generate irregular waves. The barque slapped and bel-
lied through these waves.

Thru woke up and rolled out of his bunk. The deck
beneath his feet was moving in a difficult, corkscrew
motion. He went up on deck.

Old Juf was leaning on the rail, studying the waves.
"The boat never likes this patch of water. We come
through here time and again, and she always bucks
and pitches."

"Hood rocks are over there." Thru pointed toward
the shore, where waves were breaking.

"Rough water, but Mentu says we'll be in Dronned
by dusk."

"Well, I'm sure he's right. He nearly always is."

Just then, Janbur, up in the crow's nest, cried out,
"Sail ho, windward."

Thru and Juf raced up the yards to join him.

"More than one sail," said Janbur, putting down
the spyglass.

"Man ship," breathed Juf.

Thru studied the white dot on the horizon. Even his
keen vision could not resolve it into a sail, but with
the spyglass he saw at once that it was the tops of two
masts. Then a third hove into view. The tops of three
masts, all bearing sails.

"Three-master, and coming this way."

Mentu had come up at the first cry. He studied the three topmasts and then considered their course past the Lower Alberr rocks and into the long Dronned reach.

They had reduced sail while they negotiated the rocky shoals of the Lower Alberrs. Now they increased it once again. Mentu studied the shoal water on their lee. The *Sea Wasp* was a tight sailer with little tendency to drift leeward even in a much stronger wind, but those shoals spoke of rocks ready to rip out a boat's bottom.

"She's spotted us," said Mentu calmly.

"It's a frigate," said Thru.

"And a swift one; I can see the mainsail now, and he's gaining."

There began a period of slow-rising tension. The *Sea Wasp* negotiated the channel through the shoals and then turned shoreward. The frigate was hull up over the horizon by then, and they could even see occasional white breaking from her bows.

On the open water, with more regular waves, the *Sea Wasp*'s motion became calmer even as she increased pace. Now the frigate saw the shoals ahead and changed course.

"She's trying to go around the Alberrs and then come back in."

"They don't know about the Widow's Rocks?"

"I expect they do," said Mentu. "They'd have been charted by the fleet surveyors years ago. The ship's going to try and cut in close around the rocks. It's a risk."

"But it shows how badly she wants to catch us."

"The *Sea Wasp* will stay the pace. With this kind of wind, we can match her."

And so it proved. The frigate fell back below the horizon as it turned north to pass around the Widow's Rocks. The *Sea Wasp* sped straight across the bight in the direction of the headlands of Dronned. It began to look as if they would beat the frigate handily to the harbor.

But the wind died away to a very slight breeze and began backing around to the northwest. Their progress slowed, and to the north they saw clouds massing.

Mentu studied the approaching weather with a careful eye. "Looks like our days of free sailing are just about over, shipmates."

"Still think we'll be in Dronned by dusk?" asked Juf with a grin.

Mentu chewed his lip. "No. The wind is backing into the north."

They held up fingers to the breeze. The approaching dark mass of clouds signified a sudden northern squall, a common hazard at this time of year. The *Sea Wasp* was a fine ship, capable of sailing close into the wind, but a northern squall would certainly slow things up.

They were all still chewing over that, when Janbur called from the crosstrees. "Sail ho, ahead."

They saw the *Old Skate,* a fishing cog out of Dronned, putting back into the harbor after a day of fishing on the outer Alberr Banks. The *Sea Wasp* swiftly caught up to the fishing cog and relayed her news. An enemy ship had been spotted out by Widow's Rocks.

The response was immediate. The *Old Skate* put up her topsail and three jibs. But, with unfavorable winds, it made little difference. The cog was easy prey for the frigate if it should spot her.

Mentu spread his hands, then signaled the others for the *Sea Wasp* to change course. They headed back out to sea, while still heading north. Within twenty minutes they could see the tops of the enemy frigate's sails again.

Mentu turnd the *Sea Wasp* to the west and, riding the wind on her beam, made good progress. The frigate was all too happy to clap on sail and follow. Behind them, the *Old Skate* struggled on toward the harbor with the vital news of an enemy vessel haunting their shores once again.

When they were well out to sea, the *Sea Wasp* drew the frigate on. The larger ship, designed for speed, gradually began to gain. The *Sea Wasp* turned north again and shifted the contest to one of sailing into the wind, tacking sharply back and forth while the headlands of Dronned receded, and they coursed out into the upper part of Dronned Bay.

The clouds were soon overhead and, with nightfall, came a sudden onset of heavy rain. The frigate kept up the pursuit, gaining slowly but steadily through the waning light. Then the squall broke out of the north and swept over them. In minutes, the seas rose, and soon there was spray sheeting across the bow. They quickly lost sight of their pursuer in the general murk.

Soon the darkness became absolute, and they were reduced to steering by guesswork. Mentu turned westward, out into the broader sea, determined at the very least not to end up on a leeshore with the cliffs of Dronned awaiting them. The winds continued to gust fiercely, and after midnight they backed farther into the east. By dawn, the storm was behind them, and the wind was coming from the south and east, much less forcefully.

The *Sea Wasp* had come through the night unscathed, with her sails close-hauled. They saw no sign of the frigate. Mentu turned them back toward land. He hoped to pick out the Dronned headlands shortly.

Instead he caught sight of Cormorant Rock, the headland on the northern end of Dristen Bay. They had been blown farther north than he'd expected. Blue Hill and Bear Hill rose up ahead, with cliffs curving in and out around their bases. Beyond Bear Hill the Dristen estuary opened into the sea.

After adjusting course, they began to sail close to the wind, working their way southward. Suddenly Thru felt his heart freeze in his chest.

Inland, a thick pillar of black smoke was rising into the sky.

"Sail ho, to the south, three ships," called Juf from the upper crosstrees.

Mentu hurried up to study the situation. Thru, manning the tiller, kept his eyes pinned on the smoke, which was still rising from the far side of Bear Hill. Alas, only Warkeen village lay in that direction.

"It doesn't look good," said Mentu after climbing down from the crosstrees. "There's a big four-master and two three-masters, one of which might be the frigate that chased us yesterday."

The *Sea Wasp* changed course, running in toward the shore but just out of sight of the big ships anchored in the Dristen estuary.

Thru was torn. On the one hand, the message he carried was possibly vital and meant for the general himself in Dronned. On the other hand, his family, the village, all lay just over Bear Hill. Finally, he could stand it no longer.

"Mentu, my friend, take this to General Toshak. Tell him that I'm sorry, but I had to go ashore and see if I could help."

"I will go with you," said Janbur. "Our people do evil here, and I must help you stop them."

"Evil indeed, my friend, for I have seen the results of a raid like this. I can only pray that the villagers kept up the watch during the storm last night. But I will go alone. Mentu needs both of you to run the *Sea Wasp,* and there's no point in two of us being taken captive or killed."

Mentu and then Juf tried to change his mind. The risk was great. What could he hope to achieve? But they knew they were arguing in vain: Thru would not be kept from seeing what had happened at his village. So they set him ashore on the beach at the northern side of Bear Hill and watched him climb the back path that led inland along Lupin Stream. Janbur wondered aloud if they would ever see their friend Thru Gillo again. Then they turned the *Sea Wasp* back out to sea and set sail for Dronned.

Chapter 17

Admiral Heuze hadn't been on land in months, prefer-ring his own realm aboard the *Anvil* to the recognized empire in exile of Aeswiren ashore. The hulking grey sheds, the untidy sprawl of shacks and shops on the muddy streets, everything was so flimsy and careless that it upset him. The bustle in the streets was too untidy for his sailor's eye, used to a tightly run ship. And, strangest of all, was the sight of a few of the monkey folk moving freely among the people. The world had turned upside down.

The Emperor's peace was absolute, however. Seven men had been hanged over the winter for killing mots, usually in the course of a robbery. There was a great hunger in the colony for the finery made by the na-tives. On this island—now called Mauste, the native name widely used by the men—there had existed a long tradition in cloth making. Everyone wanted to wear the warm twisted wool and bushfiber coats and trousers. Admiral Heuze disliked the practice and did his best to discourage it aboard the fleet. But ashore? Monkey-made clothing was universally worn now.

Seeing the folk clothed by the monkeys, but living in these shacks and the hulking tenement sheds, it was hard for even the admiral to avoid the comparison with the monkey cities. Heuze had seen them himself; indeed he'd burned a couple. He knew how strangely lovely the little cities were, with their centuries-old architecture, parks, monuments, tree-lined avenues, and open central squares. Now his own people appeared like barbarian vagabonds, living in rude structures and increasingly dependent on the monkeys for clothes and utensils. It left Heuze smoldering with frustration and anger.

But the rule of Aeswiren was popular with the people. They were eating better, staying warmer, and working toward the goal of returning to Shasht. Just about everyone wanted that more than anything. The land of the monkey folk was better left to its original inhabitants. The conquering spirit had gone out of the colony.

And now, he thought, a crisis was upon them. The news he carried had the potential to change everything.

Aeswiren had built a modest, two-story, block house with eighteen rooms, part fortress, part administrative center. The Emperor lived in a single room, just like everyone else in the colony. His room was a bit more lavish than anyone else's, but it was a far cry from the imperial luxury of Shasht. By this, Aeswiren assured his people that he was dedicated to the cause of returning home.

Heuze was ushered past the guards who recognized his peg-legged limp the moment he entered the hallway. Aeswiren only used the throne for large formal meetings. Most of the time he was to be found in his office, a small, cozy room decorated with woven mats and rugs given him by native weavers. Aeswiren was said to be especially fond of the brightly colored mats depicting lifelike scenes. It was an art form unknown in Shasht and taken to a very high level.

Heuze studied a piece titled "Mots at Prayer" on the wall. It was new, done by someone with considerable flair. Heuze bought and sold his share of these kinds of pieces, and he could see that this one was especially valuable. Even though he shuddered at the thought of cooperating with the monkeys, he knew that these works were of astonishing quality. If pressed, as by his friend and confidant Filek Biswas, he would cheerfully admit the inconsistency of his position.

He recalled a recent conversation. "Damn it, Biswas, first I was told that they were fornicating monkeys. I've killed as many of them as I possibly could. Now I'm told that they're not monkeys but natives, and that I have to be nice to them? Well, all I can say is that that's asking a lot."

Nothing Filek could say could break the admiral's front on the issue.

The doors opened into the inner sanctum. The Emperor, dressed informally in a grey tunic and slippers, was dictating to his favorite scribe, Simona of the Gsekk. The admiral was waved to a seat while Aeswiren finished dictating a letter to the King of Sulmo. Simona copied it and then set it in the packet with the others that were due to leave that evening aboard the frigate *Cloud.*

The Emperor clapped his hands. Almost immediately a pot of hot tea was brought in by an orderly. Cups were poured.

"Well, Admiral, I have heard the outlines of this news. What more do you have for me?"

"The count is now thirty-one major ships, Lord, including as many as eight frigates."

"Eight?"

"Yes, Lord, they must have stripped the harbors of Shasht."

"They've done that, Admiral, and they've stripped the treasury, too. The first fleet cost five years' revenue but still left just enough to keep the Empire stable. This new fleet has gone far beyond that." Aeswiren moodily pounded his fist into his palm and continued, "They have come to force our hand. It isn't the way I wanted it, but so be it. We have some advantages. This is our ground, we have experience here, and we are allied with the natives. With only thirty-one ships they cannot have much beyond twenty thousand men. With the natives, we can match that."

Heuze felt a rising tension. He found the thought of fighting alongside the monkeys blasphemous. He almost missed the days when they obeyed the priests and their harsh views concerning the natives. Now, the priests were reduced to lives as simple men of the cloth, taking care of the poor and conducting the new style of services that Aeswiren had decreed for them. There were no more Red Tops and Gold Tops. Their days of terrorizing the public were over.

"With roughly equal numbers, I know we shall give them a very hot reception," the Emperor concluded.

Heuze had to agree. Aeswiren had brought the elan back to the army. What had been a beaten force, riven by cynicism, was now reforged, unified and rededicated. Once again they drilled with the wondrous precision with which the men of Shasht had always drilled. Their weapons were ready, polished, practiced. Indeed Aeswiren had added new weapons, including an array of catapults of various sizes. The men were ready to take on anyone.

"So, Admiral, where are these twenty-three ships and eight frigates?"

"Most of them are at sail in the northern bay, Lord. Twenty ships now keep station eighty miles off the coast of Flem. Some of the locals' fishing boats have been taken by the frigates. Their crews have perished, as far as we can tell."

"Alas that it should be so. I hope we can make our enemy pay in blood for all that he has shed."

"Yes, Lord," Heuze murmured.

Aeswiren unrolled a map across the table. "So," he

mused aloud as he studied it. "It is just as General Toshak expected. Our enemy makes his first thrust at the mots in the North."

The Old One clearly hoped that by gaining a quick victory over the mots, he might avoid a fight with Aeswiren. He would expect that Aeswiren's army would not fight if the mots were already destroyed.

"It may be so, Lord, but so far only two ships have gone in close and landed forces. All advantage from surprise has been surrendered."

"Two ships only?" Aeswiren continued to study the map. "Where?"

"The estuary of the river called Dristen by the, er, natives."

"And what are they doing there?"

"They sent ashore a party of men with horses. They burned part of the village and then went inland. The last report put them well beyond contact with the ships."

Heuze thought this behavior bizarre. The monkeys would soon mobilize an army. This small raiding force would probably never see the ocean again, even if they were all mounted. The mots would find ways to kill them. They were very resourceful in that way.

The admiral studied the map. A piece of monkey work, it was beautifully done. The terrain was painted in green and brown, the rivers and sea in blue. He could see the rivers crawling across the green toward the snow-capped peaks of the mountains that cut the Land away from the dry plains of the east.

Aeswiren was just as puzzled as the admiral. "Cavalry, eh? Well, I had expected that. But why land a small force there? Why give up the element of surprise?"

Heuze knew that if he was in command of this new fleet, he would have put ashore his entire army. They would need at least that to be secure. The damned monkeys were hellishly good at fighting in the woods. Once you moved inland, you were at risk of being cut off and surrounded.

"I have wondered about that since the first news was brought in, Lord. They have the benefit of all the letters we sent back describing the place. They know the dangers. It's not a scouting mission, not with two ships' complement. Nor is it secret. They burned several houses in that village."

Aeswiren scratched his chin and studied the map. "Well, Admiral, we will move at once to embark the army, but"—Aeswiren tapped the map—"we won't sail quite yet."

Heuze nodded. A little caution might be called for in this situation. "Yes, Lord."

Chapter 18

Thru moved at a steady trot, keeping to the deer trails on the ridgeline. Over his shoulder he carried the bow and the quiver he'd taken from the abandoned Geliver house in the village. He kept moving, running on raw willpower. His constant travel for Toshak had hardened him to marching, but to keep up this jogging pace for hour after hour was a test of endurance.

Ahead and far below, the riders pressed on up the narrow road that ran beside the river Dristen. Thru had counted at least eighty riders, and with them were a dozen captives, mots and mors taken somewhere on the road below Juno village. These poor folk were tied, back to back, and placed over horses at the end of the line.

Among the captives Thru had identified a handful from Warkeen, mostly older folk like Disha Mux and lanky old Moon Chapin, but he had also seen the pretty face of Iallia Tramine, the mor he had loved in his youth.

He'd had the chance to identify them when the raiders stopped at Juno village to water the horses. Thru had caught up, and from the hill above he'd used the spyglass Mentu had given him. The captives were taken in a group to the pump and forced to drink like animals from the trough. Then they were dragged out of sight again.

The men were Shasht soldiers. Thru knew the type

very well. They wore steel helmets and leather armor. They carried spears over their shoulders and swords at their belts. A few, with green ribbons on their coats and no armor plate, carried long bows.

Thru understood what he was seeing. Mentu had long before explained to him the concept of cavalry. He had seen horses in Shasht and even driven a team of them hitched to a wagon at one point during his epic escape. He could see that these men had a professional, skilled manner with the horse animals. Such men would be deadly foes to a battlefield, able to move quickly across the terrain, strike, and then withdraw before any counterattack could be made.

Thru made sure to stay out of sight as he followed the path of the riders. Fortunately, the hooves of so many animals set up a vibration in the ground that he could often detect when he couldn't actually see them. He stayed on the slopes above, keeping to the deer trails.

There were no other mots around. The alarm had passed swiftly up the valley, and the folk had dropped everything and run for their lives. Thru imagined that Toshak had already heard of the incursion and was organizing a response.

Still, the question remained: What were these men up to? They had known by now that all the villages around were emptied of their populations. And they were surely aware that getting back to the coast and the safety of their ships would be highly hazardous. The woods would be alive with ambushes.

The whole thing seemed quite mad. Even the destruction in Warkeen village had been haphazard, almost halfhearted. A few houses had been burned, among them that of the Gillos, but most of the village had been spared. Thru had never heard of this pattern before. Usually the men burned the whole village if

they had the chance. This time they didn't bother to
burn any of the other villages they passed through.
Instead, they would stop to water their animals and
do some looting. They would eat, sometimes lighting
a cooking fire in the kitchen of a mot house. Then
they'd mount up again and move on.

This was the pattern they'd kept up all day. Thru
had managed to stay close to them by dint of a prodi-
gious effort.

Ahead of them, around the curve in the valley, the
village of Round Pond came into view. The famous
pond—broad, deep, and perfectly circular—glistened
in the late-afternoon light. No smoke rose from any
of the chimneys, though. The folk and the animals
were long gone.

Thru turned up onto the hilly ridge that rose on the
northern side of the village, which, like nearly every
village in the Dristen Valley, was built close to the
river, often around a bridge.

He worked his way around to a point where he
could see down to the main square. The men teth-
ered their horses in groups along the cobbled main
street. They broke into the houses and pulled out
furniture, mats, pottery. Some they burned on a big
bonfire. Some they rolled up and put among their
things. Others they despoiled or smashed with glee-
ful laughter.

The captives were not in sight. Thru assumed they
had been put in a cellar somewhere under guard.

The bonfire blazed. Some kind of biscuit was
handed out to the men who ate it greedily, hungry
after a long day in the saddle. The biscuit was accompanied by a wineskin. The cooks were working up a
huge pot of porridge.

Suddenly the crowd stirred, and voices began chant-
ing something. A huge figure, their leader, so Thru
had decided from previous observation, shouldered his

way close to the fire. The leader said something, and
the men roared with laughter.

More furniture was thrown onto the fire. Thru saw
a fine old dining table, no doubt an heirloom centuries
old, tossed into the flames. Meanwhile, other men had
rolled out a barrel of ale from the tavern. It was
quickly broached and mugs were handed around. The
leader took a mug and quaffed it and then made a
joke and all the men laughed.

He raised a hand and commanded silence. The huge
man paced about the inner ring around the fire, staring
into the men's eyes. Then he bellowed something at
them. Thru caught the word "monkeys" and guessed
at least part of what the huge man was saying. If Thru
could get within bowshot and had a decent steel point,
he'd be happy to show this man what the monkeys
could do.

The leader finished speaking, and a group of men
went to the door of a house a little farther up the
street and returned, dragging old Disha Mux behind
them. Disha screamed when she saw the fire and the
crowd of boisterous men.

The leader caught hold of Disha by the neck and
pulled her off the ground so she dangled beside him.
She looked like a doll in his huge hand; he shook her
and made jokes that provoked gales of laughter from
the men.

Thru stared, horror-struck, as the huge man took
hold of one of poor Disha's arms and began turning
it in the socket as if he was dejointing a rabbit for
the pot. Disha's shrieks rang off the hills while her
arm was torn from the socket and waved above the
fire.

The men howled with mirth at the old mor's agony.

The giant shook Disha like a rag, snapping her neck
and cutting off her awful screams. Then he tossed her
body to the men by the fire. Thru's gorge rose as he

watched them gut the old mor and clean out her viscera before they skinned her and cut her into pieces that were set on sticks over the coals. The odor of roasting flesh began to rise into the air.

A second captive was brought out, a mor whom Thru did not recognize. This time a hatchet was used to dispatch the victim, a single blow smashing her skull from behind. Her head was then cut off, and the process of turning her into meat unfolded as before. Thru forced himself to watch to the bitter end.

Doing so, he witnessed something strange. The arm that had been torn off poor Disha was cooked over the fire and returned to the giant man. He nibbled on it and then passed it around the group standing beside him. It didn't take too long before the arm began to come apart. As they split at the elbow and then disassembled the arm bones, each bone, gnawed and clean, was handed back to the giant. He examined each one, then handed it to a servant who stood behind him collecting the bones in a small sack.

Intrigued, Thru watched until the servant took the bag away. Another layer of mystery had been added to that surrounding this strange, grisly expedition.

The fires burned down eventually. Not a scrap of old Disha or the other mor survived. There was nothing to be buried. Their bones had been tossed into the flames, except for the arm bones of poor Disha.

Thru waited until dark, then crept down carefully into the backyards of the houses at the base of the hill. The men, who had eaten their fill, had gathered around a small group who had removed their helmets to reveal the gold and red painted scalps of the priesthood of the Great God. The men knelt and began their evening prayers. To Thru it was an incongruous sight, these savage brutes who had just eaten two of his people, kneeling and offering prayers to a deity. With their droning in his ears, he made his way carefully along the back of the village.

In one house he found some dried bushpod curd, which he pocketed, plus a small jar of cooking oil and some dried beans. In another house he found a trove of bushpod cakes, which he wrapped in cloth and tied to his belt. Then he went on.

He reached the end of the row of houses. Across the street he could see into a larger house that was being used by several men for a billet for the night. They had unrolled blankets and made themselves comfortable on the fine pillows and mattresses of the mots, brought down from the upstairs rooms. Thru heard the men chattering with each other and understood some of what he heard. The men were in a cheerful mood. They would ride on the next day, wherever their great leader wanted. They would kill whoever he wanted them to kill. They were quite content.

Thru slipped across the street, a swift invisible shadow, skirting the house inside which the men were congratulating themselves on a good day's work. Eventually he found the house with the other captives. They were confined in the windowless cellar, and there were a dozen men in the rooms above. He knew why the captives were being held; he'd heard the men discussing whether the mots were to be eaten every day, as treats. The hot, sizzling flesh was tasty to these men, who had otherwise nothing but biscuit to look forward to.

He could do nothing for the captives, so Thru crept on. He studied the horses and then the place where the huge leader was sleeping, one of the largest houses in the village, with several guards standing at the door and in the front yard, armed and awake.

At last Thru withdrew into the hills, ate some bushpod curd, chewing slowly because it was very tough, and then curled up to sleep in the base of an old oak tree. He woke at dawn, ate some bushpod cakes, then drank from a spring not far from the tree.

In the village the men were stirring. A fire was lit and food prepared, and within an hour the men were in the saddle and riding out. Above them, in the hills, Thru followed.

Chapter 19

Eight days later, a much thinner Thru Gillo climbed a rocky trail that brought him over the summit of Garspike Ridge. Far below to the south, the river churned through a deep gorge and then flung itself over the spectacular Angel Falls, dropping five hundred feet into the deep, dark pool at the foot of the Garspike.

The riders had come this way. The mark of their passage was clear enough, even down to the scattered horse dung.

Up ahead, miles away, he heard the wolves howling again. The packs were concerned about the column of men riding through their territories. Thru sympathized. To the wolves, men and horses were both alien creatures, never seen before.

Their howling was fortunate for Thru, for he had fallen far behind the horsemen. The wolves had become a vital link, keeping him in touch with the progress of the column. Of course, the horsemen were also moving more slowly than they had in the beginning of this mad march into the mountains. They'd left the road behind days before, and all vestiges of civilization had soon disappeared.

Thru's boots had worn out even before then, but by fantastic luck he'd found a pair of replacements in one of the last villages in the upper valley. Someone's spare pair, probably worn only to prayers at the fane.

They'd fit him well, too, which was fortunate, for they were immediately pressed into service for twenty miles that day.

The men showed no inclination to stop. Eastward they hewed, keeping to the valley of the Dristen and then to the most eastward-trending stream in the high country. Without roads or paths, they pressed on up the game trails made by elk and deer over thousands of years, up to the alpine meadows where the animals browsed in the summer. The horses had slowed to a walk, with rests several times a day for feed and water. Still, they'd outpaced Thru after the first few days. His respect for the abilities of men on horseback had grown. Over journeys of many days, they had a clear advantage over mots on foot.

The wolves ceased calling. Thru stopped, ears straining against the quiet sigh of the breeze through the pines. To the south rose the vast mass of one of the peaks of the Drakensberg mountains, with shoulders covered in snow far above. To the north, beyond the hill, he knew there was another, and directly east, just visible above the next hill, loomed the white crest of Iggipatnapa, the second mightiest of all the Drakensbergs. With its sharp spire thrusting forth from the central mass, it was well-known all over the Land, immortalized in countless paintings.

What were these men doing? Were they mad, or simply ignorant? They were riding deep into the central Drakensbergs, dangerous country, not only because of the occasional brown bears but also of bands of pyluk, the green-skinned lizard-men of the east, armed with long wooden spears and throwing sticks.

The trail wasn't hard to follow. The horses had churned up the soft areas. Thru kept up his slow but steady pace.

Earlier that day, he'd passed the ruins of an old mot hunting chalet, abandoned long before. Only the stone walls remained, the wood having long since rotted. An ancient haw tree had grown inside and now thrust gnarled limbs above the ruins.

Such places had been abandoned because of the danger of pyluk, which had grown steadily in the Drakensbergs over the last few centuries.

The men were numerous enough to overawe any band they might meet, but the pyluk would hunt them from concealment. A man and a horse represented so much meat that pyluk could not ignore them. Then, once they'd been targeted, the long wooden spears would flash forth, men would topple, horses would go down, and pyluk would prepare for the feast. Slowly the men would dwindle, picked off from the shadows day by day. In the end, none would ever see the lowlands again. Thru was sure.

Yet he followed, intent on trying to rescue the captives, if it was possible.

Again, the wolves howled, distant and faint, over the next hill. Thru went on, hefting his bow over his shoulder, peering around him carefully, ears pricked, nose keen.

And then he heard it for the first time, a heavy kind of throbbing, the beating of drums. He paused and listened carefully. It was distant but quite clear. The wolves continued to howl for a while, then quietened. The drums continued.

The drums continued to throb, hour after hour, while Thru pushed forward, moving very cautiously. Any pyluk in the region would be drawn by the noise. He didn't want to stumble over a band of the greenskinned spear throwers in the thickets. Accordingly, he paused frequently to crouch and listen. As he sank into a state approaching meditation, his sense of hearing grew so acute he could hear bees at work on the clover in a nearby meadow and water splashing over stones in the stream running along the bottom of the valley.

After listening, he spent several more minutes

studying the ground ahead and around him, looking for the slightest thing that might be out of place. Only when he was certain that he was alone did he continue.

When the sun slid behind the western hills, he was moving up a trail onto the lower slopes of Mount Iggipatnapa. The broadleaf trees had given way to stands of pine and spruce. He emerged onto a high meadow and surprised a small herd of deer that had been standing silently in the shadows. Disappointed, he watched them bound away, white tails bobbing in the orange evening light. Since he was down to the last day or so's worth of bushcurd in his pack, one of these deer would have been very helpful. But their tails disappeared into the trees on the far side of the meadow, and he was left alone.

The drums throbbed on. He crossed the meadow, pulled some boughs down to make a shelter, and prepared himself for sleep. First he broke in half one of the pieces of bushcurd and chewed it slowly, letting the creamy flavor fill his mouth. The taste brought back memories of his mother's bushcurd pie, one of Ual's most wonderful confections. The scrap of curd barely dented his hunger, but he restrained himself from gobbling the rest.

As dusk fell across the mountain, he saw a tiny light break forth in the darkness far ahead, under the looming mass of the mountain. Staring at the light, he wondered what the men were doing there. Why had they come so far? What drove them to this madness? He prayed that the captives were alive and that he would be able to find some way to free them.

At last he settled himself to sleep, wrapped in his blanket, sword and bow to hand in case he was disturbed by bear or pyluk in the night. He slept fitfully. Several times in the night he awoke and found the faraway fire still burning while the drums throbbed on.

They were still beating when dawn broke over the Drakensbergs. Amazed at such persistence, he roused himself, rolled up his blanket, and took several deep breaths of the cool air. The early light had cast a magical pink spell upon the hillsides. The beauty of the scene was breathtaking. He drank from a small stream splashing across the hillside and ate a little more bushcurd. Then he pushed on, moving down into the valley until he came on the rocky streambed on its center. He looked about carefully. The drums and the firelight would have drawn pyluk from miles around by now.

After progressing for a few miles up the streambed, clambering over the boulders, Thru felt the nag of some sixth sense inspiring caution. He flattened himself into a crevice between two rocks where the water ran at ankle depth. Closing his eyes, stilling his own breathing, he listened.

Upstream, he heard several runners, slapping barefoot over the rocks. A splash told him a foot had gone into the water. Cautiously he raised his head to study the terrain ahead. He glimpsed the ends of long spears above the bushes fifty yards ahead. Then they were gone.

Thru knew whom those long spears belonged to. He recalled the time he had collected some and thrown them off the cliff by the small temple in the Farblow Hills. He recalled the ferocity of their owners.

He crouched down and froze in place for a long time, listening intently for any sound, while he nocked an arrow and readied himself to die fighting. However, the minutes ticked away with no further sounds, and eventually he emerged from cover. He stepped forward to the point where the pyluk had crossed the streambed.

Here he found their tracks, at least seven individuals, perhaps more. The tracks showed the long, narrow feet with the distinctive claw marks. Now he had no doubt about their presence. They were out there around him.

Still the drums throbbed, beating like some primordial pulse in the Land, reverberating off the hillsides, pulsing over the stones.

Late in the day, he finally came over the crest of a hill and was rewarded with a clear view of the men's camp about half a mile away. In the center burned a large fire tended by a clump of men. Surrounding it was a circle of a dozen tents, one of which was significantly larger than the rest. Farther off, a crude corral had been erected from fallen tree limbs. The horses made a dark mass inside. The smell of wood smoke was mixed with the smell of roasting grain cakes. Thru found himself salivating while his belly rumbled. It had been days since he'd eaten more than small amounts of bushpod curd.

Forcing thoughts of food from his mind, he concentrated on studying the camp, searching for some sign of the captives.

In front of the large tent, four men pounded on long, tubular drums. This was the source of the steady throbbing that echoed back from the hills. A few other men could be seen engaged in various tasks. One seemed to be putting bags of feed down for the horses.

The sight of this camp produced more questions than answers for Thru, however. He'd tracked these men for many days, climbing all the way up into the mountains, and now they had pitched camp and begun beating drums? It made no sense.

A sudden sound behind him caused him to duck down behind a massive fallen pine tree and freeze. Listening carefully, he heard stealthy footsteps approach. Soft thuds, heavy exhalations, and then a burst of guttural, hissing speech sent a chill down his spine.

Nearby, perhaps just on the far side of the tree, was a party of pyluk! Feeling like a mouse among a gang of cats, Thru crouched there, scarcely daring to breathe.

The pyluk had not seen him. They remained on their side of the thick trunk of the tree while they hissed and gabbled together in their harsh tongue as they studied the camp. Gradually, Thru became aware of their odor, a sharp smell like wet leather. He wondered if they would smell him out, too.

At one point they broke into a bubbling sound, akin to that made by frogs in the spring. Appalled, Thru realised this was pyluk laughter. It stopped after a while then started again. Whatever had amused them, it was very funny. Finally the weird noise ceased altogether. The pyluk muttered among themselves a little more, and then Thru heard them rise as one and file away quietly, back into the trees. Scarcely daring to breathe, he raised his head to scan the surroundings. They were gone.

With extreme care, he worked his way down the hillside, through scrub and small trees, toward the men's camp. He had observed that the men had just three lookouts posted, set around the perimeter of the camp. Clearly they did not fear attack by the bands of pyluk that they had drawn to them with their crazy drumming.

He had also noticed that an old tree had fallen quite close to the edge of the camp, near the largest tent. Its roots lay in the forest, but the broken top of the trunk lay quite near the back wall of the large tent. When he got to within a hundred paces of the tents, he saw that this fallen tree was hollowed out. He realized that if he could get to the tree, he might be able to crawl unseen to within twenty feet of the tent.

Now he could see that the drummers were stripped to the waist, pounding on the drums with long sticks tipped with white cloths. Their bodies were strangely rigid, their faces taut with tension.

He had reached the camp's perimeter. Some sixty paces to his right stood one of the lookouts. After studying the man carefully, Thru turned his attention back to the fallen tree. The lookout kept his gaze on the hillside above. He seemed to be fighting off boredom.

Slowly, Thru slithered toward the near end of the hollow tree trunk. The approach was hidden by a dense stand of spiny bushes. Working his way in under these bushes cost Thru any number of prickles, but he kept at it and managed at last to get into the cover of the hollow tree trunk without being seen.

It was dark and quiet inside the tree. Even the boom of the drums was muffled. There was a strong smell of wet ground and mold. Thru crouched there in silence for a while, then crawled forward. The hollow part of the tree ended with an opening at one side, filling the interior with a dim light. In some places there was just enough room to crawl on his belly, while in others he could get up on his knees.

Eventually, after considerable effort, Thru reached the opening. From this vantage point he could look along the side of the tent and on to the fire and the men tending it. Cooks had set up large iron griddles and small trestles, on which they worked. Other men came and went, fetching wood to the fire or wheat cakes from the cooks.

Thru noticed that the light was fading from the sky. The sun had set. He had arrived at a good time. When the darkness had fallen, he would see if he could move closer, perhaps get a look inside the nearest tent.

Then he saw a figure stroll past the fire, and for a moment he felt his jaw drop.

It was a mot! There could be no doubt about it— the fur covering the head and shoulders was unmistak-

able. A mot was wandering through the men's camp
unharmed, unmolested, unchallenged.

The mot went on, past where the cooks labored
over biscuits, and disappeared into a tent. Thru stared
after him with bulging eyes. A traitor? How could a
fellow mot betray the Land to these terrible men?
Thru felt as if he'd been kicked in the stomach. It was
hard to breathe.

He was still struggling with what he'd seen when
the huge man, towering over everyone else, emerged
onto the scene. Thru imagined that the man had come
out of the big tent, the front entrance of which lay
out of Thru's line of sight.

The giant rubbed his hands by the fire. The men
looked up to him with something akin to reverence.

"Well, boys," he said, "I can feel them. They're
out there, hundreds of them. They're watching us and
thinking about eating us."

The men laughed nervously. Thru understood the
man's Shashti perfectly well. The occasional word
stumped him, but he got the gist.

"I'm serious, boys. It's like I told you: These fellows
aren't like you and I; they happily eat their enemies.
But we don't have to worry about that. Tonight we
will play the flute of bones."

The men responded with a forced sort of good
cheer, applauding their massive, towering leader. Thru
wondered if he'd heard correctly, and if he had, what
it might mean.

The evening swiftly faded on into darkness while
Thru crouched inside the hollow tree. It was uncomfortable, but he had developed an iron resistance to
discomfort long before, and he drew on that now.

While he watched, the men went about their business. Some worked on equipment, others on the
horses. The cooks were busy much of the time, cooking up cauldrons of stew and hot grain stirabout. Occa-

sionally one of the cooks would take food and water over to the drummers, who continued to pound out the rhythm hour after hour.

A horn was blown. More wood was thrown on the fire and it blazed up. Men came out of the tents and gathered round. Their leader appeared. He spoke to them about their mission and how they were going to help exterminate the monkey men.

"They must die, all of them!" roared the giant man.

"Death to the monkeys!" the men hurled back at him. They kept shouting this for several minutes until the huge man bellowed at them to be quiet.

"They must die, because they pose a deadly threat to the pure blood of Man. If we left them to breed, they would create a swarm and in the end they would come to Shasht and devour our children before our very eyes. They must be annihilated to stop this threat! So says He Who Eats!"

The men shouted their allegiance to the Great God.

Now the leader spoke more casually. He called out to some of the men by name and told jokes. He spoke of the good lives they would lead someday, when the new lands had been cleansed of the monkeys and all their works. They would be back home in dear Shasht. They would have titles and lands. They would have many women and even more slaves.

The men roared their appreciation of this vision of their future.

While they cheered, Thru abandoned the safety of the hollow tree and crawled quickly across the ground to the back wall of the tent.

No shout of alarm came. The drums continued to throb. The leader had begun his harangue once more. Thru lifted the tent wall and peeked underneath. A lantern gave a dim light. He glimpsed camp chairs, a bunk, a heavy wooden chest. On the farther side of the tent, huddled together in a crude pen, was a small group of mots.

Noticing something, Iallia raised her head. For a moment their eyes locked. Thru raised a finger to his lips and slipped under the tent wall. Just then there was a noise from the front entrance, the flap was pulled back, and the leader pushed inside.

Thru froze in place behind a folding chair. The leader did not notice him. His attention was fixed on the captives, crouching in the pen. The man stood over the mots, rubbing his hands together while the captives shrank back in fear.

"Wriggling won't save you, my little worms. Some of you will be honored tonight. I will dance in your blood."

The huge man leaned forward and seized three of the captives. He pulled them out of the pen and stood them before him, where they trembled in abject terror. Two older mots and a mor, none of them known to Thru.

"Yes, you'll do," said the giant man to himself. "You will have the honor of being trampled into the mud by my lordly feet. Such a privilege is not given to all."

He herded the mots ahead of him and thrust them outside the tent. The mor gave a shrill wail as she was shoved into the open. Then the tent flap fell back behind them.

Thru was about to get to his feet when the tent opened again and the man came back in. Thru crouched down behind the folding chair and prayed he would not be seen.

The huge man went to the chest, opened it, and removed a small box. From it he pulled out a complicated object. Thru had but the briefest of glimpses. Then the man set the box on the table, closed the chest, and went out once more.

Thru breathed a huge sigh of relief.

Iallia whispered, "Thru." He again put a finger to her lips to quieten her. The others, a handful of older mots and mors, stared at him with wondering eyes.

"They killed everyone but us," whispered one of them.

"I know." Thru bowed his head for a moment in sorrow and reached out to the captives in the pen. Their hands all came together. "Be brave. We'll get you out of here."

There was a loud surge of noise outside. Thru crept to the front entrance and peered outside.

The mots were being held in front of the fire by men. The leader stood beside them, arranging his fingers on a set of handpipes. He appeared to be practicing the fingerwork for some tune or other and was quite concentrated upon the task. The mor wailed as one of the men took hold of her ears and tugged her head out straight.

The leader saw that everything was ready. He handed the odd-looking pipes to a Red Top and drew a large, shining knife. With chill nonchalance, he slit the mor's throat. The men lifted her body and held her so that her blood ran out on a patch of ground in front of the fire.

Thru noticed that this patch of ground had been covered with a circle of white powder. The blood spattered down in the center of this small area, about six feet across, and slowly formed a red slick.

Meanwhile, the two mots were held in a similar way and the knife applied to their throats. They were drained into a large cauldron, however, which was then set over hot coals.

Thru shivered. The works of Man the Cruel were often horrifying, but this seemed incomprehensible. The bodies were cut up by the cooks. The great ring of men beyond the fire were intent on the spectacle before them.

The leader stepped forward and raised one hand. In the other he clutched the small set of pipes.

The drumming suddenly stopped. For the first time in days.

Only the flames crackled in the fire. The whole world seemed breathless, awoken to a new and deadly peril.

The huge man had removed his boots and leggings. He wore only his tunic and loincloth. He raised the pipes to his lips and blew upon them. There came a long, sharp note, then another, and then a longer, lower one, which he held and then let tremble into vibrato.

The giant stepped forward to the edge of the space covered in the white powder, now slick with a pool of blood. He lifted the pipes again and began to blow an odd little tune, eerie in its cheerfulness. It rose and fell a few times, coming to a short encore section once again, and he hopped forward and began to dance upon the blood-soaked ground.

The dance was strange, unnatural. He jerked his head from side to side, hopping from one foot to the other, bending the leg deeply, then hopping again to the other foot before straightening for a moment.

The blood mixed with the powder and spattered up onto his legs, even to his belly, while he danced.

Like everyone else, Thru was held spellbound by the scene, until he remembered the captives. He turned away from the flap. There was no better time to make the attempt.

The pen was easy to demolish, and the ropes that bound the captives by the neck were quickly cut. But getting the older mots across the tent and under the tent wall was not easy. They had been kept on their knees for a long time and were very stiff and weak.

Thru realized that some of them would not survive the next few days.

Outside the tent, there were more immediate perils to face. The guards were not a problem, since their attention was captured by the giant man. But Thru

had no idea what was lurking in the woods around
the camp. He kept them all together in a group as he
led them to the hollow tree trunk. They climbed inside
and crawled forward, and he brought up the rear. No
cry came from the guards; they were all riveted upon
the strange scene playing out by the fire.

The Old One danced in the sacred mud, sanctified
with the blood of sacrifice. He played the ancient
tune, and out in the woods his children stirred. The
men watched the ceremony without comprehension,
aware only that some awful power was being conjured up before them. Their hair rose on end, shud-
ders ran down their backs, sweat broke out on their
temples, but still they stared, captivated by the bizarre sight.

Out under the trees, the effects of the dance were
far greater. The throats of the bull pyluk constricted,
their eyes watered, and their hands shook. Some fell
to the ground and writhed helplessly.

Suddenly, from hundreds of leathery throats, came
harsh babbling sounds. The hills resounded as if from
a vast crowd shouting one name, as if the very hills
had come to life. The men around the fire stared at
one another in wonder. The babbling resolved into a
strange song, a creaking, groaning tune that matched
the music of the pipes.

In a vision from some rent in the fabric of the universe, the pyluk emerged from their hiding places and
approached the fire. They came in a wave, tall, hideous figures, their long throwing spears in their hands.
They marched up to the fire and stood there, en-
tranced, swaying to the tune.

The appearance of the pyluk sent a convulsion
through the men. Some drew their swords. Others
looked to their tents where they had left their weapons. They had been warned to expect something
strange to come out of the woods, but this invasion

of huge lizard-men went far beyond anything they could have dreamed.

The things were bigger than men. They wore crude shell decoration and carried long, untipped spears. Their heads were like those of small crocodiles but perverted by a brain case almost as large as that of a man or a mot. There was intelligence in those yellow eyes, but it was not like that of men, mots, or anything else in the world.

As more and more of them emerged, fear began to swell in the hearts of the men. Hundreds of the things were coming. If the situation turned ugly, the men might all die here.

As the crowd of green-skinned monsters grew until it was twenty or thirty deep, the men on the other side of the fire looked about them with bulging eyes. All felt the same question burning in their minds: How could so many of these creatures have approached so close without being detected?

While the men grappled with these thoughts, a small group of mots and mors, gasping from the effort, struggled up the hill path in the opposite direction.

Again and again they flattened themselves to the ground or behind trees as parties of pyluk emerged, spears in hand, the very stuff of nightmares for mot children down the ages. But these pyluk took no notice of the easy meat to be had. Their attention was entirely given to the dancing god by the fire.

At the top of the hill, old Kurtha knelt down, unable to go any farther.

"You'd best kill me."

Thru shook his head.

"No, I mean it. I can't keep up."

Thru would not listen. He paused only long enough to get Kurtha over his shoulders before driving on to the top of the hill. Then he stopped to look back.

Down below by the fire was a scene from some

portrait of the damned. A great wedge of pyluk had taken over half the area of the camp. The men had retreated into a tight knot on one side of the fire. The giant man continued his hypnotic dance.

Suddenly Thru understood what was happening, and a great chill sank into his heart. He turned to the others with fire in his eyes.

"Up now; we must go on. We must warn the folk."

Chapter 20

General Toshak and his immediate staff stood on Bear Hill overlooking Warkeen village. Off to their right far out in the bay, they saw the sails of the enemy. With a spyglass the great ships could be studied in detail where they tacked back and forth, marking time. They'd been there for more than a week, contributing to the mystery of what this new invading army of men was up to.

From his vantage point Toshak could see far inland as well, up the valley of the Dristen. When he looked that way, the sense of mystery deepened.

Again he considered what was known. A party of scouts or raiders had been set ashore. They had done some damage to houses in Warkeen, but had not burned the village, and then gone upstream, riding on the backs of enormous donkeys, or animals that looked like donkeys. Toshak knew they were horses. He had learned about them from the Assenzi.

The folk of the valley had fled to safety, though there was a report that a band of stragglers had been taken near Juno village. Toshak's men had since moved most of the refugees down the coast to Dronned. His army, nine thousand strong at this point, was spread all over this area. Every day reinforcements arrived as regiments of recruits came up from the mustering at Donned. Everything on that front was going well. Building on the core of veterans from the previous campaigns, the new army of Dronned had formed up quickly and efficiently. Toshak had been quietly pleased by the response.

He had a brigade placed in the village, another in reserve a little farther down the road, and a third up on the hill. But as of yet they'd had no enemy to fight, just the fleet crisscrossing back and forth across the mouth of the bay.

In the meantime, Toshak had received messages from Aeswiren, brought in down the coast by swift-sailing frigates. The Emperor had embarked his own army on Admiral Heuze's ships. They had crossed the Sea of Geld and were last reported off the coast of Sulmo. They wouldn't reach Dronned for a week or more, but at that point Toshak would have ten thousand battle-hardened men as reinforcements.

Then Toshak would face the situation he had been dreading. In his heart, Toshak could not shake entirely his suspicion of men, any man, even though he had met the Emperor and come to like him. There was also the problem of the two armies joining together. There were mots who hated all men with a passion, and there were men who had not lost their previous hatred for the "monkeys." The two armies in close proximity was a combustible mixture.

So far, though, the enemy had done nothing. One raiding party had disappeared into the distant mountains. It was all very mysterious. It made no sense at all. The mountains were beautiful but dangerous, haunted by pyluk and giant bears. What could the men possibly be doing in such terrain?

He noticed a sudden stir amid his guard. Up the path toward them came a party of three mots. One of them wore the red pins in his lapel that marked him as the quartermaster general of the army of Dronned.

"General Meu." Toshak clapped his quartermaster on the shoulder. "You have good news for me, I take it."

"Yes, sir, we have assembled enough local supplies for the army for at least three days. By then we should have a wagon train in from Dronned."

"That's a relief. One thing we don't have to worry about."

"Yes, sir. And I have word that the wagons with the catapults will be here tomorrow morning. They're camped six miles south."

Toshak nodded. The catapults would be a nasty surprise for the enemy fleet if they came in close enough to shore.

"Sir, have you had any word of Thru Gillo?"

"No, Meu. I know he is a friend of yours, but we have no word from Colonel Gillo."

All that was known was that Gillo had gone ashore from the *Sea Wasp* to track the raiders. He had disappeared up the valley in the wake of the enemy. Nothing more had been heard or seen of him.

The *Sea Wasp* had slipped out to sea to get around the enemy fleet and had brought the first detailed news of the landing to Dronned. The trusty vessel was now shadowing the enemy, part of Admiral Heuze's scout force, along with two frigates, the *Duster* and the *Cloud*. The enemy ignored them, though they had six frigates of their own and could have given chase at any time.

Thus the situation rested, baffling and enigmatic, and Toshak hated it. He hated most of all being on the back foot, waiting to see what the enemy would do next.

The chase continued through the glittering light of late afternoon. The hills were aglow with the setting of the sun, but, under the trees, hunters and prey alike were oblivious to these fleeting glories. The prey, a small group of mots, staggered along a well-marked deer trail, spent and close to collapse.

Thru, desperate to get out of a foot race with the

pyluk, looked off to either side of the path. They were
on a ridgeline, chased up through the thinning ranks
of trees toward a mountain that Thru suspected was
Garspike itself. Once they were up there, they would
have little chance of escape from the fleet-footed
pyluk and their throwing spears. Even if they had to
risk sliding down on their backsides, they had to find
a way to get down from this ridge.

There! He saw, ahead a little ways, a gravel-filled
wash sloping away between the tangled roots of some
trees. Quickly he drew his companions to the spot.

"It is our only hope."

Freese, the oldest mot, shook his head. The gravel
slide was steep, and it went down out of sight.

"Come on!" Thru would brook no opposition. "It's
this or the pyluk."

Faced with that choice, the mots slid. Freese followed Iallia and the others, and Thru came last. The
pyluk were still far enough behind not to be able to
see them. The slide was fast and rough. Thru felt the
stones kicking against his buttocks and back; he car-
omed off a tree root, shot down a chute between boulders, and then fell six feet vertically to land in a rocky
streambed. That final drop was hard. Thru almost
turned an ankle. Old Freese had broken his leg.

Aghast, Thru stared at the old mot. He'd known
this might happen, but he'd had no choice. The leg
was twisted badly, the broken bone protruding
through the skin below the knee. Freese knew his time
had come.

"Kill me," he breathed.

Thru looked at the others. They knew it had to be
done. Already they were starting to move away, leaving it for Thru to finish.

"I'm sorry, eldermot. I tried."

"I know, and you have my blessing, but don't leave
me for those things."

Thru wielded the knife in a smooth stroke. As he moved down the gulch, he thought to himself of another sad consequence of the coming of men: He had learned to kill like an expert.

They had left the pyluk several hundred feet above them. The streambed took them around a curve then through a craggy canyon and out onto the southwestern side of Garspike Ridge. For a short distance they had a wide view off to the south. The valley swept westward, the hills rose up, and another great mountain bulked up into the sky. The trees began to thicken again, and the ground was soft in places—there was no possibility of hiding their trail.

They stumbled on, Iallia and Thru helping the older ones where they could. Thru did not know this country, and being up in the high hills like this left him anxious about being trapped atop some unexpected cliff face.

An old mor, Gefeeler, had to stop. "Breath, I have to get more breath," she said, leaning against a tree.

The others stopped beside her. Thru could see that none of them could go on much longer.

He climbed a tree and tried to spy out the way ahead. The forested hillside curved away beneath the Garspike. Downhill, the woods thickened further. Above them, they thinned out on the rockier slopes.

He looked back. The pyluk were not in sight. Carefully he scanned the high slopes, up where the ridgeline trail had been leading them.

Suddenly he caught sight of a group of vertical sticks in motion along the top of the crest. Thru crouched down, hiding beneath the leaves. The pyluk were perhaps two hundred feet above them, moving along the rocky path at the top of the cliff. He watched, rigid with tension, as those spears continued to move along the ridgetop, heading west. When they were gone, he climbed down.

At the base of the tree the others were all stretched out, barely able to move. Thru thought hard.

He did not know the lay of the land very well, but he did know that he'd come up the Garspike on the other side. And that the river broke over the northwestern side of the ridge. To head downslope directly would take them south into the valley below, which trended west. The valley would lead to the main Dristen Valley, which lay two or three days' journey to the west.

He amended that. With these old mots and no food, it would take more than two or three days to get out of these hills. Again the hopelessness of the situation rose up to overwhelm him. For a moment or two he found himself staring into the darkness, his mind frozen.

Iallia came and sat beside him. "Thru, you have performed a miracle. Don't give up now."

He made no reply. Iallia had already told him the most shocking news imaginable. His old enemy, Pern Treevi, was with the men, was in fact virtually one of them. Iallia's mere presence dredged up memories that Thru found painful.

"Thru, there is something I must say: I love you. I always have."

Thru wavered a moment. He knew this was not true, but once upon a time he had most certainly loved Iallia. That younger Thru seemed like another person to him now, a figure in another life in which he had never heard the terrible name of Shasht and its grim empire. A life in which he wove mats and traveled with Nuza's troupe hitting the small white ball for the crowds.

"You married Pern, Iallia," he said as gently as possible.

"I was a fool. Pern hates me, Thru. He used to come and gloat over us, telling us who would be killed the next day. He told me I was to be kept for last."

"Why does he hate us all so much?"

"I don't really know. He keeps everything bottled up inside. He wanted power, Thru. That's all he ever said. He wanted to make the village a cloth village, and he intended to own it all. Power and the wealth to do whatever he wanted, that was what he told me back then. I was so young, so foolish. I thought he really loved me."

Thru did not believe this either, but he smiled. They had all been young and foolish once.

"Well, Iallia, all I know is that Pern hated me from our days in school, maybe even before then, though I hardly knew him."

"I know, Thru. He always hated you. You were the only mot in school who he knew he could not intimidate with his family's wealth. That day at the bat-and-ball game changed him." She paused for a moment. Both of them felt the memory of that strange day when Thru Gillo became a young legend in Dronned for hitting seventy-seven runs at the ball game tree.

"Something inside him snapped that day. He was already slipping into evil, but that day sent him over the cliff. His hate consumed him, Thru."

And now, Thru thought, Pern was one of the men, in spirit if not in the flesh.

"Then he must answer to the Spirit when the time comes. But it is not for us to say what shall be done with him, unless I come upon him in battle, in which case I will do my best to slay him. As I know he will me."

Iallia's eyes glistened in the dark. He felt her hand find his. Though he was reluctant, he allowed the contact, and she was comforted.

"Rest now. We will move again when it is dark."

While the others slept, Thru sat with his back against the tree listening carefully to the sounds of dusk, mulling over their options. He heard deer moving down into the valley some ways off. Geese called as they headed over Garspike Ridge for the lakes beyond.

To go down into the valley like the deer would only slow them down in the dense thickets. He decided they had to climb again. Upslope there came a point where the trees petered out beneath a stone cliff. If they could get up there, they could proceed westward no matter how dark it was, and when the moon came up there would be light enough to see where they were going.

After an hour, he woke the others and helped the oldest back onto their feet.

"Hold the hand of the person in front of you. Try not to get separated."

"We can't see five feet under these trees," said old Gefeeler.

"Nor can the pyluk."

The moon had not yet risen, so they stumbled forward, following Thru, who wove a path through the trees. He moved slowly, allowing everyone behind him plenty of time to plant their feet as quietly as possible. Still they made noise. If the pyluk were listening, they would hear them. Thru gambled that the pyluk were asleep. Creatures of the daylight, pyluk rarely hunted at night.

Thru called halts every few minutes while he carefully listened to their surroundings. Apart from an occasional call by either owl or wolf, the forest was almost silent. Once two mice, fighting under a log, gave them all a start with their sudden fierce chittering, but that was all.

After a while, the moon rose and bathed the woods in gentle light. Thru could move more quickly, and they quickened their pace.

The trees thinned out, and they emerged onto a zone of broken rock mounded along the base of the cliff. Nothing grew here, and the moon's light sent jagged shadows across the fallen stone.

Thru studied the terrain ahead before he pulled his charges out of the trees and hurried them along at the margin, where the ground was easier to walk on than on the stone. A few clumps of trees struggled to survive here.

Thru grew uneasy. Something was stalking them, he was certain. He settled his small band in the trees while he turned back to scout.

He'd gone only twenty paces when a slight sound froze him in place. The sound was repeated, and he heard a stealthy tread above him somewhere, thirty feet up.

The pyluk were directly above them.

He heard more steps, and soon there were at least a dozen of the brutes up there, sniffing the air. Thru barely dared to breathe. A long half minute or so passed and then he heard a guttural mutter and the pyluk withdrew.

He waited for several minutes before returning to the others. They had also heard those growls. They knew how close the pyluk had been. They were crouched together, frozen with terror, and he had to cajole them to get them moving again. By the time the sun rose. Thru wanted to be as far west, and as far away from the pyluk, as possible. So, with persuasion and even some shoving he got them going forward once more.

They crossed the scree field at the base of the cliff and gradually came around to the western face of the ridge. They began to hear the thunder of Angel Falls to the north. Thru needed to start looking for a way down. While the moon was up, they would try to descend into the valley and under the cover of trees.

Looking out into the western valley, limned with silver moonlight, they were all struck by the sinister beauty of the scene. Thru thought he detected a way down, through a gap in the thickets below. They

started toward it, negotiating their way over rocks
and boulders.

Alas, after perhaps thirty yards, old Gefeeler tripped
on a loose stone. With a sharp cry of fright, she slid
down into a gully. Thru jumped down beside her to
press his hand over her mouth.

But it was too late. Nearby he heard the sound of
heavy bodies running their way. Upon on the cliff top
he could see the tips of pyluk spears approaching the
western end.

Harsh baying calls rang out into the night and, to
his horror, they were answered by other pyluk coming
up from the valley below.

"Trapped!" said Iallia.

Thru looked around them in desperation while pulling Gefeeler back to her feet.

"Can you run?" he asked her.

"No, I am spent."

"You must run, or the pyluk will have you."

"Then," she sobbed, "I will run."

And so they ran, along the scree-strewn slope, heading north. The roar of the falls grew louder each time
they came around another bend in the cliff. The pyluk
on the cliff top easily kept pace with them, calling to
their brethren in the forest below. The air had grown
damp with the mist of the falls, and trees grew right
up to the very edge of the vertical cliff face.

Thru tried to think of a way out. Should they hide
in the forest? The pyluk would winkle them out in no
time. Should they double back? How could that work,
with pyluk above observing their every movement?

A stone whistled past his head, cast by a pyluk bull
up above. There was no likelihood of escape.

With a roar of triumph, another pyluk sprang from
a tree behind them. Turning, Thru drew an arrow,
took aim, and released. The pyluk gave a sharp cough
of dismay as the arrow suddenly sprouted from his

shoulder. Yet another green-skinned monster appeared behind the first, and more were coming.

The mots ran, but they had nowhere to go. Another hundred steps brought them to the cool cloud that edged the ridge above Angel Falls. The rock was slippery and wet, cold to the touch. The river, here about fifteen feet wide and five feet deep, arched out into nothingness and then fell to the bottom of the gorge far below.

"Jump," said Thru. "We have no choice."

The mots stared at him, eyes drained of hope.

"It is death to jump," whispered Gefeeler.

"Maybe. But it is a worse death to stay here."

A spear flew forth from the trees and flashed over Thru's head.

The mots and mors jumped, launching themselves out into the curving waters.

They fell for what seemed like an eternity, plummeting down past glistening black rock. Thru did his best to lock into a dive, hands outstretched to break the water's surface. He toppled but recovered and then struck the water hard. The shock was terrible, and after that he plunged into cold and dark. He touched bottom and looked up to a shining surface that seemed impossibly far away. A profound sense of regret overtook him. There was so much to do, but it would have to be done by others now. Then blackness closed over him.

Chapter 21

The Emperor Aeswiren had brought his army to the North. Once again, Admiral Heuze's fleet hung off the shores of Dronned, sails glittering in the sun. The flagship *Anvil* was third in the line of the first echelon. There were three echelons, all told, each of six great vessels, with the frigates farther out, upon the seaward flank.

This time, however, they came not as enemies of the folk of Dronned but as allies in time of war. The irony of this was not lost on the admiral, or the Emperor either.

Aeswiren had studied the shoreline with the spyglass and now stood with the admiral over the chart.

"The best landing place would appear to be right there, at the mouth of the river." Aeswiren brushed the chart.

"Aye, Your Majesty, that is exactly where we attempted to force a landing in the first year."

"And that was where General Uisbank was taken captive."

"That is correct."

"A ridiculous plan. What was the man thinking?"

"Begging your pardon, Lord, but Uisbank was not the most thoughtful of men, if you see what I mean."

"Mmmm, perhaps I do, Admiral, perhaps I do. And now Uisbank has refused my personal request that he return to duty. He's quite free to return, you know.

But he claims he has important work to do where he is and has declined my request that he report to me in person."

"Well, Lord, deplorable as that is, I might suggest that it is quite understandable. He probably expects to be put to death if he does."

Aeswiren nodded, accepting that this was not an unreasonable concern for General Uisbank. "Yes, I expect you're right. In his shoes, we'd probably feel the same." Aeswiren sighed and squeezed his eyes shut for a moment, oppressed by the lack of trust shown by his missing general.

"But, Lord, I should point out that there is a difficulty in using that site to land the army."

"We will not be opposed by the mots."

"No, but the enemy fleet is capable of sailing down on us to give battle at any time. It would make the operation of landing the army hazardous."

Aeswiren pondered this a moment, then agreed.

"Very well then. We will have to march farther on foot. Put us ashore as close to the city as possible."

"A day's march, Emperor, that is the best I can do without risking the fleet."

They exchanged a look, and Aeswiren gave a slow nod. He was not inclined to risk the fleet, not yet, not when the battle had not even taken shape. But he did want to get his men ashore. Their supplies were running low and could only be augmented by joining up with General Toshak and the mot army.

And in the back of his mind, Aeswiren was also concerned about getting his men to cooperate with the mots. There would be friction, inevitably, and it would take a little while for the two armies to work out methods of operating together.

Aeswiren had heard enough reports of the prowess of General Toshak's army to be confident in the mots' abilities. His own men were battle-hardened veterans, and he was confident that the two armies together would be strong enough to shatter any host the Old One might land from his fleet.

But first he had to get ashore.

"All right, Admiral, a day's march will do. The enemy is waiting for something, some portent, some sign from his god, I know not, but while he waits we will act."

"Could it be that he awaits another fleet?" said Heuze, deeply uneasy.

"Very unlikely, Admiral. Just to produce the fleet they have, the shipyards must have been working flat-out since I left Shasht. There's very little that I don't know about our shipyards; there just isn't the capacity to build more than that. Our enemy must have gutted the treasury to build this second fleet so quickly."

Admiral Heuze still had questions. "Begging your pardon, Your Majesty, but what the hell is he doing? It makes no sense. Why does he wait there, idling his ships, while we have the time to sail up here and join forces with the monkeys?"

Aeswiren sighed and unrolled the chart farther. Inland, the terrain rose slowly, through hills and dales up into higher hills and then to the great sweep of the high mountains.

"I wish I knew."

When his eyes opened once again, Thru felt like part of a miracle unfolding. He was alive! Not only that, he was warm, indeed almost hot, and he wasn't wearing a stitch of clothing. All around him was softness, warm and dry and carrying a smell that was familiar from childhood. A dim light came from somewhere above.

He shifted position and gave a groan of pain from the soreness along his left side. As he reached around himself, his hand brushed against a solid mass of woven twigs. His other hand brushed against someone's arm. Ignoring the pain, he pulled himself to a sitting position, causing his head to graze a woven ceiling of more twigs.

In the dimness he could just make out the legs and torso of another mot lying beside him. He leaned closer. It was Iallia.

His nearness awoke her.

"Thru?"

Her eyes gleamed, a sign of life in this strange netherplace.

"Are we dead? Is this the afterlife?"

Thru considered the question. Could it be? Could this be the realm of the dead? The Assenzi said that after death one's spirit returned to the Great Spirit that breathed throughout the world, but perhaps they were wrong.

Then he laughed. The sound seemed strangely loud and yet hushed by the soft down that they lay upon. The source of the slightly sweet, almost nutty smell had come back to him at last.

"No, we're not dead. We're in a chook nest."

Iallia's eyes blinked, an effect that was almost comical in those conditions. "Chooks? But how? We're miles from any village."

Thru had no idea, but he squeezed past her and crawled across the floor of the nest until he found an opening to the outside world. There was dim light, filtered by the enormous mass of twigs set atop the nest. He found an opening and wormed his way upward until he could get his head out into the open air, at once colder and filled with evening light.

It was just as he'd thought. They were in a wild chook nest, built in the low fork of a big oak tree about six feet from the ground. The nest was a huge mass of branches and twigs, woven together into an immense basket and lined with dry leaves and chook down for warmth.

After examining his side as best he could and determining that he had no broken bones, Thru clambered out of the nest and stood on the low branch that it rested on. He noted that, placed as it was, the nest was relatively safe from wolves, who would have a hard time scrambling up to get to the lower branches. Long before wolves could do that, the wily chooks would have scrambled higher, out of reach.

Before him was a narrow glade set among oaks of magnificent girth. He saw no sign of the builders of the nest but plenty of evidence of their coming and going. The ground was heavily marked by their tracks.

Iallia popped her head out of the top of the nest.

"Where are they?"

"Good question. There must be several of them living here, judging by the tracks they've left."

"Not to mention moving us here from the river."

Thru shook his head slowly in wonderment. Chooks had no arms, no hands to grasp with, but they did have strong beaks and neck muscles.

"It must have been quite a job."

"And what about the others?"

Only then did Thru realize that he and Iallia were alone.

"I don't know."

"And where are our clothes?" said Iallia, who clearly didn't relish emerging naked from the nest.

Before Thru could answer, he heard a sudden disturbance in the undergrowth close by. He whirled around, prepared to defend himself. However, nothing more threatening than a pair of big yellow chooks emerged from the brush.

"Hello!" they chorused in cheerful chook voices. "We are Chenk and Mukka, and there are also Pikka and Dunni, but they are behind, bringing food."

The big birds came bouncing forward to stand on either side of Thru. They examined him with their big, black eyes.

"You will be wanting your clothes, we know. But they are still drying out. You were very wet when we found you."

"We give thanks that you did, friends. I am Thru, this is Iallia, and we are from the coast. But tell me, did you see any others? There were more of us."

The chooks exchanged looks and bobbed their heads several times in unison, a sure sign that they were uncomfortable. "Yes, we found others. All dead. We have been burying them. Would you like to see?"

Thru closed his eyes. His attempt to rescue the old mots and mors had failed.

"Yes. I am sorry for that news."

"You fell from the top of the mountain, very far, too far for them, almost too far for you."

"Yes, we fled from the pyluk. There are many pyluk up there."

The chooks stared at them with big eyes. "Will they come down here?"

"Soon, I think they will. It would be best if we were all a long way from here by then."

"Can you travel?"

Thru hesitated. He could feel bruises and soreness all down one side, probably from the impact with the water. "I think so. We don't have much choice in the matter, not if we want to live."

The two chooks looked at each other again and bobbed their heads.

"If pyluk come here, we cannot stay."

"True. We must all go down the valley. You will not be safe here."

"We came here when everyone fled from our village, Chumsley."

Two other chooks emerged from the woods, each bearing strings of berries in their beaks.

"Look, here are Dunni and Pikka, with vine berries for you."

Pausing only to eat some of the berries, which were

very red and sweet, Thru accompanied Chenk and Mukka down the path to another clearing where the chooks had laboriously scraped shallow graves and placed the bodies therein.

Thru knelt beside the graves and offered up a prayer for the oldsters who had been torn from their lives, driven into flight, and then caught up in the nightmare of capture by men and abduction into these mountains.

When he was finished, Chenk and Mukka reappeared, carrying Thru's and Iallia's clothing. "They are almost dry. The coat is still damp, but it is close enough."

"Thank you, friends. You have saved our lives, and in so doing you have helped to save the Land, because I have very important information that must be brought to General Toshak."

The chooks, already solemn in the light of all that had happened, grew round-eyed at these words. "We hear you, and we are ready to do our part."

"Yes, chimed in Mukka, "you have big information. We help."

Thru put his clothes back on, thankful that his boots were still wearable. "You must help, friends. And in case something happens to me, you must go to the general yourself."

Chenk and Mukka blinked. "But we are only chooks!" they said in unison.

"Chooks are people, too."

"But the general is a mighty person. He will not have time to listen to a couple of chooks," protested Chenk.

"Not so, my friends, not when you tell them you have a message from Thru Gillo."

"What is the message, Thru Gillo?"

"You must tell them that the enemy is raising an army of pyluk. They will come down the valley with thousands of pyluk warriors, and we must be prepared."

At these fell words, the chooks gobbled and ducked their heads.

"We will stay in your nest tonight, and tomorrow we must all head downstream as fast as we can go. The fate of the Land depends on us."

Chapter 22

"Sergeant Rukkh, come in, stand easy. Take a cup of tea?"

Rukkh entered the Emperor's tent with not a little awe. He had served this man all his adult life, but he had never met him like this, nor expected to.

"Yes, Your Majesty."

"Good. Make yourself comfortable. We have a couple of minutes."

The Emperor took up a dull metal teapot and a tin mug and poured the tea with remarkable gusto, keeping the pot at least two feet from the mug. Rukkh observed that not a drop was spilled.

"Look, I'll get to the point. You're a good man, Sergeant, been in the army most of your life, been with this colony army since its inception. You have plenty of experience."

Rukkh sipped the tea, unsure whether he was supposed to say anything or not. He was awed that the Emperor knew anything about him at all. Rukkh had always thought of himself as just another grunt in the army of Shasht.

"So, what I want from you, Sergeant, is information. You know how the men are thinking, and maybe even why they're thinking it. I want to know all that, too, understand?"

Rukkh took a breath. This was beyond anything he had imagined. The Emperor wanted his services. He nodded. "Yes, Lord."

"Good. See, I know we're in for a difficult time here. Only a short time ago we were fighting these people, what you were calling monkeys until very recently. Well, I know you're still calling them monkeys."

The Emperor had a conspiratorial smile on his face.

"I know how soldiers think. I rose from the ranks, Sergeant, never forget that."

"Yes, Lord."

"So I know where the salt is kept hidden, understand? But now we have made common cause with the monkeys. They aren't our enemy anymore. We're allies against our real enemy who sits in that fleet offshore and threatens us all with annihilation."

"Yes, Lord."

"So we have to cooperate with our former enemies, and I know that there are many men who still bear a grudge. We've all lost good friends here, and that can leave hard feelings."

Rukkh nodded. He'd heard plenty of harsh words about the monkeys from the men during the voyage north, and now that they were actually camped on the old battleground where so many had fallen in the first summer of the war, fresh veins of bitterness had opened.

"But that has to change. We have to fight alongside these people now. Our real enemy is too powerful for us to do the job on our own. We need the monkeys now, understood?"

"Yes, Lord, I think so. But, if I may be so bold, I would like to ask something."

"Go ahead, Sergeant. When you meet with me like this, you can say anything." Aeswiren let a grim little smile flicker across his face. "Well, almost."

Rukkh grinned. The Emperor was a soldier first and foremost, and he had long since earned the respect and love of his troops. Meeting him like this, Rukkh could see why.

"Well, Your Majesty, this enemy, out there on the

ships, who is he exactly? We have been told some things, but there is still confusion. Who is this enemy?"

Aeswiren tented his fingers together and touched them to his lower lip as he considered the question.

"He is a sorcerer, Rukkh, an evil thing that has lived far beyond his time. It has been hidden behind the priesthood, and so it was invisible to the common people. It created the hierarchy of Red Tops and Gold Tops. It used them to rule us, while all the time hiding in the darkness, sucking our blood."

Rukkh heard the barely repressed fury in the Emperor's words.

"How could this enemy have hidden itself for so long?"

"Because it ruled by murder and intimidation. Only Emperors were made privy to the secret. Each Emperor was confronted with the knowledge that if he moved against this thing, it would kill him. When I refused to obey its wishes, it tried to have me killed. It unleashed the priests against me and fomented treachery among my own forces. That is why I am here."

Rukkh swallowed. These were weighty matters for a sergeant in the Blitz Regiment. "And why has this thing come here?"

"To kill me, to annihilate the native people here, both of which it sees as threats to itself."

"It is a sorcerer? You have seen it?"

"I have met it many times. It is ancient, and it despises all men. To it we are little more than ants. It has forced the men of Shasht into lives of misery for uncounted generations, and it could not care less. If we can kill it, then our descendants will have far better lives than we."

"Well, Lord, I will do everything in my power to help you."

"Good. I knew I could depend on you, Sergeant. This is how we will work together. I will send for you every other day or so. It will be nothing more than one of my men giving you a look or a tap on the shoulder. I don't want everyone knowing what you're up to or you'll be isolated in no time. When you get the nod, then I want to see you within the hour. Just find a way to reach me. My guards will recognize you. Be discreet, though, and whatever you do, don't tell anyone about this meeting."

"Yes, Lord."

"And now, tell me, honestly, how do the men see the situation?"

"Well, Lord, it's like this: We fought the bloody monkeys for years. We beat them sometimes, and they beat us sometimes. We've lost a lot of good friends here, buried a lot of good men."

Rukkh felt strong emotions rising in his chest.

"Right here on these sand dunes, Lord, we fought a hell of a battle. Lost a lot of good men. We all remember it well. And now we're going to fight alongside them. So we all feel a bit confused. But we don't look on them like we did years ago. We've had to respect them, 'cuz they are brave little fuckers. They fight hard. And they're hard to kill. When we first fought them, we always killed three of them for each of ours, but by the end of the war it was more like one of ours for one of theirs."

Aeswiren was listening carefully. "They learned to fight."

"That they did, Lord. And we have to respect them for it. But there are still some of us who hate them. It's hard to forget all that's gone before."

"I know."

"But more than that, we all want to get this over with and go home. The men are ready to fight, and they're ready to fight for you. We all believe that you're the real Emperor and that you're going to get rid of the priests, and we all want that."

"How do they feel about the colony here?"

Rukkh made a dismissive gesture. "Nobody wants to stay here. Well, maybe there's a few, but nearly everyone wants to get home where we belong. Kill the sodomistic priests and start new lives outside the army."

"Good, because we'll all be going home when this is done. I expect we'll have to knock a few more heads back home before it's all really over and done with, but in a year or two I expect most of the men will get their discharge. I plan to force through a land redistribution program and give every veteran thirty acres."

Rukkh whistled. "The men will fight through hellfire for that, Lord."

Aeswiren grinned. "I don't expect it'll be quite that bad, but we're likely to have a scrap before this is done. You'll all get the chance to wet your blades."

As the sergeant was leaving, slipping out of the back entrance of the Emperor's tent, he came face to face with a slim figure, a woman, but without the head covering of purdah. The next moment recognition bloomed in his mind. It was Simona of the Gsekk.

Her family had haughtily refused Rukkh's overtures, and then he had seen her one day, dressed in this open style, with no covering, nothing demure about her whatsoever, and he had felt hatred for her.

And now? He was confused, and curious about her presence here, in the Emperor's quarters.

"You?" he said clumsily.

She had seen him; she knew who he was. Her eyes were unreadable. She moved to step around him. He put up a hand to stop her. For a moment his fingers rested on her arm.

Simona's eyes flashed fire at him, and his own anger was rekindled.

"You wear no covering in public?" he said.

For a long moment she stared at him, as if weighing her words carefully.

"You cannot understand," she said at last. "But I refuse purdah. I am my own person. I do not belong to any man."

Then she was gone, twisting away and passing through the inner flap of the tent. Rukkh could not go back, the guards were already in place. Then it hit him that she had gone into the Emperor's tent without even a challenge from the guards.

Shaking his head, Rukkh hurried back through the lines, making sure to return to his own squad's position from the direction opposite that of the Emperor's tent. He was to be the Emperor's trusted informant, and he must not jeopardize this gift from on high.

Yet there was an edge to his feelings. He had long dreamed of that red-mark girl, seeing her on the women's deck of the old *Growler*. He had hoped to one day win her hand and make her his bride. Together they would have founded a family here in the new land where such things as birthmarks were less important than the ability to bear children and tame the wilderness.

Now that dream was gone and the girl was a woman and taken by the Emperor. Well, at least it showed that Rukkh had good taste when it came to women! He spat on the ground. What was done was done, and he would give it no more mind.

"Good tasty beetle—try?" Chenk had caught another leaf hopper and proffered it to Thru.

He grimaced, then shrugged and took the big bug. Insects were not his preferred food. With all those legs and things they felt weird in one's mouth. But they were edible in a pinch. Thru crunched the thing up, finding that it tasted a little like fried bushpod but

oilier. He tried to ignore the legs and feelers as he
chewed them up.

Iallia wrinkled her nose in disgust. She was hungry,
but she was holding out for some berries, or anything
but bugs. Iallia had led a privileged life and had never
known hunger before this nightmare.

Mukka had returned from her ramble through the
laurel bushes with another big hopper. "Eat good beetle, tasty," said Mukka, offering it to her. Iallia shuddered and turned away. Thru could not resist a grin,
though he was concerned that Iallia keep up her
strength. They still had days of hard marching ahead
of them.

They were traveling west along the north bank of
the river Dristen. They had left the mountains behind
and were wending through the lower foothills. Thru
estimated that they could reach the coast in five or six
more days, depending on the pace they were able to
keep up.

He knew a village was not too far ahead, where
he'd found some dried bushpod curd before. But until
they reached it, they had nothing except what they
and the chooks could find. Thru had lost his bow and
quiver in the plunge over the falls—indeed, he
counted himself fortunate to have retained his knife—
but he had fashioned a little sling, and with some of
the roundest pebbles he could find he'd hunted for
small game. His efforts had brought them a couple of
small birds, a squirrel that was astonishingly tough,
and one young rabbit, which he let Iallia eat mostly
since she couldn't stomach the insects.

Roaming through the woods like this with chooks
had proved a revelation. Thru had known the big, in-
telligent birds all his life, but he had never hunted
alongside them for food. They didn't miss a thing
when it came to bugs or useful leaves and berries.
There was a constant murmur from them everytime

they found a clearing filled with bushes and small trees:

"This leaf is good to eat, but that one is bad."

"These berries are good, but not too many or you be sick."

"Eat this! Very good."

Even Thru had blanched at the big spider with yellow veins across its back held up in Mukka's proud beak. "Uh, no, not just now," he'd managed. Mukka blinked, then gobbled down the tasty morsel while Thru allowed himself a little shudder. Hoppers were one thing, but spiders were still too strange for his palate.

Still, along the way, Thru had learned to try half a dozen wild foods produced by the cheerful chooks. He remembered hearing his grandmother and mother talk about them, things like toe tree buds and the yellowed shoots of the lippinstalk. Grandmother had used lippinstalk to wrap up pats of butter. She said it was good to eat, too, but Thru's mother never cooked it. She said it was "wild food" and not fit for civilized tables.

Thru had learned to relish the salty, fat flavor of the lippinstalk shoots as well as the creamy inner pulp of toe tree buds and the sour inner bark of the kork tree.

They had made pretty good time, and they had seen no sign whatsoever of the enemy, neither men nor pyluk. Whatever they were up to back in the mountains, they were still busy with it.

Before midday, they reached the village Thru remembered. The chooks had passed through it, too, during their flight up the valley.

"We found nuts there, but no people. All mots, all chooks gone to the hills. We go to the hills, too."

Thru had learned that they had become separated from the people of their village quite early during the flight. They had missed the point where the villagers turned away from the river and climbed into the hills above. The leading rooster, Chenk, was not the brightest spark in the fire. He had kept going up the river, hoping to find another group of refugees who could tell them something about their own village mots and chooks. Alas, they were behind the wave as the news had gone up the valley at great speed, triggering instant flight.

In the village they found flour, some sour curd, and a big store of hazelnuts. They made quickbread and roasted it in an oven, while Iallia fried the curd with some onions she found hanging in someone's kitchen.

Everyone had left in a great hurry. There were utensils left out and even uneaten meals abandoned on tables to mold and insects.

While they ate, Thru searched for a bow and some arrows. He was soon rewarded. In a sawyer's house he found an old but serviceable bow in a closet. Right next to it, hanging from a peg, was a quiver with ten good shafts, all with stone hunting points on them. He tried them out in the center of the village, placing three within a finger's breadth of each other on the front door of the tavern from fifty paces. The bow string was fresh, even if the bow itself was a little old.

When they'd eaten and filled packs with nuts for the rest of the journey they set out once more. They followed the river road now. From here on it would offer the quickest route to the coast, and with the supply of nuts they would not need to forage for a while.

The road turned westward as the river swung round in a broad curve into a wider section of its valley. The forest of oak and beech spread out wide on both sides. They hurried along, pushing tired legs to give their all.

After an hour of steady marching, Thru and Chenk felt the vibrations in the ground at virtually the same moment.

"Something comes," said Chenk, turning to the mot with anxious chook eyes.

"Horse animal," said Thru in an instant. "Hide. Quickly."

They scrambled up the bank. Iallia was struggling, so Thru picked her up and pitched her over his shoulder as he dug his feet in and powered them up and into the trees. He dropped her, threw himself down alongside, and peered back up the road.

They were only just quick enough. Around the bend far back up the road a pair of horsemen appeared, riding fast.

The chooks had vanished. Thru noticed. Then he saw they'd dropped a small sack of hazelnuts beside the trail. It was half hidden in leaf litter, but it might still be seen.

He strung the bow and quickly nocked an arrow.

The horsemen were coming. The sound of the horse hooves drummed on the road, scattering gravel. The men were scanning the road as they came, and Thru had the sudden chilling understanding that they were searching for him and Iallia.

Could they have tracked them?

Then he realized with a shiver that pyluk could. Pyluk could track anything that moved through the forest.

He kept the bow down but at the ready while the horsemen rode past. Hard-faced men, wearing leather hats and breastplates, they had bows and swords. He had fought men just like them many times.

Then they were past and they didn't slow down.

Thru let go the breath he'd been holding. They had missed the little sack of nuts.

He waited a few seconds, then darted out quickly to grab the sack. Others might be following the first two riders, and they might be more observant.

They were forced to move through the trees, and they traveled much less quickly than before. The chooks formed up on the flanks, Chenk and Mukka to the left, closer to the road, while Dunni and Pikka took the right. Iallia did her best not to step on dry branches and make noise. With Thru encouraging her, she did quite well. Their flight from captivity had already sharpened her survival skills considerably.

They went on like this for another hour. Thru judged the sun was halfway down the sky. They had kept well away from the road for the most part, but now they were forced closer as the valley narrowed and the river plunged down rapids for a few miles in a shallow canyon. The sides were breached by wide gulleys choked with alder and birch. Their progress was slowed negotiating these gulleys, and the footing was tricky in many places, for the rocks were covered in slippery moss.

At intervals they halted while Thru scouted forward, closer to the road, looking for any sign of the two riders. But nothing showed itself. Nor had they heard any other parties of riders come down the valley. Thru was tempted to return to the road; if they stayed in the thickets, it might take weeks to reach the coast.

He came around another bend. The river broke out of the canyon into a wider valley once more, but for the first section the road ran directly through an alder swamp. One look at the densely packed trees, the bogs and muddy pools, and Thru decided they would risk crossing the swamp on the road. On the far side, they could go back to working their way along through the woods.

"We must use the road for a mile or so. The bogs would take all day to negotiate. But when we get out there we have to hurry. Don't want to be spotted if we can help it. Those two riders may have gone all the way back to the coast, who knows? Perhaps the pyluk have eaten all the other men and horse animals. Nothing would surprise me by this point."

They readied themselves and then moved out onto the road, first along the side, moving from cover to cover as long as possible.

Soon enough the ground opened out into the bog. The alders rose in a thick mass, but the road ran virtually straight across, and Thru could see clearly right across to the far side of the swamp.

Thru studied the woods there, but saw nothing to give him further pause.

"Come on!" he cried and led them out onto the road.

As they ran, the chooks surprised him again by the determined pace that they maintained, their heads down, lunging forward on long strides of their legs. Iallia was the one struggling to keep up. Thru stayed with her, encouraging her to keep up a steady jog. It seemed to take an eternity crossing that open space. But at last they edged up a slight slope out of the bog and back under the trees. The road curved down to find the northern bank of the river, with which it kept company through the valley to the next village, some miles farther downstream.

Thru felt a surge of elation. They'd made it across the bog. Now they could make reasonable time under the cover of the trees. He decided to trust to their luck, and so they stayed on the road.

It was nearly their undoing. The attack came as a surprise despite all his care. An arrow whipped past his face, and he felt the wind of its passage. Another arrow sank into Pikka's chest, and she fell down with a squawk of agony. Thru saw the two riders suddenly urge their mounts out from between the trees nearby. The men had swords in hand. With whoops they came cantering down the short slope to the road.

The chooks fled in panic. Iallia tripped over her own feet and fell. Thru advanced to meet them alone.

As they came on, he held position between them.

Then, at the last moment, he sprang to his right, putting himself on the far side of the horse from that rider's sword arm. That also drew their attention away from Iallia, who was just getting back to her feet.

The man swung his sword over in a practiced move, however, and should have cut Thru's neck to the bone except that Thru did not stay still to be cut. He swung aside, dodging the slashing steel, then took Iallia under the arm and shoved her toward the trees.

The riders had halted in a cloud of dust. Then they turned their mounts and came back, whooping some more.

Hidden from their view, Thru took his bow from around his neck and fumbled an arrow to the string. The riders came confidently up the slope, swords twirling in their hands.

Thru's arrow sliced out of the shadow and sank into the leather breastplate of the leading rider. Alas, the stone point did not penetrate all the way, and the rider received a shock but no more. He kept coming.

Thru was forced to dive for safety under a bush. The horse went by. The sword sliced through the bush but missed Thru by a hair's breadth.

He rolled out from under. The other rider had caught up with Chenk. The sword flashed high, but Thru was too busy dodging to follow what happened next. His ankle turned on a root, and he went down on one knee. The horse struck at him, and even as he dove to the side of the tree he felt a heavy blow on his right shoulder. He rolled, wincing from the pain.

The rider was trying to get the horse to trample him, and Thru did not have time to get back on his feet. Then Iallia came whirling in with a fallen branch in her hands. She thrust it up into the man's face. He gave a startled cry and toppled backward, falling from the saddle. Thru twisted aside from the horse's hooves, got to his feet, and hurled himself at the man.

Iallia swung her branch again, but it was semi-rotten and it snapped softly across the man's shoulders. He caught her a terrific blow to the belly with his fist and sprang to his feet, sword in hand. Iallia dropped like a rock, clutching her belly, unable to breathe.

Before he could finish her, though, Thru was there. They came face to face, chest to chest, grappling. The man snarled, spit, and snapped at him. The man was the bigger, stronger of the two. He tried to knee Thru in the crotch. Thru slipped the blow and sagged sideways, pulling the man slightly off balance. Then Thru's hip turned, getting under the man's thigh, and in a moment the man was down on his back.

Thru evaded a wild slash with the sword. The man rolled over, desperate to get back on his feet. Thru sprang on his back. His knife came round and sliced across the man's throat.

Thru had only started to regain his feet before he had to dodge wildly as the other rider arrived on the scene. Thru heard the man's sword take a chunk out of the wood just above his head. The horse was carried past by its momentum. Thru turned back, wrenched the dying man's sword from his hand and took his stance again.

The horseman turned, but he held his horse back. He hesitated, not liking this change in the odds. After a moment's thought he turned his mount and moved down to the road, where he spurred it to a gallop, back up the road, back to the mountains.

Thru turned his attention to the others. Iallia was back on her knees, recovering her breath and clutching her belly. Ten yards farther on though he found the chooks. Chenk had survived, and Dunni and Mukka, but poor Pikka was dead, and Dunni was inconsolable.

There wasn't time to bury Pikka properly. Instead, they consigned her body to the river and watched it float out of the shallows into the stream where it was picked up and carried away.

Then they went hurrying down the road.

Getting to the next village was everything now, so Thru cast caution to the winds and pushed his little party down the open road as fast as they could run.

The fact that the surviving rider had ridden back toward the mountains told Thru that the man expected to find the rest of the horsemen back there. In other words, something incredible had taken place in the mountains, since the army of pyluk had not killed and eaten the men. It also informed him that the riders had indeed been seeking them. The chook nest below the falls must have been discovered and their tracks followed eastward. Once that rider returned to the main party, the enemy would know that there were fugitives ahead and that they were taking news of what had happened in the mountains down to the coast.

Thru knew the pursuit would be relentless.

So they struggled on. Iallia was close to being spent. She was tottering, staggering, and Thru had to help her stay on her feet again and again.

Chenk and Dunni were also slower than before, and poor Dunni wept constantly for his dead Pikka. Only Mukka matched Thru in possessing her old energy. Every so often Thru allowed them to stop while he put his head down to the ground to listen. No hoofbeats were to be heard, yet. They crossed another section of alder swamp, after which the road curved gently to the south while the river Dristen settled out in a proper river again. They came around a last curve and there, a mile ahead, stood the village.

Thru gave a shout of triumph. "They have boats!"

He pushed them on, impatient to board one of those boats and head downstream. From this village on, there were no more rapids on the Dristen.

"Hurry."

He could see at least three small boats, the round-bellied kind of dinghy popular on the river. With a relatively shallow draft, these boats could work through swamps and shallows with ease. They usually had a pair of oars, and larger ones might hoist a sail.

The houses, a half dozen humble stone buildings with slate roofs, were empty. No one had ventured back since Thru had passed through days before.

A quarter mile from the village, Iallia stumbled and fell. She lay there like a dead thing.

"Come on, Iallia," said Thru. "We can't delay."

Iallia barely raised her head. Thru took her arm and hauled her to her feet.

"Come on," he said fiercely. He started dragging her down the road.

And then they all felt the rumble underfoot.

Horses!

"They're coming!" cried Chenk, bouncing up into the air in alarm.

"Run!" shrieked Mukka.

Somehow Iallia found new strength. They all did, in an exhausted, almost demented way, weaving along the road.

Well before they reached the village, though, they heard a roar of triumph behind them. Thru looked back. A thick knot of dark shapes had come bounding around the bend.

Iallia gave a moan of terror. She would have crumpled to the ground again to await death, but Thru would not let go. The chooks gave sharp squawks of dismay.

"Run," croaked Thru.

Fortunately for the small band of fugitives, the horses had already covered many miles at a hard pace. They, too, were exhausted and had to be whipped on.

The village drew closer with agonizing slowness. Thru

was half carrying Iallia, half pushing her along. Chenk even added some shoves from his blunt head.

And then, at last, they were among the houses. Thru looked back. The horsemen were still two hundred yards behind.

"To the boats!" he rasped.

At a simple wooden dock, the boats were tied up on the downstream side. Iallia virtually fell into the middle boat, which was the only one large enough to take them all. The chooks jumped in, too, and the boat began to drift away from the dock at once.

"Jump, Thru," urged Mukka.

But Thru instead jumped down into one of the other boats and threw its oars into the river. He climbed back onto the dock and did the same thing with the other boat. Then he cut both boats free and pushed them out from the dock.

The delay was nearly fatal. He heard Iallia scream a warning. When he turned around, one of the horsemen was galloping right out onto the dock with a long spear aimed for his heart. Thru had barely time enough to throw himself into the water as the man rode past.

He fell in between the boats and swam out to the far side. Before he surfaced, he saw another figure break the water in a cloud of bubbles.

The horseman was after him.

Thru was exhausted, but he was an excellent swimmer, like all the watermots of the Land. The cool water revived him, and he turned easily, swimming like a fish, and then floated between the boats as they drifted along, hidden from the man swimming toward them.

He heard the clatter of another horse on the dock and shouts from the village streets. "The boats!" he heard a voice scream in harsh Shashti. "Get the goddamned boats!"

Thru ducked below the surface and swam down.

The man had stopped just on the other side of the two boats, treading water while he searched for Thru.

Knife clenched between his teeth, Thru dove under the boat.

The man didn't see him until it was too late. Thru was able to drive his knife home in the man's belly. Blood billowed in the water while Thru swam on, curving back toward the boats, which had continued to drift away from the dock. The boat with the chooks and Iallia aboard was leading the group by at least twenty paces.

The screams of the dying man alerted the rest to a danger in the water. But another man dove in anyway and began to swim with ungainly strokes toward the leading boat. The men on the dock called out warnings.

Thru took a deep breath and submerged. Under the surface he could clearly see the man's legs kicking clumsily in a cloud of bubbles.

More noise came from behind, and Thru glanced back. Additional men had jumped in. He had to finish this and get aboard the boat and row it down the river. The archers would be at work very soon, and the boat was still in range of the shore.

He came up beneath the nearest swimmer, but somehow the man was warned, some sixth sense perhaps, and he lashed out with a wild kick that spun Thru around in the water. The knife missed his belly by a fraction.

Thoroughly frightened and angry, the man drew his own knife and slashed at the water around him. Thru didn't have time to deal with him, so he surfaced and swam for the boat. An arrow sank into the water just ahead. He instantly submerged once more and swam below the surface.

More arrows fell around him, but he went deeper where they could not harm him. He surfaced for air and drew more shots, but they went wild. Then he came up near the boat, and with a few strong strokes he pulled himself to its side.

He had an arm up inside and was hauling himself out of the water when he was suddenly grappled from behind. A man had wrapped an arm around his waist. The man's knife was coming up. Thru flung himself backward, aimed a punch with his left hand, missed, and fell back into the water. The man's knife stroke went nowhere.

Thru tumbled through the water. Other swimmers were coming.

His own knife came out, and he pushed himself down five feet before curving back up right behind his attacker. He surfaced and buried his knife in the man's back. Then Thru was gone, leaving the man struggling while his blood stained the water. Thru swam for the boat. Again he got an arm over the side and heaved himself up. The archers were holding their fire because of the men who were close to the boat.

One man got an arm over the side and began to haul himself out of the water. Chenk slammed his beak down into the man's hand, producing a shriek of pain, and then he was gone, slipping behind them.

Thru set the oars in the oarlocks and dug in for a powerful stroke.

An arrow sank into the wood of the boat's side.

"Get down," he hissed to Chenk and the others, and they crouched as low as they could.

He dug in again and heaved the boat onward. The men in the water receded quickly as the boat picked up speed. But Thru knew they would capture the smaller boats and follow as soon as they fished the oars out of the water. He could not rest.

Suddenly Chenk and Dunni moved to stand in front of him.

"We can help!"

"I don't see how."

"Like this," said Chenk. The big birds crouched in front of Thru and on either side of him. As he brought the oars forward, they swayed back, and as he began to pull them toward himself, the chooks pressed forward, adding their strength to his own. The stroke grew deeper and faster.

As the boat shot ahead, Iallia sat up and took hold of the small tiller that helped to steer the craft. Now they were moving at a good pace and with some direction.

A final flight of arrows sank into the water around them, and then they were effectively beyond range from the dock.

While the archers remounted, Thru and the two rooster chooks drove the oars as hard as they could manage. The dinghy flew across the water, angling to the far side of the river where a channel ran down between small islets and the farther shore. There were rocks here and snagged trees, but the range for the archers would be close to their limit.

Meanwhile, the swimmers had captured the two smaller boats and found that their oars were gone. There was much shouting back and forth with the men ashore as they began a search for the oars.

Thus it was a race between the boat and the bowmen, and Thru and the chooks, aided by the current, were gaining slowly but steadily. They were aided by the fact that the river swung southward around a rock crag, while the road went inland two hundred yards before it passed through a natural break in the rock formation and went on to rejoin the river farther down.

Iallia gave a shriek and leaned hard on the tiller, and the boat barely dodged a boulder that rose in midstream before they shot back into the middle of the river. Beneath the crag were other rocks, and the current picked up as the river moved sharply downstream.

Thru knew that soon the river flowed into a lake. They would be safe from archers while they crossed it. They might even outdistance the horsemen, because the direct route across the lake to the point where the river began again was much shorter than the road.

The boat swung around the crag, and they curved back to the north. The bowmen were through the gap in the rocks now, but still too far for a shot.

"Come on!" cried Thru. "We can do it!"

The chooks responded magnificently. With each stroke of the oars, they pressed their breastbones to the oars just inside of Thru's hands. As he pulled they pushed, and the oars dug into the water hard and pressed them forward again. Iallia steered for the far side of the river once more to take them out of range.

A few minutes later, the river widened into the lake. They pushed on, heading across the broad expanse of water to the far side where the river went on into the west.

Chapter 23

The message had been sealed with that imperial *A,* and she had hesitated before replying, consumed with doubt. They had seen each other a few times since Aeswiren had brought his army to Dronned, but never in private.

All her time had been taken up by the task of setting up the hospital, organizing a staff of nurses, while at the same time attending the classes given by Filek Biswas, with Simona as translator, concerning medical science. At times Nuza had thought her brain would simply burst with all the knowledge she was trying to cram into it.

She had given little thought to the man she owed her life to, who was sitting outside the walls of Dronned in that camp with ten thousand armed men.

She was uncomfortable sometimes when she remembered the closeness that had existed between them. Had she let him come too close? Certainly, she had never told Thru all that had gone on between herself and the Emperor. But, then, what else should she have done, alone in that far-off land with no friends except one, and he the mightiest man in the entire country?

In the end she swallowed her doubts and made her way into the Shasht camp on the old battlefield. The warrant with the imperial seal was enough to get her past the guards, and her ability to speak Shashti took care of the one guard who was inclined to question it.

She found him waiting for her, barefoot on a lovely rug, a lush version of "Mots at Prayer" in the style of the great Misho.

"I have missed you," he said, typically blunt and to the point.

"And I you, Lord, Great King of Shasht."

But he knew she hadn't, not really, and he understood. He was man, she was mor, and they were of different kind under the sun.

"Now, don't lie to me. Remember, I know you well."

She recalled how penetrating those eyes of his could be. "No, Lord, I will not deceive you. I owe you too much for that."

"And I owe you everything, Nuza of Tamf."

She blinked. He had never called her that before.

"Tamf was burned to the ground by your soldiers."

"Yes, and we are helping to rebuild it. We will do what we can to make amends."

Again their eyes met, and neither wavered.

"I would have killed myself that day but for your intervention," he said at length.

"I am very glad that you did not, Lord."

Impelled by some unknown emotion, Nuza stepped forward and kissed Aeswiren on the cheek. It was not so strange. She had done it many times before when they had been together on the ship. She felt affection for this man, despite the chasm that separated them.

He put his hand to the spot, then kissed his fingers. "Thank you, Nuza of Tamf."

She felt uncomfortable once again. "What do you want from me, Lord?"

"Other than just to see you once more and talk like we did in the old days?" He smiled, seeing her unease. "No, fear not, I have no heavy demands to make of you, dear Nuza. I understand that each of us must go his or her own way in this world. We were not made to be together. I was infatuated with your beauty—it gave me solace in a desperate time. But that is behind us. You need not fear me."

The small cloud that had settled in her eyes was dispelled again, and he was pleased.

"But, yes, I do have a purpose for seeing you. An excuse, if you like."

"Good, because as you know, I have little time for anything other than my work these days."

"Yes, yes, I know. We are both slaves to the machinery of this war, but you, my dear, you are bringing something new and wonderful into the world, while I, well, I merely continue to practice the art of war."

She waited, watching him carefully, wondering what he wanted from her.

"All right, yes, I want your help, dear Nuza. I need information."

Her big eyebrows rose at these words.

"It is not so strange a request, surely? I am here on the sufferance of your people, of your King and General Toshak. And though I have a good rapport with the general now, that is not the case with the rest of his army. There is bad blood between our peoples. We have incidents now and again that threaten our alliance. Where I can anticipate such problems, I warn my men. I have laid down strict rules to keep us separated. Yesterday a man was given forty lashes for stealing a cask of ale. But, while I can try to control my men, I cannot know or control your people. I feel sometimes that outside the perimeters of this camp is a world of which I know almost nothing. I need someone I can trust who can tell me what is happening among the mots. What they feel about us. How they will react in this difficult situation."

Nuza studied him closely. "You want me to be your spy?"

He grinned. "Oh, my Nuza, so quick, so sharp. Spy?

Not so. I do not need a spy, because I trust General Toshak. No, I need an informant. A different role entirely, not spying on your soldiers but telling me what your people are saying, how they see this situation. Will you help me?"

Nuza knew she could not refuse him.

"Of course, Lord, I will do anything to help you win this war."

"Good."

"And I will bring you reports. Or shall I give them to Simona?"

"Best if you can come here in person, of course, but I understand how busy you are with your work, so if you can tell Simona, or give it to her in writing, then do that."

"That stolen cask of ale, by the way?"

"Yes." His head came up, his eyes tightened.

"The general opinion I have heard is that men are thieves by nature. They steal from each other, steal from the land, steal from the sea and the air, and are beggars because of it. Another opinion I heard expressed was more favorable. Men are trying to learn how to brew ale like ours because their own brewing arts are so weak."

"Ah-ha, well, already that is invaluable. Your people have a low opinion of us, then."

"What else would you expect?"

He nodded glumly.

"And the punishment, the whipping of the thief?"

"Yes?"

"That, too, has been much commented on. Among us, the penalty would have been less severe but more accurately connected to the crime."

"And what would that have meant?"

"Someone who stole beer would be made to work for the brewer for a period that matched the severity of his misdeed. A barrel stolen might be repaid with a week's work mashing wort in the brewhouse."

Aeswiren chuckled, enjoying the thought of Puugil, the soldier who'd been lashed, being condemned to a week mashing hot grain in a brew cellar. Aeswiren knew the men would rather take a lashing any day than be demeaned by performing slaves' work.

"I'm afraid in this army we don't have the resources for such a punishment regime, and my men would rebel if I tried to introduce it. But he'll wear those forty stripes for at least a week and be proud of them, too."

Nuza could not understand this, but Aeswiren assured her that it was so.

"My men are soldiers, dear Nuza, not brewers, and they touch no tools except their weapons. That is the way it is among us."

The talk turned to the city and its people and to Toshak and finally to Thru Gillo, her beloved, who once more was lost from view on a dangerous mission. Nuza tried to keep her fears in check.

"I fear for him, but at the same time I feel that the Spirit truly watches over him. He survived a journey across Shasht, passing through great dangers. Surely he will survive this, too."

"If anyone can, it is he. I have dealt with him now many times, my dear, and I have rarely met anyone of my own kind who seems so capable."

They finally parted at the entrance to the tent.

"Farewell, dear Nuza, and please come to tell me what your people are saying when you have the opportunity."

They clasped hands a moment and she left him.

The drums thundered anew as the Lord Leader, the Great One, the High Master of the World, stepped back from the stakes and the men who were tied to them. He had cut the three men's throats with smooth strokes of his long knife. Their blood ran hot and red down their naked chests, carrying their lives away with it and pooling on the ground atop the magic circle of powdered bone.

The Old One spoke the words of power and felt the very ground tremble beneath his feet. The magic took hold.

The drums thundered. Thousands of pyluk bulls stood before him, a great mass of green-skinned terrors, their yellow eyes staring, their bald pates glistening. In their hands they clutched their long spears. At the sight of the blood flowing down the men's chests, thousands of jaws lined with sharp teeth opened, and a massive hiss of appreciation rose into the air.

To the rest of the surviving men, now numbering sixty-three, the collective hiss brought on a shudder. This mission to the mountains had long since become the blackest of nightmares.

The Leader had taken Frob, Nump, and Pagliro because they'd fallen behind the day before on the march through these accursed mountains. It was hardly their fault. Their horses were exhausted. But the Old One was not interested in excuses.

This was the pattern that had developed. Each time they stopped, the Leader took two or three men, convicted them of some crime or other, and killed them in this sorcerous fashion.

Then he played his pipes and sent that strange tune echoing away into the hillsides. Soon more of the hideous, terrifying lizard-men would come down and join the swelling mass that had already gathered.

Now the pipes were playing while the giant man danced on the ring of blood. The horde swayed in place and sang with him. A great bubbling drone arose, accompanying the magic pipes.

Soon small groups of new pyluk appeared at the edges of the clearing. Their eyes swelled and popped at the sight of the mass of their own kind awaiting them.

Never had there been a horde like this! The new-comers shook with anticipation. The horde was huge. The prey would be huge, too. There would be gorging. The terrible hunger that dominated their lives would be sated.

The newcomers stared at the cluster of men and hungrily fingered their spears, but pyluk chieftains, wearing woven bibs, stepped forward with harsh barks of dominance. The newcomers crouched submissively.

As soon as the newly arrived pyluk had been mar-shaled into a single group, their Master, Lord Leader, came to them. He stood as tall as a pyluk bull with scalp sacs inflated and loomed before them, wreathed in a cloud of dark glory. Small lightning flashed and flickered above his head. Bright green sparks flared from the tips of his fingers, even from his eyebrows.

The newcomers were awed.

He spoke to them in their own tongue, and his words carried the great magic he had made. Power went out from him and into them, and they became his children, as it was of old.

Chapter 24

Sergeant Rukkh was taking a nap when the first crisis came. It was one of those rare quiet days that left him with an hour free in the afternoon, a perfect opportunity for forty winks. He'd toured his section, checked at the cook shack to check on any problems regarding the evening meal, and then lay down on his cot and pulled the blanket over his head.

The blissful peace was shattered ten minutes later by young Neaps who came hurtling into his tent, shouting about a fight with the monkeys.

"Where?" said Rukkh, sitting up and rubbing his eyes.

"In the woodlot behind the camp. Some of us went over there to get some firewood. There were monkeys there, and they attacked us."

"Damn!" growled Rukkh, now on his feet, automatically buckling his sword around his waist. His perfect afternoon had definitely been ruined.

"Take me there," he snapped, grabbing his helmet as they left the tent. Neaps led at a run. Once they were near the woodlot, Rukkh could hear the fighting, mostly a lot of yelling but with the occasional ring of steel. Rukkh didn't like that. They were supposed to be getting along with the monkeys. They were allies now, even though that seemed crazy to half the men. They were not supposed to be fighting them with drawn swords.

When they finally emerged into a cleared space, he could see the outline of a looming disaster. A dozen men were squared off against a larger mob of monkeys. A few of the men had drawn swords, as had a few monkeys, and with a rush of dismay Rukkh saw that blood had been drawn, for several men and mots were down.

He hurled himself into the fray with a roar of anger, grabbed the nearest men, and threw them back. "Stop it! Stop fighting, now!" he bellowed.

Men put up their swords. These were all boys from the Blitz Regiment, under his command more or less. But they weren't happy with his interference.

"Aw, c'mon, Sarge, we can't back down from a bunch of fornicating monkeys!"

"Yeah, Sarge, they already cut Fidibi bad. He's not gonna make it."

"Shut up!" roared Rukkh, pushing them back, ignoring their protests.

A handful, led by Romioli, were still too pumped up. They wouldn't back away until Rukkh whacked a couple of their helmets with the flat of his sword.

"Romioli, you want to be working on slops the rest of this campaign?" Rukkh snarled as he dragged the offender back.

Romioli finally gave it up as Rukkh's threat sank home.

That left the mob of mots standing there, swords and axes held ready if the fight resumed. Their fur was standing on end, their eyebrows were up, and they looked ready for battle. Rukkh had seen monkeys like this quite a few times now, and the sight gave him the shivers. When they were worked up like this, the monkeys made fierce opponents.

Since his men were all boiling over, too, this confrontation could easily explode again. Worse, other men were running up, itching for a fight. A lot of the soldiers had not really accepted the Emperor's words on this thing. To them, the monkeys were still the enemy.

Meanwhile, the monkeys had sorted out the men and mots who had fallen. All but one mot and one man managed to get back on his feet, albeit a little shakily in some cases. The man was Fidibi, who had a nasty stab wound in the thigh.

"You, Neaps, put a tourniquet on Fidibi. Good and tight," snapped Rukkh. "You, Bemeek, run to the surgeon's tent and make sure he's ready."

Rukkh took a look at the fallen mot, lying there in a pool of blood. That really didn't look good.

"Damned . . . fornicating . . ." sputtered Fidibi while Neaps went to work with a length of thong.

"Shut up, Fidibi!" roared Rukkh, bending down to take a quick look at the wound.

Fidibi was lucky; he would probably live. Rukkh wasn't so sure about the monkey.

"You idiots!" Rukkh growled at his men. "What was the orders, eh? What was they?"

They hung their heads.

"Uh, to, uh, treat the monkeys as allies, Sergeant," said someone in a toneless voice.

"Right! And what do I find? I find you fools have gone and killed one. You'll be lucky if the Emperor doesn't have more than just the skin off your backs, all of you."

More men had joined them. A couple were ready to pitch right in, and Rukkh had to yell at them to desist. A lot more monkeys had come up as well, and they were making excited cries and waving axes, spears, and swords above their heads. Rukkh was starting to feel overwhelmed. Even while he was yelling and pushing the men back, the mass as a whole was still edging toward the monkeys. The men coming up from other regiments didn't know him that well, and they were slow to heed his orders.

Then some big, bald-headed fool from the First Regiment arrived and pitched straight into the monkeys with a roar. He had sword and shield, and he immediately became the center of a knot of monkeys striking back.

He would have gone down in a moment if Rukkh hadn't reached in, grabbed him by the collar, and lugged him out of there.

"What are you doing?" said the aggrieved bald one just before Rukkh slugged him on the chin with a strong right and dropped him. The monkeys stared, then put up their weapons.

Rukkh turned back to the others. "All of you shut up and stand back!"

Neaps and some of the others were carrying Fidibi away.

The fallen mot was being tended to, but it didn't look good. He'd been stabbed in the belly.

More newcomers charged the monkeys. One was knocked headlong by a brilby with an ax handle. The others swung in, cut and hewed, and then jumped back when the monkeys turned on them with a hedge of spear points. The monkeys could have killed the one who was down, but they stepped over him and left him behind.

"Stop it!" Rukkh shoved more men back, knocked down their swords, and cursed them to hell and back.

Still the mass of men edged forward. Their eyes were bulging with hate. They were just itching to let go. After all the disappointments from the fighting of the previous few years, it was impossible not to want to settle old scores.

Rukkh could see with sudden, terrible clarity that he was losing control of the situation. It was all going to dissolve into fresh violence.

Then everything was transformed in the most inexplicable manner. A slim figure, wearing only a singlet and trousers in some monkey-made material, thrust itself into the middle of the fight. When it turned to face him, arms raised, firm breasts jutting out from the chest, Rukkh felt his jaw drop. It was a monkey woman.

The men began to guffaw but were silenced when she spoke in loud and commanding Shashti. "Stop fighting! It is forbidden by the order of your Emperor."

Every man stood rooted to the spot, scarcely able to believe his ears.

"It spoke!" said one in amazement.

"I don't believe it," said another grizzled veteran.

"Believe!" replied the monkey woman. "I speak your language. I learned it while I was held captive in your homeland."

"By the great purple ass," said someone in a stunned voice.

With an effort, Rukkh pulled himself together. Intense, confused whispering was going on among the men who were trying to come to grips with this astonishing new development.

Rukkh pushed forward to meet the mor. "Begging your pardon, uh, miss."

"My name is Nuza. You are an officer?"

"In a manner of speaking, yes," said Rukkh, taken aback by her commanding tone of voice.

"Good, then I hope you can make these men back off. The mots here are very angry. It looks as if poor Jelli will die."

Even as she said this, several mots turned toward Rukkh with rage in their eyes. They pointed down to the fallen mot, still lying in a pool of blood while friends tried to staunch the bleeding.

"They ask why your men do this thing."

"I don't know. I wasn't here." Rukkh felt uncomfortable and defensive.

"They ask why they shouldn't kill all of you."

Rukkh ground his teeth. Damn, it was hard keeping the peace with these monkeys. But he was saved from having to answer by the arrival of a second female figure, this time a human, her head bare, wearing a robe of imperial purple, marking her as Aeswiren's own. That purple required respect from them, though a woman without head covering was a shocking sight.

"What is the meaning of this?" she said in a voice crackling with anger.

Rukkh looked past the purple and realized with a start that it was Simona of the Gsekk. His confusion grew. Her bare head and voice of command aroused all his prejudices against women acting outside the protection of purdah. His first urge was to damn her to hell and tell her to go back inside and stay there. But that imperial purple checked him. She was Aeswiren's confidante, probably his courtesan.

Meanwhile, to his amazement, the monkey woman and Simona had fallen into a lively conversation in the monkey tongue. They embraced, hugging like old friends.

Simona turned back to him. "Sergeant Rukkh, you have done well. I shall report so to the Emperor himself. This is Nuza, personal envoy of General Toshak."

A lifetime of military habits carried Rukkh to safety. He swallowed his first angry reply and made a stiff salute. "Honored to meet you," Rukkh said to the mor, while part of his brain continued to be astonished by the whole mad business—talking to monkeys!

"One thing, Sergeant Rukkh." Simona leaned closer. "We must get this wounded mot to my father's surgery. Perhaps he can be saved; if so, it would be a great help. The Emperor would want this."

Rukkh looked her in the eye. As at their previous meeting, there wasn't a shadow of recognition of their old relationship to be seen there. Still, he knew that she spoke the truth. The Emperor would indeed want this wounded monkey seen to.

"Right!" Rukkh saluted her crisply and spun around.

"You, Peglek, and you, Muhub, get some others and help carry the wounded monkey to the imperial surgery. Improvise a stretcher. Two spears and two cloaks ought to do it, just like on the battlefield. If you're lucky and he survives, I'll recommend you get twenty lashes less than the others are gonna get."

The men leaped into action. In short order, spears and cloaks were lashed together. They stepped forward and laid them on the ground beside the wounded one.

The other mots were listening intently while Nuza explained what was happening. Some were plainly unhappy. They shot angry looks toward the men and held their swords and axes at the ready. But other men bent down and lifted the wounded Jelli onto the improvised stretcher. They lifted it, one at each corner, and bore it away toward the camp.

Some of the monkeys cried out at this, but Nuza shouted to them in their own tongue and they quietened.

Suddenly the men parted as if by a knife. Coming through were three new figures. Rukkh saw men snapping to attention and throwing up the imperial salute. Aeswiren was in the middle of the three.

"At ease, Sergeant Rukkh," said the Emperor in a quiet voice that still carried enough for the men to hear. The Emperor knew who Rukkh was, which was enough to impress some.

"Tell me, Sergeant," said the Emperor, drawing him aside slightly and speaking in a lower tone. "What happened here?"

"As far as I've been able to ascertain, sir, some of

our men came here to cut firewood. They took the wrong direction. Started cutting outside the area designated for us. These, er, allies came over to stop them, and it brewed up into a fight."

"As simple as that, eh?" The Emperor was clearly angry.

"I'm afraid so, Your Majesty. I haven't had time to find out who the hell got it wrong, but when I do, someone will pay."

"Yes, I'm afraid they must. We can't have this, Sergeant. We just can't have it."

They looked up to see they had been joined by yet another small group, this time five mots, all in that effective wicker armor they made. At their head was General Toshak himself.

Aeswiren turned to Toshak and extended a hand. "General, my apologies for this mess. The men strayed over the line. I don't know how or why, but believe me, I intend to find out."

Toshak took Aeswiren's hand. "They have taken the wounded mot, Jelli. Where are they taking him?"

"To the surgery. It was thought that Filek Biswas could save him, if anyone could."

Toshak nodded thoughtfully then issued a stream of orders to the mots on either side. Runners were dispatched at once, bearing messages.

"I have acted to inform all units about this. It is the best way of stopping the spread of stupid rumors."

Aeswiren thanked the gods that he had someone as sensible as Toshak as his ally in command of the native forces.

"That is an excellent idea. I will do the same."

In his surgery, Filek Biswas was surprised by the sudden arrival of the wounded mot. He was also intrigued. As he pulled out the tools of his trade and swabbed them with alcohol to sterilize them, he wondered what he was going to find out about mots.

Surgery was such an interesting exercise sometimes!

Chapter 25

For a day and a half they continued downstream, making good speed most of the time. Thru rowed as much as he could, with help from the chooks, and Iallia took her turn at the oars as well.

After the sun set, they kept going as long as they dared. Thru worried about striking a snag or floating log, so eventually they tied up on the southern shore of the river. Thru was concerned that riders might still be pursuing them down the river road on the far side, so they kept a watch.

Of course, they had nothing to eat, and they were very hungry. In the early morning the chooks foraged in the nearby woods and returned with some wild grapes and some plump beetles in their beaks.

Iallia ate the grapes but spurned the beetles. Thru accepted both gladly. Dunni wept at times for his poor Pikka, and when he could, Thru sat by the crestfallen chook and did his best to comfort him. Thru also saw that Iallia did the same while Thru worked the oars. The bereaved rooster was a forlorn sight, hunched down in the bow of the boat, feathers ungroomed, comb deflated.

They passed down a long reach of the river amid dense forest and reached the abandoned village of Groote Humly. They stopped briefly and foraged for scraps of food. They found some bushpod and some dried curd, and they ate this as they rowed on.

In the afternoon, they endured a brief shower that drenched them and then left them floating in a thick mist. Thru noticed that the current's pace was slackening, and after a while, as the mist burned off, they found themselves drifting through a wild-water swamp.

Humly water was the largest area of wilderness on the middle Dristen, ten miles of meanders, bogs, and pools where waterfowl in vast numbers lived and bred. The woods receded on either side and were replaced by huge stands of reeds and bullrushes. The clean smell of the river was replaced by the dank odor of the swamp, and, wherever trees grew, they were thickly festooned with the huge nests of ospreys, fish eagles, and herons.

"If we get through this today, we'll get into the reach of the river above the Cleansdale. After that we'll be in the lower Dristen."

"And then we'll be home," said Iallia happily.

Thru said nothing to dampen her spirits. Whether they had homes to ever return to was still in doubt.

Iallia took over the oars then, and Thru curled up to sleep in the back of the boat. In his exhausted state he slept longer than he should have, and when he awoke, he found that Iallia had lost the main channel and taken them off into a backwater.

They turned around at once but were confronted by a swarm of small islands with no clear route to the main channel. They struggled through narrow, twisting channels, oxbows, and dead water. Before long, they managed to ground the boat on a snag in quicksand. It took the best part of an hour to free themselves and to work the boat back out of the dead water.

By then the sun was halfway down the western sky. Thru took stock and then used its position to guide them back toward the main channel. Keeping their course to the east as much as possible, they wound their way through the reeds. Huge flocks of geese and

ducks rose from the quiet backwaters as they pushed
along. For an hour or more, they worked their way in
and out of narrow, snaking streams, hidden beneath
great stands of reeds and bullrushes, each time recoil-
ing in frustration from another dead end, and then, at
last, they found a wider channel that gave onto a lake.
From that they found another channel that eventually
rejoined the main river. With the sun sinking toward
the treetops, they hurried west once more, having lost
half a day in the wild water.

Darkness was falling as they came around a bend
and discerned a bridge across the river a mile downstream.

"What village must this be?" wondered Thru, trying
to recall where in the middle Dristen they were.

The chooks had no idea, for they were from an
upland village far to the east and had never ventured
this far from home before. Iallia thought it must be
Meadow Mill, and she pointed to a large building,
visible by its square bulk against the sky on the southern side of the river.

"That must be the mill."

Most of the village was on the northern side, where
the river road ran, and Thru recalled that he had
found food in this village on his trek upriver to the
mountains.

If it was indeed Meadow Mill, they were close to
the top of the Cleansdale. Past that they would enter
the lower Dristen.

As they drew closer, Thru studied the huddle of
houses, dimly visible in the darkness. Not a light
showed, nor could he detect any smoke. The inhabitants had yet to return.

He kept the boat moving straight for the bridge,
which had two arches and a central pillar of stone. He
chose the western channel and let the current take
them down the last stretch before it.

The bulk of the mill rose up beside them, its water-wheel turning slowly, with moonlit spillage scattering down its side. Thru was so taken with this beauty that he didn't see the movement above them on the bridge. Suddenly Mukka screamed. Arrows flashed down into the boat and the water at their side.

Thru looked up, saw the gleam of teeth, heard the hiss of arrows. The right-side oar was knocked from his hand and a shaft sprouted there instead. Without missing a beat, he took the other oar and poled the boat away from the central pillar and under the cover of the bridge.

Mukka was hurt, and Chenk was crying in alarm. Iallia almost fell out of the boat when she stood up. Then a second boat appeared, swinging in from downstream, with men aboard and a faint gleam of steel in the dark.

Thru ducked instinctively and felt the whisper of an arrow past his head. As he came back up he pulled the oar from the water and swung it from the hips and felt it slam home, knocking the archer in the other boat off his feet.

A moment later, the two boats rammed into each other hard, and everyone still standing fell down.

Thru pulled himself up. The chooks were crying, and Iallia was still struggling to right herself. He found the oar, seized it, and poled the boat toward the mill wheel. The men were cursing; one of them had fallen in and was splashing furiously.

"The boat is sinking," said Iallia in alarm. A moment later, Thru felt the water rising to his ankles in the bottom of the boat.

"Onto the mill wheel. Ride it to the top," he said.

"The chooks?"

"I don't know. Can you help them?"

The boat banged into the mill wheel and began to spin away. Thru grabbed hold of one of the wheel's

ribs and was hauled into the air. He moved hand over
hand to the side of the wheel, and as it tilted up he
swung a leg over onto one of the paddles. In another
moment, he was borne to the top of the wheel, where
he jumped off onto the gallery that ran around the
mill house.

The gallery overlooked the bridge. Two archers
were standing there, aiming down into the boat. At
that range, they couldn't miss. Thru didn't hesitate but
hurled himself off the gallery directly at them. He
heard a shout, and as he slammed into the nearest
fellow they all went down in a heap.

The impact was bone-jarring, but there was no time
to waste trying to get his breath back. Somehow he
got to his knees. One of the men had rolled over and
was pushing himself up. The other had hold of Thru's
shoulder. There was a flash of steel, and Thru twisted
away just as the knife came down. He flung out a
hand, felt the man's face under his palm, and pushed
him away. The knife missed again.

Thru got his feet under him. The other man was
back up, drawing a short stabbing sword. They came
together. Thru reacted with the kyo moves he had
learned so well from Master Sassadzu at Highnoth.
The sword missed his belly, but his fist snapped into
the man's throat.

The first man kicked Thru's legs out from under
him, and he fell heavily. Rolling desperately, he
avoided the stamping blow aimed at his throat. He
started to get up, but the man caught him with a heavy
kick to the ribs that knocked him over. He saw the
knife in the man's hand and realized he might die here
and all his efforts would have been in vain. Again he
struggled up, but the man's boot quickly lashed out.
Thru tried to grab it and twist the leg, but he was too
slow. The man loomed over him. The knife swung
down.

Suddenly a big ball of white and yellow feathers cannoned into the back of the man's legs, throwing him off balance. Thru kicked upward, felt his foot connect, and the man fell. Two chooks hurled themselves on top of him, delivering hefty kicks with rooster claws. Iallia appeared as well, with the other man's sword in her hand.

The men were down and not likely to get up soon. Thru took a bow and found it heavier than a mot bow but usable. He tore a quiver free from the man he'd punched in the throat.

"Hurry," he said to the two roosters, who were helping the wounded Mukka get down from the mill house gallery. An arrow jutted up from her back between the shoulders. Thru was amazed that Mukka had managed to get up the mill wheel.

"Mukka is hurt," said Chenk angrily.

"How bad is it?" Thru bent down beside the wounded chook.

Mukka winced but held her head up. "Pull out the arrow," she said, "and I will fight!"

Thru grinned. "That's the spirit," he said. "Now, hold your breath for a moment. This will hurt." He took hold of the shaft and eased the arrowhead out of Mukka's back. She gave a single sharp cry and then was silent. A moment later, the arrow came free.

"There," said Thru, breaking the shaft and hurling it away. "It did not go so deep."

Mukka's sides were heaving, but she made no further sound.

Thru examined the wound. There was a little flow of blood, but nothing life threatening. The arrowhead had not severed a major blood vessel.

"We will treat the wound later, when we have more time."

"More men are coming," said Iallia, pointing toward the village. Horsemen could be seen charging past the houses.

"Into the woods," Thru called out as he headed past the mill to the dark mass of the trees.

They ran, chooks in the lead, Thru at the rear, carrying the bow and an arrow in his hand and the quiver over his shoulder. Having a bow, even an unfamiliar one made by men, gave him renewed confidence. Let the riders come after him in these trees—he would make them pay.

They emerged onto a narrow lane that ran between woodlots on one side and vegetable gardens on the other. The gardens were fenced and terraced down to the river's edge in a style that was common in the middle sections of most rivers in the Land.

Thru urged them off the lane and into the woodlots. Progress was slower, but they were less likely to be seen by the pursuit.

The darkness was complete, and they slowed even further as they worked their way through dense stands of young trees on woodlots that had been clear-cut in recent years. The big white and yellow birds went first, and Iallia and Thru followed.

They had gone perhaps a mile when they heard the riders coming down the lane, horse hooves pounding, men calling encouragement to one another. Not far from the little band, someone struck a light, and a lantern was lit. Men were dismounting. Another party of men came down the lane.

Thru clearly heard a commander say, "Find them: The Master wants them dead or alive."

Thru understood that the enemy knew the information they carried was vital and was determined to prevent them from bringing it back to General Toshak.

A second lantern was lit, then a third. More men pushed into the woodlots. Thru, Iallia, and the three chooks retreated deeper into the trees, away from the river. Ahead, Thru could sense the ground was rising toward the hills that bound the valley.

The men came on, one group upstream of them,

another downstream, both working into the woods
with lanterns raised to guide themselves.

Thru considered shooting the men holding the lanterns, but he held his fire since it would confirm
their presence.

They came to a shoulder-high fence of poles with
another lane beyond it. The woodlots gave way to a
strip of polder created where an old outlier of the
swamp had once curled between the trees. The water-
brush had been harvested, so there was no cover.

The fence was an obstacle for the chooks, who had
to be helped over. Mukka in particular found it difficult. Just as Iallia and Thru were helping her across,
they were spotted by some of the men in the woods.

Thru vaulted over and sent the others hurrying
down the road. He himself took aim at the man carrying the lantern. His first shaft went wide, but not
by much. His second arrow struck home, and he was
rewarded with a shriek and the sight of the lantern
falling to the ground and going out.

The other men were still coming, though, and Thru
took to his heels down the rutted lane.

The strip of polder continued for half a mile before
giving way to woods once more. Thru glanced back.
Men were climbing over the fence. Then he saw a
lantern emerge from the woodlot on the right farther
down, ahead of the chooks. Men were climbing over
there as well.

"Into the polder!" Thru shouted.

The chooks needed no further encouragement. They
were already on their way. Iallia leaped down behind
the chooks and ran after them.

Thru strung an arrow, took aim, and let fly at the
men firing at the chooks. The range was extreme but
his shaft came down among them and caused them to
halt and take shelter back behind the fence.

With men coming up from behind, he couldn't stay

where he was. He, too, was forced onto the polder. He crouched low, arrow nocked, knowing that the men were watching the fleeing chooks, still dimly visible in the dark.

The men were being more cautious now. One of them had already paid for being overbold, and so they had no lantern. Thru heard them arguing over what to do.

"One of them's got a bow. Hornsli's dead for sure."

"Can't see a damn thing."

"Over there!" came another voice. "Come on."

The group of men lurched forward into the polder, and Thru rose up and sent an arrow into their midst. One of them screamed and stumbled coughing into the muck.

The others turned toward the mot.

"There's one! After him! Get his head!"

Thru fired again but missed, and then he had to run. An arrow sang past his ear as he dodged through the waterbush stumps.

"Kill him!" screamed a man from behind.

Far ahead, bouncing through the rows, he could see the chooks and Iallia. Beyond them a darker mass in the general murk delineated the hedge at the far side of the polder. He increased his pace, splashing through the muck. But he could hear the men, close behind him, and they were gaining. Another arrow zipped past, too close for comfort.

The chooks and Iallia reached the trees and disappeared. Thru concentrated on pushing himself the last few yards. He launched his body into the air, seeking to dive over the hedge and into the woods beyond.

His stomach briefly scraped the top of the hedge. His leg caught, and he fell heavily on the other side.

As he lay there partly stunned, bodies all around him rose up. In sudden terror he struggled to get to his feet, but a calm voice said, "Stay down, brother.

We're ready for them." And he saw that he was surrounded by mots in the uniform of the army of Dronned.

They had found a patrol.

The mots stood up, leveled their bows, and released at short range. Screams erupted from the charging men, taken by surprise. The mots surged over the hedge and pitched into the men. Soon they had them running for their lives back across the polder.

Thru allowed himself to be guided into the woods by another mot.

"This is Captain Dinan's patrol group. We've been looking for any sign of the riders that went up into the mountains."

Behind them came more shouting as the victorious mots gathered back at the hedge.

"I am Colonel Gillo, on a mission for General Toshak himself. I have vital information that must reach the general as soon as possible."

"Then you have found the right unit, Colonel. I will take you to Captain Dinan at once."

Chapter 26

"Thank you, gentlemen. You know the situation, and I know how you're feeling. Let's get on with our business."

The Emperor stood up and left the table in the big tent. His senior officers filed out, heads filled with potential battle plans plus a few reinforcements of Aeswiren's favorite dictums during this campaign, mostly concerning the need to get along with the native people.

Tempers had improved over the past few days. The fight in the woodlot had helped concentrate everyone's thoughts on the essential problem of getting former enemies to cooperate. Six men had received forty lashes apiece. Aeswiren was not overly fond of the lash, but sometimes it was necessary. He had the feeling that the men understood that, too.

Thankfully, Filek Biswas had saved the injured mot, Jelli, who was recovering in Nuza's hospital. During heroic surgery, Biswas had repaired the mot's intestines and sewed him up after cleaning the wounds with alcohol. The mot had survived all this, and Filek gave him a good chance of surviving. Following the news that Jelli would probably recover, there was a marked warming of relations with the mots.

Aeswiren was quite encouraged by the situation, in fact. The regiments were drilled, practiced, and ready, and from what he understood from his informants their morale was pretty good. Plus the grumbling about fighting alongside the monkeys had declined. Eating big, regular meals, courtesy of those same "monkeys," had helped quite a bit, of course.

While he was crossing between tents, he caught sight of Sergeant Rukkh, lurking as inconspicuously as possible at the side of the small white tent where the Emperor's personal staff worked. Aeswiren turned to Klek.

"See that Sergeant Rukkh is brought to me at once."

"Yes, Lord."

Once inside his own tent, Aeswiren kicked off his boots and hung up his jacket. As always on campaign, he wore the same military-issue clothes as his men. He kept the gold-plated breastplate only for those occasions when he had to give a formal address.

On the floor of the tent was spread a magnificent woven mat, a gift from the burghers of Dronned. It depicted a group of mots praying at a shrine. Their upturned faces were illuminated in yellow light, and their surroundings were rendered with remarkable skill. The weave was sumptuous, giving him the same sense of well being that he always got from a nice Nisjani carpet back in Shasht.

Servants brought in some hot biscuits and tea, and the Emperor took a few minutes to eat. At the same time, he went through the stack of messages that had piled up over the past few hours.

The bell attached to the front flap of his tent tinkled. The guard looked in. "Sergeant Rukkh to see you, Lord."

"Good."

The sergeant entered, saluted, and stood at ease, as he had done on many occasions since Aeswiren had recruited him as an informant.

"Tea, Sergeant?"

"Thank you, Lord. You asked for a report on the aftermath of the fight in the woodlot."

"Ah, yes."

Tea was poured and sipped, and then, and only then, was Rukkh allowed to proceed.

"The wounded are recovering well, Lord. The ones with stripes on their backs, too. The general feeling is that it was all just a big stupid mistake. Considering all the history between us, everyone feels that something like this was inevitable. But nobody got killed, and so the whole thing is now becoming a bit of a joke. Meanwhile, everyone is eager to get this campaign over with before winter sets in. If that means a real fight, then all the better."

"And everyone understands that we'll be fighting against men like ourselves?"

"Of course, Lord, everyone knows that."

Aeswiren mulled these words over for a moment. "Well, this is good news you have brought me, Sergeant. Thank you."

Rukkh was turning to go when the bell tinkled again. The guard lifted the flap. "Lord, it is your messenger from the city."

"Show her in. Remain, Sergeant, I want you to meet this person."

A moment later, Nuza entered, wearing a hooded robe to disguise herself, almost as if she were a woman of Shasht wearing the cloth of purdah. Aeswiren noticed that Rukkh stiffened at the sight of her.

Rukkh had the prejudices of his people, thought Aeswiren.

Nuza pulled back her hood.

"It's the monkey woman," said Rukkh without thinking. "Begging your pardon, Lord."

Aeswiren did not react to the slur. He knew it would take time to change the minds of men. "Sergeant Rukkh, this is Nuza of Tamf. She is a good friend of mine. We met while she was in captivity."

"Lord, I have met her myself. At the fight in the woodlot."

"Yes, you were both there when I arrived. I should've known you'd have met."

Nuza reached out to take his hand. "Greetings, Sergeant Rukkh. You were the hero of that stupid business."

For a moment, Rukkh was struck dumb, just as he had been back at the fight in the woodlot. Rukkh had seen a lot of monkeys, but never one like this. The world was turning upside down in poor Rukkh's head.

Aeswiren grinned. Nuza had that effect on men. The combination of her beauty and the odd differences between her and a beautiful woman could be very disturbing.

Nuza turned to the Emperor. "However, I must cut this short. I bring very important news. This comes directly from General Toshak." She handed Aeswiren a small scroll, fastened in the mot manner.

"What is it?" asked Aeswiren, then, seeing her hesitate, added. "You can speak in front of the sergeant. He will be hearing about it soon enough, I expect."

"Lord, Thru Gillo has returned from the mountains. He saw our enemy perform magic and recruit an army of pyluk."

Many clues suddenly slid into place for Aeswiren.

"Damn. He's raised an army of these, um, lizards?"

"Yes, Lord. Pyluk stand taller than mots, or men, and carry club and spear."

"Well, that explains the mysterious landing party." Aeswiren broke the seal and snapped open the scroll. "I thought those things were uncontrollable. They eat their own young, don't they?"

"That they eat each other helps keep their own numbers down," said Nuza in a cold voice. "They are predators, nothing more. They cannot be reasoned with."

Rukkh finally found his voice. "Pyluk are the lizard things we've heard about that live in the east?"

"Yes, have you seen them?"

"A couple were captured back in the first year. Big, fierce-looking things, like no animal I ever saw."

"That's right."

"Didn't think they could form an army."

"Spears and clubs, according to our informant here," said the Emperor.

"Big brutes, heavily muscled. Funny flaps on their heads that inflated when we teased them up a bit."

"An army?" pondered Aeswiren aloud, rubbing his chin. "Probably don't have real military discipline. Be useful for a single all-out attack. A wild charge to panic us."

Rukkh understood. "Yes, sir, I see the point. But they'll not be a surprise to us now."

"Yes, Colonel Gillo has seen to that."

"Still going to be a bit of a handful, Lord. An army of big lizards like that."

"Yes, Sergeant, we will see how sorcery does against discipline."

"Yes, Lord," said Rukkh. "We've faced sorcery here before. I think we've learned a few lessons. We won't be fooled again."

Rukkh left with instructions to pass on the news of the pyluk army. Aeswiren wanted the men ready for this new foe.

"And, my dear, how goes the hospital?"

"We have fifty-six nurses, all with some training. Surgeon Biswas is teaching twelve of us the skills of basic surgery."

"You've moved very quickly. I wish I could come and see the place."

"We've already taken over two whole buildings on

Fleek Street. They were tenements owned by the King."

Aeswiren nodded. "I had heard that the King is a great patron of yours."

"It couldn't have been done without his help. The Queen, too, has been very helpful. She is quite influential behind the scenes in the city."

Once again the guard called from the front of the tent.

A message was brought in from Admiral Heuze. Aeswiren opened it and rubbed his hands together.

"The enemy has made his move. Their fleet is sailing north."

Chapter 27

Drums were beating from Dronned to the Dristen. Clouds of dust rose from the narrow roads as the regiments of Toshak's army moved north. Morale in the regiments was high, though the excitement was tempered by grim experience. Half the army was made up of veterans of the previous campaigns. They knew what facing men in battle was like.

While the regiments marched north, civilians flooded south, along with a tide of game animals. Again and again, to the amazement of one regiment or another, a herd of elk or deer would suddenly flood the road, fleeing the dreadful rumor of the pyluk.

Behind the mot army, Aeswiren's army, nine thousand battle-tested men, was also on the march. The two forces kept a distance of two hours march between them, which Toshak estimated gave them the greatest flexibility. Meanwhile, he had sent scouts out across the middle Dristen and up in the northern hills seeking contact with the oncoming pyluk horde.

The enemy's plan was obvious to everyone. He would land his human forces on the shore somewhere north of the Dristen and seek to link up with the pyluk horde as it poured westward. Pyluk could not be used for disciplined battlefield maneuvers, but they would serve as a battering ram, to break a defensive line. Equally clear was Toshak's objective; to catch one of these forces alone and smash it before they could join together.

Thru Gillo hurried northward, passing the regiments along the road. He'd left the hospital in Dronned that morning after completing several days of rest and recuperation. Nuza had supervised his rest herself, relieved that he had survived the journey into the mountains.

She had also seen to the care of Iallia and the chooks. Mukka was recuperating from her wound. The roosters were lodged in Fleek Street. Dunni was still inconsolable over the loss of his Pikka. Iallia had recovered her own strength quite quickly and had volunteered to help in the hospital.

With his cuts and scrapes starting to scab over, Thru knew his place was at Toshak's side. He was basically fit to travel. He held the rank of colonel, and he had more combat experience than most. Plus he had the best working knowledge of the language of men of anyone in the Land. He shouldn't be skulking in bed. Knowing that Nuza would try to stop him, he slipped away after breakfast, leaving a note for her.

Back on the trail again, he marveled at what a few days of rest and some solid meals had done to put strength back into his limbs. The feeling of being half dead was gone.

Soon he came on the rear elements of Toshak's army. Lines of wagons and donkey carts, with their drovers cussing the animals to keep them moving through the muddy conditions. Passing the regiments, acknowledging salutes from mots who saw the red pin of his rank on his collar, hearing the cheers, Thru sensed the excitement that infused the army. Instead of an endless conflict, they faced a final battle, and they were sure they would win. General Toshak always won.

There were all sorts of rumors, too. That night he slept on the trail with units from the Fourth Regiment. Around the campfire the talk was all about the horde of pyluk that were coming to fight on the enemy's behalf. Some mots scoffed, others expressed unease, but few admitted to fear. Thru knew very well the capabilities of the pyluk, but he also knew that a disciplined force could defeat them. Toshak had made that clear from the beginning of Thru's military education. A disciplined force would always defeat an undisciplined force, as long as it held its formations and kept its nerve. Still, fighting off a column of pyluk would be a fearsome task. Before he drifted off to sleep, he recalled his own experiences with the pyluk back in the Farblow Hills.

Too tired to dream, he slept through until dawn, then awoke, grabbed some breakfast, and went on up the road. He came over the South Hill before noon and found the village of Warkeen bustling as it had never bustled before. Lines of tents were set up in the fields. Hundreds of mots, donkey carts, and oxen were packed into the road leading to the bridge. The village smithy was going full blast, and every hammer in the shop was in use.

Cooking fires were lit in every house and every courtyard, too. The village was serving as cookshop to the army as it passed through. Thru kept his eyes open but saw no sign of any of the villagers, or his own family. But, with their house burned to the ground, they would have had no strong reason to return yet. Thru suspected they would all be with his mother's relatives in Dronned country, south of the city.

Of course, the mystery about the odd pattern of burned houses in the village had been cleared up the moment Iallia told Thru about Pern Treevi's presence among the enemy. He was still musing on the strange malevolence that had taken hold of Pern, as he came up the hill to the big house that Pern had built for Iallia Tramine.

It was still too big, even ugly by the standards of

Warkeen village. A big slab of a place, with all the trees cut down to give it room.

But, ugly or not, it had its uses. General Toshak had set up his command center there, because it had room enough for his staff to work in one place.

Thru gave his name to the guards at the door and was soon beckoned inside. He found Toshak looking over an area map with with three regimental colonels.

Toshak looked up, saw Thru, and gave a cry of welcome. He came around the table and shook both Thru's hands. "Welcome back, Colonel Gillo, the hero of the hour."

"Thank you, General. I was not alone on the trek."

"Indeed, we have read the whole thing. Chooks helping you row! It sounded impossible, but I'll take your word for it."

"Without them we would never have got out of the mountains."

"Congratulations, Colonel," said the closest colonel on his right, Reetti of the First Regiment.

Thru thanked them making no effort at false modesty. The trek to the mountains had been arduous and dangerous, and he had survived. There was no point in pretending to anything else.

"How was the hospital?" asked Toshak, drawing Thru over to the table.

"A busy place, but what would we expect, with Nuza running it? I slept for three days, then I woke up and started eating."

"Expect you were pretty hungry by then."

"Couldn't stop, even though it was the same three things every day."

"You weren't expecting to dine in the manner of the Land, were you?"

"Nothing is up to that standard anymore," said Reetti with a sigh.

"The hospital is a great step forward for us. We are

indebted to the surgeon Filek Biswas for his inspiration."

"Besides the chooks, there was a mor in your party, I believe," said another colonel, Vleveld of the Third Regiment.

"Yes, indeed. She once lived in this very house. In fact, it was built for her by Pern Treevi."

Toshak caught the name and growled. "The mot who has gone over to the enemy?"

"Yes."

"It is hard to believe that anyone would go over to the men," said Reetti.

"Pern Treevi hated his own village. If anyone could do this, it would be him."

Toshak was nodding. He had personal experience of Treevi's hate. "Every village has a lockup, even if it's only a single room and not used one year to the next."

"Indeed, General, but to take up arms against your own race. It seems beyond the pale."

"No argument there, Colonel. Now, Gillo, take a look at this map. You grew up here, so you will know if my mapmakers got it right."

Thru cast his eye over the map. Cormorant Rock and the river Shell were the northern limit, South Hill the southern. Inland it ran as far as Juno village.

"The wild water below Juno village isn't quite as big as they have it there. Also, there's a trail that runs around this hill, which is called Stag's Head by some and the Dunnet by others. It's a useful trail, but it's not marked here. There's a pond here and another one here that aren't on the map."

For a few minutes Thru went over the map, indicating things he knew were wrong. Mostly they were minor details, like Anglu's Pond on Swamp Hill. Toshak listened carefully while his eyes seemed to devour the map, imprinting it on his mind. Colonel Reetti wrote little notes on the map where Thru indicated changes should be made.

When he was done, Toshak made a final inspection. "Good. The mapmakers did well, but we have just seen how important local knowledge of the ground can be, eh?"

The colonels nodded in agreement.

Toshak's hand moved to brush the estuary of the river Shell, just north of Cormorant Rock. "Here's a good place for making a landing, eh? There's only a single bridge, and the river is wide enough to be impassable at high tide. We will move some of our strength north to be ready, just in case."

The colonels made ready to depart, but Toshak asked Thru to remain behind. When they were alone, Toshak rolled up the map.

"Well, Thru Gillo, are you ready to return to active duty?"

"Yes, sir."

"Would you like a regiment to command?"

"Well, sir, of course, I am trained for that."

"Indeed, you are, Colonel. Better than most of my officers in this army. You've even commanded an army."

Thru blinked but did not deny the charge. He had been forced to take command of half the army of Sulmo when its commander was slain at the battle of Chenna.

"Did a very good job, too. Your escape from Chenna is used in our training courses now."

Thru blinked again; this time from surprise.

"But before your head starts to swell too much, I've got to tell you that I'm not giving you a regiment to command. There's a surplus of regimental commanders now, and you, my friend, have unique skills."

Thru nodded. It was what he'd expected. He'd been Toshak's chief emissary to Aeswiren for months.

"Indeed, you are the perfect mot for this next job. I want you to accompany Utnapishtim to a meeting with the Great King of Shasht. Utnapishtim will explain to the Emperor why he should send his fleet to Sulmo."

"To Sulmo?"

"Sulmo promises four thousand mots under the command of General Ter-Saab."

"General Ter-Saab," Thru repeated. "Excellent choice."

"I thought you'd say that."

Simona knew she was impressing the Emperor as she marched behind him among his personal staff. She kept up easily, did not tire, and was fresh enough to chat with him in the mot language at the end of the day.

"Where did you learn to endure like this, Simona of the Gsekk?"

As usual, he was disarmingly frank with her. His eyes were twinkling.

"During the winter in Shasht, when I was alone with Thru Gillo."

The Emperor's nod had contained an element of respect that she had not seen before. "This mot, Gillo, he's a remarkable fellow. His latest adventure brought us warning in good time about this threat of the, um, pyluk."

"He is an artist, did you know?"

Aeswiren smiled again. "Yes, the Assenzi told me. He weaves fine mats. His work is held in high esteem, I was told."

"Oh, yes, Lord. I once saw him weave a pattern on an old loom out of old thread he found locked up in a summerhouse."

"Mmm, tell me more."

She did, with the ease of their accepted familiarity,

even though he was the Emperor of all Shasht and she was but a young woman of a minor aristocratic family. They spoke the language of the Land and occasionally added Shashti words when their mot vocabulary fell short.

The next day, Aeswiren had her march with him for part of the way. The road was typical for the Land: six feet wide, cobbled in the lower lying areas, and left as gravel elsewhere. It wound around the crags, through undulating terrain covered in juniper, laurel, and dwarf pine.

As usual, the Emperor turned the conversation to his brother, Mentupah, with whom she had spent so many months during the voyage from Shasht. He asked her many questions, and Simona could hear the guilty anguish in his voice. She answered honestly, as Aeswiren had always requested that she do, and spared him nothing.

Later, while they were awaiting tea and some hot biscuits, word came that emissaries from General Toshak had come to see the Emperor.

When they entered the tent, Simona was excited to see Thru Gillo was one of them. The other was the ancient Assenzi Utnapishtim. Aeswiren, alone among his staff, showed no unease in the presence of the Assenzi.

"Greetings, ancient Master," said the Emperor with a smile and hands held out in greeting. "What brings you here?"

"Thank you for your warm welcome, Emperor Aeswiren. I have a message from General Toshak, which should be for your ears alone."

"I see. Come closer." Aeswiren waved to his staff, who withdrew a discreet distance.

Utnapishtim turned to Simona. "And greetings to you, Simona of the Gsekk. It is unusual for a woman of Shasht to march with the army."

"Greetings, Utnapishtim. I march at the Emperor's request, of course."

"Of course. And you know Colonel Gillo, do you not?"

The ancient being's words were lost on her, for she was staring at Thru's face while a train of memories and emotions played in her mind.

She remembered his scars, which could inflame and grow white when he was gripped by excitement. And his eyes, their alien greyness and keen but friendly intelligence. And then there was his fur. That fur, which she had once clutched to herself, naked in a cave.

"Hello, Simona," the mot greeted her.

For a moment, she struggled to speak. "It is so good to see you again, Thru. It has been too long."

They reached out to grasp each other's hands, then became aware of the interest they had inspired in both Utnapishtim and Aeswiren and drew back with bashful smiles.

"I'm sorry, Lord," said Simona.

"No, not at all," Aeswiren replied, beaming. "It is heartwarming to see such friendship. It is what I hope for between our peoples."

Simona wondered what Aeswiren would say if he knew the truth, the whole truth, about her and Thru. "Thank you, Lord." She bowed low to cover her temporary confusion.

She and Thru drew aside while Utnapishtim moved closer to the Emperor to speak of the need to send some of Heuze's ships south to Sulmo.

While the Emperor was engaged, Thru passed on the details to Simona in a quiet voice. "There are four thousand mots waiting, all volunteers."

Simona knew that these mots were overcoming deep-seated fears of men's ships. "After all that has happened, with all the infamy that is associated with those ships, I find it very touching that these mots are prepared to do that."

Thru smiled for a moment. "Well, they might not be prepared to go aboard those ships alone, but a thousand strong and well armed is a different matter."

"I hope they get here in time to help us. Aeswiren's army is not as strong as it once was."

Thru was quick to reassure her. "There will be time. Neither side can afford defeat, and it is to our advantage to hold off from battle. We do not wish to take risks. Our enemy has a problem with feeding his army, and they will go hungry soon. When they are starving, that is when Toshak will strike."

Simona nodded. The great mot general was known for daring moves and bold execution, but she could see the logic in this caution.

Everyone knew what the coming fight represented. If the enemy won, not only would the mots of the Land be exterminated, but the men of Shasht would forever groan beneath the heel of the Old One. Caution was the only sensible policy.

Utnapishtim and the Emperor were still engrossed. A scribe was writing a message for Aeswiren. Another was drawing up a schedule.

"I heard that you were back aboard the *Sea Wasp* with Mentu."

"Toshak asked me to return to duty."

"How is the ship?"

"As good as ever she was. Mentu is much the same, too."

"And Janbur?"

Thru shrugged. He knew that Janbur had sought to court Simona and had been turned down. "He is quieter. He has lost much, and he feels it. But I think he is happier now."

"And poor Juf?"

"Ah, now there's a happy mot. He drinks no wine

or even beer, and he never talks about the life before
the men came. But he loves roaming the seas."

"I am so glad to hear that he has found some kind
of peace. After he lost his family and everything."

They looked each other in the eye. Aeswiren and
Utnapishtim were still in deep discussion.

"And how are you, Thru?"

She saw the weariness plain in his face. After that
long winter in which they had lived together in very
close quarters, she knew his face so well she could
read him just as if he were a man. Living with him
for those months, and the voyage on the *Sea Wasp*
that came afterward, had dissolved the line between
man and mot for her.

"You know me, Simona. When this is over I will
retire to my loom and stay there."

"With dear Nuza." There, she'd said it.

He glanced at Utnapishtim again, then back to her.
"We survived, Simona. You and I, who have seen and
done so much. Who by rights should have starved to
death in those hills."

"Yes, Thru, and more than that. We have grown
wise."

A handclap interrupted them. They looked up to
see that Aeswiren had summoned a messenger.

"Take this to Admiral Heuze," the Emperor said.

The messenger hurried away.

Utnapishtim turned to Thru. The Assenzi was
clearly satisfied. "I leave for Sulmo on the tide. It has
been good to see you once more, Thru Gillo, and you,
Simona of the Gsekk."

The huge, ancient eyes seemed to probe them both
for a moment. Simona wondered if Utnapishtim had
even a glimmering of what had gone on between her
and Thru.

"With luck, I will be back with enough reinforcements from Sulmo to ensure our victory over our evil

enemy," Utnapishtim said by way of a farewell, and left the tent.

The Emperor wasn't quite finished with Thru Gillo, however. With a smile he called him to his side.

"Colonel Gillo, I have been meaning to ask you about my brother's state of mind, but we have both been too busy. So, if you don't mind, now that we finally have a moment to spare, I will ask after Mentu."

"Yes, Great King, I know your brother."

"Oh, you know him a lot better than I do. All I know about him now is that he hates me, the brother who kept him alive all these years."

"You put him in prison for twenty years. He is bitter about that."

"If I had left him to live in the village as a fisherman, he'd have been kidnapped in the first year. If it wasn't done by someone angling for the throne, it would've been done by our enemy. Mentu looks so much like me, he could be easily passed off as me."

Thru nodded soberly. "Actually, he looks younger than you."

Aeswiren started, then chuckled. Thru Gillo had yet to learn flattery, and for the Emperor it was refreshing.

"Ah, yes, perfectly true, I'm sure. He lived a quiet life in that tower while I fought to keep the Empire in one piece. But, if I had brought him to the city, he would have been seduced by evil men with designs on the throne."

Aeswiren paused a moment, caught Thru's look, and smiled. "I see you are outraged by this idea. Look, I know Mentu is a good fellow. He would have tried to resist, but such men would stop at nothing. There would have been the constant threat of their machinations."

"Yes, Great King, so he has told me himself."

"So he knows I had no choice except to put him away somewhere or have him killed. Heaven knows, many men would not have shrunk from that task, and Mentupah would have been dead these past twenty-three years and more.

"But, even though he knows this, he will not even come to my side to embrace me, his only brother. His Emperor!"

"Lord, he once told me that he didn't know if you would ever let him leave again. 'My brother has a tight grip,' he said. 'Once he has you, he never lets you go.' "

The Emperor sighed. "Mentu is perfectly correct. Being at the center of great power changes everything, including the way one must show love for one's brother. After all is said and done, my brother and I appear to be sundered forever. I could send men to kill him and rid myself of a danger, but I will not. That kind of evil counsel I reject utterly. So, he will stay on that boat of his, and I will leave him to it. He is a good seaman, no question of that."

"Yes, Lord."

"Ach. It breaks my heart. You first met him at that tower I sent him to, I believe."

"Yes, Great King. He saved my skin. I was on the run, and if they'd taken me, I'd have been for it one way or another."

"You must understand that I never bore my brother any ill will. I put him in that tower to keep him alive."

"Lord, I think Mentu fears you more than he hates you."

Someday," murmured Aeswiren, "I hope I can make my peace with Mentu."

The following days were filled with tension and rumor. Toshak and Aeswiren continued to hold their position around the Dristen Valley, while four of

Heuze's ships were sent south to Sulmo. The weather deteriorated, and for three solid days there was constant rain and driving wind. Movement became difficult, almost impossible, as roads and trails turned to mud.

Finally, when the skies cleared on the third day, it was learned that the enemy fleet had vanished. An immediate search was begun. Heuze sent out his frigates, accompanied by a swarm of native cogs. For a while, the hope was harbored that the enemy fleet had ended up on the rocks, perhaps on the Alberr Isles, whose western approaches were treacherous.

At the same time, precautions against an enemy landing were increased. That night watchfires were lit all along the hilltops north to Nurrum and south to New Tamf.

But no trace of the enemy fleet was found.

All through these days, a keen watch was kept on the movements of the pyluk horde, which had slowly worked its way north into Shellflower. Where the pyluk went, they slaughtered the game or sent it fleeting toward the coast. Behind the tramping columns, the woods were left empty of everything that ran on four legs. Nothing remained but piles of bones beside the ashes of huge bonfires.

Toshak shifted some regiments farther north, over the Dristen, up to the river Shell, and into the Shellflower country itself. The land there was mostly wild—an upland terrain, much carved into hills and crags. The few roads were narrow and wound about the landscape connecting the scattered villages of mots.

Toshak's scouts kept him well informed of the pyluk and their movements, but he did not undertake a campaign against them, not while the whereabouts of the enemy fleet was unknown. Toshak's first priority was to repulse an enemy landing.

Thru Gillo had just returned to Toshak's headquarters after carrying a message to Aeswiren. After tramping the wet roads all day, he had a fine coating of mud from his waist to his boots. Thru sipped hot tea, letting it revive him, while Toshak read the Emperor's reply.

Toshak set the message down. "What's it like over there, Colonel?"

"Wet, sir. Wet right through. Even the Great King's tent leaked last night." Toshak nodded. The rain the previous night had been unrelenting. "But his men don't seem too downhearted. They had fires going, were cooking up a meal while I was there. The Great King was in good spirits. He said he trusts your judgment regarding the conditions."

"Yes, so he says in his message."

"He asked me again if he shouldn't add his scouts to ours."

"I sympathize. I would want my own scouts, too. But in this situation I think it best that we not mingle our forces. Considering all that's gone before, I think it would be unwise to have parties of men moving around on our perimeter. We'd have constant rumors and who knows what else."

"So I told him, sir."

"I'm sure he understands. Anyway, that's the way it's going to be. Our scouts will do the job. He'll get his chance to fight his enemy soon enough, I wager."

"You're sure the enemy will land?"

"He hasn't brought all these pyluk out of the mountains only to sail away now."

Thru nodded. "Yes, of course."

"It's clear he hoped to use them as a surprise weapon. You spoiled that. But they are numerous enough to remain a threat, something to keep us worried. Anyway, all we can do now is keep our eyes open and wait for our enemy's next move. And you, Colonel, you can get some sleep."

Released from duty, Thru found his bedroll and a dry place in the equipment tent and lay down. Regular sleep had become a thing of the past since he'd become the courier of choice between the two armies.

His mud-soaked trousers and jacket were taken away and clean ones left for him by the equipment tent orderlies. One youngster even scraped the mud off his boots and gave them a spit and a polish. Thru knew nothing of any of this. As soon as his body achieved a horizontal position, he was asleep.

In his dreams he returned to the world before the war. A lazy summer day and a long game at the ball field. Iallia was there, and so was Nuza, which was confusing. For a moment, Pern Treevi's hate-filled face filtered past but then it was gone, and Thru was concentrating on hitting the next ball as it hurtled in toward the tree.

This idyll ended abruptly with a violent shake of his shoulder. Thru struggled to wakefulness and stared around him. The familiar yet unfamiliar surroundings of the equipment tent greeted him, along with a goggle-eyed orderly.

"There is news, sir! General Toshak wants you at once, sir!"

Shaking sleep from his eyes, Thru dressed and made his way to the command post.

"There you are, Gillo. Good. Enemy made his move. A surprise attack this morning on the Great King's fleet at anchor. They've taken six of his ships, and they've also taken the admiral."

Thru sucked in a breath. "Where are they now, sir?"

"Don't know, really. Last report had them sailing back out to sea with their prizes. There's confusion in the rest of the fleet now, possibly a mutiny on one ship. We don't really know yet."

"So, no landing was attempted?"

"None. They looked in at Dronned, but they sailed away again."

Thru nodded at these words. The enemy was canny. He must have studied the first battle of Dronned. He wanted to land on better ground for a fight.

"Please take this message to Aeswiren." Toshak handed him a scroll. "And this one to King Belit. Plus this one to whichever Assenzi you find in residence at Dronned."

Thru was on the road south within a few minutes.

Chapter 28

The cold water hit his face, and he came back to wake-fulness with a sad groan. He was still in the stocks.

"Wake up, pig!" snarled an all-too-familiar voice.

Heuze blinked and looked up into the circle of Red Tops grinning down at him. Already it seemed as if they'd been torturing him for years.

The one with the big red nose poked him in the head. "Wake up and answer the questions."

Another one, with two front teeth missing, chipped in, "The excellent Muambwi Gold Top will conduct the questioning today."

Today? Had he slept all night? Had there been a night?

Confined belowdecks, Heuze had lost all idea of night and day. All sense of what was going on. He could barely think straight.

Damn, he thought, but he was in up to his neck in the excrement now.

And it was his own fault. That was the worst part. He'd gone to sleep at the tiller of his fleet. He'd never dreamed the enemy would be so daring as to attempt an attack on his anchored fleet, coming out of the mists at dawn. He'd been caught unawares, and before he could effectively respond, there'd been two enemy ships grappled to his sides and the *Anvil* was swarming with boarders.

More cold water splashed over him, to the guffaws

of the young Red Tops. The muscular pair who
wielded the mallets were grinning broadly. These two
really loved their work.

They were good at it, too. Heuze was pretty sure
he'd never use his right hand again. It was already a
purple pancake, coated in crusted blood. The nails
were gone, and the joints were swollen grotesquely,
flattened by the pounding of the mallets.

The pain? Ah, the pain—Heuze had come to know
all about pain and its various levels. He flexed his left
hand, which was still recognizable as a human hand.
The pain from the broken bones was excruciating, but
he hardly winced anymore. He'd felt far worse.

At least, he told himself, they hadn't done a thing
to his remaining foot. Why, he didn't know, but he
was thankful for it with the thanks of a man with one
leg amputated already.

They had taken away his peg leg, of course. And
used it to break his fingers the first time round. Oh,
they'd enjoyed that. The Red Tops knew who he was;
they knew his reputation. The word had gotten back
to Shasht about how Admiral Heuze had broken the
priests of the colony and put the Gold Tops to the
sword. The Red Tops had been castrated and sold
down into slavery. Oh, yes, they knew all about him.

The Gold Top arrived. The Red Tops fell silent and
assumed their positions. One on either side of him to
seize him and shove his head in a bucket or pull his
ears or slap him rhythmically on the cheeks, whatever
the Gold Top indicated. The pair with the mallets
leaned their weapons on their shoulders, and a third
pair behind them would join in for those occasions
when the Gold Top wanted them to kick the admiral
in the crotch and belly.

Muambwi Gold Top sat delicately on the stool,
ready to begin. This one was a skeletal fellow, with a
long horse's face and cheekbones sticking up under

the skin. Heuze longed for the chance to get in one punch, one solid punch, even with his broken hands.

"Admiral Heuze, I hope you will answer promptly and truthfully today. We have much ground to cover, and I would like to get this over with."

Heuze tried to speak, and coughed through his dry throat a moment or two. Muambwi waited, eyes expectant. Finally, Heuze managed, "Yeah, let's get it over with."

It was hard talking normally when your cheeks and lips were as swollen as his. When your nose was broken and some of your teeth had been knocked out. His broken nose felt enormous on his face.

"Good, then we're agreed."

Muambwi opened a folder made of stiff parchment. "Admiral Heuze, you said yesterday that you were ordered recently to send four ships south. You said you did not know why the ships were sent."

"Yes," said Heuze in a dull voice.

"I will repeat a question from yesterday. Four ships were sent. Where were they sent?"

"Not my orders. I received sealed orders that I gave to the captains concerned. I was not told anything more than that."

He was sticking to his story. First lesson about lying: Never budge from your first line of deceit.

"Who had sealed these orders?"

"The Emperor."

Heuze intended to take the secret of the ships' destination to his grave. Let them tear his heart out of his chest, he would never tell them where those fornicating ships were going.

"What does this seal look like?"

"A capital letter *A* impressed in the wax."

"Is the letter enclosed in a circle?"

"No."

Muambwi paused, riffled through the sheets of

paper inside the folder. "So, the ships were chosen by the Emperor?"

"Yes."

"And what was your role supposed to be in this?"

"I don't really have a role. As I said, I passed on sealed orders. I am merely a servant of the Emperor, as is lawful and just."

Muambwi's eyebrows came together for a moment. "The Emperor sits in Shasht and is named Norgeeben the Second. There is no Emperor here."

Heuze stared doggedly into the dark eyes of Muambwi Gold Top. "So you say. But I am not in Shasht. I am on the other side of the world, and I do not know what is truly happening in Shasht. But I do know that the Emperor Aeswiren is here. I merely obey orders from the Emperor Aeswiren."

"You dissemble! You think you can deceive us?"

Muambwi made a cutting motion with one hand. Instantly, the pair of Red Tops kneeling on either side of Heuze began slapping him hard across the face. Heuze felt his head rock back and forth for what seemed an eternity while his cheeks stung and his head rang like a bell. He'd already taken too many beatings like this and soon it felt as if his head was about to fall off his shoulders and roll along the floor.

At last it stopped. His head sagged, and he struggled to breathe. His ears were ringing. His already swollen cheeks stung as if they'd been opened with a razor and bathed in acid.

"Now, Admiral Heuze, tell me no more lies!"

Muambwi sounded as if he had enjoyed the last couple of minutes.

"The fugitive, the so-called Emperor Aeswiren, is no longer blessed with the authority given by the Great God. The true Emperor is Norgeeben, who sits the throne in Shasht."

"Whatever you say," said Heuze with difficulty.

"Correct. So, tell me again what you thought your role was in this matter of these ships that were sent south."

"Very little, really. I just handed them the orders sent me."

Muambwi pursed his lips and studied Heuze for a long time. "What were the names of these officers?"

"Captain Low of *Fierce,* Captain Herrigs of *Flying Spume,* Captain Dace of *Auger,* Captain Brisbask of frigate *Sunset.*"

The Gold Top was writing the names in the folder. Heuze felt a momentary triumph. He was sure now that the four ships he'd send south had not been intercepted by the enemy fleet. Otherwise they'd know well enough who they had.

He gritted his teeth. It was even more important that he steer the enemy away from the truth.

"All right, Admiral, we'll go along with this little effort at deception you're making. We'll ask you where you think these ships are being sent, not where you know they're being sent."

Heuze shrugged and winced as he hurt both hands, still trapped in the stocks.

"I suppose they're going to Mauste. We have built our main base there. Perhaps you have seen it yourself?"

"Perhaps." The Gold Top suddenly became aware that Heuze was winkling out information from him. His eyebrows came together angrily.

"Admiral, you fail to understand the tenuousness of your position. If you fail to satisfy the questioning, you will be given to the Great God."

Heuze blinked then laughed mordantly. "What are you saying? That I won't be given to the Great God if I satisfy you? Are you saying that the tradition of centuries will be forgotten in my case and I'll go free? Are you trying to pull my leg? Hah, pull the other one, it's still got a foot!"

Muambwi's face contorted with anger and then resumed its normal look of haughty insolence. "It won't have a foot for very long if you keep that attitude."

"Look, I'll come clean with you, if you come clean with me. You're going to kill me no matter what you say. I know that, you fornicating sodomite!"

Muambwi's brows collided once more beneath the gleaming crown of gold paint. He made a chopping gesture. The Red Tops who did the kicking jumped forward and put their feet into Heuze's crotch and belly a few times.

When they'd finished, Heuze vomited weakly, blood and spittle dripping down on the ruins of his shirt and trousers.

Muambwi Gold Top leaned forward once more. "Admiral, you will save yourself much discomfort by remembering your place and speaking to Questioners with respect."

"Yes, yes, of course, foolish of me—"

Heuze didn't complete the rest, not wanting those mallets to come into play again.

As the questioning continued, Heuze found his mind wandering at times, and he could scarcely remember what they were asking him about from one minute to the next. He tried to fashion credible answers, but he knew he wasn't convincing them of anything.

Muambwi was replaced by Chushi Gold Top. Chushi was a thick-necked fellow with a bulbous nose. Chushi was even more unpleasantly small-minded than Muambwi.

"Hello, Chushi," said Heuze through broken teeth and swollen lips. "I bet my nose is even bigger than yours today."

"Be silent, slave of He Who Eats!"

Chushi was not pleased. Muambwi had been unable to wring more than the captains' names from Heuze, who had babbled for hours about all sorts of things but not the information they sought: the destination of those ships.

The mallets rained down on Heuze's hands. He screamed. He roared. He howled. He bled. Eventually he was silent, no matter what they did. Even when they put hot irons to his flesh, he opened his mouth but no sound came forth.

They threw cold water on him to no effect. In disgust they left him, and he slept.

When next he awoke, it was to be summarily dragged from the stocks and up the steps to the quarterdeck. Officers were there. No faces that were familiar to him. All looked at his battered state with dismay. The pride of the navy was being besmirched by this treatment of an admiral, and worse yet, the admiral had brought it on himself.

No fault of mine, boys, he wanted to shout, but his voice no longer served him. It wasn't what I wanted to happen, he would have added.

Ropes were attached to his wrists, and he was hauled up to hang below a yardarm. Sails billowed above him, as the ship was making good progress under a breeze from astern. Despite everything, Heuze felt a certain renewal from just looking on the sea. He had spent most of his life at sea, and on such a fine day, with such a useful wind, he could not help but feel that elemental bond with the waves that he had always felt.

Why they'd hung him up like this he had no idea. It hurt like hell, of course, but it made a change from the foulness down below, being slapped around by the sodomistic Red Tops. He craned his head down and studied the quarterdeck from a position he'd never looked down from before.

He saw no sign of Captain Pukh. He hoped Pukh had dived overboard or something. He didn't want to think of his old friend Pukh being taken by the Red

Tops because of a stupid mistake of his. There was no sign of any of his own officers. All had been replaced.

Damn, it was all his own fault. Even with an enemy fleet so close at hand he had neglected to set a good enough watch. To be taken as he'd been was more than stupid—it was humiliating.

He looked up as a shadow fell over him.

Streaming up from the southwest were dark clouds. Peculiar clouds, shaped like daggers, and so dark they looked like ink spilled across the sky. One after the other they slid across, leaving narrow strips of blue in between, until at last they all joined together and the sky became a black vault, utterly blocking out the sun.

Heuze had never seen anything like this in all his years at sea. Everything had gone cold. A sudden flash of purple-tinged lightning flared in the west, and a heavy boom rocked the ship.

Accompanying the dark came a chill wind that brought with it a premonition of horror. Heuze trembled in the cold breeze while uncontrollable fear spread through every man onboard. They were nought but rabbits in a field, pursued by swift beasts with mouths of fire.

The fear mounted, growing stronger and wilder with each passing second. Beneath him he could hear shouts and incoherent shrieking. Men ran here and there like brainless dolts.

Heuze felt his own mind slip its moorings. Whether his eyes were opened or shut, he experienced a terrifying hallucination.

Enormous creatures, pink-skinned, like men but without heads, surfaced around the ship. With arms that ended in huge nests of struggling tentacles, things that looked like worms writhing on a frying pan, they stood above the water. They had legs as mighty as the towers on the walls of Shasht.

Their huge mouths opened, and they bellowed

something unknowable to the sky. The tentacles writhed and revealed that they were tipped with mouths filled with sharp teeth. The tentacles swung toward Heuze. The vision changed in an instant. A gold flash blasted through his eyes, and then he saw into a dark, necrotic vision. Rotting faces drifted slowly down from the sky like ghastly snow. Skulls piled up on the surface of the sea, floating in great drifts. The sun had gone black. Heuze's mother emerged from the skulls and held her arms out to him.

Heuze wept. He would have liked to go to her arms, but he couldn't move. In the next moment, she was blown away in the winds, torn to pieces, shriveled and then gone.

His father's face appeared. A cold man with dark eyes, he had sent Heuze to sea at the age of thirteen. The father frowned, and a shaft of cold passed through Heuze. Then the father faded.

There was a curious implosion of sound.

The enormous manlike things were gone. The ship floated on a sea of blood. White worms the size of whales coursed through the blood. A terrible sense of desolation rose up. All was lost, all was ruined.

Heuze felt overwhelmed, crushed, broken inside. The darkness pervaded everything, and consciousness became blotted out completely.

How long he hung there, lost in the shades of terror, he never knew, but when he came back to himself, he found a scene of panic down below. He was still swinging from the yardarm, and the ship had drifted perilously close to the rocky shore.

Just three hundred feet away the waves were slamming into the rocks. The cliff towered above them, a dirty white mountain of chalk.

Officers were bellowing orders. Feet thundered up the stairs.

The sun shone once more, but the world of darkness

lay just behind them. When he looked back, he could see that the edge between the two was clear and hard. Away to the south beneath the black cloud there was just the darkness and an occasional distant flash of purple lightning.

The vast white cliff swung slowly before his eyes as the ship came about. All hands were in the rigging. Sails were furled and unfurled with frantic speed.

Voices continued to bellow orders, but the ship was no longer drifting toward the rocks. The ship was changing course, moving back out into the bay, although one outlying spire of rock was still in their way.

Slowly, rigging creaked as the sails caught the wind. The great ship swung her nose past the rock, and then they were sliding through the waves just fifty feet from doom. Seabirds lifted off the top of the rock with harsh cries.

Ahead, Heuze could see other ships, a great mass of them moving around the chalk headland. Here was the enemy fleet, and ahead was the site where they were going to land their army.

And behind the ship lay the grim, eerie darkness blanketing the world.

Thru Gillo was hurrying up Bear Hill from Warkeen when he first noticed the strange black clouds forming in the southeast. He was carrying yet another reply from Aeswiren to yet another message from Toshak. Being Toshak's messenger to the Emperor was harder work than it had ever been now that the two generals were within five miles of each other.

At times Thru wondered if it wouldn't have been better to just have the two headquarters together in the village, instead of having Toshak on Bear Hill just north of the river and Aeswiren on South Hill on the other side. Certainly that would have made it easier on Thru's boots, which were falling apart again.

Yet, he also understood that keeping the two armies apart was a good idea. The alliance between mot and Man was a very young and tender shoot. Every time he passed through the perimeter of Aeswiren's army and found himself surrounded by men, Thru felt a certain oppression. By instinct his hand strayed to his sword hilt when he caught hard glances directed his way, and as he passed by, he often heard muttered curses and insults. Many men clearly hated the folk of the Land, just as the folk of the Land hated the men.

When next Thru looked up, he saw that the black clouds had slithered farther up the sky. He hurried his footsteps. He'd missed lunch, but he still had hopes of finding something to eat at the headquarters cook fire. If there was bad weather coming in, he'd rather be in the cook tent than out here in the open.

The path up the hill and over to Cormorant Rock had suffered from the passage of Toshak's army. The ground was cut up with ruts, the bushes and trees hemmed back to let the wagons through. The pathway was almost an analogy for the Land itself, torn and beaten ever since the men first arrived.

A shadow fell over him as he crested the hill. Toshak's tents were just ahead. He glanced up and saw the clouds had spread right up the sky. They were like long fingers, each separated by a narrow band of blue sky, but the blue was being squeezed out as more and more of the flat, opaque blackness flowed up from the south.

The clouds rolled on. The light was dimmed and then virtually obliterated by the time he reached camp, delivered Aeswiren's message to the headquarters tent, and got across to the cook fire.

"Got anything left?" he said as he poked into the various pots and cauldrons.

"Oh ho, back for seconds, are you?" said the cook,

an older mor missing her right eye. Her fur was whitening at the tips on top of her shoulders and the back of her head.

"No, I wasn't here for lunch."

"Well, in that case, here, take some porridge and some bushpod cake."

She slopped a ladle of porridge into a bowl for him.

"Here, eat it quick. Looks like we've got bad weather coming in. I'll want to close the flaps tight."

"Thanks."

"Odd-looking storm. I've never seen anything like it."

It was very strange. The black fingers had passed on, and the whole sky had gone dark. The sudden flash of purple lightning away in the south dazzled them. After a few moments a heavy boom rolled over their heads.

Thru felt his fur standing up. More lightning flickered out to sea.

"Ooh, this is going to be nasty," said the cookmor.

Thru knew in his bones that sorcery was at work here. He'd seen their terrible enemy. He'd witnessed the demonic dance that summoned the pyluk from the hills. Now it seemed this warlock could summon a storm at his whim.

He ate the porridge in a few gulps, darted out of the tent as the cookmor battened down the hatches, and hurried across to the headquarters tent, still chewing the pod cake.

He was halfway there when a cold wind struck. With it came an overpowering feeling of unease, even of fear. Something dreadful was hunting them, something that promised annihilation.

Toshak had finished the noontime meeting with his regimental commanders. They were filing out as Thru came in. He knew most of them well and exchanged nods and a few handshakes.

"What the hell is happening out there?" said more than one as they stepped out of the tent.

Inside, Thru ran into the Grys Norvory, his one-time enemy. The Grys wore the red pin of a regimental commander. He had given Thru an apology for the misdeeds of the past at an earlier meeting, and now they were on cordial terms.

"So, you got your freedom from the palace," said Thru with a nod to the pin.

"At last. Think I've served my time as a bureaucrat."

Another great boom of thunder rolled overhead.

"This storm seems unnatural," said the Grys with a look out the door at the darkness above.

"Sorcery, I'd wager," said Thru.

"That's what we have to expect, I suppose. May the Spirit preserve us."

"May it keep our sword edge sharp, too."

Toshak appeared from the back of the tent. "Thank you, Grys," he said, taking Thru's arm. "Gillo, come here a moment."

Toshak moved over to the open front of the tent. The sky was pitch-black except for blast after blast of purple lightning out to sea.

"What do you think the purpose of this storm is?"

Clearly, Toshak understood that this strange weather was the work of their enemy.

"Our enemy seeks to frighten us," said Thru.

The wind was increasing in fierceness, and the tent flaps were closed by the orderlies. In short order the papers were slid into the travel binders and the maps into their waterproof tubes. Thru and Toshak went over to a side flap so they could continue to peer outside.

All across the camp, mots and brilbies were hurrying to tie things down. The wind rose steadily until it was fairly shrieking through the trees. All the fires had been put out and covered with shovelfuls of sand.

Leaves, branches, and bits of bark were blown out of the forest and right over the tents. The wind rose to a maniacal screech. Here and there a tent collapsed. The tent set up for the orderlies to sleep in lost its pegs at the rear and was torn from its place and hurled away. The orderlies' things went flying after it.

The cook tent was barely holding on. One peg had come up, and a corner of the tent was flapping madly in the wind. Thru could hear the imprecations of the cookmor, even over the general howl of the tempest, as she fought to control the loose corner.

Then came the rain. The first few drops were huge and heavy, making loud splatters on the canvas. A deluge followed. With a sudden drumming roar, the rain lashed down across the Land. Thru hesitated a few moments and was soaked to the fur by the time he pulled his head in and sealed the tent flap.

The noise diminished a little. Inside the tent, the poles creaked as the wind buffeted its walls. Orderlies did their best to hold poles in place. Rain smashed across the top of the tent in violent bursts, as if it were being hurled from the heavens by an angry god.

Suddenly the ring at the top of one of the poles ripped free from the tent. The tent itself ripped along a seam for almost a foot, and water poured in, bucketsfuls in a matter of moments.

"Seal that tent!" came the frantic command.

The orderlies threw themselves at it, but it was a nigh impossible task. Thru and Toshak joined the group, taking hold of the tent pole while an orderly climbed onto a chair and strung a thong through the torn opening and laced it together.

By the time it was done, everyone was wet, and the floor of the headquarters tent was a muddy mess.

Outside, it was still howling. Lightning struck all around them in the forest, huge flashes that lit up the interior of the tent in bright purple light.

The thunder was deafening. It came in peal upon

peal, enormous blasts and booms in a continuous roar that obliterated their voices.

Toshak and Thru were now standing in mud, the tent still heaving and starting to leak under the relentless downpour. Several orderlies were showing the strain. One was weeping, terrified beyond sense by it all. Their enemy was showing them his power, and his power was very great indeed.

But not even this storm could keep up its malevolence for long. After a few more minutes, the wind began to lessen and the rain had dropped to a more normal range. The thunder continued, but the lightning was now striking inland, up above Bear Hill for the most part.

Thru was just about to open the tent flap and take a look outside when it was rudely torn open. In stumbled a soaked, blood-stained wretch. Fur matted with mud, eyes wild with fear and exertion.

"They are coming. The pyluk."

Chapter 29

The attack had been artfully timed. When the tempest was at its height, a column of two thousand pyluk emerged from the woods of Lupin Valley. They had infiltrated the valley the previous day and night, moving with the utmost stealth, while sorcery had distracted the minds of the scouts on Stag's Head and in the Bell House above Snoyps Pond.

Once hidden in Lupin Valley, less than a mile from Bear Hill, they had hunkered down in glades and stream bottoms. They had remained frozen in place all day, in the grip of the same sorcery that had controlled them since they had first come down from the mountains.

Their stillness had kept them hidden, and the advent of the storm was the signal that brought them back to wakefulness. As one they rose up, took up their clubs and spears, and set off toward the coast.

They swarmed over Toshak's screen of pickets at the base of Bear Hill while the thunder and lightning were still crashing overhead. The pickets barely had time to look up before they were overwhelmed by a solid onrushing mass of the lizard-men. Long spears took those who attempted to flee.

Fortunately, a few mots farther up the hill heard the commotion and saw the horde of pyluk pouring through the trees below. The mots could scarcely believe their eyes, but they had the sense to run for it.

Thus the mots of the Third Regiment got a few minutes' warning, but not much more. The pickets came bolting into the camp, screaming, "Pyluk!" at the top of their lungs.

The Grys Norvory, newly appointed to the regiment, was making a tour of the tents when the word came. He'd expected some kind of deviltry, and here it was. In a matter of minutes, he was getting his soldiers out of their tents and formed into a combat line in the middle of the camp.

The pyluk burst out of the trees. The mots, torn from cowering in their tents under the fear and the overpowering energy of the storm, now found themselves confronted by an overwhelming mass of lizard-men.

Perhaps the abruptness of the attack helped the Third Regiment. They simply didn't have time to panic. Despite everything, they stood their ground.

The pyluk drove forward onto the pikes and spears. Pyluk bulls with three or four arrows jutting from their flesh thrashed against the mot shield wall, before they succumbed to sharp steel. Nowhere did they break the line.

The mots bent before this storm of flesh as the struggle went on. Their line was driven back here and there, but reinforcements coming up behind hurled themselves into the fighting at these places, and the pyluk were stopped in their tracks. For a precious ten minutes, the Third Regiment held its ground until the huge column of pyluk completely surrounded them. At that point the pyluk left them and went on across the hilltop toward the sea. The Third Regiment was left like an island of survivors amid mounds of dead.

But for the gallant stand of the Third Regiment, the rest of the army would have taken a death blow that day. But with those few minutes' warning, Toshak and Thru managed to rouse three more regiments and get them into a rough line, northwest-southeast across the center of Bear Hill.

As soon as that line began to form, Thru left the job to the sergeants and ran over the hill. The Sixth Regiment, which had been camped on the south slope, was forming up to march, and Thru shouted to them to hurry while he ran past and down into the village. He tore through the streets of Warkeen and over the old bridge. Folk were scurrying to their stations as he passed. At Aeswiren's perimeter the guards saw him coming and waved him through.

He found Aeswiren's army already forming up. Aeswiren's scouts had heard the uproar from Bear Hill.

The Emperor listened calmly to Thru and then sent him back to Toshak. "The men of Shasht will march at once to Bear Hill. We will seek to position ourselves inland of General Toshak's line. And if he's left any of them for us, we'll be happy to engage these pyluk."

Thru and Aeswiren exchanged a strong handclasp, and Thru turned and ran back the way he'd come.

The regiments of Shasht were already in motion, rank after rank of veterans of many wars. Watching them march, with a swift, economical stride, Thru felt renewed confidence. He'd fought against these men often enough. Now they would fight on his side for a change. He shook his head at the strangeness of the thought.

He took a deep breath and started jogging. He needed to get back to Toshak at once with his message. Back through the village he went, warning them that Aeswiren's men were coming through. The village shutters started coming down in a hurry. On the other side of the village, donkey carts were jammed on the road. Thru ordered them to pull their animals to the side.

"Let the men through. They're fighting on our side now."

Naturally, it took a few minutes for this to be done, and by then the first Shasht regulars were in sight, swinging through the village to a beat of a drum. The cartmots redoubled their efforts. Thru ran on, toiling up Bear Hill, with Aeswiren's army coming after him.

The effects of the earlier run, coming on top of the long walk before that, slowed his pace before he reached the top. Gasping for breath, he halted at the crest of the hill to survey the scene.

Somehow the mots had survived the onslaught. A great tide of green warriors still stormed against the front of Toshak's army, and the roar of the fighting continued, but, crucially, the line had held. The pyluk had swarmed out of the trees and fallen on the mots, but discipline and good weapons had brought them up short. Toshak's mots had never panicked.

The pyluk charge had lost its impetus. The stabbing swords and spears of the mots were taking a grim toll on the unarmored lizard-men, whose clubs and long wooden spears were not designed for close-order combat.

Behind the regiments were the wounded, dozens and dozens of them, and here and there a pyluk lay where death had taken him. On the road, Thru found a group of older mots loading wounded into donkey carts. A little ways on, he found a huge pyluk bull lying on its back, a spear driven into its immense chest. This was the farthest the enemy had come. More bodies were lying nearby, pyluk and mots mixed together.

Thru found Toshak on a hillock, set about a hundred yards from the former headquarters tent. The general had a fixed, determined look in his eyes, but Thru could tell he was worried.

General Toshak listened to his brief message from Aeswiren and then turned, nodding slowly, back to surveying the battle.

The mot regiments were pressing forward, pushing the pyluk back on their heels. The pyluk had no training and no techniques for this sort of fighting, and they paid heavily. Mots and brilbies with pike and spontoon took many pyluk when they tried to fight while moving backward.

"Well," said Toshak after a moment, "we've held this attack. But something doesn't smell right to me. Why would he make this solitary assault? It seems meaningless."

"Meaningless? It could have destroyed our army."

Toshak shook his head. "No, it wasn't strong enough. If our scouting reports are to be believed, he used barely a third of his strength."

Both looked up at the same time.

"A landing!"

"Of course, it makes perfect cover for a landing."

As Toshak whirled toward his orderlies, Thru drank a mug of water and got ready to run like the wind once again. By the time he'd drained the mug, Toshak was thrusting a packet into his hands.

"Tell Aeswiren the enemy fleet must be attempting a landing. Probably farther north. I'd say the river Shell would be most likely. Aeswiren must march his men right through here and engage the enemy before they can all get ashore. We will finish off these pyluk and then join him."

The pyluk were not reinforced. Toshak's army broke up the assault column, turned it into a fugitive mass, and drove it back down into the Lupin Valley where much of it was lost, slaughtered in the dark thickets by mots with pikes and bows. The few hundred survivors escaped across the moor beneath Stag's Head. Scouts followed them and ascertained that the remnants had rejoined the main mass of pyluk bunched along the river Shell.

Seeing that he was not needed in this fight, Aeswiren, with Thru Gillo among his headquarters group, marched straight north, past the recent battle-field, and on toward Blue Hill. The Shell debouched to the sea on the far side of the jagged pinnacle of Cormorant Rock.

Mot scouts, passing back from the river, were met by the pickets of Aeswiren's force. There was a certain amount of tension initially, but Thru was able to calm them. The mots told him what they'd seen and then loped away to find Toshak. Thru turned quickly to Aeswiren.

"They are landing, as we expected, on the north shore of the Shell. Many thousands."

Aeswiren's eyes hardened at the news. The Old One had shown a calculated blend of tactical and strategic moves.

On they went. Aeswiren's men were all veterans, with iron-hard determination settled in their minds. They weren't going to fight monkeys this time. They weren't even going to slaughter these lizard-men. They were going to fight men! Men who had the misfortune to be the slaves of the priests. Nothing united these soldiers more than their hatred of the Red Tops.

Thru sensed the ferocity lurking in the ranks around him. He had marched with several armies and had felt everything from boisterous anticipation to terror, but never had he sensed this hardened murderousness. "We are as strong as they are," he thought, "but we are not driven by the same demons, for we did not arise on our own. We were made by Man."

Thru thought again of the pattern he had invented, "Men at War." He liked the work. If he lived, he would weave it again. It was a portrait of Man as he really was. Men had been warriors since the beginning of time. If they hadn't been, they wouldn't have survived. And thus they were filled with an elemental fury that the mots and brilbies could never match.

This insight lifted his spirits for some reason, and

he marched along, head high despite the lingering winds and occasional sharp showers of rain.

The storm was lifting. The strange dark clouds had drifted away inland. Cormorant Rock loomed up in front of them. Its sharp upper spike suddenly caught the sun. Thru remembered a day, years before, when he'd turned away near here to get down to the creek. He'd been in pursuit of some sea lilies for little Iallia Tramine, the mor he'd been so in love with then.

He shook his head with amazement. All of that seemed like part of someone else's life now. A world that had only known men as the disembodied Man the Cruel of the old prayers from the Book.

They dipped down to the crossing of the Rocky Canyon and over the stream. If young mots were ever to come here in the future, seeking sea lilies for their beloved, the coming battle had to be won.

As they came up the far side of the canyon, on a trail that switchbacked up the last two hundred feet, they began to notice something strange. At the crest of the hill, all signs of the recent storm stopped. It was as if a line had been drawn across the land. On one side, the trees were wet and torn by the wind; downed branches littered the ground; pools of water glistened in the returning sunlight. On the other side, there was none of this; no rain had fallen.

Thru felt the hair on his neck stand up. This could only have been done with sorcery. In his mind's eye, Thru again saw that strange, horrific little dance performed by the giant man before the mob of savage pyluk.

The men muttered about the strange line, but they never wavered, continuing over the top of the ridge with a will.

At last, they caught sight of the enemy. The estuary of the river Shell was laid out beneath them, and it was filled with shipping. On the far side of the river, the massed troops of the enemy were visible. The water was dotted with hundreds of small craft, ferrying men and supplies ashore. Helmets and shields by the thousand caught the sun.

Thru realized that the enemy had already succeeded in getting his army ashore. Then he saw a party of men riding horse animals along the far bank of the river, and a shiver went through him. Fifty strong or more, they galloped down to the narrow bridge that spanned the river a mile from its mouth. There was no village on the Shell. It was a wild river, left to the creatures of the Land, so it had only a trader's bridge, wide enough for a single donkey cart. If the enemy wanted to cross the river, though, that bridge would be essential.

He became aware that sharp orders were being announced up and down the marching columns. Aeswiren's army came to a halt, and the Great King himself pushed forward to take a good look a the scene before them.

Less than a minute later, more orders came down. The army was to retire from the ridge top and move off the road and into the woods. The enemy was not to discover their presence.

Thru was impressed by the speed and skill the men showed in following these orders. They vanished from the road, slipped back between the trees, and did their utmost to hide their passing.

Aeswiren and his staff came hurrying back along the road, pointing out places where thousands of feet had worn trails on soft ground. More orders were given, and teams of men worked over all these places with rakes and spear points, laying leaves and broken branches to cover the worst.

Thru took the opportunity to go forward and, keeping behind cover, to take another look at the enemy.

There was no sign that Aeswiren's forces had been spotted. The landing continued. Small boats thronged the shoreline. Units of men were forming up on the shingle above. A couple units were already marching inland, up the narrow donkey path to the bridge.

The horsemen were at the bridge and they were beginning to cross.

"My enemy has won this round," came a voice beside him, speaking in the tongue of the Land, and Thru started at finding that Aeswiren had come up so quietly behind him.

"You are too late to stop him landing."

"Yes. But we have to destroy him, and we cannot do that until he offers battle."

"He has greater numbers than you."

"Not once General Toshak arrives."

"And the pyluk are out there." Thru gestured inland, across the Shell.

"True, we will have to be on our guard for them."

Aeswiren rubbed his chin for a moment as he studied the scene down below. "We will have a degree of surprise in our favor, too. All in all, I am confident."

The Emperor heard something and took a look down the trail to the bridge, which lay a couple miles distant.

"Better step into cover."

Thru needed no further urging, and along with the Emperor and his staff, he moved back under the trees and hid himself from view. A screen of archers was set out in front of them under cover.

Aeswiren sat down with his back to a tree. He had his sword out and was examining its edges.

Thru squatted close by.

Everyone kept strict silence for several minutes while the cavalry scouts rode over the crest of the hill, right past the waiting regiments of Aeswiren's army, hidden two hundred paces back in the trees.

When the sound of the hoofs had faded, Aeswiren gave a chuckle.

"You know we never could have pulled that off if we had any horses of our own. There'd have been at least one horse that gave us away. Horses always do that."

Chapter 30

"What is that bit of land down there called?" Aeswiren asked Thru as they watched the enemy army crossing the bridge about two miles away. About three thousand men had crossed by this point, in Thru's estimation.

The ground was open in places, covered in forest in others. The river had changed its course many times there, creating a braided channel.

"That is Shelly Fields, on either side of the river Shell."

"A beautiful spot. Good land, too, and yet no one plows it?"

"Shelly Fields has always been left to the wild. The Spirit tells us that we should leave some of even the best land unfarmed."

Aeswiren expressed surprise. "Wilderness, you say?"

Thru understood what Aeswiren was thinking. The only wilderness left in Shasht was high in the mountains.

The enemy continued to pour across. Their regiments were clearly visible, bunched along the road.

Thru watched Aeswiren count the enemy and then make his decision. The Emperor gestured to his chief of staff, Gottbix. Immediately orderlies were dispatched to carry prepared orders for the regiments.

Aeswiren clapped Thru on the shoulder.

"The game has begun, Colonel Gillo. When the situation begins to clear, you should return to General Toshak and bring him up to date. Though he should join us before much longer."

"Yes, Lord."

Thru watched as the regiments sprouted up from cover and returned to the road. He noted that they carried their shields turned down and wore no helmets. As far as possible they covered every bit of bright metal. Thru was impressed by how quiet they were as well. There was the inevitable stirring of undergrowth and the like, but no metal struck metal and no one raised his voice. Men knew these things about war by some deep instinct, it seemed to him.

Once on the road, they formed up quickly and hurried away down the narrow track toward the bridge. When they reached the bottom of the hill, the regiments broke out, one to the left and one to the right. The ground there was a forest of oak and pine, with hemlock on the stream edges. There was little undergrowth, allowing the regiments to form up a good line and expand the front for the attack as they quickened toward the enemy lines.

The enemy horse scout noticed the onrushing regiments when they were about three quarters of a mile from the narrow bridge.

Bugles rang, drums thundered, and Red Tops roared at the men under their command. A rough and ready line was formed up, weighted toward the road. The horsemen, two hundred strong, pulled themselves together off to the right, ready to threaten Aeswiren's flank as his force pressed forward, but the force already across the river was plainly taken by surprise.

Long before the enemy was ready, Aeswiren's men came forward in a charge. The battle cry of "Aeswiren!" rang across the fields.

The two sides came together with a roar that sent a chill down Thru's spine. The last time he'd heard that sound had been at the battle of Chillum.

This battle was different, he knew, for this was war between men, but beyond that it had the same sounds: the howls of men, the clatter of weapons and shields, and the screams of the wounded.

Aeswiren kept his command post on the top of the hill, and Thru had a good view of it all. Orderlies and messengers were in constant motion between the hilltop and the regiments. As ever, Thru was impressed with the speed and efficiency of the Shasht infantry. In a matter of minutes, Aeswiren's army had extended its line to wrap itself around the smaller enemy force. That force, working just as skillfully, backed up to the banks of the river, forming a bridgehead. Meanwhile, their cavalry force charged Aeswiren's men and forced the right flank to peel back and form a wall of shields with spears extended to stand off the horsemen. There were only a couple hundred of them on that side of the river, and the river was too deep and swift to be forded. Later, when the tide went out, they would be able to cross, but for now the bridge was the only way over.

While the fighting continued, Thru saw the enemy begin moving his force back over the bridge, withdrawing from the unequal struggle with all of Aeswiren's army.

Then, abruptly, that movement stopped and reversed itself. Thru tensed and studied the trees past the right flank. The Emperor also had seen the change. He immediately sent orders to the regiments to look out for a flank attack out of the woods on their right.

The hard fighting continued. Aeswiren's men would charge, engage the stiff lines of the enemy, then break away, regroup, and charge again. Thru knew that no regiment of mots was capable of such cohesive work.

Within a few more minutes, two scouts arrived with word from the inland side of the battle that pyluk had been seen moving stealthily forward.

More scouts soon arrived, and the picture quickly took shape. Three columns of the lizard-men, at least a thousand in each column, were moving on Aeswiren's right flank.

Aeswiren remained silent, studying the field. Thru could see the problem. The Emperor's men were keeping up the pressure on the enemy bridgehead and bottling the enemy up on the far side of the river. To pull back enough men to fend off these pyluk would ease the pressure, but eventually enough of the enemy might get across the bridge to link with the pyluk, and then the enemy would have a larger force than Aeswiren on the field.

More scouts came in. The pyluk were close.

Aeswiren prepared orders for the right wing to pull back to cover itself.

"Well, Colonel Gillo," he said, "do you think General Toshak will be much longer?"

Before Thru could reply, there was a stir among the staff, and then two mot scouts were brought forward. They both had the look of barely restrained terror on their faces. Thru lunged through the press of men and spoke to them.

Their relief was so obvious that Thru heard Aeswiren chuckle behind him.

"Dear friends," said the Emperor in the tongue of the Land, "do not fear us. We are your allies now."

The mots' astonishment was writ large on their faces. Thru saved them from further embarrassment by asking for their reports.

Toshak was hurtling up the road. He would be with them in few minutes.

Aeswiren took this news, whirled back to study the field down below, then shook his head. "Can't risk those damned lizards getting on my flank."

Orderlies were sprinting down the hill a few seconds later.

Thru hurried back down the trail with the scouts

and soon found himself among the vanguard of Toshak's army. Behind them came the regiments, rank after rank of seasoned mots and brilbies with spear, pike, and sword, ready for war.

He found Toshak striding along with his staff beneath his personal banner, a red pennon, that marked his position for all his troops to see.

Hastily, Thru explained the situation.

Toshak understood at once. He had been over that bridge several times.

"Hurry back to the Great King and tell him that I'm going to strike to the right of his force and clear those pyluk out. We will then swing around to take on the enemy force on his front."

Thru legged it back to the Emperor's command post. Already the mot regiments were filing through that area. The men around Aeswiren were all noticeably nervous at being in such close proximity to thousands of armed mots. So, Thru thought to himself, men felt the same fear mots did . . .

He passed on the message, then looked out over Shelly Fields. Down below, Aeswiren's right flank had retired and turned outward, ready to repel the expected flank assault. The enemy had taken advantage of this to expand the bridgehead and gain more room for maneuver.

Gottbix, the chief of staff, hurried past with more messages for the waiting line of orderlies. They were already looking tired; some of them had run up and down the hill three times already. Thru knew how they felt.

Then Aeswiren was standing there beside him. "Your general is very quick on the uptake. I like him."

"Thank you, Lord. We all revere great Toshak."

Aeswiren studied Shelly Fields. "Well, his timing is impeccable."

The mots had reached the bottom of the hill and

were turning off the narrow road and moving across the open ground toward the trees on the right.

"And so, Colonel, we are in battle once more. I had thought that I would never know this taste again. This blend of strength and fear, hate and anxiety. A harsh brew, and one I would not have missed."

"You put it very aptly, Lord. I've not been privileged to see a battle fought from command headquarters before."

"Yes," said the Emperor, "I expect you were in the thick of things before. Different perspective up here."

Drums began booming loudly inland in the depths of the woods. Within a minute, a mass of pyluk came pouring out of the trees closest to the river. They were joined by other groups, rough-hewn columns pouring forth from positions farther back.

As they came on, the front of Toshak's regiments prepared to receive them. Mots in the front line raised spear and shield. In the second line they carried pikes, and in the third shield and sword. Archers let fly a cloud of arrows at the approaching pyluk, and many tall green figures slumped to the ground. Moments later, the pyluk rammed into the mot line. The lines sagged here and there but quickly stiffened. The sound of fighting roared up louder than ever.

The mots and brilbies had fought pyluk already once that day. They had learned valuable lessons, and they put them to work right away. The pyluk were soon stopped dead, and then they were slaughtered.

The drumming ceased. The pyluk wavered. On their front, they were dying, speared, cut down, outfought by the mots. Behind them, the drum, the urging of their strange Master, was gone. They fell back. Soon a gap opened between the two forces. Then the pyluk turned and withdrew.

Toshak did not hesitate. The three regiments closest to the river stood back, formed up, and turned about.

They marched rapidly up past the turned-back flank line of Aeswiren's army until they came in sight of the line formed by the enemy along the riverbank.

With a sudden bark of horns, whistles, and shouted orders, the mots charged, hurling themselves at the enemy.

Aeswiren gave a whistle. "Your general is an aggressive fellow, no question about it."

Once again the roar of battle raged up from Shelly Fields.

This was the first time the men of the Old One's army had engaged the mots of the Land. They had been told over and over again that the mots were vermin, monkeys of only limited intelligence. Now they discovered that the mots had emerged from a hard school of military training and were very capable fighters.

For the mots, this was their first crack at men since Aeswiren's peace. Having warmed up on the pyluk, they were more than ready for the chance. The charge drove home. The regiments of the Old One held their ground briefly, but in a matter of minutes they were being forced back, step by step. With the river at their back, they faced annihilation.

Drums and bugles summoned reinforcements. Men were pulled away from the lines facing Aeswiren's men and thrown into the fight on the flank being chewed up by Toshak's mots. The fighting grew ever fiercer, taking a horrendous toll of men and mots, but at last the advance was halted. Toshak's forces fell back to regain some semblance of order.

That did not mean there was any let up. Aeswiren sent his men forward once more, and again the pressure on the Old One's lines intensified. The battle around the bridgehead grew very hot. The enemy understood that they could not retreat, unless they were to swim the wide, rushing river. The bridge was too narrow and would become a bottleneck and a death trap. Faced with those choices, they fought like cornered rats and died where they stood.

The rest of the Old One's host had gathered on the far side of the river, but until the tide went down, and it was now ebbing, they could do little more than watch as their compatriots fought for survival.

For an hour, perhaps, the battle went on like this. Aeswiren's men attacked then rested while Toshak's mots drove in on the right. The enemy men fought and died, and bodies mounded up in front of their lines.

Then, when their strength was beginning to fail and it looked as if Aeswiren and Toshak would finally overwhelm them, the men on the south bank were saved by the tide. It had finally ebbed low enough for the Old One to put most of his precious horsemen across, downstream from the fighting, at a place where the river channel was braided among small sandy islands, encrusted with the shells for which it was named.

The appearance of cavalry riding in on his left flank forced Aeswiren to pull back into a defensive posture.

Toshak continued the pressure on the right side of the bridgehead and was rewarded with a steady withdrawal of that force back across the river, using both the bridge and, when pressed into it, the expedient of men swimming back across the now shallow stream.

The enemy horsemen rode around the allied army and then disappeared into the woods where the pyluk had gone before. Aeswiren and Toshak took stock of the situation as the sun sank in the west.

Thru was present when the two generals met on the field between their two armies. Aeswiren and Toshak exchanged a firm handshake.

"An historic day, General."

"A good day, Great King, but we have not beaten him yet."

"True, but we have learned to fight together. This will disturb our enemy more than anything else from this day."

"Today, we disturbed him. Tomorrow, let us finish him."

Chapter 31

Admiral Heuze was taken down from the horse. His hands, two purple pancakes of pain, were tied in front of him. He had no peg leg and without it he had to be carried. So the Red Tops picked him up, and they were none too gentle about it, treating him like the proverbial sack of potatoes. They carried him into the Lord Leader's tent and dropped him on the floor.

He lay there, groaning softly to himself. Everything hurt. He wondered how long he had left before they killed him.

He felt a heavy tread nearby. Despite everything, a shiver ran down his spine. The giant was there again. The giant they called the Lord Leader, the giant that Heuze knew had to be the Old One that the Emperor had warned of.

But foul sorcery of some kind had been employed, because the Old One, in Aeswiren's words, was "weak, sickly, an ancient parasite." This young giant of a man with ferocious black eyes was instead a mountain of muscle that radiated health and vigor.

Still, the Emperor had said he was a sorcerer, and Heuze had no doubt of that.

Hands lifted him and placed him in a chair. Someone held a silver jug of water to his parched lips.

"Yes, very good, revive our battered admiral," said the big voice, filled with false cheer. Heuze glimpsed the giant, surrounded by messengers, guards, and advisors who barely came up to his shoulders.

"I want the report from the bridge," the giant rumbled, studying a scroll under a lantern. "And send for General Seezil."

Heuze wondered dully if the fighting was still going on. He couldn't hear it anymore, but he didn't know where they'd taken him. It had been a bewildering day, from the moment they'd taken him ashore.

From the atmosphere in the tent, and from the feel of things at the other place, atop a small hill behind the beach, Heuze was sure the battle had not gone quite as the giant leader had expected.

The water was blissful, cool, wet in the bruised desert of his mouth. His parched tongue became flexible again. Gods, he barely had any teeth left. His mouth was a ruin. So was his nose. He could hardly see out of his left eye, everything had swollen so much. The jug was pulled away. He groaned sadly, burped, and shivered. How long did he have left? Before they finally tore the heart out of his chest and held it up to their damned god?

A huge shadow fell across him.

"Well, well, Admiral, you have survived the ride, I see."

A big hand scrunched his shoulder. Heuze winced. Those muscles had been stretched for hours hanging in the rigging.

The giant face was all smiles. Heuze kept his eyes locked on the other's.

"Sorry to disappoint you, whoever you are."

"Oh ho!" boomed the giant. "You remain so wonderfully defiant! Excellent! I need spirit. I shall use you for the spell that I must knit tonight."

Muambwi Gold Top had entered Heuze's field of view behind the giant's smile. Muambwi grinned malevolently as he heard the Old One's words. Clearly the Gold Top would enjoy watching whatever horror was to be perpetrated on the hapless admiral.

"Yes, dear Admiral, I shall smear you with the

black paste of expungement. Then I shall boil the meat off your bones with the white fire."

Heuze spat weakly and replied in as steady a voice as he could manage, "Well, whoever you are, I'll be dead by then, so I won't know anything about it."

"Oh, but you will, for the tension of your life force seeking to depart is exactly what I will be playing on."

Heuze shivered. Whatever the insane giant was raving about, it didn't sound as if it was going to be much fun.

The leer was back. "So, tell me, Admiral, as I prepare the black paste, what does it feel like to be a broken man? An empty vessel, drained and waiting to be thrown on the fire? A doomed captive without hope? You never expected this, I'll wager."

The huge man was breaking up a black substance into a golden bowl held in front of him by two slaves. As the substance fell into the bowl there were strange sparkles in Heuze's vision and he heard uncanny little tinkling sounds at the very edge of his perception.

Heuze saw how the game might be played. Confidence, that was the thing. "Actually I do have hope."

The giant paused, his eyes wide. "Really? You astonish me. What hopes can you have? Do you refer to an afterlife? You aren't a religious man. No, no, I've seen the reports. You have many marks against you. A blasphemer, it is plain. You don't believe in an afterlife."

"You're right, I couldn't give a fart for your religion. All bunk, and you know it. My hopes rest, actually, on your undoubted intelligence. I know a lot of things that you don't, and I could tell you those things, if you were to spare me."

The giant's smile widened, if that was at all possible. "Oh ho! You know things that you haven't told us. Muambwi, how can this be?" The big man whirled on the spidery Gold Top like a bird of prey stooping on a pigeon.

"He lies, Great One . . ." Muambwi cringed.

"Maybe he does. Let us see."

Heuze tried to grin at Muambwi. It hurt too much. He let his face sag again. That at least didn't hurt quite so much.

"Well, well, well, you have hopes, Admiral, you really do. Because if you do give me something worthwhile, something I do not already know, then I will spare you."

A huge hand scrunched his shoulder again.

"I will take Muambwi Gold Top instead."

Heuze scarcely dared to believe what he'd heard. "Really?" he mumbled.

"Yes, yes, indeed." The giant man turned and snapped his fingers to the guards. He gestured to Muambwi. "Bind him for sacrifice."

The guards seized the startled Gold Top and bound his wrists behind his back.

"Now shut the tent. No one is to be admitted on pain of death. If there are urgent messages from the front, you will call me from outside, understood?"

"Yes, Lord."

The look on Muambwi's face brought a grunt of amusement from Heuze. The giant's eyes twinkled.

"Now, Admiral?"

"Well, you know that Aeswiren commands the colony army. And you know that the monkey army is commanded by this fellow Toshak."

"Yes, I have heard that name. The monkeys under this Toshak's leadership have done extraordinarily well against you, Admiral Heuze. Drove you back to your fleet once or twice, I believe."

"Yes, well, they're tricky, especially in the woods. So, anyway I have met with this General Toshak. You see, the Emperor, er, the ex-Emperor"—Heuze hurried on when he saw the huge brows knit in a frown—"he demanded that we sit down with the monkeys and pretend they're human and everything. And we were supposed to talk about what we were going to do. How we were going to get along in this campaign."

"Not your idea, eh?"

"Oh, no, your lordship. I prefer my monkey after it's been cooked."

"Very good! That's the spirit. You may have your fill of grilled monkey very soon—if my lizards leave any!"

"Yes, your lordship. It became very apparent to me that this Toshak is the key to the situation. See, he's some sort of natural leader. There's no one else like him, except the little old demon things."

"Yes, I know those that you refer to. So you say this monkey general is unique. He is their guiding genius, eh? Without him, their horde will disintegrate."

"Yes, your lordship."

"So how do I find this monkey general?"

"Well, it just so happens that I know how you might find him."

"No, Lord, do not listen to him!" cried Muambwi, horrified by this turn of events.

"Silence!" roared the Old One, who slapped the Gold Top across the mouth so hard blood and spittle flew across the tent.

The huge man turned back to Heuze. "Yes?"

"Well, I have to bargain with you, don't I? You kill that Gold Top first, do your spell, and then I'll tell you."

The giant smiled, but the eyes were most unkind. "Hmm. You think to bargain with me, do you?"

"You need the information. I need to live."

"I could hammer it out of you."

"I could hold it back until it's too late for you to use it."

The evil leader's eyes filled with calculation. He turned and went to the front flap of the tent.

"Bring my pet monkey," he snapped to the guards

before turning back to Heuze, now holding the golden
bowl in his hands.

"All right, Admiral, it's a bargain."

Heuze watched with a mix of awe and horror as the
Old One stirred sparkling powder into the bowl and
then handed it to a slave, who crouched down and
held it steady.

With a casual grasp, the giant seized the bound
Gold Top and lifted him into the air as if he were no
more than a chicken. Muambwi wailed with terror.

The huge man held Muambwi upside down by his
ankles. A knife flashed in his massive hand, and the
priest's wails cut off abruptly into choking noises. The
giant held the Gold Top by the ankles and let his
blood drain down into the golden bowl.

As the blood flowed, the sorcerer muttered a collec-
tion of guttural phrases. The words meant nothing to
Heuze, but they seemed heavy with sibilance.

Heuze began to feel a charge rising into the room.
The hair on his neck and then all over his body stood
up. A strange chill ran down his spine. Suddenly a
thick black whisker writhed up within the bowl. Something about the motion made Heuze's skin crawl. The
tendril was joined by another, and then more, until it
seemed that some giant spider must be lying on its
back inside the bowl, waving its legs in the air.

The tension continued to build. Heuze heard odd
little sounds, squeaks and chirrups, coming from the
bowl. The whiskers waved frantically.

Heuze noticed a horrible smell, as if something long
since dead had been brought inside the tent. The smell
got stronger and stronger until his eyes were beginning
to smart and he was gagging.

There was a sudden explosion, and a flash of red
light seared his eyeballs.

The stench still hung in the air, but now it began
to diminish.

The giant man was standing still, his hands clutching the top of his skull as if he were holding it on with every ounce of strength he had. The slaves that had held the golden bowl were lying prostrate, dead by every indication.

With a loud gasp, the huge man let go of his head, opened his eyes, and extended his arms upward. He gave a great, deafening cry and then lowered his hands.

Heuze realized he'd been holding his breath and let it out. Damn, but this was getting to be bad for his nerves.

"The monkey is here, Lord," said a guard outside the tent.

"Good, send him in."

The giant man spoke as if nothing had happened inside the tent.

More slaves appeared, who dragged away the comatose forms beside the golden bowl.

A mot entered. Heuze found himself being introduced to the creature a few moments later.

"Admiral, meet my translator, my guide to the ways of the native folk. This is Pern Treevi."

Heuze had spent enough time around mots to see at once that there was something strange in this mot's eyes.

"Now, tell us all about this Toshak."

Chapter 32

Through the night, the armies labored on Shelly Fields. Thru delivered his last message to Aeswiren in the fourth hour of darkness and was relieved of duty for the while. He stopped for a moment at the crest of the hill and studied the pattern of fires on the far side of the river. The enemy was not resting.

But Toshak knew all this. Thru turned away from it. He had something more important to attend to.

The trails were crowded. Mixed groups of men and mots were carrying their wounded to the field hospital set up on Blue Hill. Around him, Thru heard the groans of pain and the murmurs of encouragement in both his own language and the tongue of Shasht, mingled together as he'd never heard them before.

A donkey cart, piled with wounded men, was being driven by a big brilby wearing a captured enemy helmet. Thru worked his way around them.

The trail was a morass of mud where the storm had soaked the ground. Thru found he could make better time working his way through the woods, even in the dark. Eventually he crossed the rocky stream and struggled up the slope of Blue Hill. A city of tents had sprung up here. A big fire was blazing farther along, and he checked there.

Hundreds of wounded men and mots had already been brought in. Others were being operated on at that moment. Screams and cries echoed in the dark-

ness. Up the muddy trail struggled a steady stream of
stretcher bearers. A young mor, her fur streaked with
blood, was drinking a mug of tea. In her eyes was the
look of exhaustion.

"Nuza?" she said when Thru spoke to her. "Must
be resting somewhere. I haven't seen her for a while.
She worked so hard to get us all up here."

He went on, looking in the tents, finding scenes of
horror and scenes of heroism as young mors struggled
to help the wounded. Often the wounded men, deliri-
ous from pain, would panic when they found themselves being handled by mors. But Thru heard more
than one of these mors respond gently, "Be calm, we
will help you."

They spoke Shasht, and he heard incredulous excla-
mations as the men realized that they were being
cared for by the "monkeys" that they had hated for
so long.

At the entrance to the largest tent of all, he ran
into Simona.

"Thru?" She was stunned to see him there, and he
was equally surprised.

"Simona."

It was simply natural to hold each other close,
though it awoke memories of another desperate time,
and after a few moments they pulled apart.

Thru felt suddenly awkward, unable to speak. Simona recovered first.

"You're looking for Nuza, of course. Silly me."

Thru peered past her into the tent. Under a lantern he saw Simona's father at work, covered in
blood.

"He has worked wonders," said Simona. "My father
is not a strong man, except when he's working like
this."

Thru shivered. "I think it's easier to take lives than
it is to save them."

"They took Nuza to the blue tent, over there. That's where we sleep when we can't go on any longer."

Thru saw the lines of exhaustion on her face. "Thank you. How long have you been here?"

"I don't remember. Mentu brought us up on the *Sea Wasp*. Sailed in right under the nose of the enemy fleet. They know they can't catch the *Sea Wasp* so close to shore."

"Mentu is here?"

"Yes. He wanted to fight, but they rejected him. He knows nothing of war and, besides, he's too old."

"How was Nuza?"

"She is amazing. I have never seen anyone work so hard. Moved this entire hospital here from Dronned. Forty donkey carts, sixteen ox wagons, and more are coming. She will save hundreds, maybe thousands, of lives."

Thru was already gone, though. Simona looked after his retreating back before turning back into the tent. Despite everything, she found she had tears in her eyes.

Thru searched the blue tent, where a few exhausted mors and older mots were asleep, but Nuza was not among them. One of them suggested he try at the cook shack where a fire was blazing. Though he had missed her on his first pass, he spotted her at last, huddled alone on the far side, sipping a mug of tea and staring into the fire with blank eyes.

He slid in beside her and took her into his arms.

"You're alive," she said at last, relishing this confirmation in her faith in providence.

"I haven't been in the fight this time. More likely you would have been hurt than me."

"Silly! What harm could befall us back here?"

"The enemy has horsemen. They're out there in the woods."

"Aeswiren has a company here to guard us."

"Or, you could have killed yourself with overwork."
She started to laugh but stopped.

They were silent again. Treasuring the precious moment snatched from the battle, a quiet point of stillness in the midst of the vast storm.

"It's not the work, Thru, it's the heartbreak. There was a young mot today. He was done for, a sucking chest wound. I keep hearing him ask me if he had a chance. I lied, and he knew I was lying."

She let out a sob then steadied herself and sucked in a deep breath. "Sorry, that was weakness. It's hard sometimes . . ."

Thru just held her quietly in his arms. "The Spirit has some plan for both of us, or we wouldn't still be around."

"Trust you to put it that way," she laughed, brought back to her normal self. "That's Thru Gillo, always seeing the silver lining in the clouds."

But Thru wasn't listening. For he had felt a sudden change.

"What is it, Thru?"

"Listen."

Across the hills, over the trees, they heard it. A great moan that went on and on, an unbroken sound, neither rising nor falling for many seconds, until at last it cut off with a strange sob.

Silence fell across the Land, while every man and every mot felt his or her being shiver to its core. Some dropped their weapons and sprawled witless on the ground. Others crept into the trees and tried to hide.

A vast red light lit up the north, and they became aware of the sound of enormous drums beating in the hills.

"It is him. The crisis is upon us."

Nuza held up her hands as if for rain. "What is it?"

Thru saw the light pulsing with the sound. "Black sorcery, that is all I know."

With a last embrace he left her and started back to the front.

The climb over the hills seemed to take an eternity. The red light pulsed in the sky, the great drums throbbed, and a terrible gloom settled over Thru's spirits. Men, mots and donkey carts were all mixed up on the trail, with some trying to get up the hill and others seeking to get down to the village.

Suddenly Thru felt a sizzling sensation in his hands and feet, and then terrifying, alien images rushed into his mind. He cried out, one in a multitude of others who cried as well. The images did not let up. At first they were almost meaningless, shapes like those of bats or knives or perhaps simply clouds, but they filled his mind and blocked his vision.

Thru stumbled into someone and recoiled from a blow. Dimly he heard voices cursing in both the tongue of the Land and in Shasht. His vision cleared, and he saw himself surrounded by men and mots holding hands to their ears, some who had fallen to their knees in the mud.

A donkey cart had turned over; the donkey was kicking in the stays and the wounded men had spilled out into the brush. No one seemed capable of restraining the struggling animal or helping the wounded. Thru staggered toward the donkey, then stopped dead, blinded by a terrifying hallucination.

He waved his hands to force it away, but it would not leave him.

He stood on a shadowy plain. In the company of thousands of other doomed souls, he was marching forward to a line of great anvils. Behind the anvils stood enormous men wielding huge bloody hammers that rose and fell in time with the throbbing drums. As the doomed came up to the anvils, they laid their heads meekly on the gore-soaked metal, and the hammers came down.

Thru struggled to clear this monstrous vision from his mind, but it held fast. The sense of the inevitable grew in his heart. Why continue with the struggle when death was the only certain reward? Why resist the great power of the enemy that towered above them?

The hammers were rising and falling. The sound of their blows on the anvils throbbed in his brain. Thru heard himself screaming, but it was almost as if he were already a ghost and separated from the real world by a membrane across which sounds filtered only weakly. Strange, sickly images continued to torment him. Bones and graves, corpse flesh hanging from hooks, a pile of skulls with green light glowing in the empty sockets—all paraded across his vision.

Then the spell was broken. A flash of white light erupted across the plain, splitting the darkness like a knife. The anvils disappeared, the hammers vanished, and Thru was back, crouched over the mud on the slope of Blue Hill, holding his head in his hands with tears streaming down his cheeks.

All around him, mots and men were recovering. Someone took hold of the donkey's reins. Others struggled up from the mud. Thru shook himself free of the horror and went on, plowing through the mud and the chaotic crowd of mots and men on the trail.

As he came over the crest of the hill, the red light fell upon him in full fury. The source of the light was down in the Shell Valley, and it glowed like the sun. The throbbing of the great drums continued, and Thru could see that the battle had begun again. Arrayed across the valley were serried ranks of spears, helmets, and shields, and he could hear the harsh music of war coming from where the enemy's thrusts across the river had driven into Toshak's formations.

The trail was still full of mots and men moving away from the fight, but Thru pressed on and eventually found Toshak and his staff perched on a knoll thrust out of the northern slope of the hill.

"Colonel Gillo, good to see you. Our enemy decided not to wait for morning."

"Sir. I was delayed."

"By the hallucinations, I expect. Well, not your fault, that's for sure. We all had them, until the Assenzi did something that cut them off."

Thru recalled that blinding flash of white light. "Thanks be given to the Assenzi," he said.

"Yes, indeed, but the enemy crossed the river during that period, took our front ranks by surprise, and drove us back from the river. Now he's massed enough troops on this side to give us a real fight."

"What about those horsemen?"

"Not seen them yet, but we will. I have a regiment in reserve on the flank."

"And the pyluk?"

"The same. We know they're in the woods upstream, but so far we haven't seen any indications that they'll be attacking soon."

Toshak was studying the ground beneath his observation point. Thru could see that the mot front line had bent back in a bow shape under the pressure of two large assault columns, one at either end of the line. In the center there was relative quiet.

"I think our enemy thought his hallucination would last a while longer and disrupt us more than it did."

"It disrupted me, all right. I could barely walk while it was going on."

"Yes, there's no question that this sorcerer has great power, but the Assenzi knew how to break the spell."

As they watched, they could see the enemy attacks losing impetus and beginning to subside.

Suddenly the red light cut off and the drumming slowly faded to nothing.

Without that awful light it was hard at first to see what was happening. As their eyes adjusted, they noted that the enemy had pulled back both assault columns and was consolidating a position about two hundred yards south of the river, approximately half the distance to the base of the hill on which Toshak and Thru were standing.

Toshak turned his attention to the woods and sent messengers forward to instruct two regiments to move to the right flank and strengthen the flank guard.

"I don't think he will want to rest on that line. If we were to break him there, we could destroy his army against the river when the tide comes in later."

"He will attack again?"

"He must do something. He can't stay where he is."

"He likes to disguise his attacks with sorcery."

As if summoned by the word, a pair of spindly little figures appeared out of the darkness. Melidofulo, the patron Assenzi of Dronned, was one. The other was Estremides, who had been sent by Cutshamakim of Highnoth to assist Toshak during the campaign.

"Greetings, Masters," said Toshak with a bow.

"Greetings, General, Colonel. Karnemin's spell of blinding darkness has been broken, I am glad to say," said Melidofulo.

"Quite dispelled, we might add," said Estremides with a hint of levity.

Thru, most familiar with Utnapishtim of all the Assenzi, smiled at Estremides's jest.

"But we can be sure he will try something else." Melidofulo stared down through the darkness toward the river where the enemy army was massed.

"Colonel Gillo and I were just discussing how the enemy likes to use his sorcery to disguise his army's movements."

"He is a master of these things," said Melidofulo in a somber voice. "But we can be sure he will vary his approaches. Do not grow complacent, ever, when dealing with this enemy."

No sooner had the Assenzi said this than they heard horns blare over to the right. A mud-spattered scout appeared shortly afterward to inform Toshak that the pyluk were moving about in the forest. So far there appeared to be nothing organized about the movements, but they were enough to have alarmed the Grys Norvory, in command of the Third Regiment, which held the right flank.

Thru was sent to the Grys with a message.

"By the time you get there, I'm sure this message will be irrelevant, Gillo, since the Ninth and Thirteenth Regiments will have joined Norvory on the flank, but it will serve to assure him that I'm keeping an eye on those pyluk, and those horsemen, wherever they are. Moreover, I want you to study the flank and then report back. I'd like to go myself, but think it's better I remain here where I can see the whole field and react quickly to any fresh developments."

Thru took the message, drained a flask of tea, and turned to go. Almost immediately he bumped into his old friend Meu of Deepford, now the quartermaster general of the army of Dronned.

"Meu! Or, General Meu, sir!" said Thru with a smile and a salute.

Meu grinned back. "Stand easy, Colonel." They both laughed. "Well, well, old friend, good to see you. I caught a glimpse of you one time a few weeks back at the palace in Dronned, but you were hurrying away and I was hurrying in to speak to the King."

"Oh, Meu, that's been the way of it since this campaign began. I've covered a thousand miles and gone through another pair of boots."

"Where are you off to now?"

"The right flank. The Grys Norvory holds it with the Third Regiment. General Toshak wants a detailed report on the situation there."

"Good luck. You'll be glad to know that I've got twenty wagons full of meal coming up the back side of the hill. There should be a very good breakfast for us all."

"We'll need it. I expect we'll see some hard fighting this day."

"When this is over, we must sup at the Laughing Fish in Dronned. I have so many questions to ask you about your adventures in the land of the men."

They parted with a handshake and went their way.

Thru hurried down the muddy track to the bottom of the hill and then through Shelly Fields to the right flank.

By the time Thru found the Grys Norvory's command post, the right flank had been strengthened by the arrival of the Ninth Regiment under the command of Colonel Flares and the Thirteenth under Colonel Fladgate. They had taken positions on either side of Norvory's Third Regiment.

Thru found the regimental commanders gathered at Norvory's post, set up on a hillock that gave a reasonable view of the ground around them. He received a warm welcome and passed on Toshak's message to Norvory while adding a few verbal comments.

Norvory read the message then sealed it again.

"Well, General Toshak assures us he's looking out for the pyluk and those men on the horse animals. We can expect some kind of attack before long, I'm sure."

"Indeed, Grys, the enemy can't accept the position he's in now. His back to the river with the tide coming in during the morning—it will put him in a very dangerous situation."

"And if I know General Toshak," added Colonel Flares, "he will be looking for a way to exploit that, and at first light, too."

"No doubt he will," said Thru. "He also asked me to study the ground here so I can inform him in detail about the situation on your front."

"Well, can't see much right now, but it will be dawn in an hour or so."

Thru surveyed the scene. On the immediate front, the ground was mostly open. A pattern of dark patches of bare rock mingled with lighter areas where mounds of shells had built up. Small trees, dwarf pines, and oaks were clustered here and there where they'd found suitable soil. About two hundred yards away, the trees thickened and the forest quickly reasserted itself. By three hundred yards out, the forest was a dark mass.

The regiments were lined up in three ranks, each consisting of two hundred with a mobile reserve of another hundred kept at the back, ready to plug gaps or assist if the regimental front was flanked.

"Looks perfect to me, almost like being on the parade ground."

"It's good ground for fighting, quite clear and open. If the enemy attacks us here, we will make him pay."

"What lies farther upstream?"

"It's all wild water for miles. No polder on the river Shell."

"So there are no roads either—"

Thru's rumination was interrupted by the resumption of the sullen, throbbing drum from the far side of the river.

"It begins again," said the Grys Norvory.

"It appears so. We must be ready for the worst."

Thru walked the length of the flank force position, studying the gulleys and hillocks that broke up the flatness of the plain. The three regiments were well placed on slightly higher ground. Between the left flank of the Ninth Regiment, placed closest to the river, and the right flank of the next regiment over, in the main army position, there was a gap of twenty yards, easily filled by reserves in the case of an attack. Looking along the line of the main army front, Thru dimly saw regiment after regiment in the darkness, waiting for the next move. Pennons flapped in the predawn breeze, but otherwise it was quiet on this side of the river.

The drums throbbed on, however.

On the right side of the flank position, farthest from the river, the Thirteenth Regiment filled the ground right up to the thickening forest that marked the beginning of the hillside.

Thru could find no fault with these dispositions. After a final chat with Norvory, he turned back and started up the hillside to Toshak's position.

The drum had been joined by a whistling sound, like that of a flute played off-key. It scratched and irritated the ears of all who heard it. Slowly it mounted in intensity.

Thru stared at the river. A mist was rising there, but beyond the dark masses of the enemy troops facing the lines of Toshak and Aeswiren's armies, it was impossible to see any detail or where the strange drumming and whistling was coming from.

He turned back to the trail. It was muddy and quite steep in places, and coming after all his exertions the day before and through the night, it made him aware of just how tired he was.

The whistling continued to rise in volume. As it mounted higher and higher, it approached the shriek of a boiling kettle. Thru knew that the noise must have become close to unbearable for the mots closer to the river, let alone the enemy formations beyond them.

Then the first light of dawn broke through the

clouds in the east, and with it came new terror. Thru caught sight of a strange chilly gleam on the ground and turned to look eastward.

Where the warm, pink blush of dawn should have been, there was instead a silver-etched blackness that grew in intensity with each moment. Thru, and indeed the multitude of men and mots standing on the plain of Shelly Fields, gazed at this phenomenon with awe.

With the cold, dark light came a chill wind. Thru felt it stir the fur on his face, and he shivered. He turned, with an effort, and continued across to Toshak's position. The strange light from the east limned every blade of grass and every hummock with silver while casting the rest into shades of dark grey to black.

The whistling from the far side of the river had become a maniacal shrieking, and the drumming had increased in power until it seemed to throb inside Thru's head.

His legs felt weak. His hands were chilled as if it were midwinter. Then the first edge of the sun rose above the eastern hills.

Instantly, all who looked in that direction were blinded.

A great moan of mingled fear and horror rose from the ranks of mots and men on Shelly Fields. Accompanying it came a new sound, bugles and whistles in the ranks of the enemy. They had been warned not to look eastward and to screen the deadly light of dawn with their shields.

With a roar of "He Who Eats!" the army of the Old One thrust forward in attack. Thru had missed the deadly flash of dawn's light, but he saw its effect on those around him. The mots in Toshak's post were crying out and falling to the ground, unable to see.

Thru hurried forward and found Toshak shaking his head, grimacing, and rubbing his eyes.

"General. Thru Gillo reporting."

"Gillo? Can you see?"

"Yes, sir."

"I can only see with my left eye, and that in part only. It's as if my vision were blanked out with black ink."

Thru had put two and two together. A handful of others were still sighted, like him. "It is deadly to look at the sun—it blinds."

"Though I was not looking directly at it, the eye closest to the sun is most affected."

"That confirms it," said Thru.

"And now?"

"He attacks."

Below, on Shelly Fields, the enemy host crunched into the front ranks of Toshak's and Aeswiren's armies. Blinded, many mots and men were hardly able to either defend themselves or flee. They were cut down by the hundreds.

From the forest on the right flank came another dreadful sound, the hissing roar of five thousand pyluk bulls. Out from the trees they came, a great mass of charging lizards, their spears waving above them.

The front of the allied position collapsed. The blind staggered about until they were cut down. On the right flank, where Thru had spoken with the confident regimental commanders only half an hour before, there were even fewer with sight remaining. The pyluk fell on the flank regiments and broke them up in a matter of minutes.

Here and there on the main front there were nodes of resistance. After a few minutes, the worst effects of the blinding light passed, and many mots and some men regained their sight. The fighting turned from an all-out rout to a bitterly fought retreat across Shelly Fields. The Grys Norvory and a company of survivors from the Third, Ninth, and Thirteenth Regiments fought a desperate battle to slow the pyluk onrush.

All of this was plainly visible to Thru, standing on the hillside above, who observed the Grys's personal pennon still flying there.

"Are there any regiments asleep?" he asked Toshak.

"Yes, I sent the Tenth and the Fourteenth to sleep just an hour ago."

"Where are they?"

"Back on the crest of the hill."

"Then I will bring them here. We must stop them on this hill." Thru set off at a run.

Toshak, able to see with one eye, had found two messengers who retained their sight. In moments, they were on their way to Norvory and whoever they found in command of the main force, now trying to hold a line about a hundred yards from the base of the hill.

Thru quickly came to Aeswiren's command post. He found much the same situation as at Toshak's. Aeswiren was less affected, however, as were his personal staff.

"I knew it was some evil weirding from the first gleam, and I told everyone not to look."

"The right flank is almost lost. The pyluk came on the heels of this evil light."

"Those cavalry will be up to something soon as well. This is a well-planned assault."

"Two regiments were sent to sleep in the hour before dawn. I'm going to fetch them. We hope to hold a line on the hill."

"We will join you there. It will take all our remaining strength to hold such a position. And I expect those horsemen will make it that much more difficult, too."

Thru went on. He found the Tenth and Fourteenth awake and forming up in a marching column. Colonels Gevery and Besh were aware of the peril and busy kicking life into their regiments.

The throng of wounded and stretcher bearers had

pulled off the track to let the regiments through. As Thru charged by, he called out to the bearers to turn back and follow the regiments.

"Every mot, every man will be needed. March to the sound of the fighting. Pick up weapons where you can find them."

When he returned to the hill, he found the battle had progressed to the very lip of tragedy.

Mots and men mixed together were fighting in a rough line about halfway up the slope of the hill. The hillock that Toshak had used as a command post was now in the midst of the fighting. To the left side were the main masses of Aeswiren's men, still fairly well organized in regiments and holding quite well. On the right, besieged by a vast flood of pyluk, were the mots, who had suffered badly from the blinding light and then the flank assault. Regimental organization had broken down almost completely. They formed an irregular line, in places only a single soldier deep.

In their favor was the equal degree of disorganization among the pyluk. The struggle between mots armed with sword, shield, spear, and pike and pyluk armed with club and wooden spear was usually settled in favor of the mots.

Thus the line held. Thru could see Norvory's pennon still flying on the right end of the line. But the situation was dire.

The Tenth and then the Fourteenth Regiments were coming, and, as they crested the hill and saw the situation, they broke into a run and closed up quickly on the thin line of defenders.

Behind them came another group, perhaps three hundred stretcher bearers and even some of the walking wounded, who understood that if the fight was lost here, then they would die come what may. Their enemy intended nothing but annihilation for them. So they had dragged themselves back to face death with weapon in hand.

Thru ran over to greet this group. "Any officers among you?"

A few mots emerged. Thru bade them take charge. "Form into a company, three lines. Take what weapons you can find. We're going to use you as a reserve force."

Thru left them and hunted for Toshak. He found the general's standard flying from a position under a ledge, about a hundred yards back from the front line.

"Look upslope, Colonel," said Toshak as Thru arrived.

Thru saw three of Toshak's catapult engines being wound.

"We will show the enemy that he's not the only one with deadly surprises up his sleeve, eh?"

At a shouted command, the catapults were loosed. They flung their spears, each seven feet long and tipped with a heavy stone point, over the heads of the mot line and into the approaching masses of the enemy.

Thru applauded, but the scale of this assault was so small compared to that of the enemy's sorcery that it merely accentuated the gap between their powers. Still, it worked as Toshak expected, sowing seeds of concern among the Old One's men down below them.

The fighting stabilized. Reinforced and with the slope of the ground favoring them, the battered remnants of Toshak's army were no longer retreating. They held their ground and fought the attack to a standstill.

The pyluk had by then withdrawn. They were of little use in regular fighting, and against the mots they had taken terrible casualties once the impetus of their charge had failed.

When the enemy made one final effort, a concerted attack right along the front, there came a threat of a breach in the gap between Toshak's line and Aeswiren's. A dip in the ground there became a void in the line, and the enemy pressed through and began to peel back Toshak's left flank.

The reserve company was hurled into this fight. It managed to stem the enemy tide and then turn it with the fury of their counterattack.

At the same time, Aeswiren threw in his own reserve force, a motley crew from the Blitz Regiment mixed up with the Third Regiment. They drove a wedge into the enemy's line and brought his renewed attack to a halt. After a quarter hour of fierce combat, the enemy was called away from the line and stood back fifty yards. Mot archers flooded the lines with arrows. This barrage proved too expensive for the enemy again, and they withdrew another hundred yards, putting them at the extreme edge of the archers' range.

Now the battle wound down from exhaustion on both sides.

Thru looked to the sky. The sun's light was slowly changing from the deathly dark energy of the first hour and resuming its warmth. The battle was less than two hours old, and their situation had changed drastically for the worse. Thru estimated that Toshak's army had lost a third, even half its strength. Aeswiren's men were badly hurt, too, reduced by perhaps a quarter in the catastrophe.

The enemy also had taken casualties, particularly among the pyluk horde, which had lingered too long in combat with the mots. But, all in all, the enemy's losses were not half those of Toshak's alone. Barely enough men and mots remained to hold a defensive line against the enemy.

Some good news came from the rear. The enemy's horsemen had emerged from the forest and made an attack on the hospital. The company of guards there had been unscathed by the dawn light, and they had engaged the horsemen, forming a line with grounded pikes. The horsemen had tried to panic the defenders, then fired off arrows from a distance, and finally wheeled away and made another attempt to get in among the tents. After being frustrated five times, the cavalry pulled back and retreated into the forest once more, leaving half a dozen dead behind.

Thru would have liked to go back and reassure himself that Nuza was safe, but he was kept busy working with the Grys Norvory on reshaping the right wing of the army, digging in and setting out a screen of pickets.

Toshak and his staff worked like demons to pull the army into some sort of shape and improve positions with a trench and sharpened stakes.

The catapults were firing as fast as they could be wound up and released, and their long spears were capable of killing well beyond the range of the archers. The enemy was unhappy with standing there being shot at with the huge spears. Their lines wavered and had to be ordered to stand still. Toshak increased the pressure when another set of catapults were finally brought into operation. They had been trapped on the crowded trail from Dronned during the fighting. Now there were six of the things in action, and that meant a near constant rain of long spears into the enemy ranks.

Eventually, the enemy gave in and shifted even farther back, although the catapults were still taking a toll. By late morning, they were seen digging their own trenches and erecting protective fasciae.

The battle had ended, if only for the time being. Both sides were worn out from the exertions of the dawn hours. Slowly, as the day wore on, those who had been blinded began to recover their sight. At first they saw in fits and starts, and many were cursed with dark flecks and spots in their vision, but hour by hour things improved. By early afternoon, only those who had stared full into the rising sun at that deadly moment were still affected. Alas, many of these victims had been slain in the first fury of the battle.

By then Thru Gillo had received some of that breakfast that Meu had promised long before. Afterward he promptly fell asleep, wrapped in his cloak, behind Toshak's command post.

Chapter 33

Sergeant Rukkh rested the butt of his spear on the ground and let his shield lean against his thigh. Like the rest of the men in the line, he was bone-tired but too wound up to sleep. The day had been a strange one.

"All this hocus-pocus gives my belly the gripes," said Ladwaller, a big man from Grezack.

"Gives us all the gripes," said Rukkh.

Worse than that, of course, because it had made about twenty men in the company stone-blind that morning when they had bad luck to be awake and looking eastward when the sun first broke over the hills. In that, the company had done better than most: in some outfits on the far right of the line, as many as half the men had been blinded.

"Goddamned lizard-men, bad dreams, and this blindness. It's a bad situation," continued Ladwaller.

"Shut up, Ladwaller," said Belzec. "We're all in this together."

"Don't I know it," said the big man.

Rukkh kept quiet. Letting the men grumble was part of being a good sergeant. Especially a sergeant who was now running the whole company since the officers had been killed. The lads were a solid lot. They'd been in the Blitz Regiment since the beginning of the war and represented the best they had left in this army.

"Least the blind are getting their sight back now."

"No thanks to He Who Eats for that!" said another soldier. Rukkh grunted to himself. The religion of the Great God had really taken a nosedive in the Blitz Regiment over the past year. Once they'd been given the chance to take out the Red Tops, all interest in Orbazt Subuus had dried up. Rukkh made a mental note to inform the Emperor about that the next time he was summoned to report on the mood in the army.

"Sergeant," called Chimikin, a youngster drafted into the Blitzers from the Ninth Regiment, "something's happening over there."

Rukkh sighed and shifted position to look down into the valley. His company was holding a section of the army's line, set halfway up the hillside. Their former position, all nicely dug in, could be seen clearly about three hundred yards downslope. They'd worked hard the previous day to fortify it, but all their efforts came to naught when the monkeys had been overwhelmed in the dawn attack and the whole army had been forced to shift back up the hill.

Now he could see the enemy moving forward again, this time to face the men of Aeswiren's army.

"What are they up to?" Ladwaller asked suspiciously.

"I don't know, big man, but I'm sure we're going to find out before it's all over."

More and more of the enemy army was advancing, dressing out their line to their right and giving every indication of forming an attack column.

"All right, men, take notice of what's going on down there. Our enemy has got his wind back, and he's ready to take us on again. This time it looks like he wants some of our metal in his guts instead of the monkeys'."

"Be glad to oblige him," growled Ladwaller.

Armor clanked as the men stood up, drew their

swords to inspect them, arranged their shields, and put on their helmets after scratching their heads.

The enemy was massing right along Aeswiren's front.

"Seems weird to me," said Belzec.

"Why's that?" said Rukkh.

"Well, a frontal assault like this? Right at us and us all ready for him? He usually comes up with some kind of trickery, right?"

"Yeah, well, maybe he's run out of tricks."

Belzec snorted disbelievingly at that.

"It's starting again. Listen," said Ladwaller.

And it was. The damned drums were going again, throbbing insistently over on the far side of the river.

"Look, they're raising their shields over their heads." Belzec pointed. Rukkh saw what the enemy was doing and immediately gave the order for everyone to do the same. He turned on his heel and sprinted to the command post of Colonel Begeluse, now commanding the regiment.

Begeluse wasn't the brightest spark in the fire, but he'd come to realize that the enemy's tricks were dangerous. Not only did he repeat Rukkh's suggested order to the whole Blitz Regiment but he passed on the advice up the chain of command.

Aeswiren instantly concurred, and within half a minute every man in the army had his shield raised. The monkeys were starting to imitate the men when another sound rang out, piercingly loud, echoing off the hillsides, as if a hammer had struck a bell.

The echoes of the sound were just fading away when the flash came. From one end of the sky to the other on an east-west axis exploded a vast bolt of blue fire. For a long second or two, the whole world was hidden in the blinding glare of that fire. If they hadn't had their shields raised over their heads, they would have been blinded a second time.

Yet the sorcery wasn't primarily intended to blind.

Instead, every man felt his limbs grow heavy and his heart grow weak.

"What in the name of hell is this?" snarled Ladwaller.

Rukkh felt as if his arms had turned into lead weights. He wanted to sink down on the turf and just sleep forever.

"They're coming!" shouted Chimikin.

The lad was right. The enemy obviously hadn't suffered from the disabling power of the blue flash, because they were charging up the slope at a steady trot, spears at the ready.

"All right, everyone, suck it up. We can still fight. We ain't gonna lie down and let the fornicating sons of bitches kill us that easily."

Rukkh spoke bravely, but his arms really did feel almost useless.

"Fine for some to say," muttered Belzec, who was struggling just to hold on to his shield.

"Shut up, Belzec, or I'll gut you myself," growled Rukkh.

The enemy was closing in. Archers on both sides lofted arrows into the ranks opposite. Rukkh lifted his own shield as shafts began falling among them. There was a cry of pain somewhere off to the left and then a gasp much closer, and he found Fonson limping and staggering, with an arrow that had pierced his knee.

Rukkh whistled for stretcher bearers and worked to keep everyone in the company steady. But from the groans and sighs he knew the men were struggling with the terrible weakness they felt. They could barely raise their weapons, let along wield them in a fight.

Rukkh had a bad feeling about this, but he had to hope that by raising their shields and blocking off the worst of the blue flash, they had a chance of recovery. The enemy's men had also endured the blue flash. Surely they could not have escaped all of its effect.

A messenger ran down the line, shouting to each company as he went: "Form in three-man defense line."

The men struggled to comply. Rukkh could see they were all making a big effort. "Good thinking," he said to himself.

The lead man held his shield with both hands. The second man set his down and took up the spear of the lead man, while holding his own in reserve. The third man had his shield and spear ready to aid the other two when the clash came. It was a tried-and-true method for the men of Shasht, who were well trained in its uses.

"Hey," shouted Ladwaller, "I can feel it fading. My strength is coming back."

"You hear that, boys?" Rukkh called out to his men.

They heard him. The leaden-armed feeling was only temporary. They just had to hold on as long as they could until they got their strength back.

"Hell, this is just like a charley horse."

"Something weird from that fornicating wizard they got over there."

"He's behind the fornicating Red Tops."

"Damn their sodomistic souls to hell."

"Heh, heh, we took care of those bastards."

A sense of shared satisfaction spread among them. Everyone in the army had really enjoyed putting the Red Tops to the sword.

But the enemy was still stepping smartly toward them.

Still weakened from the wizardry in the sky, Aeswiren's men buckled here and there along their line at the first shock. The enemy thrust hard into these places and at one point, where the Sixth and Third Regiments butted up next to each other, forced open a break.

The enemy poured through the gap.

Right in front of them was the Emperor's command post.

Rukkh's company had met and broken the first charge on their front. But they were pulled back when the Third Regiment was forced to shift position to cover the flank that was exposed to the breakthrough. Rukkh saw the Emperor's banner flying over a scrum of battle. Without a second thought, he pulled half the company out of the line and led them in a charge into this fight.

His legs still felt heavy, but his right arm was back in use and his left was improving. Plus, there wasn't time to think about things like that. Rukkh flung himself into the fight, spearing a man in armor and tunic very much like this own. As the fellow sank down, cursing him for being a sodomistic slave of the demons, Rukkh had a strange moment of recognition. The foe was someone very much like himself a few years earlier. Someone who believed his mission was to kill Aeswiren's men and the natives, to take this land and make it theirs.

Rukkh forgot about all that as another man stabbed at him with his spear. He pulled his own out of the dying man's chest and fought the next man off. They stabbed, and their shields absorbed the blows. Beside him, Rukkh heard Ladwaller triumphantly smash down another foe with a shield blow. Ladwaller's spear soon brought a scream from the downed man.

Rukkh thrust low, got under the other's shield, and pinked him in the leg. The sergeant slammed his shield against the other man's and recoiled. He had still not recovered enough strength to handle this. A spear head missed his face by a fraction of an inch the next moment.

Ladwaller gloated again as he whacked down another man. Chimikin, the youngster, killed another.

"We are the Blitz Regiment, you fancy little sodomites!" roared Ladwaller.

"Your fornicating wizard didn't cut off our dicks," screamed Belzec, "so we're still gonna kill you."

Rukkh broke through a minute later and found himself among the Emperor's guards and staff. They had formed a tight cordon around the Emperor, who had drawn his sword and taken up a fallen man's shield and was ready to defend himself.

Two of the staff orderlies were cut down just to the Emperor's right, and a spear man thrust at Aeswiren. He met the spear with his sword, deflecting it and then following through with the clash of shields. Aeswiren did not fall, absorbing the blow with skill. Striking hard at his foe, he forced him back, then kicked him in the shin, taking him by surprise. The youngster squawked and hopped backward. Aeswiren slashed at him, driving him back another step. His bodyguard, Klek, fighting alongside his King, stabbed the youth through the hip and took him down.

The body thrashed, but Aeswiren was already engaged with another soldier.

Rukkh cut down a man who got up in his path, then thrust another aside with his shield. His spear reached out to take a third man in the side.

The momentum had gone out of the enemy's thrust. The Third Regiment had mounted an assault into the side of the attack column, peeling it away from the flank of the Sixth Regiment just to the other side of the gap.

Ladwaller killed another with a crunching blow of his sword, cleaving the man's helmet in two with a flash of sparks. Then the attack faltered. Aeswiren himself started up the cheer and drove at the retreating enemy. The Blitzers went with him, and they pursued the foe, now running to retreat through the closing gap. Men of the Third Regiment got in the way, though. Most of these attackers were crushed between Aeswiren's staff, bulked up by thirty Blitzers, and the men of the Third.

Aeswiren, with a slight flush in the face and a glow in the eyes that had been absent for many years, clapped Rukkh on the back. "Your timing, Sergeant, was excellent."

"Thank you, Lord."

"But this is not over yet."

And it wasn't. Rukkh could see that the half company he'd left behind on the line was hard-pressed by the assault of two full companies of the enemy. Rukkh drew a deep breath and then pulled his men together and got them hurrying back to that part of the line.

Aeswiren and his staff regrouped around the Emperor's banner, while the Emperor tried to pick up the thread of the conflict.

Rukkh and his men crashed into the line just in time to prevent a breakthrough. The assault was stopped dead in its tracks and then slowly shoved back. After a few minutes, the attack ended there, and the enemy withdrew.

The catapults resumed their fire, and those massive spears began to unseat the enemy's confidence.

But the battle was far from done. Over on the right, where Aeswiren's army met Toshak's in the line, another enemy assault had produced a gap. The mots were fighting hard to hold back the enemy wedge, but the impetus lay with the attackers.

The men of the Tenth Regiment were roused to throw the enemy back down the hillside. They went in hard, forcing a desperate struggle for several minutes. Still, the enemy prevailed, and the Tenth were stopped and forced back.

Aeswiren, seeing this danger, looked around for a force to plug the gap. The Blitz Regiment was expressly developed for such situations. Rukkh and his company received the call and hurried off to the right.

The space behind the line was filled with wounded who could no longer move. The sorcerous power of that light in the sky had cost Aeswiren's army many casualties in the initial contact.

Now that the deadening effects had faded, Aeswiren's regiments responded with a fury increased by the frustration of the first few minutes. They halted the enemy thrusts and turned them back once more. Where the younger soldiers of the enemy's host lingered too long, they paid with lives.

Rukkh and his men drove in on the enemy wedge. The Blitzers were too good for these youngsters, inexperienced in war. The wedge was broken up, and once the formation was shattered, the men of the Tenth Regiment pressed forward again and drove the enemy back down the hillside.

Aeswiren called the Tenth back to the line. The rest of the enemy's front was still in place, and Aeswiren was not ready to attack yet. The losses of that day had been grievous. Almost a quarter of the army had been wounded or killed. The blinding had shaken many more and left them terrified. Aeswiren needed to harbor his soldiers' strength while he studied the situation and looked for an opening. As it was, the combined allied army was now only two-thirds as strong as the enemy's main force. On top of which he possessed those pyluk; though the lizard-men had taken terrible casualties, they'd managed to grievously hurt the mot army.

Rukkh and his company were withdrawn to a position thirty yards back of the line, slightly behind the Emperor's banner. There they tended to their wounds. Ladwaller had picked up a couple of bad scrapes. Chimikin had lost his helmet in the fray and been knocked unconscious. They were still trying to bring him around. A couple of others were laid out with serious wounds. Steblemire's would probably kill him, unless the great Surgeon Biswas got to him quickly.

Rukkh set off around the company to check every man. Almost at once he bumped into Thru Gillo, who he thought of as the Emperor's monkey friend, or the monkey-who-came-in-the-night, because of the way he came and went at all hours.

Gillo nodded to him, and Rukkh felt his old assumptions crumble a little more. Rukkh nodded back then made a halfhearted salute, since he knew Gillo was a "kefern," which was their word for colonel. To his surprise, Gillo returned the salute, but in the monkey style with closed fist raised to the shoulder.

Then the mot was gone, hurrying on to the Emperor's banner. Rukkh saw him pass through the guards and disappear.

Chapter 34

On the right side of the battlefield, where Toshak was marshaling his battered forces after the early morning fighting, the blue flash took everyone by surprise. The deadening effect on limbs and minds was noted, but it faded quickly, for this magic was not attuned so well to mots and brilbies as it was to men.

Toshak and his staff watched the enemy assault Aeswiren's lines. Though Toshak readied two regiments for a flanking attack on the enemy columns, he held off from unleashing it because his army was still recovering. As they watched the battle seesaw back and forth on their left, the mots found themselves in the heretofore unheard-of situation of praying for a victory by the men of Aeswiren's army.

Even before that fighting was done with, a young mot from the Seventh Regiment came up with a message from its commander. The enemy had sent an emissary with a message for General Toshak. Even stranger was the identity of this envoy, for it was a mot of the Land, a renegade now serving the enemy who sought to destroy his own people.

Toshak showed the message to Thru and then ordered the emissary brought before him. A few minutes later, the guard parted to allow this figure, clad in man-made clothes of odd cut and appearance, to step through.

Thru felt a shudder run down his spine as he locked eyes with Pern Treevi.

"Well, well," said Pern, with a little bow in his direction. "If it isn't the amazing Thru Gillo, the gifted weaver of fine mats."

Thru did not return the bow, but his eyes remained locked with Pern's.

Pern turned away after a few more seconds. "General Toshak, I have brought you a message from His Lordship, the Great One, the Master of Shasht."

Toshak did not speak but stood still, examining Pern very carefully. The emissary carried no weapons, of course, but was obviously comfortable in the high-cut trousers and thick, woolen jacket of the enemy forces.

"What is your name, emissary of the enemy?"

"I am Pern Treevi, once of Warkeen village, until I was victimized and hounded out by rogues led by this oaf at your side."

Thru felt the blood rush to his head. "That is a lie!"

Toshak continued to hold Pern's gaze with his own. "So, everything that happened to you was the fault of others and none of your own. And because of this, you found refuge among the men of Shasht and became the creature of the dread sorcerer that rules them."

"Great is his power, as you have seen. Listen to me, General Toshak, and heed my words. The Master of Shasht desires an end to conflict with your army and our people. He wishes only to capture the hateful rebel Aeswiren and to end his usurpation of authority. If you stand aside and allow the Master of Shasht to bring all his force to bear on Aeswiren, this object will swiftly be attained. Once Aeswiren has been captured and brought to trial for his crimes, the Great One will leave the Land and retire to Shasht. There will be peace forever after."

Thru felt his jaw drop. This offer was so palpably false and deceitful that he could scarcely believe the enemy would think they would entertain it for a moment.

Toshak said nothing, however. Thru wondered at this for a moment. Then Toshak spoke. "Well, to say the least, we are surprised by this offer. However, perhaps it has merit. You say that your master will turn his attack solely upon the men under the Great King Aeswiren's command?"

"That is so."

"And that after Aeswiren has been defeated and captured, your master will leave the Land forever?"

"Yes."

"Well, this is something to think about." Toshak made a show of concentrating, while looking away to the forest on the right where the pyluk horde still crouched, threatening a flank attack at any moment. Then the general looked over to the left, where the enemy attack had finally foundered. Aeswiren's men were driving the enemy back down the hillside.

Pern's eyes glittered. Thru made a huge effort to remove any trace of emotion from his own features. He saw at once that Toshak was out to gain more time from this strange development, implausible as it was.

Toshak turned back to Pern. "Return to your master and tell him this: That I must confer with the King of Dronned, in whose service I am. That I do not reject out of hand these proposals, but that I find them intriguing. However, your master has caused my people great harm, and it strikes me as strange that he would seek peace after all that has happened here. Still, peace is better than war. So, tell him these things and then return here to hear our considered answer to these proposals."

Pern bowed once more, exchanged a final stare with Thru, and turned on his heel and departed.

When he was gone, Toshak let out a sigh. "Extraordinary. Can he really think that we would stand aside and let him destroy the Great King's army?"

"He holds us in great contempt. Perhaps he thinks we are that low."

"Perhaps he does, and if so then it is another sign of the arrogance that has helped us throughout this war. We shall use this breathing space to continue to fortify our positions and move the wounded to the rear. Meanwhile, Colonel Gillo, you will go to the Great King and explain what has happened."

Toshak then dictated a message to Aeswiren, which Thru carefully translated into Shashti script. Then he set off along the lines toward Aeswiren's positions.

Thru passed through the flank guards at the boundary between the two armies with little comment. His comings and goings had been so frequent that the guards knew very well who he was.

Thru found the Emperor in the middle of dictating a slew of orders as he worked to move regiments around and shorten his line. None of the men with the Emperor, not even the guards, gave Thru a second glance as he waited patiently with his message. When Aeswiren had finished giving his orders to the assembled regimental officers and messengers, Thru was summoned by a staff aide.

The Emperor was in good spirits and pleased to see him. "Welcome, Colonel. Good to see you're still in action."

"Thank you, Lord, and may I say the same to you. We heard that you were in the thick of it yourself."

"Ho, had you now? Well, what you heard was probably greatly exaggerated, but we did have a little scuffle here. So, what news do you bring me?"

Thru handed him the scroll from Toshak. "Strange news, Lord. The enemy has sent an envoy, a renegade from my people, to talk peace with General Toshak."

"Has he now? By the fire of the old gods, that's an odd move."

Aeswiren frowned in concentration as he read the message. "Mmm, your penmanship is getting better by the day, Colonel Gillo."

"Thank you, Lord," said Thru.

"But your *Z*s are still a little off."

"We do not even have this sound in our tongue, Lord."

"I know, but you do have plenty of *ung-ung* and *shi-shi,* and sometimes I don't remember which should go first after *ah.*"

Aeswiren grinned a moment and then turned serious. "And what does this renegade want, do you think?"

"Oh, it's simple enough, Lord. He wants Toshak to betray you. He says that all he wants is to take your head and recover your army and take it back with him to Shasht. He says that he has abandoned his scheme to conquer the Land. He calls for Toshak to form an alliance with him and to allow the pyluk through our positions so they can fall on your flank."

"By the purple ass!" growled Aeswiren. "This foul thing has misjudged your people again and again. Especially your General Toshak."

"Indeed, Lord. We know this is a tissue of lies. But we gain some time by considering it."

"So, General Toshak sent the renegade away?"

"Yes, Lord, but he returns soon for an answer."

"And what will General Toshak tell him?"

"That is what he wishes to confer with you about, Lord. He would say either that he has no interest in such low and ignoble treachery, or that he must consider it very carefully, to dissemble and keep our enemy waiting."

"Yes, I see the logic of that. Put up a smoke screen. But, of course, he will see through that."

"Yes, Lord, the entire offer is surely untrustworthy. Our scouts are working very hard on the right flank to make sure we are not taken by some surprise attack."

Aeswiren scratched his beard lightly. "Tell the general that I would say something along these lines: That he requires a token of this change of heart on the part of the enemy, and an explanation for it. Because, not so long ago, this enemy of ours insisted that your people were abomination and must be exterminated. Because the only reason that these armies of ours are in your land, shedding blood, is because he insisted that we build these fleets and attack you. So, ask that of him, and then ask the enemy to come to a personal parley himself. I would like to see him, from concealment. Prisoners say he has a new body, a huge one, young and vigorous. He has taken new flesh since last I saw him."

"Yes, Lord, I will tell Toshak this."

"May fortune continue to aid us, Colonel!"

"Yes, Lord, Great King of Shasht."

Thru saluted then left the Emperor and began to trot back along the crest of the hillside toward the lines of the army of Dronned. The brightly colored regimental flags and pennons were snapping in a sudden breeze. Men stood at easy in their lines, conversing in quiet voices; some had fallen out to work on their weapons or shields. Ahead beyond a thirty-yard gap, he saw the lines of mots, where the Eleventh Regiment, raised in Dronned city itself, held the left flank.

Thru noted the close resemblance of the mot regiment to that of the men around him and felt again the force of the changes that had been imposed on the mots of the Land by this war.

He nodded to the mot guards and went on through. Ahead he saw Toshak's personal banner waving just above the curve of the hillside and quicked his step.

He did not see the sudden commotion behind him at Aeswiren's command post. The Emperor had just been struck by a terrible premonition. He instantly gathered his personal guards and set off at a run in Thru's footsteps.

Unaware of this, Thru reached Toshak's command point. The general and his staff were studying the dispositions of the enemy in the valley below and marking them on the map spread out on a folding table. Nearby stood four guards and the mot holding Toshak's personal banner.

Standing in front of them, quite alone, was Pern Treevi. His eyes glittered momentarily as Thru stepped in front of him.

"The emissary has come back sooner than expected," said Thru to the sergeant of the guard.

"Damn his hide. Can you believe he'd betray his own kind?"

"That's Pern Treevi, Sergeant. He's not a friend to mot or mor, never has been. Lives only for himself."

"You know the creature?"

"I'm afraid I do."

Toshak was busy with the map. When a staff aide whispered to him that Colonel Gillo had returned, Thru was ushered to the map table.

"What did the Great King have to say?"

In a quiet voice, Thru repeated Aeswiren's message while Toshak nodded. No one at the table as much as glanced toward Pern Treevi, who continued to stand immobile in front of the four guards and the banner.

"Yes," said Toshak after a moment's reflection. "The enemy dissembles. There is some evil intent to all this, but for now it lets us strengthen our position."

Toshak directed Thru's attention to the hillside above, where he saw that another trio of catapults had arrived and been set up. Stacks of spears were set ready beside them.

"There are more on the trail from Dronned. We will have twelve catapults in place soon. Enough to hurt any attack, by my calculations."

They heard a shout, then another. Looking off to the left, they saw a small group of men running flat-out toward them.

"By the Spirit," said Thru, "that's the Great King himself."

"What can it be?"

"An attack?" Thru looked down the hillside. The enemy troops were either standing still down by the riverside or digging trenches and erecting protective fasciae. "No, the enemy aren't moving."

Unfortunately, one enemy had been overlooked.

As the Emperor and his men drew closer, their cries of warning became clearer. Alas, before they were comprehended by Toshak and his staff, they set in motion the very weapon they warned against.

Pern Treevi quite suddenly sprang into action, leaping up with an audible snap as if he were a spring-driven mechanical toy. The four mots of Toshak's guard were taken by surprise by the impossible speed with which Treevi moved.

One moment he was standing there as before, patiently waiting for Toshak's attention. In the next he was among them, and with a slender stiletto he had already taken one of the guard's lives with a deft stab into the heart.

The mot buckled, and Pern grabbed his spear. That was buried in the chest of the second guard in the next instant.

Screams of horror surrounded him, but he easily ducked the first spear thrust his way and wrenched that guard's weapon out of his hands and turned it on the stunned mot. The surviving guard, on the right side, got his shield in front of Pern. Pern's spear thrust slid off the wicker, but Pern caught the shield's edge with his free hand and pulled it away before kicking the guard senseless.

In five seconds, Pern had destroyed Toshak's guard. Now he sprang directly at the general.

While Thru was still drawing his sword, Toshak met the attack with the upturned map table as a shield. Pern's spear broke the table, but the stroke was deflected. Pern and Toshak came together for a moment, and then Pern flew away, head over heels upside down, tossed by Toshak's kyo.

Pern landed on his feet, however, and bounced in place as if made of rubber. A staff officer swung a sword at him. Pern seized the mot's wrist, bent his arm, and the sword was wrenched away. In a flash, the sword was thrust through the staff officer's belly.

Pern leaped for Toshak once more, covering a good four yards, five feet off the ground. Toshak's sword glittered in a beautiful arc, engaging, deflecting, and riposting Pern's death stroke.

Toshak brought all his great skill in sword fighting to bear, and he had never needed it more, for this enemy was death itself, inspired with unholy power drawn from some poor wretch's life spirit, sucked from his body by the sorcerous horror that had control over half the world.

Pern fought with an insectal rapidity, his blade flickering back and forth too quickly to be seen. Toshak defended, his own blade parrying, deflecting, nicking away the deadly strokes.

Thru hurled himself at Pern's back and succeeded in grappling with his old enemy. But Pern, with the strength of five brilbies, kneed Thru in the belly, smashed him in the face with a fist like a rock, and hurled him away.

Toshak took advantage of the moment and drove in. His sword sank into Pern's belly. Pern quivered, perhaps for a fraction of a second, then he tore the sword out, and out of Toshak's hands, and resumed his attack.

The last young guard had regained consciousness and staggered to his feet. He interposed his shield and absorbed the blow meant for the general. His spear thrust narrowly missed Pern's head. The next moment, Pern struck again, his face twisted into a curious rictus devoid of emotion. His blows hammered on the guard's shield, beating it back, breaking it, cutting through to sever the guard's shield arm. Then he hewed down once more to cleave the mot from neck to hip.

Thru had managed to pull himself to his knees by this point. He looked up in time to see the Emperor, with his guards in front of him, his bodyguard at his side, hurrying the last few yards to the scene.

The noise of the fight, the commotion in the army, all were deafening, but Aeswiren's battle challenge cut through them all. "Face me, foul creature of the Old One!"

Toshak had spun back several paces and drawn the sword from one of the fallen guards. Pern was caught between the two leaders of the allied army. For a long moment, indecision wracked his spell-driven mind. He feinted toward the charging Aeswiren and then sprang in a curious leap, like an enormous flea, high in the air, descending to within a sword's length of Toshak.

Their blades came together again. Toshak's borrowed sword was sundered in a flash of red sparks, and Pern's sword was buried in Toshak's chest the next instant.

Thru felt something inside him sag as he saw Toshak fall, blood spurting from his mouth.

Then Aeswiren and his men attacked. Klek knocked the wizard-thing off its feet with a mighty blow from his sword. One of Aeswiren's guard drove a spear into its guts, pinning it to the ground. Aeswiren himself sank his sword, two-handed, down into the traitor's chest and worked it back and forth.

"No, Lord," said Klek, "remember Hesh?"

"Only too well, dear friend," said Aeswiren, standing back.

The thing on the ground was writhing about the spear that held it in place.

"Be quick!"

Klek cut down. His sword sank into Pern's shoulder, but it was pulled from his hand in an instant.

Thru was there.

"Take the head!" roared Aeswiren.

Thru swung with every last ounce of strength, and his blade removed Pern's head.

There was a dull flash of reddish light, and Pern's head flew ten feet across the ground, tumbling as if propelled by a fountain. Blood spasmed forth, and the writhings of the thing began to subside, slowing and finally halting altogether.

Aeswiren and Thru stood together, shoulder to shoulder, as they absorbed the extent of the disaster.

"Toshak is dead," said a staff orderly.

Chapter 35

The army of Dronned, the protector of the Land, confronted the unimaginable. Great Toshak was dead.

Toshak's staff stood or knelt in a circle around his body. Some wept openly. Toshak had been more than simply the commander of the army; he had embodied this army. The great general had been the driving force behind it since its formation.

They were bereft, fatherless, orphaned, and lost.

Toshak was the one that all mots had come to respect. Toshak had saved Dronned, then Sulmo. Toshak had driven the army of Man off the Land again and again. And now he was gone.

With a sad curse, Aeswiren stood back from the corpse of the thing that had once been Pern Treevi.

"Colonel Gillo, can you take command of the army?" Aeswiren used Shashti deliberately, knowing that only Thru could understand it.

Thru sighed. This was a burden he would rather not have assumed. Then he slowly nodded. "Yes, I have commanded an army before. But I am not General Toshak."

"Nor am I," said Aeswiren with a grave shrug. "I knew him only for a short while, but in that time I learned that he was a master of the arts of war."

A crowd was gathering. The news of Toshak's death was spreading. The army faced its greatest crisis.

Colonel Bellis, of the Seventh Regiment, voiced the urgent question: "Who is in command now?"

Thru swallowed and closed his eyes a moment. Was he the only mot that could take on this burden? After a moment's thought he spoke.

"I must take command, I think. I am not the senior ranking officer, I'm sure. But I have more experience than anyone. I have commanded an army before, and no one else has worked as closely with General Toshak as I have over the past few days. Finally, I speak the tongue of the men of Shasht, and I have the confidence of the Great King."

The Grys Norvory and several other officers had just arrived at the scene. The Grys heard Thru speak and then jumped forward. "I second the appointment of Colonel Gillo to acting command. He is the obvious choice."

This prompt endorsement from Norvory, who had more experience than most, was hugely important. The others, still dumbfounded, stared at Thru in silence. Some nodded. Another voice was raised.

"Yes, Colonel Gillo is the best qualified among us."

A few others murmured together. Gillo was experienced, but he was very young, and he was not from a noble family.

Norvory pressed the case firmly. "We cannot equivocate. We have no time for it. Gillo is the mot for the job. I know that Toshak himself would have said this."

Thru looked across the bloody ground to Aeswiren. The Emperor had a tiny grin on his face, a wintry look, born from sad experience in a harsh world. He spoke in the language of the Land, accented, but quite understandable to every mot there. "Then, General Gillo, I should warn you that our enemy is about to attack. Look!"

Aeswiren raised an arm, and Thru turned his attention to Shelly Fields. The enemy regiments were massing once more.

"Watch them carefully," said Aeswiren. "If they raise their shields above their heads, imitate them. It may save all our lives."

Thru nodded, clasped Aeswiren's hand, then turned to the staff. "We need a new map table."

This mundane command broke the staffers out of their daze.

"Yes, sir!" said Captain Blen.

Thru turned to the assembled crowd.

"You have your places in the line. You heard the Great King. Watch the enemy carefully. Imitate them if they take measures to protect themselves from sorcery."

Thru took a breath. The weight of the responsibility he had just taken on was sinking in. He prayed he would not be crushed by it.

"The crisis is upon us, and we must rise to the challenge or the Land will be laid waste and our kind will be annihilated. We have no choice but to fight and to win."

His audience took his words in silence, then turned to get on with their tasks.

Thru looked around. Aeswiren and his guard were trotting away, back along the line of regiments to his own command position. The mot regimental commanders were bunched in front of him, and other officers were attending to the bodies of the fallen.

A new map table was set up. The staff assembled and were ready to proceed with the business of running the army.

Thru examined the map, then studied the enemy positions with the spyglass. The regiments were massed into two assault columns. Thru estimated that each column held six thousand men, a dozen regiments each. The enemy was not going to let the initiative pass to the allies. He was going to put everything on this throw of the dice.

Horns blared, drums began to beat. The enemy was moving.

"Return to your regiments and hold your lines. If and when movements are required, I will send fresh orders. And, please, keep me informed of changes that you observe on your front. That is particularly important for the right flank."

The Grys Norvory gave him a crisp salute and departed.

Thru returned to the task at hand. Fortunately, there was little to do just yet. Toshak had prepared these lines. Every mot knew his role.

Suddenly, Thru felt another presence. He looked up and saw Melidofulo standing among the group of mots who were tending to the bodies of Toshak, his guards, and Pern Treevi.

"Pern Treevi's body should be set aside, General," said the Assenzi.

"Yes, Master, it will be. Such sorcery was in it that we could not save the general."

"We did not foresee this. We must study the remains. Perhaps we can find a way to sense these threats."

Thru was reminded of the invisible war going on above their heads as the Assenzi strove with the Old One on the hidden fields of subtle magic.

"Well, Master, please inform me promptly if you sense a fresh threat."

"We will do our best, General Gillo."

The enemy had decided to move promptly. Sensing that his assassination attempt had succeeded and seeking to take advantage of the disorder in the mot army, he drove his pair of assault columns forward, with drums booming and horns braying.

As they came into range of the catapults, now twelve strong, primed and ready, the machines began to deliver volleys of heavy seven-foot spears straight into the column approaching Thru's front line. The spears had stone heads, but they were enough to pierce shields and armor, cutting a swathe through the ranks.

The drums never faltered, the organized chants of "He Who Eats!" never stopped, and the men kept on coming.

For the third time that day, battle was joined. This time the fighting raged all along the northern front of the allied armies. Only Thru's right flank, turned along the contour of the hill to face the pyluk-infested woods, was not engaged. The enemy attacks were fierce, but fighting upslope and against prepared positions, they made little headway. The same result was visible on the left, where Aeswiren's men held their ground and exacted a heavy toll on the attackers.

After half an hour of this, the enemy had had enough. The drums ceased their thundering and the assault columns fell back and then retreated downslope, pursued by arrows, insults, and more of those huge spears from Toshak's catapults.

Thru returned to the maps while scouts came in from Lupin Valley with reports of movements by the enemy horsemen. It was almost midday; the enemy had thrown his army three times at the allies and failed each time. Thru considered the situation carefully. They had suffered terrible casualties with the dawn assault due to the blindness induced by the sorcerer's magic, but the enemy had twice been induced to attack them head on and had suffered considerably himself.

"Well, Captain," he said to Blen, "this day began badly and has produced a tragedy for us all, but we hold our ground."

"Yes, sir. We can beat him. Everyone knows it. You can feel the confidence in the army."

The enemy must have been feeling it, too, because

the afternoon wore on with no further attacks. Scouts continued to bring in reports concerning movements in Lupin Valley by parties of horsemen, and there were occasional ambushes and pursuits out under the trees, but the fighting of the morning had exhausted the enemy and cost him too many dead and wounded.

Thru sent a message to Aeswiren, requesting a conference that evening. Neither of the allied armies was strong enough now to dare an attack of their own, but Thru wished to talk with the Emperor, who had such a deep fund of experience, and form a plan of attack together. Toshak had always emphasised how important initiative was in war.

As the day came to an end and both armies turned their thoughts to the evening meal, Thru and his staff met with Aeswiren.

The Emperor greeted Thru with a warm handclasp. "We bloodied him on that last attack. He'll not try that again."

Thru was less sanguine. "But he hasn't finished with us. He cannot stop now. He knows this is a fight to the death."

After meeting with the Emperor, Thru ate a quick meal of bushpod cakes and fish paste and then busied himself with a letter to Nuza. As he wrote of Toshak's death, he found tears welling in his eyes and cursed his own weakness. This was not the time for tears. He had to rise above that until this business was done.

Toshak had been their inspiration, and their father figure for the war. Thru felt not only alone but bereft. Self-doubt gnawed at him. Did he really have what it took to command an army in this crisis?

At length, he finished the note, sealed it, and sent a messenger away with it at once. Nuza would have received official confirmation of the horrible news, but she, of all people, deserved more.

Now it was time to inspect each regiment, study its position, and recommend improvements if any came to mind. Thru knew that the army's morale was at stake as well. They had held off the enemy's attacks, but they had been hit very hard, and now they had lost their great general.

Thru began with the left side of the army and found the Eleventh and Thirteenth Regiments in good position. The mots were quiet, absorbing all the losses of the day. Thru's visit seemed to have only a slight effect, but he told himself it was essential that every soldier see his commanding officer at such a time.

He went on through the positions in the center, where he found the mots digging under torchlight as they continued to improve the various works and trenches. Once again, Thru's presence brought only muted cheers and smiles, but he persisted. This was a sad time for all of them.

On the right flank, he found Norvory busy improving his lines.

"We have dug two trenches, and now we are setting stakes in them."

Thru studied the way the trenches slanted toward one another. "I see, you want to funnel the enemy into that tight space in the middle."

"And there we kill him."

"Yes, indeed. Toshak would have approved, I know."

"I would ask one more thing," said the Grys. "Could we have the services of one or two of those catapults? As you have them placed now, all their fire is directed toward the river."

"You would like a couple of them set to fire into this killing ground you're making?"

"Yes, sir."

"I will discuss this with the catapult master at once. Perhaps he can arrange some flexibility in their dispositions. If you are attacked, he can swing his weapons this way and add their fire to that of your archers."

"That would be excellent."

After they parted with a crisp exchange of salutes, Thru mused on the strange pathways that life provided. He and Norvory, once enemies, but now bonded as comrades in arms! They had not mentioned Pern Treevi, whose body had been taken away by the Assenzi for examination. Pern had come between them once, to poison their lives with his malice, and yet in the end it was Pern's final act that had promoted their friendship.

He talked briefly with the catapult master, Major Heeve, who came from Juno village and had played for the Juno team many a time against Warkeen.

"You asked about flexibility? Well, we have already taken steps to ensure it. General Toshak had requested this yesterday as soon as I reached this spot."

Thru studied the catapult sites and found that the weapons were set on wheeled limbers and could be turned in any direction in a minute or two. Where the ground had interfered with flexibility, Major Heeve had had his mots remove obstructions, level hillocks, and fill in declivities. When Thru looked eastward, he could see down on Norvory's positions with the V of his trenches faintly visible in the dark.

Thru returned to his command post, took some tea, and studied the scouting reports. The enemy horsemen were still active in Lupin Valley, but there had been no sign of the pyluk since they had been pulled off the battlefield in the early morning.

At last, worn to the bone by a day of upheaval, Thru wrapped himself in his blanket and tried to sleep in the small personal tent set up for Toshak. For a while his mind refused to let go, and he continued to fret about the army's positions, but eventually exhaustion overtook him and he fell into a dreamless sleep.

He was awoken hours later by a hand shaking his shoulder.

"What is it?"

"Begging your pardon, sir, but the enemy has started that drumming again."

Thru scrambled out of the tent and pulled on his cheek fur to wake himself. An orderly handed him a mug of steaming hot tea, which did wonders.

"What hour is it?"

"Middle of the night, sir."

Thru heard a single drum booming steadily on the far side of the river. There was something dreadful and malevolent in the sound, especially as they knew now what such drumming could portend.

"Any movements?"

"Some reports, sir. Down by the river, but hard to see from up here."

Thru took the spyglass and studied the far bank of the river.

The moon cast a gentle light across the scene, and its illumination was aided by that of a large fire burning in the center of the enemy camp. He saw the familiar tents and piles of materiel that he had seen many times the day before. But there were also companies of men on the move. The bridge over the Shell was darkened with masses of men. No obvious pattern could be seen from all this activity, however.

"Perhaps he is simply resting some units and moving other units to the front ranks," said Thru, setting down the spyglass. "What about on the right?"

"No reports for a while."

"Send a messenger to the right wing. Tell them to redouble their vigilance."

"Something's happening, sir!" said Captain Blen.

The enemy's bonfire had grown very bright. The pace of the drumming had increased. Dark shapes could be seen flickering across the firelight. In both allied armies, every spyglass available was studying that fire and the activity on the far bank of the river.

Thus they missed the Old One's next little surprise.

Three regiments, his best troops, had been carefully taken from the main body of the army, moved back over the bridge, and then put on boats and ferried around Cormorant Rock to a landing spot on the Rocky Canyon. Mixed in with all the other traffic between the ships and the shore, these boatloads of troops had been missed by Aeswiren's surveillance team.

The Old One himself had gone with them, and by use of subtle magic had confused and baffled the handful of guards that Aeswiren had set out there to keep an eye on the bay and report any fleet movements.

Thus, no one saw the enemy regiments climb the cliff paths and form up in the scrub on the crest of Blue Hill. While Thru and everyone else studied that blazing fire for clues to his intentions, the Old One readied a nasty surprise for Aeswiren's left flank.

When it came, it was devastating. Suddenly, pouring across the top of Blue Hill, the Old One's crack regiments swept over the flank units and raced right into Aeswiren's camp.

It happened so quickly that no one had any time to react.

Aeswiren and his staff were studying the huge bonfire blazing on the far side of the river. The distance was more than a mile. Troop movements had been reported closer at hand, too, on the left side of the line. In the moonlight it was hard to see more than that the regiments there were awake and set out in long lines. Aeswiren had immediately warned the Second and Fourth Regiments, which held the left end of the line, to be alert and ready to respond. A night attack was improbable. The risks and casualties of such an effort would be immense, but Aeswiren knew that their enemy would be increasingly desperate after the failures of his sorcery and repeated attacks the previous day.

And then, from nowhere it seemed, came a flood of enemy troops, streaming down from the crest of the hill into the rear of the Second and Fourth, and right into Aeswiren's command post.

For the second time inside a day, the Emperor himself was caught up in the swirling fighting. But this time the effect of surprise was complete. The Second Regiment, at the far end of the line, was under attack from below and from behind. The line contracted as the regiment broke and fled to the rear of the Fourth Regiment.

Aeswiren had the Third Regiment and a company of remnants from the Blitz Regiment held in reserve, but he had no opportunity to get any orders to them. He and his staff were too busy fighting just to stay alive. Fortunately, these veterans didn't need orders to see what had to be done. They drove into the flank assault and brought it to a halt, at least in the area behind the center of Aeswiren's army.

Alas, the damage was done, for the enemy had now set off a massive night attack directly at the left side of the Emperor's forces. The Second Regiment, flanked, had broken. Now the Fourth Regiment collapsed under impossible pressure. Together with the Second, they flowed to the rear, and Aeswiren and his staff were forced to go with them.

The reserve force, led by the Blitzer remnants, formed a line and slowed the enemy advance over the next few critical minutes. Captain Klutz and Sergeant Rukkh, both old-line Blitzers, acted with furious courage during this crucial period. They bought Aeswiren's army a lifeline.

While they did this, the Emperor and his personal

staff were able to fight their way free of the immediate battle. Yet, at this point, after he had survived half an hour of sword and spear fighting at close quarters, Aeswiren was hit. A stray arrow plunged from high above and sank into his shoulder through the gap between his helmet and his shoulder plate.

The arrow went deep, and though the Emperor tried to carry on, it was impossible. He collapsed and was placed on a litter and carried through the last fifty yards of danger to a new command post.

He was alive but weakening from a steady loss of blood. The arrow was too deep for anything but a surgical removal.

His army teetered on the brink of disaster and, with it, the cause of the people of the Land.

Thru was apprised of these events in short order. Even before Aeswiren was wounded, Thru had messengers leaping through his own army. He sent others south, across Blue Hill to warn Nuza at the field hospital.

Within a handful of minutes, he was able to send a regiment, the Sixth, across the hill to bolster Aeswiren's regiments. Soon he added the Eleventh Regiment, a force of country mots from Dristen. The pressure of the Eleventh on the enemy's flank at the extreme left of the line finally brought the attack to a halt. A new allied line was established, snaking across the top of Blue Hill's northern end. The right flank of Thru's army was now almost cut off on the extension of Blue Hill that it occupied. The enemy had pressed to within fifty yards of the only road on the hill, the coastal road that ran down to Bear Hill and Warkeen village and the crossing of the Dristen. Thru sent orders for the catapults to be pulled back at once and sent south to new positions on the northern side of Bear Hill.

When he heard that Aeswiren had been critically

wounded, he sent a messenger to fetch Surgeon Bis-was then left his own command post and ran at full tilt to find the Emperor. The guards, obviously shaken, bristled at the sight of him, but he reminded them in their own tongue who he was and they let him pass.

Around the Emperor he found a tight knot of staff officers. Aeswiren was propped up on a litter and his normal ruddy face was pale, but he was still alive.

"Lord, how bad is it?" said Thru as he pressed to the fore.

"Ah, General Gillo is here." Aeswiren reached out to take Thru's hand. "Everyone, take note of my words. If I should fail here, you are to listen to this fellow. He is the commander of the army of Dronned, our allies. Listen to him and cooperate to the fullest. It's the only way we'll turn this around. D'you hear me?"

The Emperor stopped talking, too exhausted to continue.

Some of the regimental commanders were gathered to one side.

Thru found himself beside two staff officers. One of them shook his hand. "Hello, I'm Major Balderi. We've met before, of course, but we haven't spoken."

Thru recognized Balderi and the other officer, Soames, who also stretched out a hand.

"We have a problem," said Balderi. "If the men learn that Aeswiren is dying, they will lose heart. You probably don't need us to remind you that this is Aeswiren's army."

"I understand," said Thru as calmly as possible. "I am in the process of extracting my force from the right side of the position. We need to hold this line for now, and then retire to the next hill south."

"This is General Toshak's plan?"

"Yes. General Toshak was extremely thorough. He had worked up a plan for an emergency like this. There are positions there, partly prepared, that we can occupy to deny the enemy access to the bridge at Warkeen."

"We will hold," said Major Soames. "But if the Emperor dies, we will face a crisis."

Thru nodded. He turned and made his way back to Aeswiren's side. "Lord, can you hear me?"

"Yes, it's Gillo, isn't it? Sorry this had to happen. Enemy really caught us napping. Must have landed a force behind us. Don't know why I wasn't warned."

"We have a new line, and we have stopped his attack. We are not beaten yet."

"That's good news. I'm afraid that I may be beaten, though."

"I have sent for Surgeon Biswas. He was at the field hospital, working with Nuza."

"Nuza?" Aeswiren's eyes lit up for a moment.

"Biswas will save you, if anyone can. But I have another idea: What if Mentu came here and pretended to be you?"

"Mentupah?"

"Yes."

Aeswiren's quick mind was still alert enough to see the possibilities. "Damn me, but it's a chance. Even if I die, if Mentu can convince the men that I'm still alive, they'll fight to the bitter end."

"They will."

"Do it."

Thru wrote out the message. He wanted to take it himself, but Mentu was at least two miles down the coast, and he could not be absent from his command post a minute longer. The fighting might resume at any moment.

He was about to send one of Aeswiren's men when

Filek Biswas and Simona came hurrying up out of the dark.

Biswas knelt down beside the Emperor.

"Thru," said Simona as she fell into his arms, weeping.

"Simona. You are just the person I need."

"What is it? What can I do?"

"The Emperor cannot stand. He may not even live through the night. But he must show himself to his men tonight or they will lose heart. The enemy is bound to attack again at dawn. He has come close to victory but is not quite there. I must hold him off until Sulmo comes.

"Until they come, this army must not lose heart. I need Mentu to come here. Mentu must face his destiny."

Simona's eyes widened. The Emperor was obviously not going to rise from that litter this night. Filek was already having the litter moved into a tent, which had been hurriedly set up behind the temporary command post. Officers from all over the army had converged there to get fresh orders. Soames and Balderi were answering questions, but clearly more was needed.

Thru took a deep breath. Simona gripped his hand.

"I will run all the way. Mentu will come. I will tell him he can do it."

"He can do it. The question is whether the army officers will accept it."

"They will listen to you, Thru. They must listen."

Simona left word with her father, then hurried away.

Thru marched over to speak to the knot of senior officers. In a few careful words he explained his plan. They recoiled. Then, after a few moments' reflection, they began to discuss it.

"It is a possible line of action," said Colonel Jejeji of the First Regiment. "Better than giving up."

"If we lose, we all go to the priests. They won't be gentle with us either."

"Well, I for one will die on my feet here, not tied over their fornicating altar."

And so Thru gained the support of the senior officers for his plan.

Inside the tent, he found Filek Biswas engaged in surgery. The Emperor was unconscious, the arrow was out, and Filek was cleaning the wound with spirits of alcohol and sewing it up.

"Will he live?" That was all Thru wanted to know.

"I cannot say. If the wounds do not suppurate, then he should live. He is a strong man, in good health. But this is a deep wound, and the arrow was in the flesh for a long time. Infection is the usual result, and it is often fatal."

Thru could not stay any longer. He left, again at a run, and crossed back to his own command post, where he found his staff frantic with anxiety over his absence.

The catapults and wagons were already in a line, slowly lumbering back over the top of the hill and onto the southward trail. Thru studied the scouting reports that had accumulated in his absence. The position was stretched tight across the top of the hill on a diagonal. He began the process of extracting the right flank from the northeast end of the hill and moving it south to line up on the right side of a new line that would stretch across the hill at its narrowest point. The right flank there would end on a steep slope, with forest all around and Lupin Valley below. The center would rest on open ground on either side of the coast road. And the left, to be held by Aeswiren's army, would be on the coastward side, which was mostly open ground with occasional clumps of trees where some soil had settled into the chalk.

This shorter line was the one that Thru hoped could

be held until General Ter-Saab and Aeswiren's fleet arrived from Sulmo. He could only pray he would have enough time. And that Simona could persuade Mentu to go along with his plan.

Chapter 36

When Aeswiren awoke, he found Nuza sitting beside his litter on a camp stool. The tent was otherwise empty and lit by a single lamp hanging from the tent pole.

"I am honored, Mistress Nuza. But surely there are many who are worse off than me."

"There are, Great King of Shasht," said Nuza in her own tongue. "But none of them are as important today as you."

"Well, in that case, perhaps you can tell me how I'm doing."

"Surgeon Biswas was able to remove the arrow. He has sewn up the blood vessels that were cut. He says you will live if the wounds stay clean."

"Well, that's somewhat encouraging. The good Surgeon Biswas is the foremost practitioner of medicine in the world, so if I have both him and yourself at my side, I must have a fighting chance."

Nuza smiled and squeezed his hand. Aeswiren studied her features and saw again the beauty that had pierced his soul.

"What is going on beyond these concerns over an old man's health?"

"I am not entirely sure. Thru Gillo is now commanding our army. I don't know who commands yours."

"What is the hour? How long have I lain here?"

"It is midnight. The enemy is expected to attack at dawn again, but this time we will be ready for his tricks."

"Well, I hope so. This enemy has a skinful of them."

"Here, Lord, you must drink." Nuza held a cup of water to his parched lips. After a few gulps, she pulled it away.

"It's thirsty work, lying here like this."

"I will bring you something to eat. You must regain your strength. We will move you to Dronned later on."

"Yes, yes, but first I must see my brother. Has he come yet?"

"No, but he is expected."

Aeswiren lay back and let his eyes feast on Nuza. The grey fur, the dark eyes with their inhuman color, so widely spaced beneath the enormous eyebrows. Her face was both beautiful and frightening in its difference. He pondered once again how he and other men must appear to her. Huge, coarse creatures with thick facial hair and naked skin. Everything about men must seem ungainly and ugly to her.

"Lord, what is it?" she said, leaning close.

"Nothing," he mumbled, but tears began to stream down his cheeks while she stared at him.

Men might wish to live among the mots of the Land, but they would never be anything but men, and if men were to infiltrate the culture of the Land, they could only degrade it. For the first time in many years, Aeswiren the Third felt a wave of self-pity wash over him.

"When I look at you, Nuza, my dear, I think sometimes that I would rather be an ordinary mot, one of your people, and therefore free to seek your hand, than to be the Emperor of all Shasht."

Nuza grinned, used to Aeswiren's affection for her. "But your people need you, Lord, and if you were one of us, they would not have you to take care of them.''

Aeswiren chuckled despite his tears. "You know how to bring me down from the clouds, my dear. And you're right. I have huge responsibilities." He tried to sit up.

"No, Lord, what are you doing?"

"Well, someone has to fetch my brother. He has a terrible job to do, and it must be done tonight."

"Lord, you do not have the strength to even stand, let alone go out in the dark to find him."

"I will get someone to help me if I have to."

As if he had heard all this, a figure wrapped in a cloak and wearing a wide-brimmed hat entered the tent. Behind him came Simona.

The cloak parted, the hat was removed, and Mentupah Vust stood there.

Aeswiren felt his breath catch in his throat. "Mentu, you came at last."

"Mistress Simona was most insistent, brother."

Both men grinned.

"She told you what's needed, I'm sure."

Mentu knelt down by his brother's litter. They clasped hands. "She did, Lord, and I fear it as much as I might fear death itself."

"You have known for more than twenty years that something like this might come."

"That's why you locked me in that tower . . ."

Aeswiren closed his eyes for a moment. "Yes, brother, that is why I locked you up. To keep you from being used to depose me."

"And now you need me to pretend to be you."

"Yes."

"And I must agree, because all else depends on this."

"The men must see that I am still their commander."

"Won't they be able to tell the difference?"

Aeswiren chuckled. "Not when we've finished with you."

When he was finally ready for his performance, Mentu Vust had bandages around his neck and chin and a heavy robe wrapped about his body.

Aeswiren pronounced him "as close to me as he can be."

Mentu would say very little to the men, just show himself and lead them in a short chant for victory before moving on. He would walk slowly, lean on a staff. It was already widely known that he had been wounded. A crier would go ahead of him to tell the troops what to expect. As long as he could wave to them, urge them to fight for victory, that should be enough.

Sergeant Rukkh would accompany him, as well as Klek, both primed to whisper things he should say to the different regiments. Most of the senior officers were in on the deception, but they had kept the secret well. The men were unaware of how close Aeswiren had come to dying from that arrow.

At the first stop in front of the hastily assembled reserve force, Mentu suffered a bad attack of stage fright, but he got over it after an initial stumble or two. Perhaps it was the way that Sergeant Rukkh behaved toward him, as if he really was Aeswiren the Third, that helped him step into the illusion himself. Rukkh never addressed him as anything but "Lord" and "Your Majesty."

Mentu was never really sure afterward if that was what did the trick, but after that first halting little speech, he found his way. For the rest of that night, moving from regiment to regiment, he became the Emperor, Aeswiren the Third. By the end, in front of the Seventh Regiment, he was shouting his lines and forgetting to lean on the staff. Klek had to whisper to him to remember that he was supposed to be badly wounded.

Well before dawn, the task was done. The men were reassured that their Emperor still lived. The regiments had moved back to the new, shorter line chosen by Thru. They found that an army of monkeys—kids, grannies, and females of all ages—had been working like beavers to dig trenches and set up protective fasciae.

This occasioned amazement all round. The men of Aeswiren's army had seen many new, unexpected sides to the native people. That they were people as much as "monkeys" was now coming to be accepted.

There was discomfort from this realization, however. Some men balked. Others were appalled at all that had gone before.

"You know we ate them, we killed the bastards and ate their flesh. How can we atone for that?"

Such a ghastly thought ended many an argument in the regiments that night. No one could deny that it had been the sudden arrival of a well-drilled regiment of monkeys that had enabled them to hold their line and then reorganize.

Back in the tent where Aeswiren lay on his litter, nursed by Nuza and attended by a select group of orderlies, Mentu sat down and felt the tension flow out of him.

"Well, brother," said Aeswiren, "what was it like to be the Emperor?"

"Like a dream. I started out pretending, and that was no good. But Sergeant Rukkh helped me believe, and then I think it went well."

Aeswiren chuckled. "Oh, it did. Everyone was impressed by how strong I sounded. 'A little unsteady on his feet,' they said, 'but his voice was strong!' "

"And what happens now?"

"We see if we can hold off this enemy until we get reinforcements. If we're lucky, he will make a mistake that we can take advantage of."

"And if he doesn't make a mistake?"

"He will have to press his advantage. He lacks supply and is operating in hostile country. His army will starve soon, so he must force a conclusion. That means he will attack. But many things can go wrong during an attack, and we must be ready to seize any opportunity that comes our way."

When dawn broke over the eastern hills on the third day, it was met with considerable apprehension in the ranks of both the allied armies. The shock of the previous morning was still strong in everyone's mind. Those who had been temporarily blinded were crouched down with their hands over their eyes to protect themselves from who-knew-what deviltry.

But the sun rose in all its customary warmth and majesty. It was a cloudless day, and off to the north a single thin column of smoke rose up into the sky until the upper air tore it apart and blew it out to sea.

After a few minutes, it became clear that there would be no dawn attack preceded by sorcery, and men and mots relaxed a little. The enemy was only visible as a line of fasciae set up beyond the range of the archers.

Aeswiren's men were tired and hungry, and underneath that they were angry. They had been taken unawares by a flank attack carried out in darkness. They felt humiliated and eager to get the chance to set things right.

The army of Dronned was also tired and hungry, and underneath that it was frightened. Thru could sense it. The loss of Toshak had undermined the mots' faith in their eventual victory. Always it had been Toshak who had led them to victory. Now he was gone.

On top of that, the night attack had unnerved them. The army of Aeswiren was seen by the mots as being the standard to emulate. Their skilled, seasoned veterans had always taken a heavy toll on mot armies. And yet that army had been taken by surprise and almost destroyed. As a result, the army of the Land had been forced to abandon its carefully prepared positions and retreat a mile and a half. Giving up that ground without a fight rankled many hearts.

What both armies knew for certain was that this would be a day of destiny. They had fought the enemy for two days and survived his worst. Could they rise up today and destroy him?

Thru had new scouting reports to study. He had not slept that night. He had worked ceaselessly to position his troops and form a clear idea of his enemy's dispositions.

The pyluk horde had moved during the night. They were now stationed in Lupin Valley, a few hundred feet below his right flank. Between the two was a steep slope, though not a vertical cliff. Attacking up that slope would be virtually impossible—except that, with sorcery in play, it was hard to know what might be possible.

Still, Thru's biggest immediate concern was breakfast for six thousand mots and six thousand men. He cast anxious eyes toward the south road. If they were going to be supplied, the food would all come up that road from Dronned and Warkeen.

His second concern was the problem of moving the thousands of wounded across the Dristen Bridge and down to Dronned as quickly as possible.

Nuza had performed miracles since she had left Aeswiren's side. But it would still be hours before they got most of the wounded into the wagons and rolling south.

The problem now was that Thru's line was barely a hundred yards from the medical camp itself. The tents full of those too wounded to move would be within bow shot if there was an attack.

One other problem had been solved, however. Simona had volunteered to take on Thru's previous job, the unenviable task of running messages between the two army commands. Because of her skill with either language and because she was intimately acquainted with both army commanders, she was perfect for the job.

She was Thru's first visitor of the new day. She brought good tidings from Aeswiren, who had slept for several hours and was now eating some gruel under the watchful eye of one of Filek's trained nurses. Mentu had done a wonderful job in the night, and the men's morale was intact. However, their food supplies had been lost in the night attack and were no doubt being consumed by the enemy.

Fortunately, Thru's next visitor was another old friend, Quartermaster General Meu of Deepford, who had brought with him the twenty wagons loaded with rations that he'd promised yesterday.

"A bit of breakfast will go some way to restoring the troops' spirits. They've had a hard night."

"Bushpod cakes, bushcurd pies, salt fish, beans, eggs, fresh bread, we've got it all. Even guezme tea!"

"Guezme! Well, I'll be."

"Came from Highnoth. Two Assenzi and three donkeys arrived day before yesterday. Amazing, eh?"

"I'll say. The Assenzi think of everything, and believe me, I hope they keep it up."

"This sorcery has been outrageous."

"Foul stuff. He kills to get this power, the Assenzi say."

Meu was another graduate of the Assenzi academy, so this frank talk of the Assenzi did not faze him. "Let's hope breakfast will help our mots defeat him."

Thru was happy to receive some toasted bushpod cakes with fried eggs and a piece of salt fish. He washed it down with a mug of guezme tea, the highest quality.

Throughout both armies, the food and the strange green tea lifted spirits and brought renewed strength. The aromas of wood smoke and toast covered the hillside.

They were still eating when the throb of the accursed drum began again in the north. As they grew aware of it, both men and mots stopped what they were doing, looked up to the sky with trepidation, and then quickly looked down again. Conversation faltered and dwindled away, leaving them with only the low, muttering throb, an evil sound booming on endlessly.

After a while it became maddening. Some were unable to stay silent in the face of this oppression. They leaped up and screamed frantic insults to the north.

The throbbing drum took no notice.

Thru sent out aggressive scouting parties. Something was coming, and he wanted to have the best possible understanding of the situation before the day became hectic. His scouts, in teams of six and twelve, clashed with the pyluk in the valley below. Another group, working northward along the steep western slope of the hill, were ambushed by men. They fought back and escaped after losing two mots.

The enemy had followed Thru up onto the top of the hill, and most of his army was set in four large divisions lined up opposite the allies. One notable addition was a fifth square, of a thousand horsemen, that was formed up behind the infantry. They were set out in lines, but most of the men were still dismounted.

Thru immediately sent Simona to Aeswiren with

this information. The enemy's intent was plain: a cavalry charge at some weak point on the allies' line. The most likely place was where the two armies joined. Thru also ordered a review of that part of the line. Pits were to be dug, stakes set in place. A special reserve force of two companies was already formed up, ready to plug any gap.

Thru drafted a message to his regimental commanders, informing them of all that he knew. On the right they had to keep one eye on that steep slope down to Lupin Valley. Those pyluk certainly were going to be used by the enemy that day.

On the left and center of the line, Thru emphasized that all the preparatory work they could do on their position would be gold once the fighting began. Dig, set in stakes, fletch arrows, make ready.

Not long after those messages had gone out, Thru received word that a small circular cloud had risen in the northern sky. It was an odd cloud, and it behaved strangely, ceasing to rise after it had ascended a certain distance. It seemed to spin in place and sparkled in the sunlight.

Then the cloud began to drift south.

Thru studied it through the spyglass. It was even stranger when seen close up. Myriad tiny flashes of rainbow came off the cloud, and its edge was peculiarly sharp. It floated south until it was right over the allied line.

Melidofulo, the Assenzi, had joined Thru by this time and was studying the cloud, too.

"What is it?" asked Thru.

"I do not know. I have never seen anything like it."

The cloud was growing larger, or expanding downward, one or the other—it was impossible to tell from Thru's position. But now he could hear a new sound, a faint hum that came and went with the wind.

Then the first of the flies appeared around them, small streaks through the air. When they alighted somewhere, they could be seen to be small yellow flies with golden eyes and sharp red mouth parts.

"Ouch!" came a cry from the front line. It was followed by others in no time. The small yellow flies were fierce biters, and there were millions of them. Any bare flesh was vulnerable, and the insects quickly took advantage.

The cries of pain, the frantic thrashing and even rolling on the ground did little to stop the assault. Only then did the main mass of the cloud reach the ground.

The air was simply boiling with flies.

The cries of pain and outrage were joined by a more general cry of terror as men and mots suffered under the relentless storm of insects.

Thru, like everyone else, was surrounded by the humming horde. Where they could land on bare skin, they bit and drew blood. Where they could land on a single layer of cloth, they chewed their way through.

There were so many that it was hard not to breathe them in. They got into the mots' and men's noses and eyes; they bit inside the ears. Some tunneled under collars and cuffs to get at bare skin.

Slapping, cursing, waving an arm before him like a maniac, Thru found the trumpeters and made them blow the alarm. Inside the command tent he managed to concentrate long enough to scrawl a short message four times, fold the papers, and hand them to messengers.

"Hurry!" he snapped when they seemed unwilling to leave the relatively fly-free confines of the tent. "The enemy will attack any moment under cover of this sorcery."

Outside, the horror continued. The sky was darkened with the insects. Troops fought to keep the things off them, even rolling on the ground, driven mad by the biting, crawling masses of flies.

Thru ran from post to post, hauling sentries to their feet, shouting warnings to everyone he could find.

Soon he heard a rumble and felt the ground tremble beneath his feet.

The horsemen were coming!

Chapter 37

"Admiral, how are you this day?"

Heuze looked up as the Lord Leader entered the tent. As before, the huge man was clad in a hauberk of chain mail and wore a sword and long dagger at his waist.

"Better, Lord, much better."

Heuze made no mention of his hands. They were wrapped in bandages, but they were beginning to swell from infection. The sorcerer had a very short temper and was easily moved to take drastic measures against anyone who annoyed him.

"You've been given a good wash, I take it."

"Oh, yes, Lord." A group of slaves had dumped him in a cold stream and rubbed him down before putting fresh clothes on him and carrying him back here.

"And you've had a hearty breakfast?"

"Yes, Lord."

He'd been given toasted buns and some roasted meat. He didn't know where the meat had come from, but he was so hungry that he ate it and shut his mind to the possibilities.

"Good, because we've got some very important business to attend to this morning, and I want you fresh and bright eyed."

Heuze didn't ask why. He had learned to keep one's trap shut around the giant unless one was asked a question.

A gang of soldiers brought in five men, chained at neck and wrist. These unfortunates were then tied down on stout boards so that they were unable to move a muscle. They begged for their lives, but the Lord Leader had other uses for them.

"None of you will be spared. Your bodies are required for another purpose than living your miserable little lives."

The men wept. As far as Heuze could tell, they were all young soldiers, and he was surprised to see them made use of like this. But surprise never lasted long when one was in the company of this insane wizard. He had a way of changing one's perceptions of things.

The horrible golden bowl was produced once more; the giant man mixed green and purple powders together. Once again, he took a life, that of the nearest of the men on the boards, cutting his throat and draining his blood into the bowl.

This time, however, the material in the bowl remained quiescent. No stink filled the tent. No curious, waving appendages appeared above the rim.

The Lord Leader spoke mysterious words that seemed to explode from his lips and leave haunting echoes in the tent. Heuze's skin itched, and he feebly rubbed himself with his bandaged hands.

There came a bubbling sound from the bowl, and the big man reached in and brought out small, glistening purple spheres. He placed them one at a time on the chests of the men bound on the boards. Heuze observed that the balls appeared wet on the surface. Then he noticed that they were wobbling a little, as if they were alive.

Then, before his astounded eyes, they broke open to reveal pale white things, like worms but equipped with dozens of small stubby legs. These things unrolled and began to wander over the bodies of the captive men. Their cries and pleas for mercy went unheard, and the grim business continued.

Sooner rather than later, each of the worm things found the man's face and forced itself into his nose, crawling up into the nostril. The men screamed as this unpleasantness continued, but the Lord Leader merely sat on his high chair and studied them.

The men's cries changed timber one by one. What had been screams of horror became shrieks of agony. Something unholy was underway inside these men.

Heuze found that he was sweating profusely. The nightmare of these past few days had swollen into something hellish, and yet he had not been tortured since he'd been delivered into the hands of this terrifying being.

The shrieks continued, and Heuze saw the men's flesh begin to shrivel and their stomachs to swell. Within a few minutes, the men had become something other than men. Their arms and legs withered to little more than bones covered in skin, while their bellies became huge and purple, as if each of them was pregnant with a baby elephant.

By this point, the screams had died away to little wispy sounds. These men were hardly men anymore.

Now came silence, except for an odd pulsing of the purple masses.

The Lord Leader spoke to his servants, who opened the sides of the tent and pulled up the flaps.

With the sound of rocks falling into mud, the purple bellies split and opened wide. Inside each was a tight ball of something glittering and golden.

Heuze found that he could not look away, even though the piteous sight of the sticklike limbs and the peeled-back purple flesh made him shiver with horror. The golden balls began to unravel, and a glittering plume began to rise from each of them. The plume thickened as the balls gave up their material to it, and a hum like that of a million bees filled the tent.

Heuze caught sight of the faces of the guards who were peering inside. Astonishment, fear, and awe were writ large there, no doubt matched by the expression on his own face.

Inside the tent was a whirling mass of little flies, hurtling around in circles until they found the openings to the outside and disappeared. After another minute or so they were gone.

The deranged sorcerer stood up and strode outside to watch the conjured flies ascend into the sky in a smooth spherical cloud. When it moved away to the south, he returned to the tent.

"Remove this mess," he ordered with a gesture to the remains of the five men, only one of whom retained any human appearance.

Heuze wanted to be sick.

"There, that went very well, I thought, didn't you?"

"Oh, yes, Lord."

"Sometimes, when I manage to work one of these things with such perfect results, I have to wonder if there are any limitations to what I might aspire to. What do you think, Admiral?"

To be used as a sounding board like this brought back a memory of the way he'd treated Filek Biswas once upon a time. Now Heuze knew what it was like to live in terror on the whim of someone else.

"I don't know, Lord. You have amazed me again and again."

"Yes, I amaze myself, too." Suddenly the huge man threw back his head and laughed out loud. "Those fools! Those absolute fools!" he thundered. "They dismissed me from their clique. They laughed at my work." The huge face turned to Heuze for a moment.

"I speak of the ancient days. When the great Groybeel Vaak would meet in the purple tower of Imels. They thought they understood the mysteries of the universe. They thought they could obtain eternity! Hah! Where are they now? Where is Pinque, who laughed in my face? Where stands Namooli of Thoth?"

The eyes glared at Heuze, who trembled. He understood none of this.

"The answer is that they don't stand. Nor do they sit!" The Old One guffawed again. "They are nothing but dust now, scattered across this old world. But I? The one they called Karnemin, the one they patronized as being their student, where am I? Hah! I am about to take complete control of this world for my own. They called me weak—they called me a scientist and not worthy to kiss the hems of their wizard gowns! But it is I, Karnemin, who lives, while they do not."

Again the great face lowered itself to Heuze's.

"I speak of the ancient time, Admiral, before the ice. When the last men still thought to hold back the remorseless work of the poison in their tissues. They locked me up! Called me a madman! But I escaped them, and I still live, and they do not!"

The huge man turned away for a moment to pour himself a mug of water, which he drank off in a single gulp.

"So I return to the oldest question. The one that inspired them all once upon a time. Tell me, Admiral, though you are a heretical unbeliever in the Great God, He Who Eats, do you have no religious feeling at all?"

Heuze hesitated a moment before replying. He didn't think it was a trick question, but one could never tell.

"Not really, Lord. Seems like something that people who need it lean on. I've always leaned on myself."

"A good trick for a man with only one leg!" chortled the sorcerer. "Have you never been curious about the world? How did it begin, and where did we come from?"

"Oh, when I was younger, Lord, I thought about such things. But no answers were convincing, so I gave up bothering."

"Not for you the notion that God began the world and that we are God's children, eh?"

"Well, I've heard that one. It's the usual idea."

"Yes, but what if it's completely wrong? What if the world, the sun, the stars, everything began on its own? What if it awaits the controlling hand of the God that grows within it, ripening like a seed of grain within the husk?"

"I'm not sure I understand you, Lord."

"Then listen carefully, fool. What if the universe is a dumb thing, an egg, a spore, awaiting the sperm to become the zygote. In other words, awaiting the rise of the intelligence that shall rule it? What if, instead of God providing the universe, the universe exists to provide us with God?"

With a sinking feeling, Heuze realized what this man—the Old One—was suggesting. "Then, you, Lord . . ."

"Yes, of course. I have a chance of becoming God. Probably as good a chance as that of any other conscious being in the universe. I have conquered death. I have transcended mortal flesh, taking it and wearing it like mortals wear clothing. I have mastered the arts of transformation and spell brewing. I will soon rule this world and from it I shall go forth to conquer every other world!"

"They are coming!" came the cry all along the line.

The rumble of a thousand horses in motion was clear to every mot and man in the allied armies.

"I see them!"

Thru could see them, too, even through the swarming flies. What appeared to be an irresistible tide was heading toward them at a steady trot. While they came on, the mots could barely stand up under the onslaught of the yellow flies.

Major Beech was in command of the two companies

drawn up to reinforce any gap in the line. Thru made his way to the major's post through the blizzard of flies, swatting and cursing like anyone else. The hum of the insect cloud was so loud that he had to shout over it to be heard.

He found Beech well aware of the threat. The reserve companies were formed up, although mightily distracted by the cloud of flies. Ahead of them, the flank guard, a company of the Seventh Regiment, was preparing to receive the charge.

Across on Aeswiren's side of their shared line, Thru could make out movements of further preparations, but through the haze of flies it was hard to see exactly what they were.

"We will wait to see if they break through, let them pass, then move in to reform the line. The horsemen are good for breaking lines, but they cannot exploit the advantage as well as infantry."

Beech nodded, slapped flies, and grimaced. "Yes, sir. We're all primed on that. Toshak spoke of this many times since we learned that the enemy had horse animals here."

The cavalry had burst into a gallop. Horns were braying an accompaniment to the thunder of hooves. A cloud of arrows rose to engulf the horsemen, and then the first of the riders were among the pits and outer works of the mot line.

Forced to slow, they became better targets. Men and horses fell there, in some cases blocking the way for those coming behind. Still, these Shasht cavalry were the best troops in the army, and they were not to be stopped by passive obstacles. They jumped their warhorses over the fallen, over the pits, and even over the breastworks.

The pikes and spears of the mot front line were the next barrier and here the toll exacted was high. Dozens of horses and riders went down and others shied from the spear points. A storm of arrows broke over the leading riders, and many more saddles were emptied.

But the main mass of the cavalry drove across the bodies of the fallen and everything else in their way. Where riders were dismounted, they fought their way to the line to engage with sword and spear. Mots began falling, and where gaps appeared, horses pushed through and their riders beat on helm and shield around them with battle-ax and morningstar.

For a few moments, the line held, but then the horsemen broke through on the extreme left end. Outflanked, the entire mot position began to fail.

At this point, the horsemen ran into the cloud of insects, which attacked them as avidly as they went after the mots. Horses panicked, riders lost concentration, and for a crucial half minute the cavalry milled about in the gap they had forced between the allied armies.

Thru and Beech conferred briefly. They were about to send the reserve companies forward to halt the retreat and close the gap when they saw formations of Aeswiren's men march out of the cloud of flies. They came in a column, six men abreast, and as they came within bow shot of the horsemen, they stopped and formed up in squares, three deep with twelve on a side. The parade-ground precision of their moves brought a whistle to Thru's lips.

The horsemen thrust forward at the first sight of these infantry, but they were too late. The troops were already in place, and the riders could only swirl about the stubborn squares, hacking at the shields below while archers and spear men within took a steady toll.

Thru saw the power of the square. The cavalry could surround such formations, but as long as they held, they could not be flanked and routed. And while the horsemen rode around them, the infantry could fight back.

"The flies are lifting," said Beech.

Thru looked around. The horrid haze was thinning. The flies were rising into the sky once again.

"Move! Close that breach in the line."

The reserve companies trotted forward, and the ragged formations of retreating mots on the flank opened to let them through. With fresh pikes and spears, they took a swift toll on the horsemen, who had lost the momentum of the charge and were now milling in the breach area.

This reversal brought a change of tactics. A party of fifty or more horsemen continued to ride around the squares set up by Aeswiren's flank force, but the rest pulled back, reformed into assault columns, and charged again.

Now, instead of trying to ram through the mots' line, the horsemen rode up, engaged the pikes and spears, hacked and cut with their axes and swords, and then retreated, trying to draw mots after them in pursuit. Where this happened, the horsemen turned about and cut down anyone pulled out of position.

Beech and his officers tried to prevent this, but the mots were not trained for this tactic, and besides, after the flies and the strenuous fighting, they were far from being able to think clearly. When a mot defeated a rider and sent the man retreating, the temptation to step out and try to ram a spear into his back or his animal's rump was overwhelming.

The line thinned, and, despite Beech's heroic efforts, the reserve companies foundered. The enemy ordered a general infantry assault all along the line. It came forward with drums booming. The horsemen reopened the breach between the two armies, and a full regiment of the enemy marched to occupy the gap.

Thru had pulled a regiment from the right side of the line, leaving its neighbors to close the new gap produced there. It was his final reserve, and he hesitated to commit it until he absolutely had to.

Fighting broke out all along the front. The enemy

pressed, but the mots, free of the horror of the flies, fought with the accumulated rage of days. The line held.

An exhausted messenger appeared in front of Thru. "Sir! Message from the Grys Norvory."

As he'd expected, the pyluk had been thrown against the right flank. The Grys was holding them, but he reported that masses of pyluk were moving farther down the valley and then climbing the hillside.

A scout appeared at exactly that point to inform him that a band of pyluk were attacking the donkey trains bearing away the wounded on the south side of the hill. A dreadful slaughter was taking place.

The enemy cavalry had reformed once more, and a solid mass of horsemen was emerging into the open space between the armies. In a few minutes, they would be in position to mount a charge into the rear of the mot army, now furiously engaged all along its front.

Thru felt the battle sliding away from him. He could sense a gathering disaster. He was about to order the reserve regiment forward to stem the break-up of the left of the line when the guards called to him. He turned to see Sergeant Rukkh and, behind him, a dozen men from Aeswiren's army.

"Sir!" said the sergeant. "We need to help you defend against the horsemen. You understand me?"

"Yes, I do, Sergeant, and thank you. What should we do?"

"Companies should form up into squares. Cavalry can't do much damage then. Whatever else they do, no one should leave the square they're in."

"I'm afraid we have neither the training for that nor the chance to do it."

"Then form a square of the whole army. Pull some units over here to form a new line. My men will help."

Thru realized that Rukkh's dozen were just the vanguard of a small column, maybe two hundred men.

"We're the Blitzers, sir. We know how to fight cavalry."

Thru wasn't sure about all of this, but he did understand that Rukkh and his men were reinforcements. He turned and sent orders streaming out to his besieged army. The rear companies behind each line regiment were to turn about and form a new line one hundred paces to the rear, facing the other direction. Thru also remembered to add a warning that there would be men fighting alongside them on this line.

The mots had practiced such formations on the parade ground, but that was a very different matter from the chaos of battle when every nerve was lit with the fire of war. And yet, with plenty of shouting and some shoving, and with help from Thru and his fellow sergeants, they accomplished it in a matter of minutes. They presented the attacking cavalry with a new line, bristling with pikes and spears.

The cavalry came on and tried to stampede the line, but the mots held. Once the impetus had gone from the horsemen's charge, some of the Blitzers darted out to hamstring horses and pull down riders. As fallen horses and empty saddles became common along the front, the cavalry were pulled back by sharp blasts of the horn.

One more crisis had passed. But another was forming, for even as the cavalry charge clattered to a halt, the pyluk were enveloping the right flank of Thru's line. Though they littered the ground with their own dead, the lizard warriors kept coming, forcing back the mots, bending their line, and lapping around the huge square that Thru's army had become.

Thru looked all about. The red-tinged maelstrom swirled around the mot army. On the right and in the rear, a swarming mass of pyluk, seemingly driven to suicidal efforts, hurled themselves against the mot lines. On the front, facing north, the mots battled the main mass of the enemy's army. On the left, they faced the horsemen, now reinforced with infantry swung across to exploit the gap made by the cavalry charge.

The sounds of fighting rang out from every quarter. The mots were beginning to sag with the fatigue and exhaustion brought on by days of fighting. The pressure of the pyluk was unrelenting. No matter how many died, more were ready to press themselves into the gaps.

A sudden surge by the pyluk sent a mob twenty strong bursting through the lines. Thru and everyone else drew their swords and plunged into the fight. There was no alternative. The fighting was savage, and Thru hardly got into it before the intruding pyluk were downed.

Suddenly Thru found the Grys Norvory standing beside him. In the confusion he hadn't seen him approach. The Grys was bleeding from a head wound.

"We're breaking down on my front. Can't hold them much longer."

Before Thru could even answer, another band of green-skinned lizard-men broke through. They stabbed and clubbed their way forward. Mots to either side stepped back, trying to avoid being flanked. The whole position collapsed in moments, and a confused jumble of mots straggled back. On their heels came a roaring mass of pyluk. Thru drew his sword. He and his staff were swallowed up in the fighting.

A tall pyluk bull stabbed at him. He struck aside the spear and knocked it out of the pyluk's hand. The pyluk reached for him with the free hand. Thru tried to dodge but bounced off the mot to his right and felt the pyluk grasp his shoulder. Thru struck up with his sword, and the blade sank to the hilt in the pyluk's belly. But these bulls were in the grip of terrifying sorcery, just as Pern Treevi had been. The pyluk ignored the sword in its guts and smashed Thru across the face.

Thru found himself on the ground. The damned pyluk was standing on his back. Another mot fell on top of him, blood squirting across the back of his head. Thru struggled to free himself. The monster was still standing on him while it fought with mots ahead of it. Thru finally managed to slip sideways under the dead mot. The pyluk lost its footing and went down, twitching, with Thru's sword still stuck in its rib cage.

As Thru pushed to his knees, a huge pyluk bull swung its club at him. He rolled desperately to his right. A spear took the pyluk in the throat, and a brilby cut through its spear arm with a terrific blow with the sword. The pyluk fell next to Thru, who had struggled back to his knees. He got up, hurdled that pyluk, and pulled his sword free of the other one.

Norvory was working with desperate energy to reorganize some of his mots and put them into a new line. Thru staggered toward him. His left hand was covered in someone else's blood.

"Got to form a new line."

"Pull back!" said Norvory.

"Right." Thru looked off to the south. There was clear ground and then the cluster of tents of the field hospital. On that side there were only a few parties of enemy horsemen.

"Retreat to those tents. Form a line in front of them!"

All the regimental commanders were given these orders. In the crush of the fighting it would be hard to retreat in an organized way, but to stay where they were offered nothing but doom.

"Now!"

The mots disengaged and ran for it. Their retreat surprised the enemy, who hesitated briefly before setting off in pursuit. The horsemen along the way spurred their mounts to take them clear of the hurrying masses of mots and men.

Two hundred yards south, Thru stopped. Toshak's banner was planted in the ground to center the new line. As regiments ran up, they sorted themselves out into a rough sort of order. Units were mixed up, but none of that mattered now.

Away to his left, Thru could see that Aeswiren's men had formed a checkerboard pattern of squares and that the enemy was content to stand off and exchange archery with them. The enemy's main effort was directed at the mots.

Yet the desperate ruse had worked. Thru's force was once again in line and extending to the left and the right. Thru found himself in the second rank, with a crew of Rukkh's Blitzers to his right.

"Well, Sergeant, here's a day you never expected, I'll wager."

It took Rukkh a moment to realize who had spoken to him. "By the purple ass, sir, this has been a fight to remember. If we live, we'll sing of this one for the rest of our lives."

"Here they come!"

The shattered mass of pyluk gave way to an assault column of men, who came forward shouting the name of the Great God. When they were fifty feet from the line, they saw the Blitzers among the mots.

"Fornicating monkey lovers!"

"Sodomistic heretics!"

"Kill the traitors!"

The enemy poured forward, and the two lines closed. The roar of battle went up once more. The enemy had the weight of numbers, and the defensive line was pressed back. Thru and his command post were swept up in the fighting. Thru hacked down a man who tried to grasp the banner. Then Sergeant Rukkh and the Blitzers formed across his front.

"We'll guard this point, sir!"

Thru was all too aware of the irony in this situation.

He and Rukkh looked each other in the eye for a moment, and Thru thought Rukkh, too, saw the strange reversal of fortune that fate had arranged for them.

But then he was torn away from the front by the urgent need to sort out his lines.

They were forced back to the edge of the field hospital. Several of the tents had collapsed and were actually underfoot. Fortunately, all the wounded had been removed. Back they went a few more steps. Then a few more, until they were halfway through the field hospital. Heaps of dead lay everywhere.

At last, the fury of the Shasht regiments began to ebb. Soon they were pulling clear and backing away while arrows flicked back and forth between the two armies.

Thru took the opportunity to run up and down the line, calling to his regimental commanders. The line was straightened. A barricade was thrown up. The mots worked frantically.

He found the train of catapults, nine of them, stuck on the trail, abandoned by their operators when attacked by the cavalry. Thru ordered the weapons pulled off the trail, spun around, and made ready. The principles of the weapons were plain, and though they were clumsier than the practiced crews, Thru's mots soon loaded the catapults and began firing the huge spears.

At this range, just a couple of hundred yards, the spears were fearsome. They flashed across the gap and sank into the massed enemy. Shields and armor were of little use. The sheer power of the impact was enough to kill anyone they struck.

At each volley Thru's army gave a cheer.

To counter them, the pyluk horde was driven forward, urged by the power of sorcery and the terrible will of he who wielded it. The lizard-men struck at the right side of the line and bent it back under intense pressure.

The enemy horsemen charged once again, reformed into a solid mass, eighty long and ten deep.

"Prepare to receive the horsemen!" went up the cry all along the center of the line.

Thru turned to the Grys Norvory, panting as he regained his breath. He had lost his helmet and was holding a Shasht shield.

"Grys, can you find a hundred mots?"

Norvory looked down the left side and then sprang away.

Thru turned back to the front. The catapults fired another volley, and their spears slammed into the onrushing ranks of the cavalry. Saddles emptied and horses rolled upon the ground.

Along the line, those few who still held pikes grounded them, the points ready to impale the horses. Others hefted spears and swords, determined not to break and flee. The Blitzers formed up in trios, as they'd been trained.

The horsemen drove in at Thru's thin line. There was a shock. In several places the overmatched mots went down, and the horsemen thundered through.

The fighting became a general melee, and all cohesion was lost except on the right where Norvory's regiment was still holding off five times their number of pyluk.

All seemed lost. The chaotic battle spilled back across the field hospital, trampling the rest of the tents into the ground, smashing equipment and supplies into the mud. Back past the catapults they went, and some took up the catapult spears to use as pikes.

Thru, wielding his sword and holding Toshak's banner with the other hand, fought his way back to a low mound at the southern end of the camp. He killed a man who came at him with spear leveled. Men with swords followed. His blade rang against the first as the others closed in. In the nick of time, he was saved by Rukkh and a handful of his Blitzers. Swords rose and fell until the enemy backed down.

"Pity your lot don't know how to defend against the sodomistic horsemen."

Thru didn't understand all of this, but he got the gist. "Hold on, Sergeant, we're not done yet."

Grys Norvory came swinging up from the left side with almost two hundred mots behind him. They plowed into the battle and drove in deep. Horses went down screaming. Others galloped headlong into the rear.

Once again, the enemy assault had been stemmed. But Thru's force was in tatters. There was no line, just a mob of mots, many of them wounded, standing around the little mound on which Toshak's banner flew.

The enemy closed around them, ten regiments of men plus the sullen mass of pyluk. Off to the north, separated by two hundred yards or more, Aeswiren's army was attacking the enemy on its front and flank, but they had yet to break through. The fate of the battered mot force seemed sealed.

Thru and the Grys Norvory, with the help of Sergeant Rukkh and the other Blitzers, worked hard to get the mots formed into three lines, set out in front of the mound with the flanks bowed back on either side. The mots responded slowly, too worn out to think clearly. Nonetheless, the lines began to form, and the flankers took up positions.

This would be the last stand. Thru knew it, and so did everyone else.

A vast clap of thunder burst suddenly from the clear blue sky.

They all looked up in wonder.

The enemy stood back; even the archers ceased firing. A strange quiet fell over the southern sector of the battlefield, although they could hear the din where Aeswiren was trying to break through to their aid.

And then, shouldering through the throng of pyluk, came another figure, huge, black-mantled, upon a horse of equal might. A shadow surrounded him, even in the sunlight. Upon his head he wore a helmet chased with gold, and under his mantle gleamed steel on every limb.

Every eye of the enemy host was on him.

Thru sensed this being's true identity. He had stood in the presence of this dire majesty once before. Anger lit in Thru's stubborn soul, and, without another thought, he stepped off the mound and pushed past Rukkh and the others to stand in front of his line.

The huge horseman loomed over him like a dark thundercloud about to spit lightning. Thru did not waver. Looking up, with his hands on his hips, he spoke in as loud a voice as he could muster.

"Who are you, and by what right are you here?"

There was a collective gasp of surprise in the enemy ranks at this audacity. Thru took no notice.

"This is not your land. We are not your people. Why do you do us these great wrongs?"

The towering man looked down at him with cruel eyes. Thru felt a slow mounting pressure on his mind. The huge man sought to compel him to fall on his knees and beg for mercy. The pressure intensified.

Thru shrugged as if dislodging a fly. Then he looked up into the face of his great enemy and sang his defiance:

"Who'd be a jolly beekeeper
And always suffer stings . . ."

The rider snarled a sudden curse, drew his sword, and raised it high.

"Silence, animal! Your time is over. Extermination awaits you and all your kind. The world is now to be mine."

From the sword came a great flash of red light. The pyluk roared en masse. The enemy forces began to beat their swords and spears against their shields. The drums began to boom.

"Prepare to meet thy doom!" roared the Old One, and every spirit on the line quailed as death rose above them like a great, unstoppable wave.

And yet the wave never fell. At that crucial moment, another sound cut across the battlefield: the scream of trumpets and with it the battle cry of Sulmo. Sulmo was come at last!

Thru and the rest of his battered little army looked south in wonder and were rewarded with the sight of banners streaming forward through the trees. Four thousand fresh troops, landed at Warkeen village that same morning, came driving forward in two brigades.

As they went, they sang out their war cry. The mots of Dronned cheered them on and raised their banners high.

Chapter 38

The Sulmese columns struck the enemy on either end of his line. On the left, the Old One's men defended stoutly and gave ground bitterly and slowly. But on the right, the mots slammed into the pyluk, and the lizard-men collapsed. They were fought out; no matter how great the sorcery that gripped them, they could not stand against this fresh assault.

The pyluk broke and ran, or died where they stood. The mots cut through the enemy's host and broke into the rear. The horsemen were caught in the process of reforming and were routed. Now the entire force facing the mots began to crack apart. Only the Old One's infantry, formed in a square, remained intact, retreating slowly and steadily while the Sulmese lapped around it.

The battered but unbeaten army of Dronned now jumped forward with a glad shout to support the Sulmese.

Thru was still standing there, amazed, barely able to cheer, when a tall figure strode up and slapped him on the back. It was a brilby with a battered face in the uniform of Royal Sulmo.

"Ten-Saab!"

"At your service, General Gillo."

Right behind Ter-Saab was Janbur of the Gsekk, his sword in hand and bloodied.

"Janbur, old friend. You came in time!"

"We had to get past the enemy's watch. Could only manage to land the troops this morning."

"Juf!"

And there was the ruined face of old Juf Goost.

"Not too late for us to get in a blow for the Land!"

Thru had no words left. He could only embrace his old companions and weep tears of gratitude.

The battle was not ended, though. The Old One on his mighty steed had withdrawn at the first cry of the trumpets of Sulmo, but his infantry had not broken. The horsemen were scattered, but they would soon reform. The allies had halted the Old One's killing stroke, but they had not yet forged a victory.

As soon as word reached Aeswiren of the arrival of Sulmo, he called on his men to make one last supreme effort. With the cry "Aeswiren!" on their lips, they surged forward and pressed hard on the enemy along their own front. The enemy wavered, their will to fight shaken by the change of fortune. In the center they cracked, on the left they gave ground, and on the right, suddenly flanked by parties of Sulmese mots, they broke altogether and streamed back across Blue Hill until they were among the horsemen. In vain did their commanders ride among them, calling on them to halt.

With the collapse on the right side, the rest tried to form a square to resist, but Aeswiren's men were ready for that maneuver and lapped around the enemy too quickly. Surrounded, companies, even whole regiments, threw down their arms and surrendered. Others, isolated from the main mass, simply fled.

Ter-Saab's columns kept up their pressure on the remaining infantry, and the collapse of the force facing Aeswiren disrupted the cavalry. Before they could reform, Aeswiren's vanguard arrived to harry them and press them hard. As a result, the horsemen never regained the initiative and instead were driven off the hill.

On the northern end of Blue Hill, where Toshak and Aeswiren had set their line the previous day, the fight teetered briefly. More and more mots came up to join in, and soon they outflanked the enemy on the right and the position collapsed once more.

This time there was no chance of a stand. The enemy broke and fled downhill. The infantry streamed in panic for the bridge, and the mots of Sulmo and Dronned pursed them with sword and spear.

At the bridge, the fugitives jammed together, panicked, and there was great slaughter made of them. Elsewhere, fleeing men abandoned their weapons and armor and swam for it. The river was high and many drowned or were swept out to sea.

Avoiding this ruin, the enemy horsemen withdrew in companies inland. They outpaced the pursuit, but alone, without support, they could offer no real threat.

As for the pyluk, their horde had shattered entirely. The survivors, barely a third of those that had marched down from the mountains, were heading eastward in small groups as quickly as they dared. The magic that had gripped them was broken. They would play no further part in the deadly affairs of other races.

The mots held the bridge and all the southern side of the river. The surviving regiments of the Old One's host were a huddled mass of fugitives on the northern bank, waiting for the boats.

When Thru reached the scene by the bridge, Ter-Saab had already made an end to the killing. His regiments were massing on the northern shore, prepared to finish the job if necessary.

The boats were at work, but there were too many men waiting on the strand. It would be hours before they were all taken off.

Thru cast about for a messenger. Simona was with the Emperor. Finally he located Sergeant Rukkh, who had stayed in the vanguard all the way to the bridge with his cadre of Blitzers.

"Sergeant, will you take a message to whoever is in command of those men?"

"Yes, sir."

Rukkh went away with an escort of six other Blitzers. He was back within half an hour.

"They agree to the terms, sir. They will lay down their arms if you will spare their lives."

"And their leader?"

"He is not among them, sir. Some claim he was lost in the fighting. Perhaps he is already dead."

And so the battle of Shelly Fields came to an end. Across the Land, the word was sent out by pigeon and fire beacon and tireless messengers running the roads from Nurrum to Sulmo and from Creton to Ajutan. The Land was saved. General Toshak was dead. The war was over.

The command of the enemy fleet faced a strange predicament. Most of the troops they had landed had been captured or killed. The horsemen had retreated inland and were out of contact. The Old One had vanished. Emperor Aeswiren commanded the victorious allied army in conjunction with the natives. To surrender to the Emperor seemed the logical choice, but to the Gold Tops this was anathema. The fleet was in the grip of several thousand fanatical Red Tops. The sailors wished to surrender, but the Red Tops refused. Fighting broke out within an hour of the surrender ashore. Ship by ship across the fleet, sailors and soldiers rose up against the hated Red Tops and put them to the sword.

The fighting in the fleet was still going on when Thru and a small party returned across Blue Hill to find Aeswiren's command post. The Emperor was lucid, and Mentu was with him. Seeing both brothers together brought a strange joy to Thru's heart.

Simona came running up to embrace him. She was weeping tears of gladness. "It is over, Thru. We have beaten him. Everything will change now. The Emperor has said so."

"Then I am sure it is so. Most of the enemy foot soldiers have surrendered. The horsemen are still at large, but on their own they can do little harm. They will have to surrender, too. The ships are a scene of conflict right now. We think the priests are losing and that the fleet also will wish to negotiate a surrender."

"It is over, General Gillo!" said Aeswiren from his litter.

Simona stepped back. Thru turned to find Nuza with a bandage wrapped around the top of her head.

Thru swept her up in his arms. "You're alive! I was so afraid when I heard that the pyluk had broken through."

"Oh, my Thru, we have come through a great shadow, but we have survived the darkness."

There was still much to be done, however. The prisoners, more than eleven thousand strong, had to be corralled and fed. The dead had to be buried, and the wounded had to be collected and brought in for care.

Thru and Aeswiren sent out a joint statement to the defeated men. They were absolved of blame. They would be given the opportunity to join Aeswiren's army. Those that did not would be shipped back to Shasht but not put down into slavery.

When this had gone out, Thru found a pair of ancient Assenzi waiting to speak with him.

"General, please accept congratulations for your work today," said Utnapishtim, squeezing his arm with joy.

"And mine, General Gillo," said Melidofulo.

"We held on just long enough. Sulmo got here in time. A new age dawns for us."

Utnapishtim held up a bony finger. "It is not quite over. Our great enemy still lives."

Chapter 39

Into the night, the victors worked to complete their victory. Scouts and strong skirmishing parties were sent inland to pursue the horsemen and compel their surender. Of particular concern was the whereabouts of the Old One. He was sought dead or alive, but no trace of him had been reported. Meanwhile, the great mass of prisoners was broken into four groups and marched south toward Dronned. When darkness fell, the prisoners were made to set up tents and crowd inside them. A strong guard of Sulmese mots was set on each group.

The exhausted army of Dronned had reorganized its own camp and was in the process of celebrating the victory. The war was over. Around their fires they danced and sang, though there was no ale and no chance of getting any for days to come.

Here and there among them were parties of Aeswiren's men. Mostly Blitzers and men from the Third Regiment who had fought right alongside the mots and now held radically changed views of their new-found friends.

The rest of Aeswiren's men were celebrating, too, relaxing around the fires or seeking treatment for their wounds at the surgeon's tent. It had been the hardest-fought battle any of them had ever seen, and they had all fought at Dronned in the first summer and remembered that battle very well. This one had lasted three days and taken them to the very brink of defeat. But the monkeys had come through in the end, and the hated Red Tops were going down to defeat on the enemy fleet.

The thought of a couple thousand Red Tops getting their comeuppance was a tremendous boost to the men's celebration. They had found and confiscated a few flasks of brandy from the enemy camp, and that was fueling their good spirits, too.

Thru Gillo had scarcely rested long enough to eat a small meal in the hours since the fighting had ended. There was so much to do. His immediate concern was tracking the fugitive horsemen. Though impotent against an army, they could still wreak havoc in the countryside if they got south of the Dristen. After that came the concern for the prisoners. Though they were disarmed. Thru wanted to get them into a secure camp near Dronned as quickly as possible. Then there were the wounded, of both sides. Three days of battle, with endless attacks and counterattacks, had taken a grim toll. Thousands of wounded had already been sent south to the city, and thousands more were collected in two huge groups north and south of the ruins of the field hospital. Nuza and her staff were struggling to cope. Filek Biswas and his team of surgeons also faced a mountain of desperate needs. More than a thousand mors from Dronned had come north to help. With their strength to call on, the army was able to place the wounded in some degree of proper care.

Finally, there was the need for proper disposal of the dead. Another army of older mots, mors, and children had also marched up from Dronned to dig pits for the enemy dead and graves for the dead of the allies. This work would go on for days. The tally of the dead stood at more than three thousand for the army of Dronned alone, and perhaps two thousand of Aeswiren's men. The enemy had suffered even greater losses, and huge mounds of pyluk corpses were strewn along the eastern margins of Blue Hill.

Thru received a set of scouting reports in the first hour after dusk. The news was mostly good. The pyluk horde continued to flee eastward without any sign of halting. Better yet, the pyluk were moving in small bands once again—their horde behavior had ended.

The horsemen had gone inland then moved north into Shellflower, and were now camped fifteen miles away. They were under constant surveillance, though they did not know it. There had been several arguments and fights among them, and there was no obvious sign of their evil leader.

Thru decided to confer with Aeswiren and his commanders about how best to approach the horsemen. He left his command post, now back on the north side of Blue Hill, and strode the two hundreds yards that separated it from Aeswiren's, which was back where it had been in the evening of the second day, with good views across the country to the north.

Several tents had been set up. Some were a bit battered following the vicissitudes of the past days, but with the Emperor's banner flying above on a new pole and with a large fire crackling in the center, there was an atmosphere of celebration here, too. Thru found Aeswiren inside the main tent. Filek Biswas had replaced the bandages and examined the wound. The Emperor was weak but able to speak clearly. By his side was his brother, Mentu.

"Hail, General Gillo!" said the Emperor, who tried to struggle up, but Filek and Simona restrained him.

"Hail, Great King of Shasht. You attacked at just the right time."

"The arrival of your friends from the south is what saved us. That was the key development. We were beaten otherwise."

Thru had come to expect this kind of candor from Aeswiren. "Yes, Lord, it did look that way."

"But now the enemy forces are truly done for. I have had news in the last twenty minutes that the fighting among the fleet is over. The Red Tops have been locked down belowdecks, and all the captains have thrown in their lot with me."

"Wonderful news, Lord. I think we have achieved an end to the war." Thru turned, his eye catching another figure. "Hail to thee, Mentupah! You found your moment of destiny, did you not?"

Mentu embraced Thru. "Exactly the moment that my brother had feared for twenty years, and it turned out to be essential."

"Vital for all our survival, Mentupah, who once called himself the Eccentric."

"Ha, that seems like another life."

"And, Janbur, it is well indeed to find you here."

Janbur had been standing to one side, waiting to greet Thru. "I'm so glad we were able to get here in time to lend a hand. I would never have forgiven myself if we had missed it."

"Never was an arrival better timed, my friend."

"Simona!" Thru embraced her next and then held her close.

"We have won, Thru. We did it."

For a moment, their eyes met and they recalled those desperate days in faraway Shasht, when a pair of fugitives fought for their lives and almost starved to death amid the snow.

"We came back, Simona, and we have defeated our enemy."

Suddenly both were aware of another presence. Thru half turned and found Nuza had arrived. She fell into their arms, so that all three of them were held close together. They stayed that way while tears of happiness ran down their cheeks.

When all had been greeted and hosannas had been sung, it was time to get down to business. Sergeant Rukkh entered the tent under guard. He came forward and, in a brief but moving ceremony, was rewarded with a gold pin from the Emperor in recognition of valor and courage above all expectation.

As Rukkh stepped back from the Emperor's litter, Thru saw a glint of moisture on the sergeant's hard-bitten cheek.

"May I be first to offer my congratulations, Sergeant." Thru shook the man's hand.

"Thank you, General. That was a hard fight we had there."

"But for you and your quick thinking, we'd have lost it."

"Well, sir, your army has done its share of quick thinking. You've come a long way since first we found you."

Thru nodded. "Our lives will never be quite the same."

"And I am sorry for all those who were killed. We should never have come here. But now your people have learned to fight. In the long run, they will be safer."

"That is so, but there are many of us who might wish never to have been stirred from our old lives."

Just then, there came a message for Aeswiren from the troops who were scouring the enemy camp.

"Great heavens!" said the Emperor. "They've found Admiral Heuze, and he's alive."

"The admiral is alive?" Filek Biswas spoke up.

"Yes, Surgeon Biswas, it appears he has survived captivity. They are bringing him here at once."

"Well, thanks be given for that. The admiral was very kind to me. Indeed, without his help, I fear I would long since have been murdered or made a slave."

Soon afterward, six men carried the admiral into the tent on a stretcher. His clothes were reduced to rags, he had no peg for his leg, and he could hardly move because his hands were swollen into red and purple lumps.

Heuze apologized to the Emperor for allowing himself to be captured. He made no excuses.

"Well, Admiral, you appear to have paid a price already. I will not exact more from you."

"Thank you, Lord."

Filek examined the admiral's hands. The infection had gone deep already.

"I was buried under a pile of bodies. The Red Tops thought I was dead, you see, and they just threw my body on the pile."

"I am afraid, Admiral, that I must take off both of your hands and the left arm to the elbow."

Heuze groaned. "By the time you're done with me, Surgeon Biswas, I fear I'll have no limbs at all!"

"That may be, Admiral, but you'll be alive."

By this point, Thru's attention had been diverted to another visitor, this time brought in by hesitant guards, obviously uncomfortable with the newcomer.

"Welcome, Utnapishtim," said Thru, taking the ancient's hand.

"It has been a very long time since there was such a momentous day, Thru Gillo, and I have always expected that you would be involved in great events."

Utnapishtim greeted the Emperor and then the others with a quick smile and a clasping of hands.

"I have come to assist the good Surgeon Biswas. Melidofulo is also present, though he was delayed on the way here. He will join us shortly."

"I am glad to have your assistance, ancient Master," said Filek, coming forward to clasp Utnapishtim's hand.

Loud voices were heard outside, and soon there began a round of singing. "What is that?" exclaimed Thru.

"That's the regimental song of the Third Regiment," said Sergeant Rukkh. "I'd know it anywhere."

A guard in put his head to announce that some veterans of the Third had come to sing their congratulations to the Emperor. The voices outside grew louder yet. The singing was loose and ragged.

"Mentu, will you go out and speak to them?" asked the Emperor.

And so, Mentupah went out to impersonate his brother once more, though this time he felt little concern that he would be found out. From the sound of them, these men were well past the state where they could have told the difference between Mentu and his brother, Ge.

The singers had composed a special verse of their song in Aeswiren's honor, and now they bellowed it forth across the hilltop.

When they'd finished, Mentu bid them farewell, commended them for their singing, and came back into the tent. "They're well liquored up, I'm afraid."

"They found some brandy in the enemy camp," said Janbur.

To confirm this there was more noise as some of the veterans objected to being moved on too quickly by the guards. Shouts, cries, even a few blows were heard before the disturbance was over.

"So it is with these fellows after a victory like this one," said the Emperor. "Hard fought, and every man screwed tight to the point where his nerve may fail. Afterward there is a need for boisterousness."

Utnapishtim stood up suddenly and held up a hand.

"What is it, Utnapishtim?" said Thru.

"I felt something, a twinge of the darkness. As if magic were being done here."

Thru laughed. "No one here is capable of that, Utnapishtim."

The Assenzi did not smile, however. He reached for a talisman that he kept in a small bag in his pocket. The stone was glowing. Utnapishtim cast about the tent, studying everyone's face with his huge, serious eyes.

"What can it be, Utnapishtim?"

"I do not know, Thru Gillo, but something stirs."

At that very moment, the admiral started screaming. Everyone turned to look and were rewarded by the sight of Heuze thrashing on the floor of the tent, while terrified shrieks came from his throat.

"Help him, someone," Aeswiren commanded.

Janbur dropped down beside the frantic body. Filek crouched on the other side. As they took hold of the admiral's arms, they were pulled this way and that by his bizarre strength. Even with only one leg and with his hands completely ruined, the man had the strength of five.

Utnapishtim dropped down beside them and held his talisman high while he mumbled verses so quickly they were incomprehensible. Everyone in the room felt a strange pressure in their ears, and then there was a popping sound in the air as if a cork had been pulled from a bottle. A green light flickered all over the admiral.

Heuze's screams stopped at once, and his body subsided to the ground.

"Admiral?" Filek leaned over Heuze and took his pulse.

"How is he?" asked Mentu, crouching down to look.

"His pulse is high but slowing. He is covered with sweat."

"This was sorcery," said Utnapishtim, getting to his feet and trembling a little.

Klek, Aeswiren's loyal bodyguard, had drawn his sword. "We have seen such sorcery before. It is a favorite of our enemy's."

"Indeed," said Aeswiren, who was now sitting up on his litter, damn the pain it caused. "Call the guard. I want the area searched."

Before his order could be sent out, the tent flap opened and one of the guards slipped in. A huge man, whose helmet seemed too tight for him.

Thru sprang to his feet, a shout in his throat.

He was too late, however. The giant man brought a hand up from inside his robe and cast something toward them as if he were tossing dice against a wall.

The huge hand opened, and sparkling dust flickered in the air.

"Close your eyes," hissed Utnapishtim, but too late. The next moment, the brilliant dust seemed to catch fire and flare with a white brilliance that blinded anyone who saw it.

Mentupah fell to his knees with a choking cry. Klek stumbled into the tent wall and fell down. Janbur had drawn his sword but could do no more than hold it out in front of himself, unable to see a thing.

Only Thru had heard Utnapishtim in time. When he opened his eyes, the white fire had died and the giant man in a stolen guard's armor and helmet was inside the Emperor's tent. His sword was out and pressed to Aeswiren's throat.

The glittering dust had covered everybody, and its magic took effect. Their clothes and skin became stiff. Within a few seconds, not one of them could move, as if trapped inside armor plate that had rusted fast.

The giant tore off the confining helmet, and Thru recognized at once the evil leader who had danced for the pyluk on a mat of bloody mud.

"Well, well!" chuckled the huge man, contemplating his catch. "Aeswiren the Third, as I live and breathe. Who can truly claim to know all the ways of twisted fortune, eh?"

The sorcerer pulled the sword away from the Emperor's throat and drew up a camp chair and sat down. "All of your companions are frozen in place, Your Majesty. Your guards are dead—I killed them myself. Yes, I can see you are astonished at this turn of events. You thought you had won a great victory. You thought you had finally gotten the better of me.

"Ha! Revenge is mine, saith the Lord, and am I not the Lord?"

The eyes raked the tent, alighting on Admiral Heuze, still lying on the tent floor. Heuze had come back to his senses and was staring up at the Lord Leader with terror. "Well, Admiral, don't you have an answer for me?"

But Heuze could not speak, could not move a muscle.

"I suppose none of you are fit to answer me, so I will answer myself. Of course I am the Lord. I cannot be defeated. I cannot be killed. I will live forever, and I will rule the universe."

Utnapishtim had also shut his eyes in time, and his hand rested on his talisman. The pale green light warred with the crystalline sparkle that covered his hand. Slowly, the crystal decayed. The green glow traveled farther, working its way up the Assenzi's arm to the shoulder and across his body.

As soon as he could move a muscle, Utnapishtim reached out to touch Thru on the shoulder. The green glow sparked over Thru as well.

"Yes"—the Old One was savoring the new turn of events—"this will indeed be a day sung of forever. I shall ensure that it is enshrined in the daily prayers of the billions that shall worship me. This will be known as the day when I took the head of Aeswiren, faithless man of Shasht. This will be the day when I crushed the rebellion and began the process of finally exterminating my enemies."

The green glow from Utnapishtim reached Thru's feet and the top of his head simultaneously. He stepped forward boldly, while Utnapishtim stepped back into shadow.

The giant man heard Thru's footfall and whirled around. "Well, well, well, if it isn't the little monkey who likes to sing for his supper!"

Thru had his sword drawn and was measuring the distance to the sorcerer in the chair. As he stepped carefully forward, he spoke: "You wore another's body then. We were prisoners in that cruel pyramid of yours. You came out on your balcony and tried to make us crawl. But we sang instead, and you went away."

The Old One got to his feet and towered over Thru. "Nasty little monkey, aren't you? You're the one that got away. Went off to the mountains and made those rug things. Very nice work, impressive skill. I'm sorry to say that I burned them. Couldn't have things like that left around, might give men the wrong idea."

Thru took another careful step. He was almost close enough. "Burn and destroy, that's all you can ever do, isn't it? You can't build anything beautiful. You can't make anything fine. You cannot create, you cannot give pleasure. All you can do is encourage the worst in the world. You cheat and lie and deceive and murder."

"Ho! Listen to the monkey preach to me. Who do you think you are, monkey?"

"I am a free mot of the Land, and I know who you are, Karnemin the traitor."

"Karnemin is it? They taught you that, did they, the little demons? Well, I will snuff them out just as I snuff out you and all your kind. When I am done, you will all be exterminated!"

Thru came forward again slowly, light on the balls of his feet.

"All you have to offer the world is cruelty and oppression. You keep men beaten down like whipped dogs. They are your slaves, and they do not even know it. They are slaves in a system that strips them of dignity and shortens their lives. Only the few who are wealthy escape the worst effects, but they suffer other things, such as the blight on their souls that comes from administering your horrible system."

"Fool! They are men. Know you not men by now? Men are weak. Oh, they have some native wit, some inner intelligence. But, left to themselves, they rarely rise above mud huts and peasant plows. It is only when I puff men up and give them strength that they can lift themselves from the mud. Without me, they would be nothing!"

"That is what you tell yourself. That is your justification. Which you must have, because the alternative is something you cannot face. You steep your mind in such lies and repeat them endlessly to yourself. You have to, because the truth is that all you have done is for vanity."

"Silence, you impudent animal! I will hear no more of this! You are nothing but a freak of nature. Frogs' eggs and rats' tails! You came from a soup cooked up in a laboratory by senile men who'd lost their way. It is my duty to expunge you!"

"You can try," said Thru in a tight voice. "But I will kill you if I can."

He tensed, about to spring.

But the Old One leapt first, exploding from the chair while swinging his sword round in a glittering arc meant to end it there and then. Thru had learned his kyo from Master Sassadzu, though, and he ducked it. The sword sank into a tent pole instead and virtually sundered it.

In the shadows, Utnapishtim's frail old hand rested on Nuza's shoulder. Her sight was already recovering from the flash, since she had looked down at that moment. The slight green glow displaced the crystalline sparkle.

Thru moved along the wall of the tent. The space was too tight for him. The giant could kill him with a single blow.

"When I have finished, there will be nothing left of any of you. Your squalid hamlets will be plowed

under. Even those ruins in the North where the little
demons dwell shall be pulled down. I will erase your
memory."

The evil sorcerer stalked Thru, his sword gleaming
in the lamplight.

Thru recalled Toshak's maxim: "Attack! Seize the
initiative whenever you can." So he thrust, knocked
aside the enemy's blade, and drove for his chest. The
giant dodged, his own sword flickered, and Thru was
forced to party. The huge man swung his free hand,
and though Thru was withdrawing he still clipped him
on the side of the head. Thru stumbled to the floor,
but rolled instantly to his right. The giant sprang forward and drove down with his sword. Thru kept rolling, and the sword missed him, smashing the lid of a
wooden chest instead.

Thru got to his feet, and their swords clashed. The
enemy tried to catch him again with his fist, but this
time the mot ducked. The Old One hit another tent
pole.

"Damn monkey! I'll kill you for that!" he howled.

He stalked forward once more with an insane leer
on his face.

Thru struck aside his sword and tried for the giant's
throat. The speed of his strike brought it very close
to success, and the Old One pulled back with a hiss.

"Venomous little monkeys, a lesson to all of us.
Nasty things should never have been allowed in the
first place. I told them they were wrong to bring their
abominations to life."

The Old One's sword whistled over Thru's head.

A moment later their blades rang against each
other. Thru was forced back by the other's great
strength. He tripped on a chair leg and fell sprawling
on his back. The giant laughed and leaned forward
for the kill.

And gave a sudden squawk of dismay. His blow

went wide, sinking through the rug into the ground beneath. The Old One turned and found Nuza there, holding up a blood-streaked dirk.

"Another one!" he growled. Then he caught sight of Utnapishtim moving out of the shadows with a small sword held before him.

"And you! The damnable Assenzi, no less, caught in the act of winding the springs on your tame monkeys!"

"Your time is over, Karnemin," said Utnapishtim in a cold voice. "The shadow is waiting to close over you."

"Never!" roared the giant. His sword whirled through the space where Nuza had stood a moment before. The Old One shifted on his feet and winced from the pain in his leg from Nuza's dirk.

He struck at her again, and then at Thru, who had climbed back to his feet. Nuza feinted but stayed out of reach of the enemy's sword. Thru drove in again. The sorcerer struck out with his foot, but Thru skipped aside. The giant swung suddenly and caught Nuza with the back of his hand, sending her flying backward. She slammed down onto Aeswiren's litter and then to the floor. As the enemy stepped forward to finish her, Thru harried him from behind. He whirled aside to evade the stroke.

"Enough of this!" roared the Old One. In a furious flurry, he drove Thru back across the tent, caught him with a punch to the chest, and drove forward to skewer him. The sword scraped past Thru's ribs and went through the wall of the tent. But Thru's own sword found its way into the giant's chest. The Old One pulled back and put a hand to his side.

"It cannot be."

Thru swung with every ounce of remaining strength— a two-handed grip on the sword as if it were a bat and he was hitting for the boundary.

The swords struck with a flash of fire, and the Old One's sword broke in two. Thru drove in again on the backhand and buried his sword to the hilt in the monster's belly.

With a great cry of disbelief, the giant toppled, bounced on the ground, and lay still.

"It is done," breathed Thru. "Our enemy is dead."

He collapsed beside Nuza. She looked up woozily, her lips swollen from the Old One's blow. Thru put his arms around her and held her tight.

Utnapishtim studied the fallen giant, then turned to wield his healing talisman stone on the others. One by one they were freed of the sparkling paralysis.

Heuze was the last, and when he awoke he cried out in wonder and in fear.

"It is over, Admiral. The thing had you in thrall of its sorcery," said Utnapishtim.

Simona sprang to Aeswiren's side. The Emperor was slower to escape the grip of the paralysis.

"His vitality is low, weakened by the arrow," explained Utnapishtim.

Filek took Aeswiren's pulse. "It is light and fluttery."

"He must rest," said the Assenzi. "There is much to do, but Aeswiren the Third has done his part. At least for now. He must gather his strength for the struggle for the future. He has much great work ahead of him."

Thru and Nuza had joined the group standing around the Emperor's litter. Klek, the bodyguard, removed Thru's sword and prodded the corpse of great Pulbeka the stone breaker.

"Will you go with him, Utnapishtim?" asked Thru.

"Yes, Thru Gillo, I will go to Shasht. Another turn in the road for old Utnapishtim."

"It is a dry land, Utnapishtim. It needs the care of the Assenzi."

"Shasht can be green once more. Aeswiren has seen the way. We will work together. It will not be done in a day, nor even in one man's lifetime. But give us three generations, and even ruined Shasht can be fruitful and lovely."

"Then it will be a marvel, and the men who live there will become wise."

Utnapishtim smiled at the optimism of the mots. "Well, by then, the men of Shasht will have at least begun to see the outline of wisdom, perhaps."

Klek returned with three guards. The others had been killed by the Old One at the end of the disturbance caused by the drunks with an urge to sing.

"Karnemin must have guided those drunks and used their presence to disguise his attack," said Utnapishtim.

With a grunt, Aeswiren finally emerged from the crystal spell. His eyes opened. "What happened?" he managed to say.

Just then, the guards and Klek took up the arms and legs of the dead giant. As they lifted it, they were abruptly hurled backward. With an astonishing jackknife motion, the great body sprang back to life and landed on its feet. It snapped erect with a strange hiss. The eyes glittered with life, and yet the thing was dead.

Klek came in first, his stabbing blade in hand. The thing caught his wrist, turned it, and hammered him with a huge fist. Klek was out cold before he hit the ground. His sword remained with the reanimated corpse.

The sword swept around and beheaded the nearest guard.

Thru had no weapon, but he snatched the water gourd from the table beside Aeswiren's litter and hurled it into the zombie's face. It burst, the water flew everywhere, and it distracted the thing. Thru struck it with foot and fist in a blindingly swift flurry of kyo blows.

The dead thing took no notice. It struck down

Janbur as he came forward with his sword. It slashed again and again, carving its way toward Aeswiren.

"The head, take the head!" shouted Utnapishtim, before he caught a glancing blow from the thing and was knocked head over heels into the side of the tent.

In the dreadful struggle, the lamp went over with a crash, and flames licked up at once from the tent floor. Screams arose and the insane thing gave off a hissing, more like a kettle than a serpent.

Thru stepped on Janbur and slipped. As he got up again, he took Janbur's sword. He ducked a sweep of the enemy's blade and struck up inside the giant's reach. Once more, he buried his blade in the zombie's body. But this time it scarcely sagged. Yellow fire leaped from its eyeballs, and the head darted at Thru, who pulled back just in time as the great jaws snapped shut where his face had been.

Thru whipped his sword across the outstretched throat. The hissing was cut off. The horrible thing staggered. Thru struck again, below the ear, and the monster pitched forward. It thrashed on the ground and emitted a terrible wail. Thru struck down. His blade went right through the massive neck, the head slid sideways, and the wailing stopped abruptly.

Mentu was stamping out the fire. Someone else lit another lamp. Filek was beside the Emperor, who had struggled up to a sitting position and had produced a dagger from somewhere.

Simona was sobbing, kneeling down beside Nuza, who lay still.

Thru gave an inarticulate cry of horror and knelt beside her.

"I don't know what happened," wept Simona.

Thru felt for a pulse. He heard a loud gasp behind him. "Nuza!" cried the Emperor in sudden despair. "Not Nuza, no!"

"It is all right, Thru Gillo, let me examine her."

Thru heard the voice in his ear, but he had gone numb. The world seemed to have receded into fog. The enemy was finally destroyed, but had he slain Nuza in the end?

Filek Biswas knelt beside Nuza and took her wrist in his hand.

Aeswiren, ignoring the pain of his wound, pulled himself across the litter until he could rest a hand on Thru's shoulder, but Thru felt it not. Thru was lost in a world without shape or form, where despair mocked him from a bleak grey sky.

Then a hand pounded on his back with excitement. "She lives! Her pulse is strong!" Filek Biswas was shouting.

Thru looked down, and the fog stripped from his brain. As he reached for her, he saw Nuza's eyes open, and she started up toward him.

Epilogue

Four years later, Thru Gillo stood back from an almost completed mat and heard Nuza on the steps to his workroom. She was coming quickly, which meant she was excited. He looked out the window to check the position of the sun in the sky. It was early for Nuza to be coming home.

"What is it?" he said as she burst in. Then behind her he saw other forms and jumped up with a glad cry.

"Mentu!" Their hands met. "Juf! You're back."

"The only mot who ever went twice to Shasht!" said Juf proudly.

"You'll become a byword, my friend, if you keep this up."

"And this!" Mentu was staring at the large mat that Thru was weaving.

"It's new. What do you think?"

Mentu studied it and burst into a rich laugh. "What a splendid joke!"

Thru was smiling. "There's always hope. Maybe it will come true."

Little Kima, their oldest child, came running in and leaped into Nuza's arms. Thru ruffled his daughter's hair and took another look at the work on the loom.

"What do you call it?" asked Juf.

" 'Men at Prayer,' " said Thru with a grin.

Juf laughed. "And how was 'Mots at War' received?"

"There was some resistance, but I have woven it twice now. Not as popular as the old styles."

"Nothing ever will be. And you must do another 'Chooks and Beetles' soon."

"I'm getting too old to do 'Chooks and Beetles' anymore."

"There is tea on the boil downstairs," said Nuza. "Unless you want to stay up here and talk weaving."

"No, no, we would love some tea," Mentu answered.

"And you must tell us all that has happened."

"Well, the war is over. Aeswiren is Emperor once again. The priests are beaten for good."

"And the pyramid?"

"They have begun to dismantle it. Aeswiren has ordered the stone to be used for new temples to their old gods, to Canilass and the rest."

"But that isn't the biggest news," said Juf.

"Oh?"

"Aeswiren has wed Simona. She is the new Empress of Shasht."

Christopher Rowley has written more than a dozen science fiction and fantasy novels, including the *Bazil Broketail* series. He lives in Ellenville, New York.